Praise for Lincoln Child and

TERMINAL FREEZE

LINCOLN CHILD
TERMINAL FREEZE

Lincoln Child is the *New York Times* bestselling author of *Deep Storm*, *Death Match*, *Utopia*, and the forthcoming *The Third Gate*, as well as coauthor with Douglas Preston of numerous bestsellers.

www.lincolnchild.com

TERMINAL
FREEZE

TERMINAL FREEZE

• A NOVEL •

LINCOLN CHILD

ANCHOR BOOKS

A DIVISION OF RANDOM HOUSE, INC.

NEW YORK

FIRST ANCHOR BOOKS EDITION, MARCH 2012

Epigraph on p. xi courtesy of the Geophysical Institute,
University of Alaska Fairbanks, Fairbanks, Alaska.

The Library of Congress has cataloged the Doubleday edition as follows:
Child, Lincoln.
Terminal Freeze: a novel / by Lincoln Child.—1st ed.
p. cm.
1. Scientists—Fiction. 2. Archaeological expeditions—Fiction.
3. Eskimos—Folklore—Fiction. 4. Animals, Fossil—Fiction.
5. Arctic regions—Fiction.
I. Title.
PS3553.H4839 T47 2009
813'.54—dc22

Anchor ISBN: 978-0-307-94707-9

www.anchorbooks.com

Printed in the United States of America
10 9 8 7 6 5 4 3 2 1

To Veronica

Acknowledgments

As *Terminal Freeze* made the long journey from concept to printed reality, many people generously lent their time and expertise. J. Bret Bennington, PhD, of the Department of Geology at Hofstra University, helped me gain a better understanding of paleoecological field-work and principles. Timothy Robbins provided a window onto the nuts-and-bolts details of documentary filmmaking. (I hasten to add that the particular peccadilloes of Terra Prime, Emilio Conti, et al. are completely of my own devising.) William Cors, MD, assisted with several medical aspects of the story. My father, William Child, PhD, former chemistry professor and associate dean of Carleton College, offered invaluable insight into crystalline structures and other chemical matters. Special Agent Douglas Margini once again helped with firearms details. And my cousin Greg Tear listened patiently and offered his usual excellent advice.

I would also like to thank my editor and friend, Jason Kaufman, for as always being an essential guiding light through the composition of this novel, as well as Rob Bloom and the many others at Doubleday for taking such good care of me. Thanks also to my agents, Eric Simonoff and Matthew Snyder, for fighting the good fight. Thanks to Claudia Rülke, Nadine Waddell, and Diane Matson for their various ministrations. An ice-cold Beefeater martini, extra dry, straight up, with a twist, to my writing partner, Doug Preston, for his many years of comradeship and for his significant contribution to the setting of this novel. His daughter Aletheia suggested a great twist. And last but most certainly not least, my thanks and gratitude to my family for their love and support.

In the early part of the twentieth century the Beresovka mammoth carcass was discovered in Siberia. Nearly intact, the animal was found buried in silty gravel sitting in an upright position. The mammoth had a broken foreleg, evidently caused by a fall from a nearby cliff ten thousand years ago. The remains of its stomach were intact and there were grasses and buttercups lodged between its teeth. The flesh was still edible, but reportedly not tasty.

No one has ever satisfactorily explained how the Beresovka mammoth and other animals found frozen in the subarctic could have been frozen before being consumed by predators of the time.

—J. Holland, *Alaska Science Forum*

TERMINAL
FREEZE

At dusk, when the stars rose one by one into a frozen sky, Usuguk approached the snowhouse as silently as a fox. There had been a fresh snowfall that morning, and the village elder stared across the gray-white arctic desolation that ran away endlessly on all sides to a bleak and empty ice horizon. Here and there, ribs of dark permafrost jutted out of the snow cover like the bones of prehistoric beasts. The wind was picking up, and ice crystals stung his cheeks and worried at the fur of his parka hood. A scattering of surrounding igloos stood unlit, dark as tombs.

Usuguk paid no attention to any of this. He was aware only of an overwhelming sense of dread, of the rapid pounding of his heart.

As he entered the snowhouse, the small band of women gathered around the moss fire looked up at him quickly, their expressions tense, worried.

"Moktok e inkarrtok," he said. "It is time."

Wordlessly, they gathered up their meager tools with trembling fingers. Bone needles were returned to needle cases; skin scrapers and flensing *ulus* were slipped inside parkas. One woman, who had been chewing sealskin boots to soften them, bundled the boots up carefully in a threadbare cloth. Then they all rose, one after another, and slipped out the rough opening that served as a door. Last to go was Nulathe, her head bowed in fear and shame.

Usuguk watched as the caribou skin fell back over the opening, blotting out the view beyond: the lonely huddle of igloos, the desolate icescape stretching on across the frozen lake toward the failing sun. For a moment he stood, trying to forget the anxiety that had settled over him like a heavy cloak.

Then he turned away. There was much to do—and little time to do it in.

Moving gingerly to the rear of the snowhouse, the shaman drew blankets off the top of a small mound of furs, exposing a box of polished black wood. Carefully, he placed the box before the fire. Next he removed a ceremonial *amauti,* folded with ritual care, from between the furs. Pulling the hooded parka over his head and placing it aside, he donned the *amauti,* its intricate fretwork of beaded tassels clattering faintly. Then he seated himself cross-legged before the box.

He sat for a minute, caressing the box with fingers wizened from years of fighting a hostile landscape. Next he opened it and removed one of the objects inside, turning it over and over, feeling its power, listening carefully for anything it might tell him. Then he returned it to the box. He did this with each of the objects in turn. All the while he was aware of the fear within him. It lay deep in his body's core like undigested blubber. He knew all too well what this thing they had witnessed, this awful portent, meant. It had happened only once before in the living memory of the People, scores of generations ago, although the story—handed down from father to son before the snowhouse fire—remained as portentous as if it had happened yesterday.

Yet, this time, it seemed so frighteningly out of proportion to the transgression that provoked it . . .

He took a deep breath. They were all counting on him to restore peace, to bring the natural order back into balance. But it was an oppressive task. The People were so diminished that there had been but a tiny handful to pass on to him the old, secret knowledge. And even they were gone now, passed into the spirit world. Of nature's secret order, only he was left.

Reaching beneath the *amauti,* he drew out a handful of dried herbs and botanicals, carefully tied together with a slender stalk of arctic balsam. He raised it with both hands, then placed it on the fire. Clouds of gray smoke began to rise, filling the snowhouse with the smell of the ancient forest. Slowly and reverently, he took the objects out of the box and arranged them in a semicircle before the fire: the tusk tip of a rare white walrus, caught and killed by his great-great-great-grandfather. A stone the color of summer sunlight, shaped like the head of a wolverine. A caribou antler, cut ritualistically into twenty-one pieces, decorated in intricate patterns of tiny awl holes, each filled with ochre.

Last of all he withdrew the tiny figure of a man, made of reindeer skin, ivory, and blanket cloth. He laid the figure in the center of the semicircle. Then, putting his palms flat on the floor of the snowhouse and letting his chin sink to his chest, he bent low before it.

"Mighty Kuuk'juag," he chanted, "Hunter of the Frozen Waste, Protector of the People. Withdraw your rage from us. Walk quietly again in the moonlight. Return to the way of peace."

He raised himself back to a sitting position. Then he reached out for the first object in the semicircle—the walrus tusk—turning it clockwise to face the small figurine. Hand on the tusk, he half sang, half chanted the atonement prayer, asking Kuuk'juag to soften his heart, to forgive.

The transgression had occurred the previous morning. In the midst of her daily chores, Nulathe had unwittingly brought the sinews of a caribou and the flesh of a seal into contact. She had been tired and sick—this alone could explain such an oversight. But nevertheless the forbidden deed had been done, the ancient rule broken. Now the souls of the dead animals—in spiritual opposition to each other—had been defiled. And Kuuk'juag the Hunter had felt their anger. This explained what Usuguk's tiny band had witnessed in the frozen wastes the night before.

The prayer lasted ten minutes. Then—slowly, carefully—Usuguk moved his wrinkled hand to the next object and began his chant anew.

It took two hours to complete the ceremony. At last, bowing one final time before the figurine, the old man said a parting blessing, then uncrossed his legs and rose painfully to his feet. If all had gone well—if he had performed the atonement prayer in the proper way of his ancestors—the taint would leave them and the Hunter would withdraw his fury. He walked around the fire, first clockwise, then counterclockwise. And then, kneeling before the box, he began to place the objects back inside, beginning with the small figurine.

As he did so, he heard cries from outside the snowhouse: sobs, shrieks, voices raised in despair and lamentation.

He stood quickly, dread pressing upon his heart. He shrugged into the parka, pulled back the caribou skin, and stepped outside. The women were there, tearing their hair and pointing at the sky.

He looked heavenward and groaned. The fear and dread, which had receded in the calming motions of the ceremony, consumed him with redoubled strength. *They* were back—and worse than the night before. Much worse.

The ceremony had failed.

But now, with a horrible creeping certainty, Usuguk realized something else. This was not the result of anything Nulathe or the others had done. It was not merely the wrath of Kuuk'juag, or some accidental desecration. Only a violation of the most serious of all taboos could cause the kind of spirit fury he now paid witness to.

And Usuguk had been warned—as had countless generations before him—what that taboo was.

Not only warned—Usuguk knew. He had *seen* . . .

He looked at the women, who were staring back, wild-eyed with apprehension. "Pack what you need," he told them. "Tomorrow, we head south. To the mountain."

1

"Hey, Evan. Lunch?"

Evan Marshall put the ziplock bag aside and stood up, massaging his lower back. He'd spent the last ninety minutes with his face inches above the ground, collecting samples from the glacial sediment, and it took his eyes a moment to adjust. The voice had been Sully's, and now Marshall made him out: a squat, slightly portly figure in a fur-lined parka, standing, arms crossed, thirty yards up the steep valley. Behind him rose the terminal tongue of the Fear glacier, a rich, mysterious blue riddled with white fracture lines. Large ice boulders lay scattered along its base like so many monstrous diamonds, along with daggerlike shards of ancient lava. Marshall opened his mouth to warn Sully against standing so close: the glacier was as dangerous as it was pretty, since the weather had turned warmer and the ice front was calving off deadly chunks at an unprecedented rate. Then he thought better of it. Gerard Sully was proud of his position as nominal leader and didn't like being told what to do. Instead, Marshall just shook his head. "I think I'll pass, thanks."

"Suit yourself." Sully turned toward Wright Faraday, the party's evolutionary biologist, who was busying himself a little downslope. "How's about it, Wright?"

Faraday glanced up, watery blue eyes oddly magnified behind tortoiseshell frames. A digital camera dangled from a heavy strap around his neck. "Not me," he said with a frown, as if the thought of stopping to eat in the middle of a workday was somehow heretical.

"Starve yourselves if you want to. Just don't ask me to bring anything back."

"Not even a Popsicle?" asked Marshall.

Sully smiled thinly. He was about as short as Napoleon, and radiated a combination of egotism and insecurity that Marshall found especially annoying. He'd been able to put up with it back at the university, where Sully was just one arrogant scientist among many, but up here on the ice—with nowhere to escape—it had grown irksome. Perhaps, he reflected, he should be relieved that their expedition had only a few weeks to play out.

"You look tired," Sully said. "Out walking again last night?"

Marshall nodded.

"You'd better be careful. You might fall into a lava tube and freeze to death."

"All right, Mom. I'll be careful."

"Or run into a polar bear, or something."

"That's all right. I'm starved for some good conversation."

"It's no joke, you refusing to carry a gun and all."

Marshall didn't like the direction this was leading. "Look, if you run into Ang, tell him I've got more samples here for transport back to the lab."

"I'll do that. He'll be thrilled."

Marshall watched the climatologist make his way carefully past them, down the rubble toward the foot of the mountain and their base. He called it "their base," but of course it belonged to the U.S. government: officially known as the Mount Fear Remote Sensing Installation and decommissioned almost fifty years ago, it consisted of a low, gray, sprawling, institutional-looking structure, festooned with radar domes and other detritus of the cold war. Beyond it lay a frigid landscape of permafrost and lava deposits spewed ages ago from the mountain's guts, gullied and split as if the earth had torn itself apart in geologic agony. In many places, the surface was hidden beneath large snowfields. There were no roads, no other structures, no living things. It was as hostile, as remote, as alien as the moon.

He stretched as he looked out over the forbidding landscape. Even after four weeks on-site, it still seemed hard to believe that anyplace could be so barren. But then the entire scientific expedition had seemed a little unreal from the start. Unreal that a media giant like Terra Prime had picked their grant applications for approval: four scientists from Northern Massachusetts University with nothing in common save an interest in global warming. Unreal that the government had given them clearance to use Fear Base, admittedly at significant expense and with strict limitations. And unreal that the warming trend itself was occurring with such breathtaking, frightening speed.

He turned away with a sigh. His knees hurt from hours of crouching over the terminal moraine, collecting samples. His fingertips and nose were half frozen. And to add insult to injury, the snow had turned to thin freezing sleet that was now slowly seeping through three layers of clothing and settling into the most intimate crevices of his person. But daylight was brief these days, and their expedition's window was fast closing. He was keenly aware of how little time he had left. There would be plenty of food back in Woburn, Massachusetts, and plenty of time to eat it.

As he turned to retrieve the sample bags, he heard Faraday speak again. "Five years ago, even two, I'd never believe it. *Rain.*"

"It's not rain, Wright. It's sleet."

"Close enough. Rain in the Zone, with winter coming on? Unbelievable."

The "Zone" was a vast stretch of northeastern Alaska, hard against the Arctic Ocean, sandwiched between the Arctic National Wildlife Refuge on one side and the Yukon's Ivvavik National Park on the other. It was a tract so cold and desolate that nobody wanted anything to do with it: temperatures struggled to get above zero only a few months out of the year. Years ago, the government branded it the Federal Wilderness Zone and promptly forgot all about it. There were, Marshall reflected, probably no more than two dozen people in all its two million acres: their own scientific team of five, the base's skeleton crew of four, a small band of Native Americans to the north, and a scattering of backpackers and loners who were too hard-core or eccentric to settle for anything but the most remote. How strange to think there were few people farther north on the planet than their little group.

A sudden, tremendous report, like the crack of a cannon, shook the glacial valley with the violence of an earthquake. The sound echoed across the tundra below them, violating the profound silence, bouncing back and forth like a tennis ball, growing slowly fainter as it receded into endless distance. Above, the face of the glacier had shorn away, tons of ice and snow adding to the frozen rubble lying along its forward edge. Marshall felt his heart lurch uncomfortably in his chest. No matter how many times he heard that sound, its violence always came as a shock.

Faraday pointed toward it. "See? That's exactly what I mean. A valley glacier like the Fear should taper to a nice, thin ice front, with a minimum of meltwater and a healthy percolation zone. But this one is calving like a tidewater glacier. I've been measuring the basal melt—"

"That's Sully's job, not yours."

"—and it's off the scale." Faraday shook his head. "Rain, unprecedented melting—and there are other things happening, too. Like the northern lights the last few nights. You notice them?"

"Of course. A single color—it was spectacular. And unusual."

"Unusual." Faraday repeated the word thoughtfully.

Marshall did not reply. In his experience, every scientific expedition, even one as small as this, had its Cassandra figure. Wright Faraday—with his prodigious learning, his pessimistic outlook on life, his dark theories and outrageous predictions—played the role expertly. Marshall gave the biologist a covert glance. Despite knowing him casually as a university colleague, and now having spent a month almost continually in his presence, he didn't really have a good idea what made the man tick.

Still—Marshall thought as he filled and sealed a fresh bag, recorded the sample's location in a notebook, then measured and photographed the extraction site—Faraday had a point. And that point was one reason he himself was collecting samples at an almost frantic pace. A glacier was a near-perfect place for his kind of research. During its formation, as it accumulated snow, it trapped organic remains: pollen, plant fibers, animal remains. Later, as the glacier retreated, melting slowly away, it gracefully yielded up those secrets once again. This was an ideal gift for a paleoecologist, a treasure trove from the past.

Except there was nothing slow or graceful about this glacier's retreat. It was falling to pieces with alarming speed—and taking its secrets with it.

As if on cue, there was another ear-shattering explosion from the face of the glacier, another shuddering cascade of ice. Marshall glanced toward the sound, feeling a mixture of irritation and impatience. A much larger section of the glacier's face had fallen away this time. With a sigh, he bent toward his specimens, then abruptly swiveled back in the direction of the glacier. Among the fractured ice boulders at its base, he could see that part of the mountain face beneath had been exposed by the calving. He squinted at it for a moment. Then he called over to Faraday.

"You've got the field glasses, don't you?"

"Right here."

Marshall walked toward him. The biologist had pulled the binoculars from a pocket and was holding them out with a heavily gloved hand. Marshall took them, breathed on the eyepieces to warm them, wiped them free of mist, then raised them toward the glacier.

"What is it?" Faraday said, excitement kindling in his voice. "What do you see?"

Marshall licked his lips and stared at what the fallen ice had revealed. "It's a cave," he replied.

2

An hour later, they stood before the icy rubble at the Fear glacier's front face. The freezing rain had stopped, and a weak sun struggled to pierce the gunmetal clouds. Marshall rubbed his arms briskly, trying to warm himself. He looked around at their little group. Sully had returned, bringing with him Ang Chen, the team's graduate student. Except for Penny Barbour, their computer scientist, the entire expedition was now assembled at the terminal moraine.

The cave lay directly ahead, its mouth black against the clear blue of the glacial ice. To Marshall, it looked like the barrel of a monstrous gun. Sully stared into it, chewing distractedly on his lower lip.

"Almost a perfect cylinder," he said.

"It's undoubtedly a branch pipe," Faraday said. "Mount Fear's riddled with them."

"The base is," Marshall replied. "But it's very unusual to see one at this altitude."

Abruptly, another section of ice front calved off the glacier about half a mile south, collapsing in house-sized blue chunks at its base and throwing up a cloud of ice shards. Chen started violently, and Faraday covered his ears against the roar. Marshall grimaced as he felt the mountain shudder beneath his feet.

It took several minutes for the echoes to die away. At last, Sully grunted. He glanced from the ice face, to the mouth of the cave, to Chen. "Got the video camera?"

Chen nodded and patted the equipment bag slung over one shoulder.

"Fire it up."

"You're not planning on going in, are you?" Faraday said.

Instead of answering, Sully straightened to his full five feet six inches, sucking in his paunch and adjusting the hood of his parka, readying himself for the camera lens.

"It's not a good idea," Faraday went on. "You know how brittle the lava formations are."

"That's not all," Marshall said. "Didn't you see what just happened? More ice could calve off and bury the entrance at any minute."

Sully looked back at the cave indecisively. "They'd want us to."

"They" referred to Terra Prime, the cable channel devoted to science and nature that was underwriting the expedition.

Sully rubbed one gloved hand against his chin. "Evan, Wright, you can stay out here. Ang will follow me in with the camera. If anything happens, get the army guys to chop us out."

"The hell with that," Marshall said immediately, grinning. "If you discover buried treasure, I want a cut."

"You said it yourself. It's not safe."

"All the more reason you need another hand," Marshall replied.

Sully's lower lip protruded truculently, and Marshall waited him out. Then the climatologist relented. "Okay. Wright, we'll be as quick as we can."

Faraday blinked his watery blue eyes but remained silent.

Sully brushed stray flakes of snow from his parka, cleared his throat. He glanced up a little gingerly at the ice front. Then he positioned himself before the camera. "We're standing at the face of the glacier," he said in a hushed, melodramatic voice. "The retreating ice has exposed a cave, nestled in the flank of the mountain. We're preparing to explore it now." He paused dramatically, then signaled for Chen to stop recording.

"Did you really say 'nestled' just now?" Marshall asked.

Sully ignored this. "Let's go." He pulled a large flashlight out of his parka pocket. "Ang, train the camera on me as we go inside."

He started forward, the gangly Chen obediently following in his wake. After a moment, Marshall pulled out his own flashlight and swung in behind them.

They picked their way slowly and carefully through the debris field. A few of the blocks of ice were the size of a fist; others, the size of a dormitory. In the weak sunlight, they glowed the pale blue of an October sky. Runnels of meltwater trickled past. As the three continued, the shadow of the glacier fell over them. Marshall looked up apprehensively at the vast wall of ice but said nothing.

Close up, the cave mouth looked even blacker. It exhaled a chill breath that pinched at Marshall's half-frozen nose. As Sully had said, it was quite round: the typical secondary vent of a dead volcano. The glacier had smoothed the surrounding rock face to almost a mirror finish. Sully poked at the blackness with his flashlight. Then he turned toward Chen. "Turn that off a moment."

"Okay." The student lowered the camera.

Sully paused, then glanced at Marshall. "Faraday wasn't joking. This whole mountain is one big pile of fractured lava. Keep on the lookout for any weaknesses. If the tube seems at all unstable, we turn back immediately."

He looked back at Chen, nodded for him to start filming again. "We're going in," he intoned for the camera's benefit. Then he turned and stepped into the cave.

The roof wasn't especially low—at least ten feet—yet Marshall ducked instinctively as he followed Chen inside. The cave bored straight into the mountain, descending at a gentle grade. They proceeded cautiously, flashlight beams playing over the lava walls. It was even colder in here than out on the ice field, and Marshall snugged the hood of his parka tightly around his face.

"Hold up," he said. The beam of his flashlight had caught a hairline fracture in the braids of lava. He let his light travel along its length, then pressed at it gingerly with one hand.

"Looks solid," he said.

"Then let's proceed," Sully replied. "Carefully."

"It's amazing this tunnel hasn't collapsed under the weight of the glacier," said Chen.

They moved deeper into the cave, treading cautiously. When they spoke, it was in low tones, almost whispers.

"There's a coating of ice beneath the snow here," Sully said after a minute. "Spans the entire floor. Remarkably even."

"And it's getting deeper the farther we go," replied Marshall. "At some point, this branch pipe must have been filled with water."

"Well, it must have frozen with remarkable speed," Sully said, "because—" But at that moment the climatologist's feet slid out from under him and he fell heavily on the ice with a whinny of astonishment.

Marshall cringed, heart in mouth, waiting for the ceiling to come crashing down around them. But when nothing happened, and he saw Sully was uninjured, his alarm turned to bemusement. "You got that on film, right, Ang?"

The graduate student grinned through his sudden pallor. "Sure did."

Sully rose laboriously to his feet, frowning and wiping snow from his knees. He had a cat's ingrained displeasure of losing dignity. "This is a serious moment, Evan. Please remember that."

They continued even more slowly now. It was intensely quiet, the only sound the crunch of their feet on the dusting of snow. The ancient lava walls to either side were dark. Sully led the way gingerly, brushing the snow away with his boots, passing his flashlight beam back and forth over the path ahead.

Chen peered into the gloom ahead. "Looks like the cave opens up ahead."

"That's good," Sully replied, "because the ice sheet's getting deeper, and—"

Suddenly he fell again. But this was no clumsy repetition: Marshall immediately grasped that this time the scientist had fallen out of sheer surprise. Sully was frantically wiping away the snow underfoot and probing his light into the ice beneath. Chen dropped to his knees beside him, the camera temporarily forgotten. Marshall came quickly forward, peering down into the ice.

With a chill unrelated to the cave's air, Marshall saw what Sully had found. There, buried beneath the ice floor, two fist-sized eyes—yellow, with black oval pupils—were staring implacably back up at him.

3

The trip down the mountain was as silent as the journey up had been chatty. Marshall could guess what they were all thinking. This discovery would change what up to now had been a quiet, unglamorous, even monotonous scientific expedition. Exactly how things would change, none of the scientists could say. But from now on, everything would be different.

At the same time, he knew, everyone was privately asking one question: *What the hell was it?*

Sully broke the silence. "We should have taken an ice core for testing."

"How long has it been there, do you think?" Chen asked.

"The Fear's an MIS-2 glacier," Marshall replied. "That cave has been buried at least twelve thousand years. Maybe much longer."

Silence settled over them again. The sun had finally succeeded in burning through the low-hanging clouds, and as it sank toward the horizon it ignited the snowpack into fiery brilliance. Absently, Marshall pulled a pair of sun goggles from his pocket and snugged them into place. He was thinking of the unfathomable blackness of those dead eyes under the ice.

"What time is it in New York?" Sully asked at last.

"Half past eight," said Faraday.

"They'll have gone home; we'll try first thing in the morning. Ang, will you make sure the satphone is fired up before breakfast?"

"Sure thing, but I'll need to apply to Gonzalez for fresh batteries, because—"

Chen stopped in mid-sentence. Looking up, Marshall immediately saw what made the graduate student fall silent.

The base lay a few hundred yards below, the long, low structure rusted and sullen-looking in the dying sun. They had followed the glacial valley in a gentle curve, and the main entrance to the base was now in view beyond the security fencing. Penny Barbour, the team's computer scientist, stood on the concrete apron between the guardhouse and the central doors, wearing jeans and a plaid flannel shirt. The air was very still, and her short, mouse-brown hair hung limply over her forehead. Beside her was Paul Gonzalez, the sergeant in charge of the tiny posting that kept Fear Base nominally operational.

Four figures in heavy parkas, trousers of polar bear fur, and animal-skin mukluks surrounded them. One was holding a rifle; the others had spears or bows lashed to their backs. Although their faces were hidden, Marshall was certain these were Native Americans from the small encampment to the north.

As they quickened their steps toward the base, Marshall wasn't sure whether to feel curiosity or alarm. Although they'd been on-site for a month, the scientists had had no interaction with the Indians. In fact, they only knew of their existence because the soldiers at the base had mentioned it in passing. Why would they choose today, of all days, to pay a visit?

As they passed the fence and empty guardhouse and approached the entrance, the group turned to face them. "This lot knocked on the door not two minutes ago," Barbour said in her broad North London accent. "The sergeant and I came out to meet them." Her plain, friendly face was pinched and somewhat worried-looking.

Sully glanced at Gonzalez. "Has this ever happened before?"

Gonzalez was fifty-something and burly, with the clear-eyed fatalism of the career soldier. "Nope." He unshipped his radio to alert the other soldiers, but Sully shook his head.

"That won't be necessary, will it?" Then Sully turned to Barbour. "You'd better get back into the warmth." He watched her head for the main entrance, then cleared his throat, faced their guests. "Would you like to step inside?" he said, slowly enunciating each word and gesturing toward the door.

The Native Americans said nothing. There were three women and a man, Marshall noticed, and the man was by far the oldest. His face was seamed to an almost leathery complexion by years of cold and sunlight. His eyes were a clear, deep brown. He wore large earrings of bone, carved with fantastic detail; there were feathers in the fur of his collar; and his cheekbones bore the dark tattoos of a shaman. Gonzalez had told them the band lived a life of unusual simplicity, but—Marshall thought, staring at the spears and animal skins—he'd had no idea just how simple.

For a moment, an uncomfortable silence settled over the group, the only noise the grumbling of the nearby generators. Then Sully spoke again. "You've come from the settlement to the north? That's a long journey, and you must be tired. Can we do anything for you? Would you like something to drink or eat?"

No answer.

Sully repeated himself, slowly and emphatically, as if speaking to a half-wit. "You like drink? Eat?"

When there was no response, Sully turned away with a sigh. "We're not getting anywhere."

"They probably don't understand a word you're saying," said Gonzalez.

Sully nodded. "And I don't speak Inuit."

"Tunit," the old man said.

Sully turned back quickly. "I'm sorry?"

"Not Inuit. Tunit."

"I'm very sorry. I've never heard of the Tunits before." Sully patted his chest lightly. "My name is Sully." He introduced Gonzalez and the scientists by name. "The woman you met is Penny Barbour."

The old man touched his own breast. "Usuguk." He pronounced it Oos-oo-gook. He didn't offer to introduce the women.

"Pleased to meet you," Sully said, as usual playing his role as team leader to the hilt. "Would you care to step inside?"

"You asked if you could do anything for us," Usuguk said. Marshall noticed, to his surprise, that the man spoke with a completely uninflected accent.

"Yes," Sully replied, equally surprised.

"There is something important you can do—very important. You can leave here. Today. And don't come back."

This response left Sully speechless.

"Why?" Marshall asked after a moment.

The man pointed toward Mount Fear. "That is a place of evil. Your presence here is a danger to all of us."

"Evil?" Sully repeated, recovering. "You mean, the volcano? It's extinct now, dead."

The Tunit glanced at him, the lines of his face thrown into sharp relief by the setting sun. It was a mask of bitter anxiety.

"What evil?" Marshall asked.

Usuguk declined to elaborate. "You should not be here," he said. "You are intruding where you have no business. And you have made the ancient ones angry. Very angry."

"Ancient ones?" Sully asked.

"Normally they are"—Usuguk searched for the word—"benevolent." He made a semicircular movement with one hand, palm open. "In the old days, all the men here, the ones with guns and uniforms, stayed inside the metal walls they built. Even today, the soldiers never stray into the forbidden place."

"I don't know about any forbidden place," Gonzalez rumbled. "But I keep my keister inside, where it's nice and warm."

Usuguk was still staring at Sully. "You are different. You have stepped on ground where no living man should tread. And now the ancient ones are angry, more so than in any memory of my people. Their wrath paints the sky with blood. The heavens cry out with the pain, like a woman in labor."

"I'm not sure what you mean by 'crying out,'" Sully said. "But the strange color of the night sky is simply the aurora borealis. The northern lights. They're caused by solar winds entering the earth's magnetic field. Admittedly the color is rather unusual, but surely you've noticed them before." Sully was acting the kindly paterfamilias now, smiling, patronizing, like a man explaining something to a young child. "Gases in the atmosphere give off excess energy in the form of light. Different gases emit photons of different wavelengths."

If this explanation made any difference to Usuguk, he didn't let on. "As soon as we saw how angry the spirit folk had become, we started on our way here. We have been walking—no rest, no food—ever since."

"All the more reason for you to come inside," Sully said. "We'll give you food, something hot to drink."

"Why is the mountain forbidden?" Marshall asked.

The shaman turned to him. "Can you not understand? You have heard my warning. You now refuse to heed it? The mountain is a place of darkness. You *must* leave."

"We can't leave," Sully said. "Not yet. But in a few weeks, two or three, we'll be on our way. And until then, I give you my word that—"

But the shaman turned away, toward the Tunit women. "*Anyok lubyar tussarnek,*" he said. One of them began to cry loudly. Turning back, Usuguk looked at each of the scientists in turn, his face filled with such a mixture of sorrow and fear that it curled the hairs on Marshall's neck. Then, pulling a small pouch from his parka, the elder dipped a finger inside and daubed a number of signs in the frozen tundra with a dark liquid too viscous to be anything but blood. And finally—intoning something in his own language with a low and prayerful voice—he turned away and joined the others already retreating across the permafrost.

4

For the two days that followed, a frigid wind blew out of the north, bringing clear skies and bitter temperatures. At 11:00 AM on the third day, Marshall, Sully, and Faraday left the base and walked across the frozen plain that stretched south endlessly from Mount Fear. It was a perfect morning, the sky a dome of arctic blue unblemished by clouds. Beneath their feet, the permafrost was as hard as concrete. The temperature hovered around zero degrees Fahrenheit, and, temporarily at least, the glacier had stopped its dreadful cracking and groaning.

Their thoughts were interrupted by a sudden low drone, strangely attenuated by the arctic chill. A speck appeared on the southern horizon. As they watched, it slowly resolved into a helicopter, flying low toward them.

Faraday sniffed with displeasure. "I still think we should have waited a few days. Why did we need to phone it in so quickly?"

"That was the deal," Sully replied, eyeing the approaching chopper. "If we'd stalled, they'd have known."

Faraday mumbled something, clearly unconvinced.

Sully frowned at the biologist. "I've said it before. Make a deal with the devil, don't complain about the consequences."

Nobody replied. Nobody needed to.

Northern Massachusetts University didn't pretend to be in the first rank of educational institutions. With grant money in short supply, the university had resorted to a relatively new tactic: securing expedition financing from a media conglomerate in return for exclusive rights and access. While global warming wasn't particularly sexy, it was topical. Terra Prime had bankrolled the team as it had half a dozen others—a group studying native medicines in the Amazon jungle, another excavating the potential grave of King Arthur—in hopes of snagging at least one science documentary worth developing. For weeks now, Marshall had kept his fingers crossed, hoping they could finish up their research and leave without attracting attention. Those hopes were now dashed.

The scientists drew together as the helicopter approached, circled over the camp, then settled onto a relatively level section of ground, rotors beating hard against the air. The passenger door opened and a woman jumped out. She was dressed in a leather jacket and jeans. Long black hair spilled over her collar, dancing lightly in the chopper's wake. She was slim and perhaps thirty, and as she turned to reach for her luggage, Marshall caught sight of a shapely derriere.

"Nice-looking devil," he murmured.

Now the woman was hoisting her bags and heading toward them, ducking beneath the rotors. She turned to give the pilot a wave of thanks; he gave a thumbs-up and, goosing the engine, quickly lifted off and banked sharply southward, hurrying back the way he'd come.

The scientists stepped forward to meet her. Sully pulled off his glove and quickly extended his hand. "I'm Gerard Sully," he said. "Climatologist and team leader. This is Evan Marshall and Wright Faraday."

The woman shook their hands in turn. Marshall found her grasp brief and professional. "And I'm Kari Ekberg, field producer for Terra Prime. Congratulations on your discovery."

Sully took one bag, Marshall the other. "Producer?" Sully asked. "So you're in charge?"

Ekberg laughed. "Hardly. You'll find that on a set like this, everybody with a clipboard is a producer."

"Set?" Marshall repeated.

"That's what it is to us, anyway." She stopped to look carefully around, as if scouring the landscape for drama.

"You're a little underdressed for the Federal Wilderness Zone," Marshall said.

"So I see. I spent most of my life in Savannah. The coldest place I've ever been is New York City in February. I'll have the crew bring me up something from Mountain Hardwear."

"Underdressed or not, you're the best-looking thing that's ever happened to this base," Sully said.

Ekberg stopped studying the landscape to glance at him, her eyes traveling from head to toe. She didn't reply, but she smiled slightly, as if in that glance she'd taken the measure of his person.

Sully colored slightly, cleared his throat. "Shall we get back, then? Careful where you step—the ground around here is riddled with old lava tubes."

He led the way, discussing the morning's research with Faraday. Ekberg wasn't in charge, and she apparently wasn't receptive to his clumsy flirtations; that was sufficient to put an end to his interest. Ekberg and Marshall brought up the rear.

"I was curious about what you said just now," Marshall said. "Our expedition site being a set."

"I didn't mean to sound insensitive. Obviously, to you this is a work environment. It's just that, on a shoot like this, the clock is everything. We don't have a lot of time. And besides, I'm sure your group wants us in and out as quickly as possible. That's my job: to advance the gig."

"Advance the gig?"

"Scout locations, arrange a schedule. Basically set up a trajectory so that when the producer and talent hit the ground, their path is already prepared."

Privately, Marshall was surprised by this talk: producer, talent. Like the other scientists, he'd assumed Terra Prime would be sending one person, or two at most: somebody to point the camera, and somebody to stand in front of it now and then. "So you do all the heavy lifting up front, then the big shots come and steal the glory."

Ekberg laughed: a clear, rich contralto that rang over the permafrost. "I guess that about sums it up."

They reached the security checkpoint, long since fallen into disuse, and Ekberg stared ahead in unconcealed surprise. "My God. I had no idea how big this place was."

"What did you expect?" Sully asked. "Igloos and pup tents?"

"Actually, most of the base is underground," Marshall said as they walked past the perimeter fence and across the apron. "They built it in a natural declivity, brought in prefabbed sections, filled in the excess space with frozen dirt and pumice. The visible structures are for the most part mechanical or technical systems: powerhouse, radar domes, that sort of thing. The architects wanted to minimize its visual footprint. That's why it was built in the shadow of the only mountain for many miles around."

"How long since the base was active?"

"A long time," Marshall replied. "Almost fifty years."

"My God. So who maintains it? You know, keeps the toilets flushing, that sort of thing?"

"It's what the government calls a minimal maintenance installation. There's a tiny detachment of soldiers here to keep things operational, three guys from the Army Corps of Engineers under the command of Gonzalez. That's Sergeant Gonzalez. They maintain the generators and the electrical grid, cycle the heating systems, change lightbulbs, monitor the level of the water tanks. And at present, babysit us."

"Fifty years." Ekberg shook her head. "Guess that's why they don't mind renting it out to us."

Marshall nodded.

"Still, Uncle Sam isn't exactly a cheap landlord. We're paying $100,000 more just to house the documentary crew for a week."

"Cost of living is high up here," said Sully.

Ekberg looked around again. "The soldiers have to *stay* here?"

"They get rotated out every six months. At least, the three grunts do. The sergeant, Gonzalez—he seems to like it."

Ekberg shook her head. "Now there's a man who clearly values his privacy."

They stepped past the heavy outer doors, through a staging area, down a long weather chamber—lined on both sides with lockers for parkas and snow gear—and then through another set of doors into the base itself. Although Fear Base hadn't been active for half a century, the military atmosphere remained strong: American flags, steel walls, utilitarian features. Fading posters on the walls listed standing orders and warned against security breaches. A wide corridor ran left and right from the entrance plaza, quickly fading into obscurity: the immediate area was well lit, but the more distant regions contained just the occasional oasis of light. On the far side of the plaza, a man in military uniform sat behind a glass panel, reading a paperback.

Marshall noticed Ekberg's nose wrinkling. "Sorry about that," he said with a laugh. "Took me about a week to get used to the smell, too. Who'd have thought an arctic base would smell like a battleship's bilge? Come on, let's get you signed in."

They walked across the plaza to the glass window. "Tad," Marshall said by way of greeting.

The man behind the panel nodded back. He was tall and youthful, with a buzz cut of carrot-colored hair. He wore the stripe of a private in the engineers' corps. "Dr. Marshall."

"This is Kari Ekberg, here in advance of the rest of the documentary team." Marshall turned to Ekberg. "Tad Phillips."

Phillips looked the woman over with ill-concealed interest. "We got the word just this morning. Ms. Ekberg, if you'll sign in, please?" He passed a clipboard out through a slot at the base of the glass panel.

She signed on the indicated line and passed it back. Phillips noted the time and date, then put the clipboard aside. "You'll give her the orientation, explain the cleared areas?"

"Sure thing," Marshall said.

Phillips nodded and—after another glance at Ekberg—returned his gaze to the book he'd been reading. Sully led the way to a nearby stairwell and the group began to descend.

"At least it's warm in here," Ekberg said.

"The upper levels, anyway," Sully replied. "The rest is reduced to maintenance only."

"What did he mean about cleared areas?" she asked.

"This central, five-level section of the base is where the officers lived and much of the monitoring went on," Marshall said. "We've got full access to that—not that any of us have had the time or inclination to do much exploring. We have limited access to the southern wing, where most of the computers and other equipment was stored and maintained. The enlisted men live there; we have clearance to the upper levels. We're not authorized to enter the northern wing."

"What's in that?"

Marshall shrugged. "No idea."

They emerged onto another corridor, longer and better lit than the one above. Ancient equipment of all kinds had been shoved up against the walls, as if the place had been abandoned in great haste. There were more lockers here, along with official-looking signboards with arrows, providing directions to various installations: RADAR MAPPING, RASP COMMAND POST, RECORDING/MONITORING. Doors with small metal-grilled windows lined both sides of the corridor. They were marked not with names but with series of letters and numbers. "We've set up our temporary labs here on B Level," Sully said, jerking his thumb toward the doors. "Ahead are the galley, the officers' mess, and a briefing room we've converted into a temporary rec area. Around that bend are the bunk rooms. We've set up a spare for your use."

Ekberg murmured her thanks. "I still don't understand why anyone would need a base like this at all," she said. "I mean, way up here, so far north."

"It was part of the original early warning system," Marshall said. "Ever hear of the Pinetree Line, or the DEW Line?"

Ekberg shook her head.

"Back in 1949 the Soviets tested a working atomic bomb. It drove us crazy: we'd thought we had at least five more years to prepare. Instead, our eggheads suddenly predicted that in a few years the Russians would have enough bombs to cripple the United States. So there was a huge ramping up of troops, aircraft, weaponry—including a crash program to develop a perimeter defense system. The Pacific and Atlantic seaboards were well protected, and it became clear that the main threat would come in as bombers, over the pole. But radar then was very primitive: it couldn't detect low-flying aircraft, couldn't detect things over the horizon."

"So they needed to bring their eyes as close to the threat as possible."

"Exactly. The military put their heads together and came up with the most likely routes the Russian bombers would take in the event of an attack. They built early warning stations as far north as they could along each route. This is one of them." Marshall shook his head. "The ironic thing is that by the time it was completed in the late fifties, it was already obsolete. Missiles were replacing aircraft as delivery systems for bombs. We needed a centralized network to address that kind of threat. So a new system called SAGE was put in place and these stations were mothballed."

They had rounded the corner and started down another barrackslike passage. Sully stopped at one of the doors, turned the knob, and pushed it open, revealing a spartan room with a cot, desk, wardrobe, and mirror. The worst of the dust had been cleared away by Chen earlier that morning. "These are your quarters," Sully said.

Ekberg glanced inside quickly, then nodded her thanks as Sully and Marshall placed her bags on the cot.

"It's a long ride up from New York," Sully said, "and if you're like us you probably didn't get much sleep on the way. If you'd care to nap or freshen up, go right ahead. The showers and head are just down the corridor."

"Thanks for the offer, but I'd better get started right away."

"Get started?" Sully glanced at her in confusion.

Light dawned on Marshall. "You mean, you want to see it."

"Of course! That's why I'm here." She looked around. "That is, if that's all right with you."

"I'm afraid it's not all right," Sully replied. "There have been several polar bear sightings in recent weeks. And those lava tubes are extremely dangerous. But you're welcome to observe it from a distance, I suppose."

Ekberg seemed to consider this. Then she nodded slowly. "Thank you."

"Evan here will take you up—won't you, Evan? Now, if you'll excuse me, I have some tests I need to complete." And with that he flashed her a faint smile, nodded to Marshall, then turned and made his way back in the direction of the temporary labs.

5

"Amazing," Ekberg said, her words smoking the air. "I don't think I've ever seen a sky such a clear, intense blue."

They were making their way up the glacial valley in brilliant sunlight. Despite fretful allusions to the pressing nature of his work, Faraday had elected to come along, and he puffed and wheezed as they climbed. He'd been making this climb at least once a day for a month: the fact he still labored at it betrayed all his sedentary years spent in a laboratory. Ekberg, on the other hand, strode forward with the effortlessness of a committed runner. Her eyes darted everywhere, missing nothing. Now and then she would murmur something into a digital recorder. She was wearing Penny Barbour's spare parka over her leather jacket.

"I know what you mean," Marshall replied. "I just wish there was more of it."

"Sorry?"

"The days are growing shorter, fast. We've got two, maybe three weeks of viable daylight left. After that, it'll be white night around here, twenty hours a day. And we'll be gone."

"No wonder you're in a hurry. In any case, Allan's going to have a field day with that sky."

"Allan?"

"Allan Fortnum, our DP. Director of photography." She glanced ahead at the glacier, deep blue framing the sharp azure of the sky. "How did Mount Fear get its name?"

"After Wilberforce Fear, the explorer who discovered it."

"Did that make him famous?"

"Actually, it killed him. He died of exposure at the base of the caldera."

"Oh." And Ekberg murmured something into the recorder. "Caldera. So it's a volcano?"

"Extinct volcano. It's quite a bizarre thing, really—the only geologic feature in a thousand square miles of permafrost. People are still arguing about how it formed."

"Dr. Sully said it was dangerous. What did he mean by that?"

"Mount Fear is really just a dead cone of prehistoric lava. Weather, and the glacier, have worn it down, made it fragile." He pointed at the knife-edged ridges of the valley, then at one of the large caves that riddled the base of the mountain. "Lava tubes like that are created when a crust forms over an active magma stream. Over the years they become very brittle and can easily collapse. As a result, the mountain's like a vast house of cards. We made the discovery in the back of one of those tubes."

"And the polar bears he mentioned?"

"Cute to look at, but extremely man-aggressive, especially these days, what with habitat shrinkage. When your people get here, make sure they don't stray beyond the fenced apron unless they're armed. There's a store of high-powered rifles at the base."

They climbed a minute before Ekberg broke the silence again. "You're a paleoecologist, right?"

"A Quaternary paleoecologist, yes."

"And what, exactly, are you doing here?"

"Paleoecologists like me reconstruct vanished ecosystems from fossils and other ancient evidence. We try to determine what kinds of creatures roamed the earth, what they ate, how they lived and died. I'm determining what kind of an ecosystem existed here before the advance of the glacier."

"And now that the glacier's retreating, the evidence—the samples—are coming to light again."

"Exactly."

She looked at Marshall with penetrating, inquisitive eyes. "What kind of samples?"

"Plant traces. Layered mud. Some macro-organic remains like wood."

"Mud and wood," Ekberg said.

Marshall laughed. "Not sexy enough for Terra Prime, is it?"

She laughed in return. "What can you do with those?"

"Well, wood and other organics can be radiocarbon-dated to determine how long ago the glacier buried them. Mud samples are processed for pollen, which in turn indicates what kind of plants and trees were dominant prior to the glaciation. See, modern ecologists are stuck analyzing the world as it exists today, which has been hugely impacted by humans over the last hundred centuries. But with the samples, the readings, the observations I make here, I can reconstruct the world as it existed *before* humans became the dominant element."

"You can re-create the past," Ekberg said.

"In a way, yes."

"Sounds pretty sexy to me. And I suppose a glacier's the perfect place to do this because it would have locked everything into a deep freeze, preserving it like a time capsule."

"Exactly right," Marshall said. He was impressed by her ability to quickly size up and understand an unfamiliar discipline. "Not to mention the fact that when the ice melts, it simply releases its contents. No muss, no fuss—and no need for a lot of work with shovels and chisels uncovering fossils and subfossils."

"A very pragmatic approach. What are subfossils? Really small fossils?"

Marshall had to laugh again. "That's what paleontologists call fossils less than ten thousand years old."

"I see." She turned to the struggling Faraday. "And Dr. Faraday, you're an evolutionary biologist, right?"

Faraday stopped to catch his breath, and the others halted obligingly. He nodded as he shifted his day pack from one shoulder to the other.

"And that means . . . ?"

"Put simply, I study how species change over time," Faraday puffed.

"And why are you doing it here, in such an inhospitable place?"

"My research involves the effect of global warming on species development."

A smile formed on her face. "So you really *are* working on global warming. While Dr. Marshall, here, is simply taking advantage of it."

Alarm bells rang faintly in Marshall's head: Terra Prime had funded their expedition with the understanding it would involve global warming. But Ekberg's smile was a friendly one, and so he just smiled in return.

They stopped a moment so Ekberg could transcribe a few more notes. Marshall waited, looking out over the horizon. Then he paused. Plucking out his binoculars, he passed them to Ekberg. "Take a look. Out there on the permafrost, to the southwest."

She peered through the glasses a moment. "Speak of the devil. Two polar bears." She stared a minute, then passed the binoculars back. "Do we need to turn back?"

"We should be fine up here on the mountain. Normally, one of us would be armed."

"So why aren't we?"

"I refuse to carry a weapon. And Wright here is absentminded. Come on, we should get going."

As they approached the glacier, Marshall looked up a little apprehensively at the glacial wall, but the recent frigid temperatures had arrested its retreat and the ice face looked much the same as it had three days ago when the cave was first exposed.

"That's the cave," he said, pointing at the black maw near the base of the glacier.

Ekberg glanced toward it. Although her face betrayed nothing, Marshall knew she must be disappointed not to see inside. He nodded to Faraday. The biologist reached into the pocket of his parka, pulled out a large glossy photograph, and handed it to Ekberg.

"*This* is what we found," Marshall said. "A print from our video recording."

She took the photo eagerly. Staring at it, she caught her breath audibly.

"It died with its eyes open," she breathed.

Nobody answered; nobody needed to.

"My God. What is it?"

"We can't be sure," he replied. "As you can see from the photo, the ice is very opaque, and we can only see the eyes, some surrounding fur. But we believe it may be a Smilodon."

"A *what*?"

"Smilodon. Better known as a saber-toothed tiger."

"Which is technically incorrect," Faraday said. "Because the Smilodon descends from a completely different line than the tiger."

But Ekberg didn't seem to hear. She was staring at the photo, wide-eyed, digital recorder forgotten for once.

"We think that because of the eyes," Marshall said. "They resemble very closely the eyes of the big cats—of all cats, for that matter. Note they are predator's eyes: large, forward-facing. There's the wide area of iris, the vertical pupils. I'd bet that an autopsy will reveal a layer of tapetum lucidum behind the retina."

"How long has it been frozen?" she asked.

"Smilodons became extinct about ten thousand years ago," Marshall said. "Whether due to the advancing ice, loss of habitat or food, or a virus that jumped the species barrier, we don't know. Given the time this ice cave was covered by the glacier, I'd estimate this was one of the last of its kind to die."

"We're not yet sure how it came to be frozen," Faraday added. His habitual blinking, his wide, watery eyes, gave him the appearance of a startled child. "The creature probably retreated into the cave to avoid an ice storm, and froze there. Perhaps it was wounded, or starving. Or perhaps it simply died of old age. More analysis may give us answers."

Ekberg had quickly regained her professional composure. "What's this?" she asked, pointing to a clean, vertical hole near the carcass about half an inch wide.

"As you can see, there isn't a clear view," Marshall said. "This ice is dirty, occluded, full of prehistoric mud. So we had our intern, Ang, bring up a remote imaging device. It sends out sonar pings and measures the echoes produced."

"Like a fish-finder," Ekberg said.

"In a way," Marshall said, amused. "A very high-tech fish-finder. Anyway, due to the condition of the ice, precise measurements aren't possible, but the body seems to be approximately eight feet long. We estimate its weight in the thousand-pound range."

"More appropriate for *Smilodon populator* than *Smilodon fatalis*," Faraday intoned.

Ekberg shook her head slowly, eyes still fixed on the photograph. "Amazing," she said. "Buried under a glacier for thousands of years."

A brief silence settled over the group. Standing motionless, Marshall began to feel the cold creeping in around the edges of his hood, biting at his fingertips and toes.

"You've asked a lot of questions," he said quietly. "Any objections to answering one?"

Ekberg glanced over at him. "Shoot."

"We know Terra Prime is planning to make some kind of documentary, but none of us have any idea what kind. We assume you're going to explain our work here, maybe end it by describing this un-usual find. Record the discovery for posterity. Can you give us more details?"

A wry smile formed on her lips. "Actually, it isn't posterity the network is concerned with."

"Go on."

"I'm afraid the details will have to come from Emilio Conti, the executive producer. But I can promise you one thing, Dr. Marshall: he views this as a real feather in his cap, something he's been work-ing toward his entire professional career." Her smile deepened. "Your expedition is about to become more famous than in your wildest dreams."

Dawn burst across the Blue Ridge Mountains with a violent explosion of color. The sun, rising over Mount Marshall, infused the autumn sky with brilliant hues normally confined to a painter's palette: naphthol and cadmium, magenta and vermilion. The sleepy peaks and slopes were furred with the deep greens and blues of oak, hemlock, maple, and hickory trees. The mountains themselves seemed to exhale the chill air, their breath settling in deep blankets of mist that cloaked the dark valleys and crowned the summits with gauzy rings like monks' tonsures.

Jeremy Logan eased the rental car up to the Front Royal entrance station, paid the park fee, then accelerated gently away. There were faster ways to reach his destination—Skyline Drive was as sinuous as a snake, with a top speed of thirty-five miles per hour—but he was early, and he hadn't traveled this road since he was a boy, camping with his father. Ahead, the parkway disappeared into a velvet haze, promising a journey of both discovery and nostalgia.

La Bohème was playing on the car stereo—the 1946 Toscanini recording, with Licia Albanese as soprano lead—and he turned it off in order to concentrate on the passing scenery. The Shenandoah Valley Overlook: they'd stopped there, he remembered, for deviled-ham sandwiches and a few snaps of the Instamatic. Next, Low Gap, Compton Gap, Jenkins Gap: each appeared in his windshield in turn, yielding up—almost reluctantly—their stunning vistas of the Shenandoah River, the freckled hills of the Virginia piedmont. Logan had grown up in the low country of South Carolina, and he remembered how—first seeing these sights through boyish eyes—he'd never imagined there could be so much dramatic scenery crammed into such a relatively small space.

At milepost 27, he passed the turnout for the hike up Knob Mountain. He and his father had stopped there, too, and made the two-mile ascent. It had been a warm day, Logan recalled, and the cold canteen hanging from his neck had sweated icy droplets against his skin. His father had been a historian, a stranger to exercise, and the hike winded him. It was at the summit he'd told Logan about the cancer.

At Thornton Gap, Logan exited Skyline Drive, following the state highway along the river and out of the national park. At Sperryville, he turned south onto Route 231 and followed the signs for Old Rag Lodge.

Within ten minutes he was in the shadow of the mountain. At more than three thousand feet, Old Rag was a relatively low peak, but the rock scrambles to its bald top were famously challenging. Yet it was best known not for its hiking opportunities but for the luxury hotel that lay in a bowl-shaped valley near its feet. Old Rag Lodge resembled nothing so much as a vast château, hugely out of place in the wild Virginia terrain. As Logan swung into the private drive and accelerated up a gentle slope, the hotel came into view, a confection of monolithic limestone walls and brilliantly hued stained glass set into mullioned casings. The rambling structure was topped with extravagant cupolas and minarets of copper.

Logan drove past a lush thirty-six-hole golf course, then over the carefully raked drive of white gravel leading to the porte cochere. He gave his keys to the waiting valet, then stepped inside.

"Checking in, sir?" the woman behind the front desk asked.

Logan shook his head. "I'm here for the tour."

"Viewings of the bunker begin at ten o'clock."

"I've arranged for a private visit. The name's Logan." And he slid a business card across the marble top of the reception desk.

The woman examined the card, turned to her computer monitor, typed briefly. "Very good, Dr. Logan. If you'd kindly have a seat in the lobby?"

"Thank you." Gathering up his briefcase, Logan walked across the echoing, domed expanse and took a seat between two vast Corinthian columns wreathed in red silk.

While the lodge had been popular for seven decades among the golfing and hunting aristocrats of the Old Dominion, in the last few years it had developed a stranger reputation. For it was here that— starting in 1952—a large, highly secret underground bunker had been maintained for officials of the United States government. In the event of nuclear war, congressmen, senators, and other functionaries could retreat to the bunker beneath Old Rag Lodge to coordinate military operations, enact new laws, and see to the continuing governance of America—assuming, of course, an America still remained to govern. Looking around the opulent lobby, Logan smiled faintly. It made perfect sense that government leaders had chosen a place like this to hunker down in: far enough from Washington to escape the worst of the holocaust, yet perfectly appointed to ride out Armageddon in comfort and luxury. Although the bunker had gone out of active service in the 1980s, it had not been declassified until 1992. Now it served as historical museum, conspiracy theorist magnet—and unlikely tourist attraction.

Logan glanced up to see a short, slightly tubby man in a white linen suit and panama hat bustle across the lobby. He wore round black glasses and his face was quite pink. He extended a hand. "Dr. Logan?"

Logan rose. "Yes."

"I'm Percy Hunt, official historian for the lodge. I'll be your view facilitator this morning."

View facilitator, Logan thought as he shook the proffered hand. *Must be what passes for tour guide at the Old Rag Lodge.* "I'm grateful."

"You're from Yale, isn't that correct?" Hunt glanced at a small folded sheet. "Regina Professor of Medieval History?"

"Yes. Though at present I'm on academic leave."

Hunt slipped the paper into his jacket. "Very good. If you'll follow me, please?"

He led the way to an arch at the far end of the lobby, which gave on to a plushly carpeted hall lined with sporting prints. "There are two entrances to the bunker," Hunt said. "A large exterior door built into the rear of the mountain—used by trucks and heavy vehicles—and an elevator behind the hotel's main conference room. We'll be entering via the latter."

They passed an indoor swimming pool decorated with faux-Grecian marbles, a banquet hall, and a ballroom, before entering the large and well-appointed conference room. Without pausing, Hunt headed toward a set of double doors in the rear, wallpapered to match the rest of the room. "Congress would have used this space to convene, assuming it remained standing," he said. "Otherwise, they would have employed the smaller chambers below." He pointed at the wall ahead of them. "This supports the blast doors protecting the bunker elevator." Opening the doors with some effort, he revealed a small space with another door at its far end. Unlocking this with a key he kept on a fob, Hunt ushered Logan into a large elevator, painted green. Closing the door, he used the same key to operate the elevator. There were no floor buttons or indicator lights of any kind.

The descent was very long. After thirty seconds or so, Hunt turned toward his guest. "So, Dr. Logan," he said, "where in particular does your interest lie? The engineering spaces? Personal quarters? Infirmary? I ask because usually researchers who arrange for private tours like this are following up some particular area of expertise. The more you tell me, the better I'll be able to assist you."

Logan glanced back. "Actually, Mr. Hunt, it isn't the bunker per se that I'm interested in."

Hunt blinked back. "No? Then why—"

"I'm here to examine the Omega Archive."

Hunt's eyes widened. "The archive? I'm sorry, but that's quite impossible."

"The information in that archive was declassified as of"—Logan glanced at his watch—"eight o'clock this morning. That was seventy minutes ago. It's now a matter of public record."

"Yes, yes, but the proper deactivation procedures—vetting, cross-checking, all that sort of thing—need to be attended to first. Requests have to go through proper channels."

"I'm only interested in a single file. You can observe; I'll read it in your presence. As for proper channels, I think you'll find this sufficient to allay any objections." And Logan opened his briefcase, removed a folded sheet stamped at the top with the United States seal, and handed it to Hunt.

The little man glanced over the letter, eyes widening farther still. He licked his lips. "Very well, Dr. Logan. Very well. I'll still need to get verbal authorization—"

Logan pointed to the signature at the bottom of the letter. "If you really want to trouble him, feel free to do so—once we're back in the hotel. I'll only be a few minutes if I'm allowed to conduct my research unobstructed."

Hunt removed his glasses, wiped them on his jacket, replaced them, adjusted his straw hat. "May I ask . . ." his voice faltered, and he cleared his throat. "May I ask what interest a professor of medieval history has in the Omega Archive?"

Logan glanced at him mildly. "As I mentioned earlier, Mr. Hunt: I'm on administrative leave."

The elevator creaked open onto a concrete tunnel with a semi-circular roof and a floor punctuated by steel grills. "Follow me, please," Hunt said, walking quickly down the tunnel. It was very chill and raw. A line of incandescent bulbs in circular fixtures, hanging from the ceiling by slender stalks, lit the way. Ganglions of green-painted pipes ran high up along the walls, snaking deeper into the bunker. Hunt set a brisk pace, apparently no longer disposed to conversation. They passed several branching tunnels, what looked like a dormitory, and a large room with television cameras and a back wall covered by a photo of the Capitol building taken in cherry blossom season, before Hunt veered off the main corridor. He led the way through a room full of electrical control panels to a small antechamber that lay beyond. Sliding away a false wall at the rear of the chamber, he revealed a heavy metal door balanced on massive hinges. Taking a different key from his pocket, he fitted it to the central slot. "The archives lie beyond," he said. "Please locate the file and review it as quickly as possible. I need to get this authorized with all possible haste."

"I'll be quick," Logan replied.

Hunt frowned, nodded. Then, turning the key, he pulled open the door. Air rushed out from the blackness beyond—stale air, dust-laden. The very smell quickened Logan's pulse.

The Omega Archive was precisely the kind of find that Jeremy Logan—for whom the title of medieval scholar was something of a genteel, if accurate, smoke screen—lived for. In the years following the Second World War, the government had taken advantage of the built-in security of the congressional bunker to store secret and top-secret military records. Though the bunker itself had been declassified a decade earlier, it had taken many more years—and much political pressure from historians, journalists, and freedom-of-information advocates—to clear away the red tape surrounding the Omega Archive. And while technically the archive had been declassified as of this morning, standard procedure was for representatives from the security agencies to examine its files—and in the process remove many still deemed sensitive—before allowing general public access. Logan had called in several favors in order to gain brief access before this final vetting process began.

The space he stepped into was utterly black, but some sixth sense told him it was large—very large. He felt along the wall, found a bank of at least two dozen light switches, and snapped a few on at random.

With a low boom, rows of fluorescents began flickering into life here and there ahead of him, creating small pools of yellow in a sea of darkness. He switched on additional lights and, finally, the entire archive came into view: row after row after row of ten-foot-tall olive-green cabinets arranged in regular columns, marching back almost out of sight. He stood in the doorway, blinking, gradually accustoming himself to the scale. The space before him was wider than a football field and at least as long. His eyes traveled over the banks of files. The amount of potentially fascinating information stored in here—official secrets, scientific patents, confiscated cultural and national patrimony, sets of sworn testimony whose contradictions would prove most enlightening—could keep him happily occupied for years.

A restless movement beside him reminded Logan he was working on borrowed time. With a smile and a nod, he took a fresh grip on his briefcase and strode forward. The file that interested him in particular concerned an event that took place in Italy in 1944. While fighting the Germans for control of Cassino, units of the American Fifth Army commandeered an ancient fortress—the Castello Diavilous. The long-deserted castle had once been home to an infamous alchemist who performed extremely unsettling experiments. Following the occupation, the castle was burned to the ground, its secret basement laboratory ransacked. Logan had been tracking the alchemist's accomplishments and the fate of his bizarre experiments. His best hope to learn more, he now knew, was here, among the moldering files of the Omega Archive.

He proceeded briskly down the tall metal ranks, peering at the labels on the cabinets at random. He quickly determined they were chronological, further subdivided by armed services branch. It was the work of ten minutes to locate 1944; five more to bracket the files related to the Fifth Army; another sixty seconds to pinpoint dossiers related to the Italian theater of operations. He pulled the appropriate drawer to its maximum. There were perhaps three feet worth of manila- and khaki-colored files related to operations at Cassino. They were dusty and badly faded, but otherwise appeared to be barely touched. A quick flip through the titles located a thick file labeled "Fort Diavilous—Tactical and Strategic."

He glanced over at Hunt, who was standing nearby, looking on like a disapproving chaperone. "Is there a reading table nearby I can use for my examination?"

Hunt blinked, sniffed. "The commissary is down the hall past the electrical substation," he said. "I'll take you there."

Logan pulled out the file, prepared to close the drawer. Then he stopped. Removing the file had exposed another behind it, almost equally faded. Its title tab had been stamped with a single word: "Fear."

Instinctively, Logan reached for it, pulled it forward. It was very thin. Behind it lay another file, identical, stamped with the same word.

Both copies of a classified file, stored in the same location? Something was very wrong here.

He shot a hooded glance toward Hunt. The man was walking down the aisle of hulking cabinets, his back to Logan. Looking back at the drawer, Logan cracked open the first of the two identical files, scanned the cover sheet.

TOP SECRET
United States Army

Report to: Internal Board of Inquiry

Subject: (1) Anomaly D-1, further analysis of

(2) Circumstances surrounding death of science team

(3) Recommendations (urgent)

By: H. N. Rose
           Officer in Charge, Fear Base
Date: May 7, 1958

REFERENCE
B2837(a)

Logan's instincts as a researcher into the abnormal were finely tuned, and now they were going off full blast. This was an opportunity, and he didn't hesitate. As stealthily as possible, he snapped open his briefcase; slipped one of the two thin folders beneath other paperwork; closed the case again; placed the Castello Diavilous folder atop the black leather. And then, closing the file drawer and arranging his face into an expressionless mask, he turned and followed Hunt, the view facilitator, out of the echoing vault and down the concrete hallway.

7

Within five days, Fear Base was transformed utterly. The three-acre apron of concrete between the base entrance and the perimeter fence had become a frantic anthill of activity. Helicopters and small transport planes arrived day and night, dropping off workers, supplies, food, fuel, and all manner of exotic equipment. The quiet, dimly lit hallways of the base's central wing now seemed like city boulevards: full of chatter, the clacking of keyboards, and the whir of machinery. Power cables snaked everywhere, waiting treacherously to trip the unwary. The base's powerhouse, until now operating at near-minimum capacity, had been ramped up to 50 percent, filling the arctic silence with its growl. Sergeant Gonzalez and his three army engineers had seemed first astounded, then annoyed by this sudden invasion that turned their once-somnolent base into a hive of demanding, high-maintenance urbanites. The small team was at work night and day, splicing broken wires, fixing leaks, opening heating ducts, and in general making several dozen rooms—largely unused for fifty years—habitable once again.

Evan Marshall walked down the mountain valley, a cooler full of specimens on one shoulder. Halfway to the base, he stopped briefly to rest and survey the small city below, bathed in early-afternoon sunlight. Although the documentary team was naturally bunking in the warmth of the base—various quarters on B Level for the grips, gaffers, publicists, and production assistants, and fancier officers' compartments on C Level for the producer, director of photography, and channel rep—there were still plenty of outbuildings cluttering the grounds. He could make out a variety of prefab huts, storage shacks, and other temporary structures. At one side, a hulking Sno-Cat—an all-terrain vehicle with massive, tanklike treads—guarded a gasoline depot that would do an army division proud. And beyond everything else, standing alone just within the fence, was a metal-walled cube: a mysterious vault about which the scientists had been able to learn nothing.

With that morning's arrival of Emilio Conti, the executive producer and creative force behind the project, the breakneck pace had accelerated still further. Conti had hit the ground running. At his order, large machines now effectively blocked the top of the glacial valley, complicating the scientists' access to their work site. From what Marshall had heard, the producer spent his first hours on-site walking around the base and the surrounding permafrost with his photographic team; studying the way the light fell on the snow, the lava, the glacier; scrutinizing everything through a dozen different positions with a wide-angle lens that hung around his neck. Kari Ekberg had been with him the entire time, filling him in on what she'd accomplished, getting him up to speed, jotting down his work orders for the days to come.

Those days promised to be interesting, indeed.

Marshall picked up the cooler again, hefted it onto the other shoulder, and continued down the mountain. He felt bone-weary:

as usual, he'd had trouble falling asleep the night before, and the noisy additions to Fear Base hadn't helped in the least.

It was hard to believe that only a week had passed since the discovery. Privately, he almost wished the thing had never been found. He was unhappy with the frantic activity, so unlike the careful, cautious approach favored by scientists. He was unhappy with how the documentary team was being coy, almost secretive, about the specifics of their project. And he was especially unhappy with how distracting it all was, how his work was hampered by so many people underfoot. Their own window of opportunity here on the ice was closing fast. The only good thing about the rush, he reflected, was that the faster the film crew worked, the faster they'd clear the hell out.

He bypassed the Sno-Cat and walked into camp. A member of the film crew went by, carrying a long metal boom, and Marshall had to duck out of the way to avoid getting brained. The entrance to the base was obscured by a knot of Terra Prime employees, their backs to him, and as he placed the cooler on the ground and opened the lid to check the samples, he could hear querulous voices raised in complaint.

"This is the worst set I've ever had to work, bar none," said a voice. "And I've worked on some shit."

"I'm freezing my ass off," said a second. "Literally. I think it's frostbitten."

"What's Conti thinking? Coming up here to the middle of nowhere, just because of some dead pelt."

"And all these dweebs wandering around, messing with our site and getting in the way."

Our site, Marshall thought with a mirthless smile.

"Speaking of wandering around, have you heard the talk of polar bears? If we don't freeze to death we're likely to get eaten."

"We should be getting hazard pay."

"The place stinks. The water pressure is terrible. And the craft service sucks. I'm used to fresh stuff—pineapple slices, canapés, finger sandwiches, sushi. Here we get prison rations: beans, hot dogs, frozen spinach."

A sudden cheer erupted on the far side of the outbuildings. A moment later, there came another. Sealing the cooler again, Marshall trotted over to investigate.

About a dozen people had just gathered outside the little steel-walled vault. They were congratulating each other, shaking hands and hugging. A short distance away stood Conti. He was short and dark-haired, with a closely trimmed goatee. He watched the celebratory group, arms folded. Beside him stood the "network liaison," or channel rep: a man named Wolff. And beside Wolff were two photographers, one with a large camera on his shoulder, the other with a portable handheld. Still another man—the one who had almost knocked Marshall over a few minutes earlier—stood nearby, holding a microphone fixed to a boom. Wires from the cameras led to a device attached to his belt.

Marshall glanced curiously at Conti. The man's reputation preceded him: his documentary *From Fatal Seas,* about research submarines exploring the very deepest depths of the ocean, had won half a dozen awards and was still routinely shown in museums and IMAX theaters. He had done a number of other documentaries, mostly dealing with the natural world and environmental crises, and they had all been critical and popular successes. With his goatee and fussy demeanor, the wide-angle lens hanging from his neck like some huge black jewel, he looked the very picture of the brilliant and eccentric director. The only things missing, Marshall reflected, were a megaphone and a white ascot. He reminded himself that looks were deceiving: this man was not only well respected but influential, as well.

"Again," said Conti, in a clipped, mild Italian accent. "More excitement this time. Remember: you've *done* it. Mission accomplished. Let me *see* it in your faces, *hear* it in your voices."

"Rolling," said the man with the handheld camera.

"And—*action,*" said Conti.

Once again, shouts of jubilation burst from the assembled group. They jumped in the air, whooped and yelled, slapped one another on the back. Marshall glanced around in puzzlement, painfully aware of his total ignorance of the project.

Ekberg stood nearby, watching the goings-on. She had been very busy the last several days but had always smiled politely when she saw him—unlike most of the crew, who clearly found the scientists annoyances to be merely tolerated.

He stepped closer to her. "What's happened?"

"It's all over," she said. "A major success."

"It's over?"

"Well, that's what we're filming, anyway."

"But—" he began. Then, suddenly, he understood. Conti was filming the crew's reaction to a successful conclusion . . . whatever and whenever that conclusion might ultimately be. It seemed the producer was filming everything he could, as quickly as he could, whether it was real or simply staged. Clearly the concept of linear time didn't exist here—and Marshall realized he had a lot to learn about documentaries.

Conti was nodding, apparently pleased by this latest effort. He turned toward the photographer with the smaller camera. "Got the B rolls?"

The man gave him a smile and a thumbs-up. Conti glanced from him to Ekberg, caught site of Marshall. "You're Marshall, right? The ecologist?"

"Paleoecologist, yes."

Conti glanced down at his clipboard, checked something off with a pencil held in one heavily gloved hand. "Good. That's next on the list." He looked up at Marshall again, more carefully this time, his gaze running up and down as if examining a side of beef. "Could you assemble the rest of your team in the staging area, dressed for outdoors? Fifteen minutes, if you please. Having all of you on hand will increase the realism of the shot."

"What shot is that?"

"We're going up the mountain."

Marshall hesitated. "I'd be happy to assemble the others. But first I think it's time you explained just what it is you're documenting here. You've said nothing specific. I don't mean to be difficult, but we've all been kept in the dark long enough."

Conti sniffed the chill air. "We're getting all the footage we can before Ashleigh arrives."

"That's something else I don't understand. Why does a host need to fly all the way up here? Why can't she add her narration back in New York, when the film is cut and edited?"

"Because we're not just talking about narration," Conti replied. "We're talking about a docudrama. A *huge* docudrama."

Marshall frowned. "What does that have to do with our work here? Or with the cat we discovered?"

At this, Conti gave a faint smile. "It has *everything* to do with the cat, Professor Marshall. You see, we're going up the mountain to cut it out of the ice."

Marshall felt a chill of disbelief settle over him. "*Cut* it out, you said?"

"In a single block. For transport back to our specially prepared vault. The vault will be sealed, the block of ice melted under controlled conditions." Conti paused for effect. "And when the vault is unsealed again, it's going to be done live, right here—before an audience of ten million viewers."

8

For a moment, Marshall felt almost too dazed to speak. And then, as quickly as it had come, the feeling of disbelief vanished, flushed away by an anger he wasn't even aware he'd been keeping in check.

"I'm sorry," he said, surprised by the calmness of his own voice, "but that isn't going to happen."

The smile didn't leave Conti's face. "No?"

"No, it's not."

"And why is that?"

As the producer asked this question, Marshall saw Sully approaching from the direction of the base. No doubt he'd heard the commotion of Conti's last shot and come to investigate. The climatologist had been fawning over Conti every chance he had, eager to curry favor and perhaps land a supporting role in the production.

"Mr. Conti has just told me the real reason they're here," Marshall said as Sully joined the group.

"Oh?" Sully asked. "What's that?"

"They want to cut the Smilodon out of the ice cave and thaw it in front of live television cameras."

Sully blinked in surprise at this revelation, but said nothing.

Marshall turned back to the producer. "It's one thing for you to take over our base, interrupt our research, let your people treat us like squatters. But I'm not going to allow you to jeopardize our work."

Conti folded one arm over the other. Marshall realized Ekberg was staring at him intently.

"That carcass represents an important—maybe hugely important—scientific discovery," he continued. "It's not some cheap publicity stunt you can exploit for your own ends. If that's why you came up here, I'm sorry you wasted your time and money. But you might as well pack up and leave now."

Sully seemed to master his surprise and hear Marshall once again. "Ah, Evan, there's really no need—"

"And *another* thing," Marshall spoke over Sully. "I've already told Ms. Ekberg here: that cave is unsafe. The vibration of heavy equipment could bring the damned thing down on your heads. So even if we didn't object to your crazy idea, there's no way we'd grant you access."

Conti pursed his lips. "I see. Was there anything else?"

Marshall stared at him. "Isn't that enough? You can't have the cat. It's as simple as that."

He waited for Conti's response. But instead of replying, the director threw a significant glance at Wolff.

Wolff cleared his throat and spoke for the first time. "Actually, Dr. Marshall, you're right. It *is* simple: we can do whatever we want."

Marshall turned toward Wolff, feeling his jaw set in a hard line. "What are you talking about?"

"If we want to cut the cat out of the ice, we can. If we want to chop it up and barbecue it, we can do that, too." The channel rep reached inside his parka and withdrew a sheaf of papers, which he held out to Marshall.

Marshall didn't take them. "What's this?" he asked.

"This is the contract that your Dr. Sully, and the head of NMU's research department, signed with Terra Prime."

When Marshall didn't reply, Wolff went on. "In exchange for underwriting your six-week expedition, Terra Prime—and by extension its corporate parent, Blackpool Entertainment Group—has exclusive and unlimited access not only to your site but to any and all discoveries you make, at our sole discretion."

Reluctantly, Marshall took the document.

"Clause six," Wolff said. "The operative word is 'unlimited.' "

Briefly, Marshall scanned the contract. It was as Wolff said: in effect, Terra Prime controlled any physical or intellectual property their expedition produced. He hadn't realized Terra Prime was a subsidiary of Blackpool, and he didn't like it: Blackpool was infamous for its sensationalist, exploitative journalism. Clearly, Wolff anticipated this moment would come: that's why he was carrying the contract around in the first place. Marshall looked more closely at the man. Even in a parka, Wolff was thin, almost cadaverous, with close-cropped brown hair and an expressionless face. He returned the look, pale eyes betraying nothing.

Marshall turned to Sully. "You signed this?"

Sully shrugged. "It was either that or no expedition. How could we know this was going to happen?"

Marshall didn't answer. Suddenly, he felt more tired than ever. Without another word, he refolded the contract and passed it back to Wolff.

9

A quarter of an hour later, a large group set off up the glacial valley toward the ice cave. In addition to the scientists, Conti, and his
small retinue of assistants, there was Ekberg, the two photographers, and the soundman. A dozen or so tough-looking roustabouts
in leather jackets followed behind, both on foot and in the Sno-Cat,
whose cargo bed had been loaded to overflowing with wooden pallets. These men were not officially part of the documentary team;
they were locals, flown up from Anchorage for a few days to do the
heavy work. Ekberg had already explained that the real rush was to
get the principal photography, the live stuff, done quickly—with
the producer now on scene and the star on the way, money was being burned through quickly, and the sets and props needed to be
built as speedily as possible.

Normally, the hike to the face of Fear glacier took twenty minutes, but today it took several times as long: Conti was forever stopping so the photographers could get shots of the mountain, the valley below, the party itself. Once he'd stopped everything for ten minutes just to gaze pensively up at the glacier. Most strangely, he later got a number of shots of Ekberg—from every angle except face-forward.

"What are those for?" Marshall asked her after the fifth such shot.

Ekberg tugged off her hood. "I'm standing in for Ashleigh."

Marshall nodded his understanding. Ashleigh Davis, the host, wasn't due for another two days—but that wasn't stopping Conti from filming her anyway. "I suppose it's as you said. On a shoot like this, the clock is everything."

"That's right." She glanced over at him. "Look, I'm sorry about what happened back there. I wish I could have warned you, but I was given strict orders. It had to come from Wolff."

"So he's top man. And here I'd figured it was Conti."

"Emilio is in charge of everything creative: the shots, the lighting, the direction, the final cut. But the network is putting up the money. So the network has the last say. And up here at the top of the world, Wolff *is* the network."

Marshall glanced over his shoulder, down the mountain. Wolff had not come along, but he could still be seen far below: a tiny figure, gaunt and wraithlike, standing motionless outside the perimeter fence, watching them.

Marshall turned back with a sigh. "Is this normal? All this stopping, looking around, filming again and again?"

"Not really, no. Conti's burning three times the normal amount of film."

"Why is that?"

"Because he wants this to be his *Mona Lisa*. His masterwork. He's risked a lot to put this together."

"And why is the Great Auteur trudging up the mountain with the rest of the unwashed? I figured he'd be riding in the Sno-Cat."

"He wants to be photographed 'on the ground,' as we say. It

looks better for the 'making-of' video that will ultimately accompany the DVD."

Marshall shook his head in quiet disbelief at the circus this had become.

They resumed the climb, and almost on cue Conti angled toward them. "Is there anything I should know?" he asked Marshall in his clipped Italian accent.

"About what?"

The producer swept his hand in a wide arc. "Anything. The place, the weather, the local fauna—any color we can add to the project."

"There's a great deal you should know. It's a fascinating geological region."

The producer nodded a little dubiously. "I'll schedule an interview when we get back."

Sully, who had heard this exchange, hurried over. "I'd be happy—in my role as team leader—to give you any assistance you need."

Conti nodded again, absently, his eyes back on the glacier.

Marshall wondered if he should tell the producer about the nearby inhabitants. They were probably precisely the kind of "color" Conti was looking for. Just as quickly, he decided against it. The last thing the Tunits wanted—or deserved—was a loud, ignorant film crew descending on their village. He didn't need to guess how they'd react if they could see how Mount Fear had been transformed over the last few days.

He glanced surreptitiously at Conti. Marshall was having a difficult time drawing a bead on the director. For all his posturing as a fey artiste, the man also exhibited a hard, uncompromising façade. It was a most unlikely combination, half Truman Capote, half David Lean. It kept one off-balance.

The ice cave lay ahead now, its dark maw obscured by the pieces of heavy equipment: a flatbed crane on balloon tires and another vehicle that Marshall could not identify. They were painted bright yellow, garish against the snowpack and the pale blue of the glacier.

While the cameramen swapped out lenses and the sound engineer readied his belt mixer, the battalion of men in leather began spreading out around the machines. Two heaved themselves up into the cabs, while others began pulling the wooden pallets from the Sno-Cat and stowing their contents onto the rear of the mobile crane. Glancing more closely, Marshall saw that they were duffels loaded with heavy steel spacers, with hydraulics for adjusting their height.

Barbour watched the men work with narrowed eyes. She held a palmtop computer in one heavily gloved hand and a digital recorder in the other. Even more than Marshall, she was suspicious of the documentary crew. "I can guess what the bloody great flatbed is for," she murmured. "But what's the other thing?"

Marshall peered at the second vehicle. It bristled with equipment that looked vaguely medieval. "No idea."

"Make a note," Conti was saying to Ekberg. "I want a four-color palette: the white of the snow, the cerulean of the sky, the azure of the glacier, the black of the cave. It should be a nocturne in blue. We'll need to use that special process when we get it to the lab." He glanced at the cameramen. "Ready?"

"Ready," said Fortnum, the director of photography.

"Ready here, Mr. C," said Toussaint, the assistant DP.

"You'll need to be very, very careful," Marshall said. "The floor is glare ice, and very slippery. And like I said, these lava tubes are extremely brittle. This whole thing is a crazy risk. One false move and you'll bring down the roof."

"Thank you, Dr. Marshall." Conti turned back to the cameramen. "Fortnum? Toussaint? If you hear any sharp cracking noises while we're inside, quickly pan over the assembled faces. Pick the most frightened you find and zoom in."

The cameramen glanced uneasily at each other, then nodded.

Conti took one final look around, then nodded to Toussaint. "Quiet on the set!" bellowed the cameraman. All chatter immediately faded.

Conti raised his eyes to the cave. *"Action!"*

A digital clapstick snapped and the cameras rolled. Simultaneously, the heavy equipment started up with ear-splitting roars. With a grinding of gears, they lurched toward the face of the glacier. Conti and his small knot of assistants swung in behind. The cameramen stood back, panning carefully, getting everything in. With a huge sense of reluctance, Marshall followed the procession toward the cave. He had a horrible sinking feeling that Conti's hubris was going to make victims of them all.

At the cave mouth, the vehicles paused to let some of the roustabouts pull a few of the canvas duffels off the flatbed. Then, powerful searchlights snapped on atop the yellow cabs, clutches popped, and the equipment rolled forward again, more slowly now, disappearing under the low roof of the cave. Marshall and the rest followed single file. The chill dry air of the lava pipe grew heavy with diesel fumes. The walls vibrated madly, and the sound of the engines was deafening. Glancing over his shoulder, Marshall noticed that—under the direction of a burly crew foreman named Creel—the roustabouts were pulling the steel spacers from the duffels and snugging them into place between floor and ceiling. This temporary bracing made him feel only marginally better.

He made his way down the tunnel. There was no need for a flashlight: the searchlights on the cabs and the camera illumination turned the cave into a tube of brilliant blue. There was a deep scraping noise ahead as one of the vehicles forced its way beneath the low-lying ceiling. Marshall noticed even Sully's resolutely bluff expression pale at this.

Then the cave widened, the ceiling rose, and the little company quickly formed a circle around the cleared spot in the ice floor. The diesels cut off, one after the other, and for a moment the silence seemed deafening. A faint staccato crackling echoed in the chamber as the ice floor settled under the weight of the big machines. The roustabouts finished buttressing the cave with the spacers, then hung back at the periphery.

For a moment, nobody spoke. Everyone looked down at the

large dead eyes that stared back up at them from the ice. Marshall glanced at the assembled company, one by one. Ekberg, frowning, looking troubled. Barbour, making brisk notations on her palmtop. Conti, gazing into the cloudy ice, his complacency clearly shaken. Faraday, blinking through oversize spectacles as he pulled measuring equipment from his pockets. Sully, beaming with something like paternal pride.

Finally, Conti roused himself. "Fortnum, Toussaint, you getting this?"

"Affirmative," said the DP.

"You've panned across the scientists?"

"Twice."

"Very well." The producer turned toward Sully. "Mark out the animal, please."

Sully cleared his throat. "Mark out?"

"The block of ice we'll be cutting from the cave floor. Be generous—we'd hate to slice off a drumstick by accident."

Sully winced, but he stepped gamely forward and—after a few whispered consultations with Faraday—made some calculations, then scratched out a crude oblong in the ice with his penknife.

"Depth?" Creel asked.

Sully looked at Barbour, who consulted her palmtop. "Two point seven meters," she said.

Creel turned to the man at the vehicle's control console. "Make it two point eight."

Once again, the cave filled with the roar of a diesel engine and dense clouds of exhaust. As the cameras rolled, another of the roustabouts used a handheld remote to guide a heavy mechanical arm on the strange-looking machine into position over the ice. Slowly, he lowered it onto Sully's etching.

"Stand back," Creel warned.

A beam of intense red light appeared at the tip of the instrument. Immediately, the ice beneath the beam began to spit and boil. "Military-grade laser," Conti said. "Very powerful, yet more precise than a jeweler's file."

Everyone watched as the laser cut slowly along the outline in the murky brown ice. One of the roustabouts snapped on a portable compressor mounted on the side of the flatbed. Holding a snorkel attachment to the lengthening hole, he siphoned the meltwater through a heavy rubber tube and channeled it down into the recesses of the ice cave. Looking on, Marshall was reminded of some kind of monstrous dental work. While the scientist in him rebelled at the very idea of such an undertaking—cutting a unique specimen out of its matrix with such brusque abandon—he was nevertheless relieved at the evident care being taken.

Within twenty minutes it was done. The oblong Sully had scratched into the ice was now a deep channel, one inch wide along two of the sides and almost six inches wide on the others. There was a brief wait while Chen stepped forward and used the remote imaging sensor to confirm the cut was sufficiently deep. Then the laser was retracted and another bizarre-looking arm telescoped out from the machine. Something that to Marshall resembled a robotic hand, thin but quite wide, was attached to its end. It came alive with an insectlike whine.

"What's that?" he asked Creel.

"Lateral drill," the foreman growled over the noise. "Tipped with diamond-silicone carbide."

Slowly, the device was lowered into one of the wider ice channels. The whine increased in urgency as, nine feet below, the drill bit into the ancient ice. The snorkel was lowered into the trench and meltwater once again began gushing down the cave floor. Yet another mechanical arm hovered nearby, ready to slip supports into position beneath the ice block.

The lateral cut took less time, and within ten minutes the drill was retracted. At a nod from Creel, the roustabouts swung two grappling hooks forward, lowered them into the trench, and fixed them to the ends of the ice block. These were further secured with lashings of thick canvas straps.

Conti looked again at Fortnum and Toussaint. "I want a clean take. We'll only get one chance at this."

Fortnum adjusted his lens, checked his radio pack, nodded.

Everything ground to a halt while Conti insisted on getting down on his hands and knees to examine the block, nose inches from the ice. Fortnum filmed the director's every move. "Let's go," Conti said at last, rising, the lens around his neck swinging portentously.

Creel signaled his team. With a fresh roar of machinery, a winch atop the flatbed was engaged. There was a series of clanks as heavy chains fixed to the grappling hooks pulled taut. For a moment, everyone watched as the engine whined and the hooks strained against the reluctant ice. Then—with a low grating that seemed to shake the mountain itself—the huge block began to rise.

"Easy," said Creel.

Conti looked at Fortnum. "Train your camera on the equipment. Your shot should be like a caress. *This* is what's lifting our treasure from its frozen prison."

Slowly, very slowly, the frozen cat rose from the bed it had lain in for thousands of years. The scientists pressed forward, making visual observations and taking hurried notes. Marshall drew in with the rest, staring intently. The block of ice was maddeningly opaque, a storm of mud and debris frozen in time, the color of dense smoke under the pitiless glare of the searchlights. The surface was ribbed in tiny, regular channels where the laser had cut it free. *Christ,* Marshall thought, caught up in the moment despite himself. *That block's got to weigh four tons, minimum.*

It rose, higher and higher, until the head of the crane bumped against the ceiling of the cave. Then at last the block swung free, tilting sharply and scraping along the snowy floor, narrowly missing Faraday, who'd been busy examining it with a sonar spectrometer. People scattered, tripping over one another to get out of the way.

"Stabilize!" Creel shouted.

The winch squealed in protest as the operator boosted power to the maximum. The block tilted, yawing wildly, then slowly settled back onto the floor of the cave. The crane operator throttled down for a moment. Then—slowly and carefully—he raised the block again, swung it around, and maneuvered it onto the flatbed. There was a sharp hiss of hydraulics. As the cameras rolled, a few of the other roustabouts secured the block to the vehicle and threw a heavy insulating tarp over it. Within minutes it was all over, the machinery was rolling back up the tunnel, and the countless spacers were being removed from their positions and returned to their canvas bags. And the cat—along with its surrounding block of ice—was on its way to the climate-controlled vault, where it would be kept securely locked until it was thawed and displayed to a live audience of millions.

Conti surveyed the tunnel, a look of evident satisfaction on his face. "We'll use the departing machinery as a keyframe," he told Fortnum. "We'll do a series of cutaways exiting up the tunnel, then a jump cut back to the base. Shoot a lot of coverage. And that'll be a wrap."

He turned to Marshall. "So. Ready for that interview?"

10

As they stepped back into the overpowering warmth of the base's entrance plaza, Conti nodded for the soundman and Toussaint to accompany them. Then he turned to Marshall. "We might as well shoot this from your lab."

"It's this way." Marshall led the small group down the central staircase, along the wide corridor, then right at an intersection, stopping at a half-open door. "Here we are."

Conti leaned in, took a quick look around. "This is your lab?"

"Yes. Why?"

"It's too neat. Where's all the equipment? The samples? The test tubes?"

"My samples are kept in a refrigerated locker down the hall. We've set up separate rooms for the scientific equipment, though we left most of the heavy stuff back in Woburn. This expedition is primarily about observation and sample collection—the analysis will come later."

"And the test tubes?"

Marshall smiled thinly. "Paleoecologists don't have much use for test tubes."

Conti thought for a moment. "I noticed that we passed a more appropriate lab a few doors back."

"Appropriate?" Marshall echoed. But Conti was already walking back down the hall, the soundman and photographer in tow. After a moment, Marshall shrugged and followed.

"Here." Conti had stopped outside a room whose every horizontal surface was covered with journals, printouts, plastic sample containers, and instrumentation.

"But this is Wright's lab," Marshall protested. "We can't use it."

Conti had raised the lens dangling around his neck to one eye and was examining Marshall through it. "Why not?"

Marshall hesitated. He realized that, in fact, there was no good reason why they couldn't use Faraday's lab. "Why don't you interview him, then?"

"Because, Dr. Marshall—how can I put this delicately?—the camera would not be kind to Dr. Faraday. You, however, have a rugged academic appeal. Now, may we proceed?"

Marshall shrugged again. He found it difficult talking to a man who was regarding him through a fist-sized lens.

Conti stepped inside and—lens still in place—motioned Toussaint where he wanted the camera placed. The photographer walked to the back of the lab, followed by the soundman. "Dr. Marshall," Conti went on, "we're going to film you walking in and having a seat behind the desk. Ready?"

"I suppose so."

Conti dropped the lens. "Action."

As the camera rolled, Marshall walked into the lab, stopping when he saw the tottering pile of papers placed on Faraday's lab chair.

"Cut." Conti swept the papers onto the floor, shooed Marshall back out into the hall. "Let's try that again."

Once again, Marshall walked through the door and into the office.

"Cut!" Conti barked. He frowned at Marshall. "Don't just come strolling in. Let's see some *excitement* in your step. You've just made a big discovery."

"What discovery would that be?"

"The saber-toothed tiger, of course. Let the audience see your enthusiasm. Let them *live* the thrill of this marvel through *you*."

"I don't understand. I thought this whole circus was about thawing the carcass, live."

Conti rolled his eyes. "You can't take up seventy-four and a half minutes of prime time with that. Please get with the program, Dr. Marshall. We need to show the whole backstory, the buildup. Get the audience to buy in 100 percent. We won't actually open the vault until the final segment."

Marshall nodded slowly. He tried hard to do what Conti asked: get with the program. He swallowed his irritation at the artificiality of it all; he tried to forget his indignation at the sacrifice of science on the altar of theatricality. He reminded himself Conti was an award-winning producer; that his *From Fatal Seas* was a landmark among modern documentaries; that having an audience of millions could only be beneficial to future research.

He stepped back out into the hall.

"Action!" Conti called out. Marshall stepped briskly in, seated himself behind the desk, and pretended to busy himself at Faraday's laptop.

"Cut it and print it," Conti said. "Much better." He stepped around the desk. "Now, I'm going to ask you some questions, off camera. You will then answer them, on camera. Remember that in the final print, it's going to be Ashleigh asking the questions, not me." He glanced down at a clipboard. "Why don't you start by explaining why you're here in the first place?"

"Sure. We're here for three reasons, really. First, we wanted to see the impact of global warming on subarctic environments, specifically glaciers. Second, we wanted an undisturbed site to conduct our analyses. Third, we had to do it relatively cheap. Fear Base fit all three."

"But why this mountain, in particular?"

"Because of its glacier. Examining glacial retreat is an excellent way to measure global warming. Let me explain. The upper part of a glacier, the part that gets the snowfall, is known as the accumulation zone. The lower part, the glacier's foot, is the ablation zone. This is where ice is lost through melting. A healthy glacier has a large accumulation zone. And this glacier—the Fear—is not healthy. Its accumulation zone is small. Dr. Sully's been recording the speed of its retreat. It took ten thousand years to form the glacier, bring it this far. But the alarming thing is that it has retreated a hundred feet in just the last twelve months . . ."

He stopped. Toussaint had lowered the camera, and Conti was perusing his clipboard again. *Time is money,* Marshall reminded himself.

Conti glanced up. "What's the scientific name for the cat again, Dr. Marshall?"

"Smilodon."

"And what was the Smilodon's diet?"

"That's one of the things we hope to discover with more accuracy. The contents of the stomach should—"

"Thank you, Doctor, I get your drift. Let's try keeping it to general terms. Was this cat a meat eater?"

"All cats are meat eaters."

"Did it eat humans?"

"I suppose so. When it could catch them."

A look of impatience crossed Conti's face. "Would you state that, please, for the camera?"

Marshall glanced at the camera and—feeling a little foolish—said, "Smilodons ate human beings."

"Excellent. Now, how did you feel, Dr. Marshall, when you discovered the cat?"

Marshall frowned. "How did I feel? Shocked. Surprised."

Conti shook his head. "You can't say *that.*"

"Why not? I was very surprised."

"Do you expect our sponsors to pay $500,000 a minute to hear you were 'surprised'?" Conti thought for a moment. Then he turned the clipboard over, pulled an erasable marker from his shirt pocket, and scrawled something on the back. "Let's try something. I'd like to hear how you sound reading this. Just for a sound test." And he held the clipboard up.

Marshall peered at the handwriting. "It was like peering into the heart of darkness."

"Again, please? Slowly, and with more drama. Look at the camera, not at the clipboard."

Marshall repeated the sentence. Conti nodded with satisfaction, then turned to the assistant DP. "Get that?"

Toussaint nodded. Conti turned to the soundman in turn. "Got it?"

"Got it, chief."

"Wait a minute," Marshall said. "I didn't say that. Those are your words."

Conti spread his hands. "They're good words."

Marshall lost his patience. "You're not interested in scientific accuracy here. You're not interested in accuracy, period. You just want a good show."

"That's what I'm being paid for, Doctor. Now, let's talk about you." Conti glanced down at his clipboard again. "I had my researchers do a little digging into the members of this expedition. Your story is particularly interesting, Dr. Marshall. You were a decorated officer. You won the Silver Star. Yet you left the army with a dishonorable discharge. Is this true?"

"If it is, you could hardly expect me to want to talk about it, could you?"

"Let's try again." Conti pressed his hands together. "Northern Massachusetts University is—how shall I put it?—not known for the quality of its academics. How does somebody like you end up a scientist—especially at a place like that?"

Marshall didn't answer.

"You qualified as a sharpshooter. So why is it you're the only member of your expedition who refuses to carry a rifle for protection?"

Abruptly, Marshall stood up. "You know what? Go find yourself another poster boy. I don't think I'm going to answer any more questions."

When Conti opened his mouth to speak, Marshall stepped closer. "And if you try to ask any, I'll knock your annoying little ass across this lab table."

There was a strained silence. Conti looked at him—the same appraising look he'd given him just before Wolff produced the contract. After a long moment, he spoke. "Let me explain something to you, Dr. Marshall. I am a powerful man—and not just in New York and Hollywood. If you decide to make an enemy of me, you'll be making a rather large mistake." He wiped the scrawl off the clipboard with the palm of his hand, then turned to Toussaint. "See if you can track down Dr. Sully. Something tells me that we'll find him more cooperative."

11

Later that night, Marshall found himself walking through the equipment-crowded corridors of B Level. In his lab and his quarters, he'd felt preoccupied and distracted—feelings not helped by the raucous conversations and clatter of passing gear. Knowing that, as usual, he'd find sleep difficult, he headed toward the surface to take the nightly walk that had become something of a habit with him.

He climbed the stairs and walked into the entrance foyer, his steps ringing on the metal-and-linoleum floor. The MP post was manned, as he knew it would be: since the documentary contingent had arrived, Sergeant Gonzalez had kept it staffed day and night, despite all the other demands on the soldiers' time. But to Marshall's surprise the sentry station was manned by Gonzalez himself.

The sergeant nodded to him as he came up. Despite being

well into his fifties, the man radiated a feeling of almost inexhaustible strength. "Doctor," he said. "Going on your evening constitutional?"

"That's right," Marshall said. He felt a faint surprise: he didn't know Gonzalez kept track of his movements. "Sleep's a little hard to come by."

"I'm not surprised—what with that frat party going on down there." Gonzalez frowned. His bullet-shaped head seemed attached directly to his shoulders, and as he shook it in disapproval, heavy bulges appeared at the nape.

Marshall laughed. "They are a little noisy."

Gonzalez scoffed. "Beg pardon, Doctor, but the noise is the least of it. There are just too damn many of them. We weren't expecting half this many, and it's putting my base under strain. The physical plant's old, it's been maintained only for light use. And this is hell and gone from light use. There are only four of us, we can't nursemaid all of them. This afternoon Marcelin found one of them wandering out of bounds, in the military operations sector." The frown deepened. "I'm half tempted to file a formal complaint."

"Things should ease up soon. I think a dozen or so are leaving tomorrow." He'd heard that once the bulk of the setup was complete, the roustabouts would be heading back south.

Gonzalez grunted. "Won't be soon enough for me."

Marshall glanced speculatively at him. *My base,* Gonzalez had called it. The man had reason to feel possessive. Now close to retirement, he'd supposedly spent almost thirty years at Fear Base, totally isolated, four-hundred-odd miles north of the Arctic Circle. It seemed almost unbelievable—no doubt the other three soldiers couldn't wait to finish their tours. Perhaps, Marshall speculated, he'd been here so long he couldn't imagine being anywhere else. Or perhaps—as Ekberg had hinted—he was just a man who valued his privacy.

Waving to Gonzalez, he headed toward the main entrance. The large external thermometer in the weather chamber displayed minus five degrees Fahrenheit. Opening his locker, he donned his parka, balaclava, snow boots, and gloves. Then he stepped through the staging area and pushed the outer doors open into the night.

The apron of concrete outside the base lay still beneath a vast dome of stars. He paused a moment, acclimating himself to the sharp chill of the air. Then he set off into the night, gloved hands in pockets, careful not to trip over the power cables that snaked underfoot. The wind had died away completely, and a gibbous moon lent a spectral blue light to the landscape. With the entire documentary staff currently inside Fear Base, the prefab huts and storage sheds were preternaturally silent. Everything seemed to be asleep. The only noise came from the powerhouse, which grumbled under the strain of supplying the power-hungry new inhabitants.

He paused at the perimeter fence, glancing carefully left and right. Since they had first arrived, there had been at least half a dozen polar bear sightings, but tonight no dark shapes could be seen prowling the endless permafrost or ugly coilings of ancient lava. Pulling his hood more tightly around his face, he walked past the empty guard post, letting his feet find their own path.

Soon he was climbing the steep valley toward the glacier, his breath streaming behind in great clouds. As he warmed to the work, his stride lengthened and his arms swung easily at his sides. A good dose of exercise, and just maybe he'd be able to sleep through all the noise the film crew generated.

In fifteen minutes, the slope lessened slightly. The hulking machinery had been repositioned and he had an unobstructed view of the glacier's tongue, a deep blue wall of ice that seemed to glow in the moonlight with inner fire. And there, in its shadow, was the small black hole of the ice cave . . .

He stopped. There were figures standing at the mouth of the cave. Three of them, shadows within shadows.

More slowly, he approached. The three were talking: he could hear the muffled sounds of conversation. They turned at the crunch of his footsteps and to his surprise he recognized the other scientists: Sully, Faraday, Penny Barbour. The only team member missing was Ang, the graduate student. It was as if they had converged here—with a single mind—at the site of the discovery.

Sully nodded as Marshall joined them. "Nice night for a walk," he said. One of the expedition's hunting rifles was slung over his shoulder.

"Beats the madness back at the base," Marshall replied.

If he'd expected the ever-politic Sully to protest at this, he was mistaken. The climatologist made a sour face. "They were filming some sequence in the tactical center, next door to my lab. Posing as us, if you can believe it. Must have done at least a dozen takes. Couldn't hear myself think."

"Speaking of films, how did your interview go?" Marshall asked.

The sour face deepened. "Conti stopped in mid-take. The sound-man was complaining, saying—get this—that I was swallowing my words."

Marshall nodded.

Sully turned to Barbour. "I don't swallow my words, do I?"

"Bloody yobs crashed the file server this evening," she said by way of reply. "As if they didn't bring enough laptops of their own, they had to steal our processing cycles as well. Gave me some chat-up about 'special rendering requirements.' I didn't half cause a fuss."

"There was only a single empty seat when I went to dinner," Marshall said.

"At least you got a seat," Barbour said. "I waited, standing, for ten minutes before I packed it in. Took an apple and a bag of crisps back to my lab."

Marshall glanced at Faraday. The biologist wasn't joining in the conversation. Instead, he was staring into the cave, apparently lost in thought.

Although Marshall knew better, he heard himself ask anyway. "So, Wright, what's your take on things?"

Faraday didn't reply. Instead, he just kept looking into the dark maw that lay before them.

Marshall gave him a gentle poke. "Hey, Faraday. Rejoin the living."

At this, Faraday glanced over. The moon had lent a spectral sheen to the lenses of his glasses, and he stared back at them like a goggle-eyed alien, looking perpetually surprised as usual. "Oh. Sorry. I was thinking."

Sully sighed. "Okay, let's have it. What's the dire theory for the day?"

"Not a theory. Just an observation." When nobody replied, Faraday continued. "Yesterday, when they were cutting the Smilodon out of the ice?"

"We were there," Sully said. "What about it?"

"I took some readings with a sonar spectrometer. You know, since the earlier readings from the remote imager, top-down, were quite imprecise, and having access to a cross-section I wanted to—"

"We get the picture," Sully said, waving a gloved hand.

"Well, I spent much of this afternoon analyzing the readings. And they don't match."

"Don't match what?" Marshall asked.

"They don't match a Smilodon."

"Don't be daft!" said Barbour. "You saw it, didn't you? Like the rest of us, and all?"

"I saw very little, in an extremely cloudy medium. The sonar analyzer gave me far more data to examine."

"So what are you saying?" Marshall asked.

"I'm saying that whatever's inside that block of ice appears much too large to be a saber-toothed tiger."

The little group fell silent, digesting this. After a few moments, Sully cleared his throat. "It must have been illusory. Some debris cloud you saw, maybe a lens of sand or gravel, trapped in a position to resemble the corpse."

Faraday simply shook his head.

"Just how much larger, exactly?" Barbour asked.

"I can't be precise. Perhaps twice as big."

The scientists exchanged glances.

"Twice?" Marshall exclaimed. "So what *did* it look like, then? Mastodon?"

Faraday shook his head.

"Mammoth?"

Faraday shrugged. "The readings are pretty clear on the issue of size. They're not as clear on, ah, shape."

Another silence.

"Those were cat's eyes," Barbour said in a low voice. "I'd bet on it."

"Sure seemed that way to me," Marshall said. He glanced back at Faraday. "Positive those new readings are accurate?"

"I ran the analysis twice. Cross-checked everything."

"That doesn't make sense," said Barbour. "If it's not a Smilodon—not a mastodon—not a mammoth . . . then what the bloody hell is it?"

"There's one way to find out," Marshall said. "I'm tired of being pushed around our own research site." And he began walking briskly down the slope in the direction of the base.

12

Conti had taken not only the base commander's quarters but the deputy commander's as well—three floors down on C Level—as his private suite. He seemed irritated to be disturbed by the delegation of scientists. When they explained their business, his irritation increased noticeably.

"Absolutely not," he said, standing in his doorway. "That vault is climate controlled, kept frozen to a very specific temperature."

"We're not going to melt the ice," Sully said.

"Besides, it's well below freezing outside," Marshall added. "Or hadn't you noticed?"

"Nobody can see the animal," Conti retorted. "Those are the rules."

"We've *already* seen it," Barbour said. "Remember?"

"It doesn't matter. It can't be done, period."

Marshall wondered exactly why the producer was being so territorial. "We're not going to steal the damn thing. We just want to take a closer look."

Conti rolled his eyes. "The vault is to be kept locked. Blackpool has issued strict written instructions on that point. It's critical for the publicity campaign that it not be opened until the live telecast."

"Publicity," Marshall repeated. "You're calling your special *Raising the Tiger*—right? You and your sponsors are going to look pretty foolish if you open up the vault on prime-time television and find a dead bear lying on the floor."

Conti did not reply immediately. He looked from one scientist to the next, his features settling into a deep frown. Finally, he sighed. "Very well. But only you four. And no cameras, no equipment of any kind—you'll be searched before you enter and watched carefully while inside. And you're to tell nobody what you see: remember, you've already signed nondisclosure agreements with hefty penalties attached."

"We understand," Sully said.

Conti nodded. "Five minutes."

It had grown colder still—almost fifteen below—and the stars gleamed piercingly in the blackness overhead. The vault stood by itself not far from the perimeter fence within a circle of tall sodium vapor lamps: a squat structure, perched some three feet above the ground on heavy cinder blocks. Thick bundles of power cables led directly to it from the powerhouse, and a backup generator was attached to the rear of the vault, ready to instantly take over refrigeration duties in case the main diesels failed. *Not that there's much need for that,* Marshall thought as he hugged himself against the arctic chill.

The little group stopped before the steps outside the vault entrance. Marshall noticed that the front wall was hinged along its left edge, the entire wall swinging open like the door of a bank

vault. Three heavy padlocks had been attached to the right side—
no doubt more for visual effect than anything else—and an oversize
dial was mounted in its center. Beside it, a bank of meters and
switches for monitoring and controlling the internal temperature
was set behind a thick metal cage, secured with its own padlock.

One of Conti's techs, a youth named Hulce, approached from the
thicket of outbuildings, heavy boots crunching on the permafrost.
He checked the pockets of the scientists one by one, found a digital
camera on Faraday.

"He always carries that," Sully said. "I think it was surgically attached at birth."

Hulce confiscated the camera, then nodded to Conti.

"Turn away, please," the producer told them.

Marshall did as requested. He heard the spin of the vault's dial;
heard the *chunk* of a heavy lock disengaging. This was followed by
three distinct clicks as the padlocks were removed. "You may turn
back," Conti said.

As Marshall turned around, he saw Hulce pull the front wall of
the vault ajar. A thick shaft of brilliant yellow light flooded out.
Conti gestured for them to step inside.

Marshall followed Sully, Faraday, and Barbour up the steps and
into the vault. Conti and the tech came last, closing the door behind
them. There was very little room to stand: the block of ice took up
almost all of the vault's space. The only other items inside were the
bank of painfully bright lights set into the ceiling and a portable
heater set into the rear wall, which—Marshall knew—would be
turned on when the time came to thaw the carcass and reveal it to
the world.

The floor felt too yielding to be steel. Looking down, Marshall
noticed with surprise that, except for two steel I beams spaced
about four feet apart, the floor was made of wood—wood painted
silver to resemble metal. It was riddled with tiny drill holes that, no
doubt, would help meltwater escape when the thawing began. He
shook his head: another Hollywood contrivance, just like the super-
fluous padlocks. The cameras would never see the floor, so there

had been no need for the expense of extra steel beyond the support-ing I beams.

Conti nodded at the tech to remove the tarp. Then he turned to the scientists. "Remember. Five minutes."

Hulce reached over and, with some effort, pulled the heavy tarp across the top of the ice block, letting it fall to the back. Immedi-ately, Marshall caught his breath, almost staggering in surprise.

"Jesus," Sully muttered in a strangled voice.

Although the sides of the block remained rough-edged and frosted, the upper face of the ice had apparently rubbed against the insulating tarp during the trek down the mountain. Now it was pol-ished to a glassy sheen. This was the side that faced forward, toward the vault door. Within the ice, the huge black-and-yellow eyes stared out at Marshall implacably. But that was not what caused him such a powerful shock.

As a child, he had been plagued by a recurring dream. In it, he would awaken at home, in his bed. He was alone: his parents, his older sister, inexplicably gone. It was late; the power was off; all the windows were open to the night. The house was full of fog. He would draw back the covers and get up, again and again with each new dream, even after he knew better. Everything about the dream was painfully, unforgettably tangible: the chill of the mist on his face, the hard smooth wood of the floorboards beneath his feet. He walked out of his bedroom and began heading down the stairs. The landing below was thick with soupy gray vapor. Halfway down, he stopped. Because creeping up the steps toward him was a terrifying beast: huge, feline, with burning eyes and sharp fangs and massive forepaws studded with cruel talons. He stood, staring, rooted by horror. Slowly, very slowly, more of the creature emerged from the mist: a lank, greasy mane; shoulders rippling with muscle. It stared at him unblinking as it came forward, and a sound emerged from deep within its chest, a sound more sensed and felt than heard: an ineffable primal growl of hatred, hunger, *desire* . . . and that was when the paralysis would break and he'd turn, running, screaming, back up toward his room, the stairs shaking under the weight of the creature and the crash of its bulk coming ever nearer and the stink of its breath warming the small of his neck . . .

Marshall shook his head, drew a hand across his eyes. Despite the arctic chill of the vault, a close, oppressive warmth flooded his limbs.

The dead thing in the ice was, in size and general shape, the precise creature of his nightmare. Even the murkiness of the vast block resembled the fog of his dream. He swallowed as he stared. Only the top half of the head and the forequarters of the beast were visible—emerging out of a storm of frozen mud—but that was enough to convince him instantly this was no saber-toothed tiger.

He turned to the others. They were all staring into the ice, their faces registering shock, disbelief, and—in the case of Hulce, the tech—something like naked fear. Even Conti seemed at a loss, shaking his head.

"We're going to need a wider lens," he muttered.

"That's a nasty piece of work, and no mistake," said Barbour.

"What *is* it?" asked Sully.

"I can tell you what it isn't," said Faraday. "It's no Smilodon. And it's no mammoth."

Marshall struggled to push his childhood terrors away, to examine the corpse as clinically as possible. "That's hair on the forelegs," he said. "*Hair.* And they're too thickly muscled—the talons are too long."

"Too long for what?" Conti asked.

"For anything." Marshall shrugged as his pretense at scientific detachment fell away. He exchanged glances with the other scientists. He wondered if they shared his thoughts. Even though relatively little of the creature was visible, it nevertheless looked like nothing else on earth, past *or* present.

For a long moment, nobody spoke. Finally, Sully broke the silence. "So what are you saying?" he asked. "That we're looking at a life-form unknown to the fossil record?"

"Maybe. But whatever it is, I think it's of vital importance *to* the fossil record," Faraday said.

Marshall frowned. "What do you mean?"

"I mean the theory of evolutionary turbulence." Faraday cleared his throat. "It's something that comes up now and then in biology. According to the theory, when animal populations grow too numerous for the ecosphere to support, or when a certain species becomes too comfortably adapted and loses evolutionary vigor, a new creature comes along to prune back the population blooms, force new changes."

"A killing machine," Barbour said with a glance at the ice block.

"Precisely. Except if the killing machine is too successful, it will depopulate its environment, lose its food source, and ultimately turn on others of its own kind."

"You're talking about the Callisto Effect," Marshall said. "The alternate theory for what killed off the dinosaurs."

Faraday nodded, glasses flashing in the brilliant light.

"That was championed by Frock of the New York Museum of Natural History," Marshall said. "But since he vanished, I didn't think anyone else had come forward to support it."

"Perhaps our Wright is the new champion," Barbour said with a grim smile.

"Sounds highly dubious to me," said Sully. "In any case, even if you're right, this corpse is no longer a threat to anybody, let alone an entire species."

Conti stirred. Most of the shock had faded from his face, and his remote, faintly disdainful expression had returned. "I don't know what you're all getting so worked up about," he said. "You can only see its head and shoulders—and a paw."

"*Ecce signum,*" replied Marshall, jerking a thumb toward the ice.

"Well, we'll all find out soon enough," Conti replied. "For now, it stays a tiger. Meanwhile, your five minutes are up." He turned to the tech. "Mr. Hulce, give Dr. Faraday back his camera. Then cover this up and make sure all the locks are secure. I'll escort our friends here inside the base."

13

Marshall was awakened by a rap on the door of the small compartment—formerly a warrant officer's quarters—that served as his bunk. He rolled over, disoriented, rolled over once more and promptly fell out of the narrow bed.

"What?" he croaked.

"Get dressed, luv," came the voice of Penny Barbour. "And hurry. You won't want to miss this."

Marshall sat up, rubbed his eyes, then glanced blearily at his watch. Almost six. As usual, he'd spent a restless night and hadn't fallen asleep until two hours ago. He stood, dressed quickly in the warm dry air of the base, then stepped out into the hall. Barbour was waiting for him impatiently. "Come on," she said.

"What is it?"

"See for yourself." And she led him down the echoing corridors and up the central stairwell to the base entrance. They suited up in the weather chamber—Marshall noticed the temperature had risen significantly since he'd gone to sleep—then passed through the staging area and stepped outside.

Marshall stopped, blinking wearily in the predawn darkness. Despite the early hour the day's work was well under way: he could hear hammering, shouts, the whine of a cordless drill. There was another sound, too, in the background: something familiar, yet elusive. Barbour led the way through the thicket of outbuildings, pausing not far from the vault, where a small knot of onlookers had gathered. With a faint smile, she pointed out past the perimeter fence.

Marshall stared into the gloom. At first he saw nothing. Then, in the distance, two pinpricks of light resolved themselves. As he watched, they grew larger: angry-looking yellow spots that reminded him uncomfortably of the eyes that had stared up at him out of the ice. As they continued to approach, other, smaller lights became visible. The background noise he'd noticed grew louder, as well. And now he recognized it: a diesel, and a big one.

"What the *hell* . . . ?" he began.

A huge eighteen-wheeler was approaching them across the snow. It grew and grew in size, until at last it drew to a stop in the pool of lights beyond the perimeter fence, its engine idling. The tires were covered with heavy chains, and the cab was laden with filigrees of frost. Ice fog lay thick on the windshield, and the headlights and the canvas-covered grill were almost completely obscured behind a densely packed coating of snow and rime.

Barbour dug an elbow into his ribs, chuckled. "An articulated lorry. Now that's something you don't see every day in the Zone."

Marshall looked at it in wonderment. "How did it get here? We're a hundred and fifty miles from the nearest road."

"He made his own road," Barbour said.

Marshall looked at her.

"I asked the same question. That lot over there—the ones who told me it was coming—sorted me out." And she pointed at the nearby onlookers. "Seems the driver is what's known as an ice-road trucker. People like him drive the 'winter road'—a road that exists only in the coldest months, a straight line over the frozen lakes, a temporary ice highway to get goods and equipment to remote camps and communities with no regular access."

"Over frozen *lakes*?"

"Not a job for the fainthearted, is it?"

"I'll be damned," Marshall said. It seemed so wildly anachronistic—a big rig here, in the Federal Wilderness Zone—he could hardly believe it.

"Normally they travel between Yellowknife and Port Radium," Barbour said. "This was a special trip."

"Why? What's so important it couldn't have been ferried in on a plane?"

"That." And Barbour pointed to the trailer behind the cab.

Marshall's attention had been fixed on the cab of the truck. But now, as he glanced back toward the load it was carrying, he saw that it wasn't the typical boxy container, but something more like an Airstream trailer—except several times larger. The sun was just now beginning to peer above the horizon, and the trailer gleamed in the newly minted light. In a perverse way, it resembled the submarines he sometimes saw berthed in the Thames when he drove through New London on the way to his parents' house in Danbury. Its metal-covered flanks rose smoothly toward a gently curved roof, which in turn sported a small forest of antennas and satellite dishes. The large windows were hung with expensive-looking curtains, all carefully pulled shut. A small balcony with deck chairs—a truly bizarre touch, given the harsh environment—was set high up in the rear wall.

The semi's engine rose to a roar again and it pulled forward, tire chains clanking. Two burly, leather-jacketed roustabouts detached themselves from the group of onlookers, trotted toward the security gates, and pulled them wide. The truck shifted into reverse and—with a succession of ear-shattering chirps—began backing its burden into the compound. Guided by the roustabouts, it crept back until the trailer was well within the perimeter fence. Then the diesel's revolutions slowed; the driver shifted into park and killed the engine; and, with a hiss of air brakes, the vehicle shuddered into silence. The door of the cab opened and the ice-road trucker—a young, thinly built man, deeply tanned and dressed in a lurid Hawaiian shirt—jumped down and began uncoupling the trailer. Then the passenger door opened and another figure emerged. This one descended much more gingerly. He was fair-haired and tall, perhaps forty-five, with a closely trimmed beard. He slid to the permafrost with obvious relief. Collecting a large duffel and a laptop bag from the semi's cab, he hoisted them over his shoulder and began walking stiffly toward the base. He nodded to Marshall and Barbour as he passed by.

"A bit green about the gills, that one," Barbour said with a chuckle.

Another roustabout appeared, unreeling heavy orange power cables from a large spool, and began attaching them to a panel in the side of the trailer.

Marshall nodded toward it. "What do you suppose it's for?"

"Her highness," Barbour replied.

"Who?"

But even as Marshall spoke he became aware of a new sound: the whine of an approaching helicopter. As it grew louder he noticed it didn't have the hollow, thin drone of the workhorse choppers that had been ferrying equipment to the site in recent days. This was smoother, lower, more powerful.

Then the bird came into sight, moving low against the brightening horizon, and he realized why. This was no puddle jumper: it was a Sikorsky S-76C++, the ultimate in luxury helicopters. And he knew instantly who "her highness" must be.

The Sikorsky came in fast, hovered over the base for a moment, then settled onto the permafrost alarmingly close to the perimeter gate, throwing up stinging clouds of ice and snow pellets. The onlookers quickly scattered, covering their faces and retreating behind the nearby structures. As the whine of the turboshaft engines eased and the ice storm subsided, a hatch in the chopper's belly opened and a blade-thin woman in a Burberry trench coat emerged. She descended the steps, then stopped, looking around at the scattered outbuildings with an unreadable expression. Then, opening an umbrella—which was buffeted mightily by the prop wash—she mounted the stairs again. Another form emerged—this one wearing what looked to Marshall like an ermine coat—and the two descended together. Marshall craned for a look at the second woman's face, but the woman in the trench coat was shielding her so adroitly from the prop wash it was impossible to see anything but the end of the fur coat, the flash of shapely legs, and the glitter of black high heels stepping over the permafrost.

The steps folded inward and the hatch closed, the whine of the turboprops increased, and the Sikorsky rose, blades slapping the air. As it moved away, quickly rising and gaining speed, Barbour scoffed audibly.

For the first time, Marshall noticed that Ekberg had been standing nearby, watching the landing. Now she came forward to intercept the new arrivals. "Ms. Davis," Marshall heard her say. "I'm Kari Ekberg, the field producer. We spoke in New York, and I just wanted to say that I'd be delighted to do anything I can to make you more—"

But if either woman—the one in the trench coat or the one in furs—heard, they gave no sign. Instead, they walked past, mounted the metal steps of the gleaming trailer, slipped inside, and closed the door heavily behind them.

14

All day the temperature crept slowly upward, past ten degrees Fahrenheit, then twenty, causing Conti to scramble his film crews for shooting a flurry of snow-covered landscapes, just in case. Under brilliant sunlight, the mood of the documentary team improved noticeably as military-grade parkas were traded for woolen sweaters and down jackets. From the direction of Mount Fear, the sharp cracking and booming noises returned as the face of the glacier began calving away once again. Gonzalez deployed his team of army engineers to replace bad bearings that had caused one of the generators to seize up. After lunch, the bulk of the local roustabouts—their initial construction work completed—were ferried south to Anchorage in two cargo helicopters, not to return until the shooting was complete. Only Creel, the burly crew foreman who looked like he consumed steel bolts for breakfast, remained on the base. Around three in the afternoon, Ashleigh Davis emerged from her über-trailer, surveyed the surrounding works with distaste, and then set off for the base—accompanied by her personal assistant in the trench coat—apparently to be briefed by Conti.

After dinner, Marshall returned to the lab where he'd spent the day hard at work, seeing no one. With the bulk of the documentary staff out of doors preparing for the following day's broadcast, the base had been relatively quiet and he'd had few distractions. Now he was bent over an examination table, so engrossed in his work that he didn't hear the lab door open softly. He didn't realize he had company, in fact, until a feminine voice over his shoulder began to intone:

> *"And soft they danced from the Polar sky and swept in*
> *primrose haze;*
> *And swift they pranced with their silver feet, and*
> *pierced with a blinding blaze.*
> *They danced a cotillion in the sky; they were rose and*
> *silver shod;*
> *It was not good for the eyes of man—'twas a sight for*
> *the eyes of God."*

He straightened and turned around. Kari Ekberg was standing there, leaning against a table, dressed in jeans and a white turtleneck. A smile played at the corners of her mouth.

He quoted in return:

> *"They writhed like a brood of angry snakes, hissing and*
> *sulphur pale;*
> *Then swift they changed to a dragon vast, lashing a*
> *cloven tail."*

"So," he said. "They're out again?"
"And how."

"You know, ever since I got here and first saw those lights, I've been waiting for somebody to quote Robert Service. Didn't think it would be you."

"I've loved his stuff ever since my older brother scared me half to death, reading 'The Cremation of Sam McGee' aloud in a pup tent by the glow of a flashlight."

"Guess my story's pretty much the same." He glanced at his watch. "My God. Ten o'clock." He stretched, glanced back up at her. "I'd have thought you'd be rushing around with all sorts of last-minute details."

She shook her head. "I'm the field producer, remember? I do the advance work, make sure everybody knows their dance steps. Once the talent hits the ground I pretty much take a backseat and watch it unfold."

The talent, Marshall thought, recalling the non-encounter he'd witnessed between Ekberg and Ashleigh Davis that morning.

"And you," she said. "I haven't seen you all day. What grand discoveries have you made?"

"We paleoecologists don't go in for grand discoveries. We just try to answer questions, fill in the dark corners."

"Then why work so late? It's not like all this is going away." And she waved a hand roughly in the direction of the glacier.

"Actually, it's going away a lot faster than you might think." He turned to the table, picked up a small yellow flower. "I found this just outside the perimeter wall this morning, poking up out of the snow. Ten years ago, the northerly range of this flower was a hundred miles south. That's how much global warming has changed things in just a decade."

"But I thought global warming helped your work."

"Glacial melt helps me collect more samples, more quickly. I can collect everything from the face of a melting glacier—pollen, insects, pine-tree seeds, even atmospheric bubbles for sampling the amount of CO_2 in ancient air. It beats the hell out of drilling ice cores. But that doesn't mean I'm enthusiastic about global warming. Scientists are supposed to be objective."

She looked at him, wry smile deepening. "And is that what you are? Objective?"

He hesitated. Then he sighed. "If you want to know the truth . . . no. Global warming scares the hell out of me. But I'm no activist. It's just that I understand the consequences better than most. Already we're losing control of the situation. The earth is remarkably resilient, she's hugely capable of repairing herself. But this warming trend is accelerating too quickly, and a hundred chain reactions are under way—" He stopped, laughed quietly. "I'm supposed to be neutral on the topic. If Sully heard me talking like this, he'd have my head."

"I'm not telling. I appreciate your speaking from the heart."

He shrugged. "Actually, it's pretty ironic. In the short term I benefit from the glacial melt. But once the glacier is gone, all the evidence I need for my research will be gone with it. Everything will be washed into the ocean. This is my one best chance to study the glacier, collect specimens."

"Hence your burning the midnight oil. Sorry to barge in."

"You kidding? I appreciate the visit. Anyway, I'm not the only one who's busy. Look at you: asking questions, doing the legwork, making the star look good. A star who, by the way, doesn't seem particularly grateful for all your hard work."

She made a face but refused to be drawn into the line of chat. "We field producers have our crosses to bear, just like you do." She glanced over. "You play?" And she pointed at a MIDI keyboard that was leaning against the far wall.

Marshall nodded. "Blues and jazz, mostly."

"Are you any good?"

He laughed. "Good enough, I guess. Couldn't make a living at it, but I play in the house band for a club back in Woburn. Mostly I love tweaking synthesizers. These days, of course, you don't have to anymore—the sounds are all pre-rolled, you just select the waveform you want from a computer menu—but growing up I loved manipulating oscillators and filters. Built my own from scratch."

"You'll have to play for us sometime." She motioned to the door. "Guess I'd better get back outside. I set up a segment about the northern lights a little while ago, and Emilio's probably filming it by now."

Marshall rose. "I'll come along, if that's all right."

Up in the weather chamber, Marshall noticed the thermometer read twenty-eight degrees. He shrugged into his lightweight parka, then followed Ekberg through the staging area, out of the base, and into a scene of controlled pandemonium. Despite the late hour, the apron was alive with sound and light. Grips were arranging camera stands and moving large trusses into position around the vault, preparing for the next day's shooting. Not far from Davis's trailer, a gaffer was setting up a sun gun to add light to the impending segment. The soundman was in animated conference with Fortnum. Wolff, the network liaison, stood motionless in the shadow of the Sno-Cat, hands in pockets, observing the scene silently. And a dozen others were just hanging around in small groups, staring up at the night sky.

Marshall looked upward, following their gaze. What he saw took his breath away. He'd assumed that the bright illumination around him was all artificial: instead, he saw it came from the most bizarre and spectacular display of aurora borealis he'd ever witnessed. The entire sky was ablaze with layers of undulating light. It seemed to have corporeal form, a viscous, mercurylike glow that crawled slowly across the heavens. It hung so low over his head that Marshall felt a crazy urge to duck. It was a color that he found hard to describe: an incredibly rich, dark crimson with a haunting, faintly radioactive glow.

"Jesus," he murmured.

Ekberg looked at him. "I'd have thought you'd be jaded by now."

"These are no ordinary northern lights. Usually you see shifting bands of color. But tonight, there's only one. Look how intense it is."

"Yes. Like wine, maybe. Or perhaps blood. It's creepy." She glanced at him, her face spectral in the reflected glow. "You've never seen these kind of northern lights before?"

"Only once: the night before we discovered the tiger." He paused. "But tonight the effect must be twice as strong. And it's so low in the sky you can almost touch it."

"Is it my imagination, or is it making sounds?" Ekberg had cocked her head to one side, as if listening. Marshall found himself doing the same. It was impossible, he knew. And yet, over the clank of equipment and the drone of generators, he could hear something. One minute it crackled like distant thunder; the next it was moaning, like a woman in pain—and always in time to the ebb and flow of the lights. He remembered the old shaman's words: *The ancient ones are angry . . . Their wrath paints the sky with blood. The heavens cry out with the pain, like a woman in labor . . .*

Marshall shook his head. He'd heard stories of the northern lights groaning and crying, but he'd always ascribed them to legend. Perhaps, because the lights were much closer to the ground tonight than normal, there *was* some kind of associated auditory phenomenon. He was about to step back inside to alert his colleagues when he caught sight of Faraday. The biologist was standing between two temporary sheds, magnetometer in one hand and digital camera in the other, both pointed heavenward. He'd obviously noticed it, as well.

There was movement to one side and Marshall turned to see the ice-road trucker and his passenger approaching. Despite the chill, the trucker was still dressed in a gaudy floral shirt. "Hell of a sight, isn't it?" he said.

Marshall simply shook his head.

"I've seen my share of northern lights," the man went on, "but this beats all."

"The Inuit believe they're the spirits of the dead," Marshall replied.

"That's true," said the passenger with the trim beard. "And not particularly friendly spirits, either: they use the sky to play football with human skulls. Legend has it that if you whistle when the northern lights are out, those spirits might come down and retrieve your head, too."

Ekberg shuddered. "Then please—nobody whistle."

Marshall looked curiously at the new arrival. "I never knew that."

"I didn't either, until my layover in Yellowknife." The man nodded at the trucker. "That's when this fellow kindly offered me a lift."

Marshall laughed. "You didn't look too happy about it getting out of the truck."

The bearded man smiled thinly. He'd recovered his composure after what had clearly been a harrowing trip. "It seemed a good idea at the time." He extended his hand. "My name's Logan."

The trucker did the same. "And I'm Carradine."

Marshall introduced himself and Ekberg. "Something tells me you're not from around here," he told the trucker.

"Something tells you right. Cape Coral, Florida. The pay up here's great, but otherwise Alaska's got plenty of nothing I need."

"And is what you don't need anything you can talk about?" Ekberg asked.

"Snow. Ice. And men. Especially men in red flannel shirts."

"Men," Ekberg repeated.

"Yep. Far too many of them. Up here, the ratio of men to women is ten to one. They say that if a woman's interested, the odds are good but the goods are odd."

They laughed.

"I've got to return to the base," Logan said. "Seems my letters of introduction didn't get here in time, and the good Sergeant Gonzalez needs an explanation for my presence. A pleasure to meet you two." He nodded at them in turn, then headed for the main entrance.

They watched him leave. "I don't recognize him," Ekberg said to the trucker. "Is he part of Ashleigh's retinue?"

"He's on his own," Carradine replied.

"What's he doing here, then?"

Carradine shrugged. "He told me he's a professor—called himself an enigmalogist."

"A what?" Marshall asked.

"An enigmalogist."

"So he's with you?" Ekberg asked, turning to Marshall.

"Nope," Marshall replied. "He's a mystery to me."

He glanced around again. There was a palpable excitement in the air that even the bizarre display of light couldn't fully explain. Despite the anthill-like frenzy, everything appeared to be running on schedule. Already, the carefully calculated thawing of the ice block had begun: he could see the occasional bead of meltwater dropping from the vault floor. Tomorrow at 4:00 PM—coinciding with prime time on the East Coast—the cameras would roll and the live documentary would begin. Ultimately, the vault would be opened. And then—Marshall realized quite abruptly—the crew would pack up, calm would descend once more over Mount Fear, and it would be business as usual for the remaining two weeks of their stay.

Marshall was very eager for that calm to return. Even so, he couldn't deny there was something special about this night, something unique and exciting that he felt absurdly pleased to be part of.

Now Davis stepped out of her trailer, accompanied by Conti, the personal assistant, and a publicity flack. They headed toward a small clearing near the old security checkpoint, where Fortnum, Toussaint, the gaffer, and the key grip were waiting. "You're sure you're warm enough?" Marshall heard Conti ask fawningly as they walked by.

"I'll be *fine,* darling," said Davis in a martyr's tone of heroic resignation. She had exchanged her expensive fur for a stylish Marmot down jacket.

"The shoot shouldn't take more than ten minutes, tops," Conti said. "We've already gotten the process shots and the backgrounds." They didn't glance toward Marshall or Ekberg as they sailed past.

"Well, I'd better make myself useful," Ekberg said. "I'll catch up with you later." And she joined the flack at the rear of the small procession.

Carradine grinned and shook his head. He was chewing a massive wad of gum that swelled one cheek like a hamster's. "What say you? Shall we stick around and watch this dog and pony show?"

"If you can stand the cold," Marshall replied, nodding at the trucker's flimsy shirt.

"Hell, this isn't cold. Come on, let's get us a pair of front-row seats." And the man grabbed two wooden packing crates, set them down in the snow, sat on one, and gestured Marshall toward the other with a flourish.

There was a final commotion by the security checkpoint; the lights came up, Ekberg gave the teleprompter a dry run; the sound check was wrapped; Davis's nose was given a last powdering before she shooed the makeup girl away with a curse. Then there was the snap of a clapstick; Conti cried "Action!"; and the cameras rolled. Instantly, the fretful scowl left Davis's face, replaced by a dazzling smile, her expression somehow becoming excited and dramatic and alluring all at the same time.

"It's almost time now," she said breathlessly to the cameras, just as if she'd been with them in the trenches for the last week. "In less than twenty-four hours the vault will be opened, the primordial mystery will be solved. And as if nature itself understands the gravity of this moment, we've been treated to a most unusual display of northern lights that is second to none in its allure and grandeur . . ."

15

Even though Fear Base turned relatively quiet—everyone abed in expectation of a busy tomorrow—Marshall as usual spent a restless night, tossing in his spartan bunk. Try as he might, he could not get comfortable. Pulling up the sheets made him too warm; throwing them aside chilled him. Now and then, the muscles of his arms and legs tensed spasmodically, as if unable to relax, and he could not escape the feeling that—despite all evidence to the contrary— something was quite wrong.

Finally, he sank into a half doze in which a succession of disturbing images moved slowly across the field of his inner vision. He was out walking the permafrost, alone, beneath the strange and angry northern lights. In his mind, they were lower than ever in the sky, so low they seemed to press down upon his shoulders. He stared at them in mingled awe and unease as he walked. And then he stopped, frowning in surprise. Ahead of him, on the torn and frozen ground, the lights actually met the land, viscous driblets flowing like wax from a tilted candle. As he stared, the forms grew larger, took shape, solidified. Legs and arms appeared. There was a moment of dreadful stasis. Then they began approaching him— slowly at first, then more quickly. There was something horrible about the way they came, their bodies alternately bulging and ebbing; something horrible about the evident hunger with which they stretched out their splayed hands toward him. He turned to run but found, with that horrible creeping paralysis of a nightmare, that his leaden feet were so terribly slow to move . . .

Marshall sat up with a start. He was sweating and the covers were twisted around him like the winding-sheet of a corpse. He stared left and right, wide-eyed in the darkness, waiting for his breathing to slow, for the vestiges of the dream to fade.

After a minute, he glanced at his watch: quarter to five. "Shit," he murmured, sinking back onto the damp pillow.

There would be no more sleep—not tonight. He sat up again, then stood, quickly dressed in the gloom of his bunk, and slipped out into the corridor.

The base was so quiet it reminded him of the first nights he'd spent here, when the labyrinthine corridors and the long-abandoned spaces seemed to overwhelm the tiny band of scientists. His footsteps rang on the steel floor and he felt the ridiculous urge to tiptoe. Leaving the dormitory section, he walked past the labs, the mess, the kitchen, then turned down a corridor into an area of the base they'd never used: a warren of equipment rooms and monitoring posts. He paused. In the distance, he could just make out the faintest strains of music: someone's CD player, he assumed; there were very few radio stations within five hundred miles, and even those tended to concern themselves with the price of diesel oil and the state of the annual moose rut.

Hands in pockets, he wandered deeper into the maze of listening posts. Try as he might, he couldn't seem to shake an oppressive sense of foreboding. If anything, it seemed to increase: a perverse conviction—given the excitement of the coming day—that something terrible was going to happen.

He paused again. The claustrophobic base, shrouded in watchful silence, just exacerbated his gloom. On impulse, he turned, threaded his way back, climbed a stairway to the topmost level. He walked to the entrance plaza, walked by the sentry post, then passed through the staging area, donning his parka as he did so. It was only eight hours since he'd last been out, but in his current frame of mind nothing was going to keep him inside this shadow-haunted base another minute. Grabbing a flashlight and zipping the parka, he opened the outer doors and stepped outside.

He noticed with surprise that the display of northern lights had grown even more intense: a deep, unguent red, throbbing and pulsating. It transformed the entire apron—with its temporary shacks and Quonset huts, tents and supply caches—into a monochromatic, otherworldly landscape. He put the flashlight in a pocket. The wind had picked up sharply, worrying at loose tarps and indifferently tied ropes, but even it could not explain the eerie cracklings and moanings he could have sworn came from the lights themselves.

There was something else that seemed odd, but it took him a moment to realize what it was. The wind was almost warm on his cheek. It felt as if a false spring had abruptly come to the Zone. He unzipped his parka slowly; he should have checked the thermometer on the way out.

He moved through the low structures, half of them backlit blood red, the other half sunken into shadow. As he did so, a low creak sounded from the small forest of outbuildings ahead.

He paused in the crimson half-light. Was somebody out here with him?

Everybody—scientists, documentary crew, and the mysterious new arrival, Logan—were bunking inside the base. The only exceptions were Davis, in her mega-trailer, and Carradine, the trucker. He glanced in the direction of Davis's trailer: it was dark, all lights out.

"Carradine?" he called softly.

The creaking noise came again.

Marshall took a step forward, emerging from between two supply tents. Now the bulk of Carradine's semi came into view. He glanced toward the rear of the cab, where the "sleeper" was. Its windows were dark, as well.

He remained still, listening intently. He heard the mournful howl of the wind, the low rumble of the diesels in the powerhouse, the purr of the backup generator affixed to Davis's trailer, and—now and then—the eerie murmurings and moanings that appeared to come from the northern lights themselves. But that was all.

He shook his head, smiling despite himself. Here he was, on the eve of what promised to be one of the most memorable days of his life . . . and he was working himself into a lather over a bad dream. He'd walk to the perimeter fence, take a turn along its length, then head back to his lab. Even if he couldn't put in useful work, at least he'd try. He squared his shoulders, took another step forward.

The creak came again. And from where he now stood, Marshall got a bearing. It was coming from the direction of the vault.

He moved toward it slowly. The vault stood alone, one wall haloed in the unnatural light, the rest in darkness. Even without his flashlight, Marshall could make out the sheen of water beneath it: clearly, the automated thawing process was well under way. Tomorrow this steel container—and its contents—would be the star of the show. Tugging the flashlight from his pocket, Marshall aimed it at the silver structure.

Then he heard the creak yet again, louder. Armed with the flashlight, Marshall identified its source: a piece of lumber, hanging down loosely into the three-foot crawl space beneath the vault.

Marshall frowned. *Shoddy workmanship,* he thought. *That'll have to be taken care of before Conti and his variety show go live.* Or perhaps something had simply broken loose from the structure. It was swaying in the wind, just above the dirty puddle of meltwater . . .

But there was something else wrong here. It wasn't so much a puddle he was looking at but a lake. A lake full of chunks of dirty ice.

He moved closer, crouched, shone his light at the pool of meltwater. Frowning, he raised the beam to the loose piece of lumber. It creaked again as the wind played with it, the lower end badly splintered. Slowly, he let the flashlight beam travel up the lumber to the vault's underside.

A hole—large, circular, and rough—had been cut into the wooden floor. And even in the shifting beam of his flashlight, Marshall could clearly see that the vault was empty.

16

In thirty minutes, somnolent Fear Base was completely awake. Now, Marshall—along with practically every other person on-site—sat in ancient folding chairs in the Operations Center on B Level. It was the only room large enough to hold so many people. He looked around at the assembled faces. Some, like Sully and Ekberg, seemed stunned. Others were openly red-eyed. Fortnum, the DP, sat with his head bowed, hands alternately clenching and unclenching.

They had assembled at the request of Wolff, the channel rep. Actually, Marshall reflected, it hadn't really sounded like a request. It was more like an order.

When first confronted with the news, Emilio Conti had been dazed, almost paralyzed, by the sudden turn of fortune. But now, as Marshall watched the director move back and forth before the rough semicircle of chairs, he saw a different emotion on the small man's face—desperate rage.

"First," Conti snapped as he paced, "the facts. Sometime between midnight and five, the vault was broken into and the *asset*"—he bit the word off—"was removed. Stolen. Dr. Marshall here made the discovery." Conti glanced toward him briefly, his black eyes glittering with mistrust. "I've spoken with the management at Terra Prime and Blackpool. Under the circumstances, they have no choice: tonight's live feed has been canceled. A rerun of *From Fatal Seas* will be aired instead." He almost spat out the words. "They will be refunding $12 million in advertising guarantees to their sponsors. That is *in addition* to the $8 million they spent to make all this possible."

He stopped for a moment, glared at the assembly, then continued his pacing. "Those are the facts. Next: conjecture. There's a mole among us. Someone in the pay of a rival network. Or perhaps someone working for a 'handler'—a dealer in exotic goods with connections to museums or wealthy collectors overseas."

Beside Marshall, Penny Barbour scoffed under her breath. "Bloody daft," she murmured.

"Daft?" Conti rounded on her. "It's happened before. This isn't just an artifact—it's a commodity."

"A commodity?" Barbour said. "What are you talking about?"

"We're talking about a commodity." It was Wolff who answered. The network liaison was standing in the back of the room beside Sergeant Gonzalez, arms crossed, a plastic swizzle stick in his mouth. "More than just an evening's entertainment. An indefinitely exploitable network resource. Something that could be repurposed many times—touring on exhibition to museums, loaned to universities and research institutions, used in follow-up broadcasts. Maybe even a future icon for the network. Or—perhaps—its mascot."

Mascot, Marshall thought to himself. Until now, he'd had no idea just how ambitious Blackpool's plans for their frozen cat had been.

As Wolff stepped to the front, Conti stopped pacing and joined him. "As a network, Terra Prime is part of a very small community," Wolff went on. "Despite the pains we took to keep things quiet, we knew word of this project might leak out. But we were confident that our vetting process would weed out anyone not one hundred percent reliable." He raised a hand to his lips, plucked out the swizzle stick. "Apparently our confidence was misplaced."

Marshall noticed most of the network staff was listening, heads bowed. Only his fellow scientists seemed surprised by this cloak-and-dagger talk.

"What are you saying, exactly?" Sully asked.

"Just a moment." Wolff turned to the sergeant. "Is the head count finished?"

Gonzalez nodded.

"Anyone unaccounted for?"

"Just one. That new arrival, Dr. Logan. My men are looking for him now."

"Everybody else? Network and expedition crew?"

"They're all here."

Only then did Wolff glance back at Sully. "I'm saying we have reason to believe that someone at this base was paid to appropriate the specimen for a third party. Either arrangements were made before our arrival, or contact was established at some later point. We will be reviewing all communications in and out of Fear Base over the last seventy-two hours to learn more."

"I thought you had all this under tight control," Marshall said. "The thawing process, the security, everything. Just how was this pulled off?"

"We don't know that yet," Wolff replied. "It would appear the thawing was hastened—obviously by whoever appropriated the carcass. It was a fully automated process, there was a backup generator—nothing could have gone wrong without external manipulation. We've checked outside the perimeter fence. There is no sign of a plane either arriving or leaving in the night. That means the asset is still here."

"What about footprints?" somebody piped up. "Can't you track those?"

"Around the vault, where the ice thawed, the ground has been churned up by so many prints it's impossible," said Wolff. "Beyond that, the permafrost is too hard for prints to leave an impression."

"If somebody stole it, why didn't they take off in the Sno-Cat?" Marshall asked. "You keep the keys up in the weather chamber; anybody could grab it."

"Too conspicuous. And too slow. The thief would use a plane." Conti looked around. "We'll be checking everyone's belongings. Everyone's quarters. Everything."

Wolff rested his oddly expressionless eyes on Gonzalez. "You have the schematics for Fear Base, Sergeant?"

"For the central and southern wings, yes."

"What about the third wing, the northern wing?"

"That is off-limits and tightly locked."

"There's no way somebody could get in?"

"Absolutely not."

Wolff remained silent a moment, staring at the sergeant as if a new thought had just occurred to him. "Bring me what you can, please." He looked around the room. "Once this meeting is over, I want everyone to return to their quarters. We'll try to conduct the search as quickly as possible. Meanwhile, be watchful. If you see anything suspicious—any activity, conversation, transmission, *anything*—come to me."

Marshall looked from Wolff, to Conti, and back again. He wasn't sure which surprised him more: the inherent assumption of treachery, or the speed with which Wolff was moving to address it.

Ashleigh Davis had been sitting disconsolately in a front-row seat, one leg crossed over the other at a sharp angle. She wore a rich silk nightgown beneath the fur coat, and her long blond hair was tousled. "Have fun playing policeman," she said. "Meanwhile, Emilio, will you please arrange for me to fly back to New York right away? If this tiger thing has fallen through, I still have a chance to cover that special about coral bleaching on the Great Barnacle Reef."

"Barrier," Marshall said.

Davis looked at him.

"Great Barrier Reef."

"I've got someone working on transportation," Wolff said, with a warning glance at Marshall. "By the way, Ms. Davis, you and Mister . . . ah, Carradine were the two closest to the vault last night. Did you hear anything, or see anything, unusual?"

"Nothing," Davis replied, seemingly annoyed at being mentioned in the same breath with the trucker.

"And you?" Wolff glanced at Carradine. The trucker, his seat tilted backward at a dangerous angle, merely shrugged.

"I'd like to speak with the two of you once this meeting ends." Wolff looked at Marshall. "You too."

"Why me?" Marshall asked.

"You're the one who reported the theft," Wolff replied, as if this act alone established him as a prime suspect.

"Just a minute," Sully broke in. "What about this new arrival, this Dr. Logan? Why isn't he here?"

"We'll be looking into that."

"It's one thing to toss orders around, confine everyone to their bunks. But it's another to start questioning my staff without my authorization."

"Your *staff*"—Wolff shot back—"will be the first to be questioned. Your people are the only ones here not cleared in advance for this network operation."

"Logan isn't cleared, is he? Besides, what does clearance have to do with anything?" Apparently the abrupt loss of any chance for television immortality—along with this bureaucrat encroaching on his bit of turf—had reawakened Sully's professional territoriality.

"It is plenty to do with it," Wolff replied. "The magnitude of this prize—not only in terms of science but in terms of scientific careers."

Sully opened his mouth, then closed it again. His face turned beet red.

"I think that covers everything." Wolff glanced at Conti. "Care to add anything?"

"Just this," the producer said. "Twenty minutes ago, I got off the phone with the president of Blackpool Entertainment Group. It was one of the more unpleasant conversations of my life." He scoured the room with his glance. "I'm speaking now to the person or persons who did this. You know who you are. Blackpool considers the value of this find to be incalculable, and is therefore considering its disappearance a gross criminal act."

He paused once again. "This theft is not, I repeat, *not,* going down as a black mark on my oeuvre. The asset is here, and you won't have a chance to get away with it. We will *find* it, we will *retask* our documentary, and we will emerge with an *even greater* work of art."

17

Marshall mounted the set of stamped-metal steps very slowly. The stairwell was narrow and dark, lit only by a single fluorescent fixture. Lightbulbs were a scarce commodity: even with the film crew on hand, much of the base remained completely dark.

He felt more tired than he had ever felt in his life. And yet it was not a physical weariness—it was total emotional exhaustion. He had seen it in the strained faces of the others, as well. After so much effort, so much buildup, the sudden inexplicable disappearance left everyone stupefied. And over the entire base hung the question: Who did it?

Reaching the top of the stairwell, he stopped at a closed, windowless door. He glanced at his watch: five minutes past eight. Fifteen hours had passed since he'd discovered the missing cat. Fifteen endless, awful hours, full of mistrust and suspicion and uncertainty.

And now, just after dinner, an e-mail summons from Faraday: "RASP room, right away."

Marshall reached for the handle, pushed it open. Beyond lay a long, low room that resembled the control tower of an airport. Windows ran around all four sides, looking out over the limitless icescape of the Zone. The room was as dark as the stairwell, and the dim light reflected off the scopes of a dozen obsolete radar stations, arrayed in regular rows. Ancient screens, each six feet tall, were pushed diagonally into the corners of the room. Before each sat a projection device, dusty and unused for nearly half a century.

This was the Radar Mapping and Air Surveillance Command Post, known as the RASP room, the nerve center of Fear Base and the highest structure within the perimeter fence. As he looked around, he could make out three dim forms seated at a conference table: Sully, Barbour, and Chen. Chen gave a listless wave. Sully, elbows on his knees and chin in his hands, glanced up at the sound of the door, then let his eyes sink back to floor.

Three evenings a week, without fail, the team had assembled here for a status meeting. Who'd chosen the RASP room for the meeting was forgotten, but the bizarre location had become a fixed ritual within days of their arrival. Except this was no pro forma meeting: Faraday wanted to talk to them, urgently.

As if on schedule, the door opened again and Faraday came in, a thin folder under one arm. The usual preoccupied look was gone from the biologist's features. He stepped quickly past the radar stations and sat down between Sully and Chen.

For a moment, nobody spoke. Then Barbour cleared her throat. "So. Are we going to have to pack it in?"

There was no response.

"That's what he told me, you know. That nancy-boy Conti. Him and his storm trooper."

"We've only got another two weeks on the project," Marshall said. "Even if they do close us up, bureaucracy moves slowly. We can get our work done in time."

Barbour didn't seem to hear him. "Pawed through every last one of my drawers. Said it was us, he did. He said we thought we were in it together. Said we wanted the specimen for ourselves, for the university."

"Penny, forget it," Sully snapped. "He's just kicking out at anybody within reach."

"He just kept after me . . . and after me . . . oh, *God*!" And Barbour buried her face in her hands, her frame suddenly shaking with violent sobs.

Marshall leaned over quickly, put an arm around her shoulders.

"Bastard," Sully murmured.

"Maybe *we* could find it," Chen said. "Or maybe the person who stole it. They couldn't have gone far. In fact, they must still be here. We'd be off the hook then, they could salvage the special."

Barbour sniffed, detached herself gently from Marshall's embrace.

"We can't do anything Wolff isn't doing already," Sully said. "Besides, he's not likely to trust us. He made that perfectly clear. I don't know why he's so fixated on us—that Dr. Logan seems guilty as hell. You think his arrival just yesterday was a coincidence? And why wasn't he at the meeting?"

"Why indeed?" Marshall replied. Privately, he had been thinking the same thing.

"While cooling my heels in my quarters I went online, did a little digging into Jeremy Logan. Seems he's a professor of medieval history at Yale. Last year he published a monograph on some genetic disorder that afflicted ancient Egyptian royalty. The year before, a monograph on spectral phenomenon in Salem, Massachusetts. 'Spectral phenomena.' " Sully spat out the words. "Does that sound like a history professor to you?"

When nobody answered, Sully sighed and looked around. "Well, this speculation won't get us anywhere. Wright, what was it you wanted to see us about? It is your latest theory du jour?"

Faraday glanced at him. "No theory," he said. "Just some pictures."

Sully groaned. "*Again* with the photographs? That's why we're here? You're in the wrong profession, you know that?"

Faraday ignored this. "After Evan told us about the theft—after the first hue and cry died down—I went out to the vault. The door was wide open, nobody seemed to care about it anymore. So I took some shots."

Sully frowned. "Why?"

"Why do I ever take shots? Documentation." He paused. "Conti seemed to be blaming us already. I thought maybe . . . well, maybe I'd find some evidence to clear us. I didn't get a chance to print them until an hour or so ago." He opened the folder, drew out half a dozen eight-by-tens, and passed them to Sully.

The climatologist shuffled through them quickly, then handed them to Marshall, clearly unimpressed.

The first photo showed a blurry interior of the vault. Chunks and blocks of ice littered the floor, but otherwise it was empty save for the heater in the rear and the large hole between the I beams. Marshall turned to the second photo. This was clearer: a close-up of the hole itself.

"And?" Sully prompted.

"People were saying the thief must have crawled in under the vault." Faraday removed his glasses, began polishing them on the cuff of his shirt. "Cut out the block of ice with a hacksaw."

"Yes, we all heard that. So?"

"Did you see that shot of the hole? Look at the kerf pattern."

"The what?" Sully asked.

"Kerf. The saw marks. If somebody was breaking into the vault from underneath, the marks should go from down to up. But when I examined the edges of the hole in close-up, the marks did the opposite. Went from *up* to *down*."

"Let me see that." Sully plucked the photos from Marshall's hand, examined them closely. "I don't see anything."

"May I?" Marshall retrieved the photos, looked at the close-up again. Although the silver paint of the floor reflected the bright light of the vault, he could immediately see that Faraday was right: the wood splinters weren't forced upward. Instead, they clearly angled down.

"Whoever it was didn't break in from underneath," he said. "They sawed their way out from inside."

Sully waved his hand in impatient dismissal. "Wolff's gotten to the two of you. You're seeing things."

"No. It's there all right." Marshall glanced at Faraday. "You know what this means?"

Faraday nodded. "It means whoever stole the cat knew the combination to the vault."

18

Until now, Marshall had been no deeper inside Conti's capacious suite than its threshold. But as the director gestured for him to enter, Marshall immediately understood why Conti had appropriated not only the commander's quarters but the deputy commander's as well. The rambling but spartan set of rooms on C Level had been converted into a sprawling, opulent salon. Leather couches, velvet banquettes, and plush ottomans were placed in complementary attitudes atop expensive Persian rugs. Draperies and postmodernist paintings in discreet frames camouflaged the drab metal walls. The centerpiece of the space was a huge, hundred-inch LCD screen in the rear, its base hidden by rows of chairs set before it: a private cinema for viewing rushes, feature films, and—Marshall felt certain—the Greatest Hits of Emilio Conti.

The director was polite, even cheery, and the only hint he hadn't slept in perhaps thirty-six hours was the blue-black smudges beneath his eyes. "Good morning, Dr. Marshall," he said with a smile. "Good morning. Come in, come in. Seven-thirty: excellent. I appreciate promptness." He'd been watching something on the vast screen—black-and-white, slightly grainy—and with the flick of a remote he switched it off. "Please, sit down."

He led the way across the room. Through an open doorway, Marshall could see a small conference table, surrounded by ergonomic work chairs. A Moviola stood in a far corner, strips of film trailing from its spools. Marshall stared at it, wondering if this anachronism was part of Conti's work flow or simply a directorial affectation.

Conti took a seat before the screen and motioned Marshall to do the same. "What do you think of my little screening room?" he asked, still smiling.

"I watched them airlift that thing in," Marshall said, nodding at the LCD. "I'd assumed it was some critical piece of documentary technology."

"It *is* critical," Conti replied. "Not only for assembling my film but for maintaining my sanity." He waved at two bookcases full of DVDs that framed the screen. "You see those? That is my reference library. The greatest films ever made: the most beautiful, the most groundbreaking, the most thought provoking. *The Battleship Potemkin, Intolerance, Rashômon, Double Indemnity, L'Avventura, The Seventh Seal*—they are all here. I never travel anywhere without them. Yet they are not just my solace, Dr. Marshall—they are my oracle, my Delphic temple. Some turn to the Bible for guidance; others, the I Ching. I have these. And they never fail me. Take this, for instance." And with another flick of the remote Conti restarted the film.

The perpetually worried-looking visage of Victor Mature filled the screen. "*Kiss of Death*. Familiar with it?"

Marshall shook his head.

Conti muted the sound to a whisper. "A forgotten masterpiece of 1947. Henry Hathaway's breakthrough film—but then you must know Hathaway's work, *The House on 92nd Street, 13 Rue Madeleine.* Anyway, in the movie, the hero, Nick Bianco"—and Conti pointed at Mature, his exaggerated face now framed by prison bars—"is sent up to Sing Sing on a minor charge. There he's double-crossed by his shyster lawyer. In order to make parole, he cuts a deal with the DA: he agrees to squeal on this psychopathic killer named Tommy Udo."

"Sounds intriguing."

"That's putting it mildly. Not only is it a brilliant film—but it's exactly the solution to my problem."

Marshall frowned. "I don't follow you."

"When we discovered the cat was missing, I was close to panic. I was afraid my documentary—possibly even my career—was in jeopardy. You can imagine how I felt. This was to be my ne plus ultra. It was to put me right up there with Eisenstein."

A prime-time documentary? Marshall thought. He decided it was better to keep mum.

"I paced half the night, worrying, debating what to do. Then I turned to these"—he waved at the bookcases—"and as always they provided the answer I needed."

Marshall waited, listening, as Conti nodded once more toward the screen. "You see, *Kiss of Death* is what's known as a 'docunoir': a hybrid of documentary and film noir. Very interesting concept. Very revolutionary."

He turned to Marshall, the screen illumination throwing the contours of his face into chiaroscuro. "Yesterday, in the heat of the moment, I was sure this was an act of theft. Now I've had time to think. And I've changed my mind. I'm convinced it was sabotage."

"Sabotage?"

Conti nodded. "As valuable as that cat is, the logistics of removing it from the base—spiriting it away—simply don't work." He ticked the points off on his fingers. "The thieves—and there would have to be at least two, the asset is simply too heavy for one person to handle—would need transportation. That would be impossible to conceal from us. And if anyone were to leave prematurely, we'd know."

"What about Carradine, the trucker? He not only has the transportation; he's one of the newest arrivals."

"His cab's been thoroughly searched, and his movements are accounted for. As I was saying, stealing the cat would be prohibitively difficult. But if all somebody wanted was for the documentary to *stop*, for our show to go away . . ." He shrugged. "Then it would just be a matter of dropping the carcass down some crevasse. Nobody would be the wiser."

"Who would want to do such a thing?" Marshall asked.

Conti looked at him. "You would."

Marshall looked back in surprise. "Me?"

"Well—you scientists. It might be you, in particular. But on careful consideration I think Dr. Sully is the more obvious choice. He seems to be quite put out that I didn't make him a star of *Raising the Tiger*."

Marshall shook his head. "That's crazy. The documentary was set to go live yesterday—you would have been gone today. Why bother with sabotage?"

"It's true: I would have been gone today. But postproduction on a successful shoot would take several days longer. Not to mention dismantling the sets, removing the equipment. When I gave Sully an estimated timeline, he didn't seem especially pleased." Conti looked at him searchingly. The smile was now gone. "Sully seems like the impulsive type. You don't. That's why I've come to you. Despite our little fracas the other day, I think you're a reasonable man. Perhaps more than your colleagues, you realize what's at stake. So: *Where the hell is that cat?*"

Marshall returned the stare. Despite the director's carefully composed expression, it was obvious that Conti was doing a desperate dance, searching for a way, *any* way, to salvage the situation.

"What about Logan?" Marshall asked, recalling the previous evening's conversation in the RASP room. "He came here out of nowhere. Nobody knows what he wants. I'm told he's a Yale professor—professor of history. Doesn't that strike you as strange—and very suspicious?"

"It is strange. So strange, in fact, that I have to discount him as a suspect. He's too obvious. Besides, I already told you: my money's on sabotage, not theft. And Dr. Logan has no reason to sabotage my documentary. So: Where's the cat? Sully would have told you, I think. Is it retrievable?"

"Sully didn't tell me anything. You're barking up the wrong tree. You should be searching among your own team."

Conti regarded him carefully, his expression slowly dissolving into something very much like regret. "That's Wolff's job." He sighed. "Listen. I've given it a lot of thought, and I can do this one of two ways. If we find that cat, I can make the film I originally intended. With my skills, I can even turn this delay into a benefit: make things more exciting, increase the audience. Everybody wins. Or—I can make this a crime story."

He jerked his thumb back at the screen. "I've always wanted to make a noir picture. Now I can—except I have a *true* story to tell. A *huge* story, documented as it plays out in real time: the sabotage, the investigation, the ultimate triumph of justice. Such a story would never die, Dr. Marshall. Imagine the publicity—positive or negative—for those portrayed. All I need do is cast it. Find the hero . . . *and* the villain."

On the huge screen, Victor Mature was crossing a busy street, the urban skyline rising behind him. "Look at him," Conti said. "An average Joe, caught up in something bigger than himself. Remind you of anybody?"

Marshall did not reply.

Conti shifted again. "So what's it going to be, Dr. Marshall: do the right thing, side with the cops, squeal on the bad guy? Or do something else . . . something much more stupid?"

As Mature left the frame, the camera panned in on another figure, hiding in a dark alley: pale, lean, all in black with a white tie, eyes strangely empty. Tommy Udo. Emerging from concealment, he looked carefully around, then disappeared into a doorway.

"I always loved Richard Widmark in this role," Conti said. "He plays such a great psycho. His mannerisms, his nervous hyena laugh—pure genius."

Now the killer was creeping stealthily up a narrow staircase.

"I was hoping to cast you as Mature," Conti said. "But now I'm not so sure. You're beginning to look a little more like Widmark."

The killer had entered an apartment and was confronting a terrified old lady in a wheelchair.

"That's Nick Bianco's mother," Conti explained.

The camera looked on, with monochromatic dispassion, as the woman was interrogated, shaken about. Widmark was smiling now, a strange lopsided smile, as he manhandled the grips of the wheelchair, steered it out of the shabby apartment and onto the landing.

"Watch this," Conti said. "An imperishable moment of cinema."

Widmark—still smiling, a pale, grinning death's-head in a black suit—positioned the wheelchair at the top of the stairs. There was the briefest of pauses. Then, with a sudden violent thrust, he sent it and its struggling occupant tumbling down on a one-way ride to perdition.

Conti froze the picture on Widmark's contorted face. "The network is calling me in six hours. I'll give you four to make your choice."

Silently, Marshall rose.

"And remember, Dr. Marshall—one way or the other, I'll be casting you."

19

In days past, the officers' mess had been full of noise and bustle, radiating the kind of irrepressible glee more common to a frat party than a remote army base. This morning it felt more like a morgue. People sat in twos and threes, picking listlessly at their breakfasts, barely talking. Furtive, suspicious glances were exchanged, as if the guilty party could be anyone. Standing in the doorway, Marshall realized this was, in fact, true: anybody in the mess might be the culprit.

His eye settled on a far table, where a man sat alone, reading a book. He was light-haired and thin, with a carefully trimmed beard. Logan, the history professor.

Marshall helped himself to a slice of whole wheat bread and a cup of tea, and then—on impulse—took a seat across from Logan. "Good morning," he said.

Logan put down the book—*Illuminations,* by Walter Benjamin—
and glanced across the table. "That remains to be seen."

"All too true." Marshall peeled open a small tub of marmalade
and spread the contents over his bread.

"I guess it's worse for them than for us." Logan nodded toward
the next table, where the two photographers, Fortnum and Toussaint, sat woodenly pushing scrambled eggs around their plates
with shell-shocked expressions. Much of the documentary crew
had been put to work searching the base and its surroundings for
the missing cat.

"That's right. Nobody's made off with *my* livelihood." Marshall
was careful to keep his tone light. "You?"

Logan stirred his coffee. "Unaffected by the events."

"I'm relieved to hear it. Professor, right? Of medieval history?"

The stirring slowed. "That's right."

"I'm fascinated by the subject. In fact, I've been reading a history
of the Counter-Reformation." This was only half true—Marshall's
nightly reading was, in fact, a book on the Counter-Reformation:
but it was with the desperate hope that the incredibly dry exposi-
tion would help him find sleep.

Logan raised his eyebrows. He had blue eyes that while at first
impression seemed almost drowsy were in fact subtle and penetrating.

"I just finished a chapter on the Council of Trent. Amazing, the
impact it had on the Catholic liturgy."

Logan nodded.

"And since it convened for the fourth time in—1572, right?—
there hasn't been another council as influential."

The stirring stopped. Logan took a sip of coffee, made a face.
"Terrible coffee."

"You should switch to tea. I did."

"Maybe I will." Logan put the cup down. "There were three
councils of Trent, not four."

Marshall didn't reply.

"And the last was 1563. Not 1572."

Marshall shook his head. "Guess I was more tired than I realized, getting it wrong like that."

Logan smiled slightly. "I get the feeling you got it just fine."

There was a brief, uncomfortable silence. Then Marshall laughed ruefully. "You're right. I'm sorry. That was really ham-handed of me."

"Can't say I blame you. I arrive out of nowhere, with a bizarre job description and no good reason to be here—and immediately all hell breaks loose."

"Even so, I had no right to play with you like that." Marshall hesitated. "Not that it's any excuse, but I just came from this really unpleasant meeting with Conti."

"The director? He and that pit bull from the network, Wolff, gave me a good going-over yesterday afternoon. I've never seen anybody so paranoid."

"Yeah. And the worst thing is, it's catching. I caught a good dose just now." And it was still resonating: some of the things Conti had said about Sully, in particular, were more persuasive than Marshall cared to admit. He glanced at his watch: he had three and a half hours to make up his mind.

He took a bite of his toast. "So why are you here, if you don't mind my asking?"

Logan pushed his cup away. "Doctor's orders. The climate, you know."

Marshall shook his head. "I deserved that."

Another silence settled over the table, but this time it was neither especially awkward nor uncomfortable. Marshall finished his toast. He found his suspicions of Logan fading. There was no logical reason for it, of course, other than the professor was almost certainly what he claimed to be. Rather, it was something about the man—a degree of straightforwardness—that made him difficult to suspect.

Logan sighed. "Okay, let's start again. Jeremy Logan." He reached a friendly hand across the table.

Marshall shook it. "Evan Marshall."

Logan sat back and spoke quietly. "When it comes to my research, I tend to play my cards pretty close to my vest. I make more progress that way. But I guess there's no reason not to tell you. In fact, you might even be able to help—so long as you don't mention it to the others."

"Deal."

"Actually, I think you'll see for yourself the wisdom of keeping mum."

"Somebody told me you were an enigmalogist. I haven't heard of that particular, ah, discipline."

"Nobody else has, either. My wife gave me that title once, in a playful moment." Logan shrugged. "It helps remind me of her."

"What does it have to do with medieval history?"

"Very little. But being a history professor is quite useful. It opens doors, discourages questions—most of the time, anyway." He hesitated. "I solve mysteries. Explain the unexplained: the stranger and more bizarre, the better. Sometimes I do it professionally, for a fee. Other times—like now—I'm on my own nickel."

Marshall sipped his tea. "Wouldn't teaching history bring in a more regular paycheck?"

"Money's not really an issue. Anyway, the jobs I do for others tend to pay extremely well—especially those I'm not allowed to write up in the professional journals." He stood. "Excuse me, I think I'll try the tea."

Marshall waited while Logan fixed himself a cup, returned to the table. He moved with easy, graceful motions more appropriate to an athlete than a professor. "How much do you know about Fear Base?" he asked as he sat down again.

"As much as anybody does, I suppose. An early warning station, designed to guard against a preemptive Russian attack. Decommissioned in the late 1950s when the SAGE system went online."

"Did you know that, while it was still in active use, it briefly housed a team of scientists?"

Marshall frowned. "No."

Logan sipped his tea. "Last week I gained access to a newly declassified archive of government documents. I was researching something else—medieval history, as it happens—and was looking for some relevant army records from the Second World War. I found them, all right. But I found something else as well."

He took another sip. "Specifically, I found a report from a Colonel Rose, written to an army board of inquiry. Rose was the commander of Fear Base at the time. It was a short report—a summary, really. He was scheduled to fly to Washington a few weeks later to make a more detailed report in person."

"Go on."

"The report had been misfiled. It was stuffed behind the file I'd been looking for, unread and obviously forgotten for half a century. As I said, it was very brief. But it mentioned the fact that the scientific team attached to Fear Base died very abruptly, over a two-day period in April 1958."

"The *entire* team?"

Logan made a suppressing motion with his hand. "No, that's not quite correct. There were eight members of the team. Seven died."

"And the eighth?" Marshall asked more quietly.

"Rose's report doesn't specify what happened to him—or her."

"What were they doing up here?"

"I don't know the details. All that Rose said is that they were analyzing an anomaly of some kind."

"Anomaly?"

"That's what he called it. And his recommendation was that the research be immediately suspended and no second team sent up to continue it."

Marshall stared thoughtfully at his empty cup. "Did you learn anything else? The name of the surviving scientist, for example?"

"Nothing. There was no other record, official or unofficial, of any science team at Fear Base. I searched carefully—and believe me, Evan, I've had a lot of practice uncovering lost or hidden information. But a couple of things particularly intrigued me." He leaned in closer. "First, there were *two* copies of the report stuffed in behind that file I mentioned—I can only assume that one was meant for the archive, and the other had been destined for the Pentagon.

Second, the tone of Colonel Rose's report. Even though it was nothing more than a sober government memo, you could almost smell the hysteria. When he made the urgent recommendation that no more scientists be sent up, he really meant it: *urgent.*"

"So what about the detailed report he made in Washington later? That must have been documented."

"He never made any report. He died ten days later, in a plane crash on the way down to Fort Richardson."

"That second copy of the report . . ." Marshall began. Then he stopped. "So the whole thing was just forgotten."

"The secret died with the scientists. And Colonel Rose."

"But are you sure? That nobody else knew about it, I mean?"

"If they did, they kept their mouths shut and they're now long dead. Otherwise, do you really suppose the army would have let you and your team use Fear Base?"

Marshall shook his head. "I hadn't thought of that."

Logan smiled faintly. "Now you see what I mean about the wisdom of keeping mum?"

For a moment, Marshall didn't reply. Then he glanced over at Logan. "So why, exactly, are you here, Jeremy?"

"To do what I do best. Solve the mystery. Find out what happened to those scientists." He drained his own cup. "You're right— this tea's not bad. Care for another cup?"

But Marshall didn't answer. He was thinking.

20

The shudder of a slamming door; a shake of the mattress; a rough jostling of his shoulder. Josh Peters stretched, plucked the buds from his ears. As his dream and the pianistic musings of McCoy Tyner both faded into memory, the sounds of reality—and Fear Base—returned: distant clangs, the incessant tapping of the heating pipes, and the impatient voice of his roommate, Blaine.

"Josh. Hey, Josh. Get the hell up."

Peters snapped off his music player and blinked his eyes open. Blaine's red, wind-chapped face swam into focus.

"What?" Peters mumbled.

"What 'what'? It's your turn, man. I've been out in that shit for an hour."

Peters struggled to a sitting position, then collapsed again back onto the cot.

"You'd better hurry up. It's past nine and you wouldn't want Wolff to catch you still racked out."

That did it. Peters got up from the bed and rubbed his face vigorously with his hands.

"The whole thing's crazy," Blaine said in a petulant voice. "We've been searching an entire day already. Nobody's going to find anything in that storm. Just do what I did: walk in circles, look busy, and try to keep your ass from freezing."

Peters didn't reply. He tugged on a shirt and stepped into his shoes. Maybe he could remain half asleep through this, then return to his bunk and pick up where he'd left off: a delightful reverie in which Ashleigh Davis had been rubbing hazelnut-infused massage oil—the edible kind—all over . . .

"When we get back, the union's going to hear about this. I mean, I'm supposed to be maintaining the digital library and logging takes, not out searching for the abominable snowman. And another thing. Why are they making *us* look outside? Why can't we be like Fortnum and Toussaint, searching the lockers?"

"Because we're PAs. Doesn't take a rocket scientist to figure that out." And Peters shuffled out, shoes untied, leaving the door wide open.

He made his way, in a somnambulistic haze, along the corridors and up an echoing stairwell to the entrance plaza. It was deserted except for the army engineer manning the security station. Peters gave a desultory wave as he shuffled into the weather chamber, opened his locker, and put on his parka. Blaine was right: this was bullshit. To begin with, half of the base was off-limits to them. If *he* had wanted to hide the carcass, he'd make sure to find a way to stow it someplace the others wouldn't be allowed to search. Or in the quarters of the army guys, maybe—they probably wouldn't be much inclined to let a bunch of faggoty film types paw over all their gear. But the bottom line was, only an idiot would stow the creature inside the base. Not only were there too many pairs of eyes everywhere, but the place was warm and humid enough to grow orchids. A carcass hidden somewhere—especially a ten-thousand-year-old carcass—would start to stink in a matter of hours. No: anybody with half a brain would have stowed it outside.

Which was precisely where he was headed.

Peters stopped to enter his name and the time into the logbook Wolff had placed in the chamber. Then he walked through the staging area, opened the main doors, and stepped outside. At the first biting blast of wind, the last clinging vestiges of drowsiness were brutally ripped away. Any hopes he'd entertained of getting back to sleep after his one-hour shift had been in vain. He'd heard about the bad weather that had come in, pinned them down, kept planes from either landing or taking off. Hearing about it was one thing—experiencing it firsthand was something else. He staggered back against the outer doors, lowered his head, leaned into the blast. Sharp cold needles stung his cheeks and he retreated farther into the fur lining of his hood. Through the tumbling sheets of ice and snow he could make out the faint silhouettes of the outlying structures. He took a tentative step forward, then another. It was so dim it seemed more like night than day. Gaffer's rigging and scaffolding swayed like giant Tinkertoy constructions, creaking with protest under the fierce gusts.

Searches in shifts: one hour on, eleven hours off. Six searchers inside, six outside—the latter number reduced to three in the stormy weather. Even so, it was hard to believe there were two other poor saps out here with him, searching uselessly in this shit. This was beyond crazy. What were Wolff and Conti smoking, anyway?

Face away from the wind, he plodded forward a dozen steps to a storage shed, its door rattling fretfully in its frame. He paused a moment, then tacked left to the outbuilding that served as temporary prop fabrication. He peered in through the window: empty, of course. Was it really just two days before that he'd lounged in there, chewing on a piece of chipotle-flavored beef jerky and scoffing at the army types and lame-assed scientists who were stuck in this godforsaken place? Now those same soldiers and scientists were inside, warm and dry—and he was out here freezing.

With a curse he moved forward again, counting the steps—ten, twenty, thirty—until he reached the ice-road trucker's cab. He huddled behind one of the huge tires, partially sheltered from the wind and snow. He'd been outside less than five minutes and he felt numb already.

Once again he wondered about the two others who were supposed to be out here, searching. He upbraided himself for not checking the logbook when he'd signed in. A little company might make the time pass quicker. He opened his mouth to shout for them, then—feeling the wind immediately snatch the breath from his lungs—thought better of it. Why waste energy when nobody could hear him, anyway?

He shuffled forward again until the heavy chain-link of the perimeter fence abruptly materialized out of the gray soup. He stopped, extending one hand to brush the fence. He'd been warned not to stray far from the base in this weather, and with polar bears roaming the tundra he planned to heed that advice, big-time. He walked another few steps to the corrugated metal walls of the deserted security station, then stepped past it. He'd make one circuit of the base, keeping an arm's length from the fence. That's as much as anyone could expect. Then he'd go hide in some outbuilding for the remainder of his hour, try to warm up.

Rounding the security station, he stepped out of the perimeter apron and onto the permafrost. The wind seemed to redouble its fury. He trudged ahead more quickly now, one step, another, and then another . . . He staggered forward like a blind man, one hand trailing along the fence, his eyes all but closed against the ice pellets. The shriek of the wind filled his head, making his ears ring strangely. Already it seemed like he'd been out here forever. Jesus, this was awful. Blaine was right: he'd file a grievance not only with the union but with the channel as well. He'd do it as soon as he could get online; he wouldn't even wait until they were back in New York. It didn't matter if he was just a production assistant: his job description didn't include anything like this, and all Wolff's talk of "emergency measures" was nothing but a crock of . . .

He paused. His hand fell away from the fence, and he looked around, temporarily heedless of the brutal cold and stinging wind.

Why had he stopped? He'd seen nothing. And yet suddenly his senses were on full alert, his heart hammering in his chest. Living well east of Tompkins Square Park had honed his instinct for self-preservation—but he wasn't in New York City, he was in the middle of frigging nowhere.

He shook his head, moved forward—then stopped again. What was that noise that seemed to come from everywhere and nowhere, that made the inside of his head feel like it was stuffed with bees? And what was that shape, dark and indistinct, in the tumbling hail of snow ahead of him?

"Who's there?" he called out, the wind snatching away the words as quickly as he uttered them.

He blinked, peered more closely—and then with a piercing shriek of terror tumbled backward, turned, and, half falling, half staggering, fled in the direction of the security station. Screaming and gibbering in sudden mindless fear, Peters made it two more steps before a devastating blow from behind knocked him to his knees, wheezing, eyes bulging—and then a violent, unimaginable pain abruptly blossomed between his shoulder blades. Yawning darkness claimed him for its own.

21

The physics and life-sciences lab was a converted sheet-metal shop on B Level. It wasn't really much of a lab, Marshall thought as he stood just inside the doorway, surveying the laptops, microscopes, and other equipment strewn across half a dozen worktables: basically, it was just enough for the most essential day-to-day analysis and observation until they could get their data and samples back to Massachusetts.

In the rear of the lab, Faraday and Chen were huddled over something, backs to him, their heads almost touching. Marshall threaded his way between the tables toward them. As he approached he saw what they were studying so intently: a rack containing a dozen or so small test tubes.

"So this is where you've been hiding," he said.

The two straightened up and turned toward him with the swift, guilty motions of children caught doing something forbidden. Marshall frowned.

"What are you up to?" he asked.

Faraday and Chen exchanged glances.

"Analyzing something," Faraday said after a moment.

"So I see." Marshall glanced down at the test tubes. They were filled with different colored liquids: red, blue, pale yellow. "Seems to have captured your full attention."

Faraday said nothing. Chen shrugged.

"What is it?" Marshall asked bluntly.

In the pause that followed, he looked around the nearby tables, more carefully this time. Faraday's eight-by-tens of the inside of the vault were scattered across one; they were now covered with circles and arrowed notations in grease pencil. On another table, a plastic bin full of what appeared to be wood chips sat beside a stereomicroscope.

Faraday cleared his throat. "We're examining the ice."

Marshall glanced back at him. "What ice?"

"The ice that the cat—the creature—was encased in."

"How? That ice melted away long ago. And the resulting water would be contaminated, useless as a scientific sample."

"I know. That's why I retrieved the samples from the source."

"The source?" Marshall frowned. "You mean—from the ice cave?"

Faraday pushed his glasses up his nose, nodded.

"You went back to the cave—in this storm? That's crazy."

"No, I went last night. After our meeting in the RASP room."

Marshall folded his arms across his chest. "That's *still* crazy. In the middle of the night? That cave's dangerous enough at the best of times."

"You sound just like Sully," Faraday replied.

"There might have been polar bears wandering around."

"I went along," Chen said. "With one of the rifles."

Marshall sighed, leaned back against one of the tables. "Okay. Mind telling me why?"

Faraday blinked at him. "It's like we discussed at the meeting. Something's just not right about this."

"I'll say. We've got a thief in our midst."

"That's not what I mean. Things aren't adding up. The sudden thawing, the creature going missing, the kerf marks..." He pointed at the plastic bin beside the microscope. "I took some samples from around the edges of the vault hole and examined them at 40x. There's no question about it: those marks were made *from the inside out,* not from somebody sawing in from underneath."

Marshall nodded. "A minute ago you said I sounded like Sully. What did you mean by that?"

"When he heard I went up to the cave, Sully went ballistic. He said it was a waste of time, that I might as well throw the samples away."

Marshall didn't reply immediately. He recalled how dismissive Sully had been about this theory—and about the photographs in general. While Faraday might have been foolhardy to collect the samples in the first place, it seemed a scientific given that, once obtained, they should be analyzed. He thought again of what Conti had said about Sully.

Chen glanced at Faraday, then nodded toward the wood samples. "Tell him the other thing."

Faraday smoothed the front of his lab coat. "When we examined the chips under the microscope, we also found samples of matted hair and a good amount of dried, dark matter caked to the sharper edges."

"Caked?" Marshall repeated. "Was it blood?"

"I haven't analyzed it yet," Faraday said. He opened his mouth, then shut it again, as if thinking better of the idea.

"Go ahead," Marshall said. "Tell me the rest."

Faraday swallowed. "Those kerf marks..." he began. "I don't know. Under the scope they don't look like they were made by a saw."

"What, then?"

"They appear to have been more ... natural in origin."

Marshall looked from Faraday to Chen and back again. "Natural? I'm not following."

This time it was Chen who spoke. "Not sawed through. More like *chewed* through."

The silence that followed this was much longer.

"How on earth can you expect me to believe that, Wright?" Marshall asked at last, trying to keep his voice from betraying his deep skepticism.

Faraday cleared his throat again. "Listen," he said, his voice lower. "When I know something for a fact—*if* I know something—I'll tell you. I won't hold it back. I just don't want any more flak from Sully."

"Sully," Marshall repeated thoughtfully. "You know where he is?"

"Haven't seen him for hours."

"Okay." Marshall eased himself away from the table. "If you learn anything, you'll let me know?"

Faraday nodded. With a final, searching look at the two men, Marshall turned and slowly made his way out of the lab.

22

Jeremy Logan ventured carefully along the narrow corridors of E Level. It had taken him almost ninety minutes of exploring to reach this, the lowest level of Fear Base's central section. As he'd penetrated deeper into the base, he'd found the passages cluttered with increasing amounts of shadowy detritus: desks piled atop one another, tools, pieces of ancient electrical equipment, decaying boxes filled with vacuum tubes. It was as if all the unused clutter of the base had literally sunk to the bottom over the years.

C Level had been primarily comprised of support services for the men originally stationed at the base: food-preparation areas, laundry, tailoring. D Level held the quartermaster's office and countless storage spaces, along with several repair bays. Unlike the suffocatingly warm upper levels, the chill down here was pronounced. The unpleasant smell of the base—inescapable even on the upper levels—was significantly worse. Logan wrinkled his nose at the musky odor.

E Level was a jumbled mélange of secondary spaces and mechanical systems. The ceilings were even lower here than elsewhere, and heavily veined with pipes and cabling. Most lightbulbs had been removed from their fixtures, and those that remained no longer worked. Logan moved slowly from room to room, his flashlight licking right and left, right and left. Many of the objects were covered with old tarps, well preserved in the cold dry air. He wondered when someone had last been this deep inside the base. It was like stepping into a time capsule.

He stopped in what appeared to be an auxiliary control room, a fallback in case the primary systems upstairs became inoperative. The black screens of the monitors and oscilloscopes winked back as his light passed over them. The silence was complete. On a whim, he switched off the flashlight. Instantly, unrelieved blackness engulfed him. He hurriedly switched the light back on. He moved out of the control room and down the corridor, wishing he'd brought along some spare batteries, or preferably a spare flashlight: it wouldn't do for the one he was using to fail.

He passed several more cramped rooms, their doorways yawning rectangles of black, before the corridor ended at a T intersection. He stopped, trying to get his bearings in this confusing military labyrinth. If he was correct, the passageway to his left was headed more or less south. He turned right and continued on.

Within twenty yards the passage ended in a heavy metal door—hatch, really—windowless and dogged shut by thick cleats. A red bulb in a narrow cage was set into the ceiling above it—unlit, like the rest on E Level—and a sign screwed into the adjacent wall: WARNING. AUTHORIZED ENTRY ONLY. F-29 CLEARANCE REQUIRED.

Logan read the sign once, then again. Then he let his light play over the metal hatch. Taking a step forward, he put a hand on the nearest cleat, gave it an exploratory tug. It held fast. Looking closer, he saw that even if he could undog the cleats it would make little difference: a heavy padlock had been snugged through a hasp on one side of the hatch.

Suddenly, Logan turned. Back to the hatch, he stabbed his light down the corridor. The base was deathly still. He hadn't seen anybody for nearly an hour and a half. And yet he was sure—completely and utterly sure—he had just heard something.

"Who's there?" he called out.

No response.

He stood there, motionless save for the hand probing with the flashlight. Was it one of the film crew, searching for the missing carcass? Nobody would be foolish enough to drag it all the way down here—or to extend the search this far.

"Who is it?" he called. Again, silence.

He might as well head back. He'd found what he'd been searching for, yet could go no farther. The hatch was sealed. Taking a deep breath, he started forward, then stopped again, uncomfortably aware that he was in a dead end. There was no other way to get back to the surface except down this corridor. Where the sound had come from.

Then he heard it again: a tread, the sound of a footfall. Then another. And then a form stepped out into the intersection. Logan's light swiveled to it like a magnet. It was Gonzalez, the sergeant in charge of the base detachment.

Logan swallowed, felt limbs that had suddenly grown tense now relax a little. He composed his face into a neutral mask.

Gonzalez came toward him slowly, his own Maglite held loose in a burly hand. "Out for a morning constitutional?" he asked as he approached.

Logan smiled.

Gonzalez let his light drift over Logan's features. "You're Dr. Logan, right?"

"That's right."

"What are you doing down here, Doctor? Are you looking for the creature, too?"

"No. Were you following me?"

"Let's say I was curious why anybody would be down here."

Logan debated asking how he'd found out. He decided the sergeant probably wouldn't tell him.

"So what were you looking for?" Gonzalez asked.

Logan aimed a thumb at the hatch behind him.

Gonzalez frowned. "Why?"

"That's the north wing, right? The science section?"

Gonzalez's expression grew guarded. "What do you know about it?"

"Not much. That's why I'm down here." Logan took a step forward. "You wouldn't have a key on you, by any chance?"

"If I did, I wouldn't use it. It's unauthorized, off-limits. Even to me."

"But scientific work went on there, right?"

"I'm afraid I'm not at liberty to answer that."

"Look, Sergeant, I came all the way up here just to learn more about what happened beyond that door. I learned about this from sifting through a pile of recently declassified papers. It piqued my interest. I'm not a spy, and I'm not a journalist. Isn't there anything you can tell me?"

Gonzalez didn't answer.

Logan sighed. "Okay. What if I tell you what I know? In the 1950s this base was used not only as an early warning system. Scientific work was going on here, as well. Whether it was research, or experiments, or what, I don't know. But something went wrong—something that shut down the work prematurely. Does that jibe with what you've been told?"

Gonzalez looked at him from behind the flashlight—a long, appraising look. "All I ever heard was rumors," he said. "From the guys stationed here before me."

Logan nodded.

"The northern wing is built deep inside the natural declivity here, basically intended as a support structure for the rest of the base. That hatchway leads to its upper level."

"The *upper* level?"

"That's right. The northern wing is completely underground. I don't know what was inside except that it was top secret." Gonzalez hesitated, then—despite their remote location—lowered his voice. "But word was that some strange stuff went on."

"What kind of strange stuff?"

"No idea. The guys here before me didn't know, either. One of them heard that a bunch of scientists got mauled by a polar bear."

"Mauled?" Logan echoed. "In the north wing?"

"That's what he said."

"How did a polar bear get down here?"

"Exactly."

Logan pursed his lips. "You don't know if anybody talked to these scientists?"

"No idea."

"Where did they bunk?"

Gonzalez shrugged. "C Level, I think. Anyway, there's extra berths there that no military ever used."

There was a brief silence before Logan spoke again. "From the background research I've done, it seems neither of the other two early warning bases had any detachments of scientists."

Instead of replying, Gonzalez pointed at the warning bolted to the wall.

"What's F-29 clearance?" Logan asked.

"Never heard of it. Now, Doctor, shall we head back upstairs?"

"One last question. How often do you come down here?"

"As little as I can. It's cold, it's dark, and it stinks."

"Then I'm sorry to have put you to the trouble."

"And I'm sorry you came all the way up here for nothing."

"That remains to be seen." And Logan gestured. "After you, Sergeant."

23

Marshall strode down the corridor toward Conti's quarters, Penny Barbour at his side. He'd wanted to bring along more of his fellow scientists, if only for a cosmetic show of numbers—to display a solidarity that, in fact, did not exist—but it had been impossible. Sully's whereabouts were still unknown. And Marshall hadn't wanted to disturb Faraday and Chen from their analysis. And so, ultimately, it had come down to him and the computer scientist.

As they stopped before the door, Marshall became aware of a murmur of conversation in the room beyond. He glanced at Barbour. "Are you ready for this?"

She looked back. "You're going to do the talking, luv. Not me."

"But you leveled with me, right?"

She nodded. "Of course."

"Okay." Marshall raised his hand to knock.

Just as he did, one of the voices on the far side of the door grew abruptly louder. "It goes beyond decency!" Marshall heard Wolff say. "I absolutely *forbid* it!"

Marshall rapped on the metal door.

Instantly, a hush fell. Ten seconds went by before Wolff's voice sounded again, calm this time. "Come in."

Marshall opened the door for Barbour and stepped in behind her. Three people were standing in the center of the elegant room: Conti, Wolff, and Ekberg. Marshall stopped, looking at them. Conti was very pale, and Ekberg's eyes were red and puffy. Both of their gazes were cast downward. Only Wolff stared back at Marshall, his narrow face inscrutable.

Marshall took a deep breath. "Mr. Conti, the deadline you imposed still has an hour to run. But I don't need any more time."

Conti looked up at him briefly, then looked away.

"I've spoken to my colleagues. And I'm convinced that none of them had anything to do with the cat going missing." This was mostly true: Barbour had almost bitten his head off when he'd asked if she knew what happened to the cat, and if Faraday was responsible he wouldn't be in his lab now, studying its disappearance. Marshall still hadn't found Sully—and the climatologist *had* been acting a little strange—but Sully surely couldn't have acted alone.

Conti didn't answer, and Marshall continued. "Furthermore, I find your bullying tactics and intimidation insulting. And this insistence that somebody sabotaged your show—that there's some conspiracy to force you into leaving the site—borders on the paranoid. Go ahead and make your revised documentary if it will help soothe your vanity. But if you say, or intimate, or allege anything about me or my colleagues that *in any way* deviates from pure fact, you and Terra Prime can expect to hear immediately from a large and very angry group of lawyers."

"All right," said Wolff. "You've made your point."

Marshall didn't reply. He looked from Conti to Wolff and back again. He realized his heart was hammering and he was breathing hard.

Wolff continued to look at him. "Now if there's nothing else, would you mind leaving?"

Marshall returned his gaze to Conti. At last the director looked up at him, nodded almost imperceptibly. It wasn't even clear whether he'd heard a single word of the exchange.

It seemed there was nothing else to say. Marshall glanced at Barbour, gestured toward the door.

"Aren't you going to tell them?" Ekberg asked, very quietly.

Marshall looked at her. The field producer was looking from Conti to Wolff, a haunted expression on her face.

"Tell us what?" Marshall asked.

Wolff frowned, made a small suppressing gesture.

"You *can't* keep it secret," Ekberg said, her voice louder now, more self-assured. "If you don't tell them, I will."

"Tell us what?" Marshall asked.

There was a brief silence. Then Ekberg turned toward him. "Josh Peters. One of our PAs, assistant to the supervising editor. He was found outside the security fence ten minutes ago. Dead."

Shock lanced through Marshall. "Frozen?"

At this, Conti at last roused himself. "Torn apart," he said.

24

The Fear Base infirmary, a confusing, claustrophobic network of small gray rooms, was located deep in the south wing military quarters. Marshall had been here only once before, for a butterfly bandage and a tetanus booster after gashing his arm on a rusty fairing. Like most of the base, the place looked like something out of an old movie set. Ancient inoculation schedules and posters warning against lice and athlete's foot were pinned to the walls. Half a dozen fresh bottles of Betadine and hydrogen peroxide had been hastily stored in glass-fronted cabinets beside ancient, semi-fossilized beakers of iodine and rubbing alcohol. And over everything lay a faint shabbiness that clung to the fixtures and furniture almost like a coating of dust.

Marshall glanced around. The space that had once served as office-cum-waiting-room was full of people—Wolff, Conti, Ekberg,

Gonzalez, the carrot-haired PFC named Phillips—making the cramped space feel even more confined. Sully had finally turned up—he had, he said, been studying weather data tables in a remote lab—along with the gloomy news that the current blizzard wasn't due to abate for forty-eight hours. He was standing in a far corner, his flushed face agitated. Nobody, it seemed, wanted to look through the open doorway to the south. The space beyond had once been an examining room. Now it was a makeshift morgue.

Sergeant Gonzalez was questioning the unlucky production assistant who had found the body: a gangly youth in his early twenties with a wispy goatee. Marshall knew nothing about him except that his name was Neiman.

"Did you see anybody else in the area?" Gonzalez asked.

Neiman shook his head. He had a dazed, glassy-eyed expression, as if he'd just been hit with a bat.

"What were you doing out there?"

Long silence. "It was my shift."

"Shift for what?"

"To search for the missing cat."

Gonzalez rolled his eyes, turned angrily toward Wolff. "Is that still going on?"

Wolff shook his head.

"Good thing, or I'd have ordered you to call it off. If you hadn't sent your people off on a wild-goose chase, Peters would still be alive."

"You don't know that," Wolff replied.

"Of course I know that. Peters wouldn't have been outside. He wouldn't have encountered a polar bear."

"You're assuming something," Wolff said.

Gonzalez glared at him.

"You're assuming it's a polar bear. This man could have been murdered."

Gonzalez sighed in disgust, and—disdaining to answer—returned his attention to Neiman. "Did you hear anything? See anything?"

Neiman shook his head. "Nothing. Just blood. Blood everywhere." He looked as if he was going to be sick.

"All right. That's enough for now."

"Who transported the body here?" Marshall asked Gonzalez.

"I did. Along with Private Fluke."

"Where's Fluke?"

"In his bunk. He isn't feeling so hot at the moment." The sergeant nodded to Phillips. "Why don't you escort Mr. Neiman back to his quarters?"

Ekberg came forward. "I'll go with you."

"Don't speak of this to the others," Wolff said. "Not quite yet."

Ekberg looked at him. "I have to."

"It will just cause needless anxiety," Wolff told her.

"What will cause anxiety is rumor and gossip," she replied. "Which is spreading already."

"She's right," Gonzalez said. "It's better if people are told."

Wolff looked at the two of them in turn. "Very well. But play down the degree of the injuries."

"And warn everyone to stay indoors," Gonzalez added.

Ekberg walked out, following Neiman and Private Phillips. As he watched her go, Marshall observed that a change had come over her. Until now, she had always been very deferential to Conti and Wolff. But in the wake of Peters's death, she seemed different. Not only had she broken rank with her bosses to inform the scientists of the killing but now she was openly challenging their orders.

He realized that Wolff was staring at him. "What is it?" he asked.

"As long as you're here, are you going to take a look?"

"A look?" Marshall repeated.

"You're a biologist, aren't you?"

Marshall hesitated. "Paleoecologist."

"Close enough. Until the storm clears and we can get a plane up here, we're going to place the body in cold storage. But first, why don't you examine it and give us your conclusions."

"I'm no pathologist. And I don't have a medical degree. You should get Faraday down here—at least he's a biologist."

Wolff shifted. "I'm not asking for an autopsy. I just want you to examine the wounds and give us your opinion."

"Opinion of what?" Sully chimed in, speaking for the first time.

"Whether they could have been inflicted by a human."

Gonzalez frowned in irritation. "That's a waste of time. We know a polar bear did this."

"We know no such thing. Anyway, Peters was a Terra Prime employee—it's our call to make." Wolff looked searchingly at Marshall. "We're all trapped up here—for several more days, at least. If there's a sociopath in our midst, don't you think we need to know—for our own safety?"

Marshall glanced toward the open door. He was hugely reluctant to step through it and confront what lay within. But he was also aware of the four pairs of eyes focused on him.

He nodded tersely. "All right."

Wolff led the way through the doorway into the examining room beyond. There was a plain wooden chair, a sink, a bench containing towels and two military-issue portable medical kits, and several cabinets full of supplies both old and new. Dominating the room was an examining table, fully reclined, on which lay a sheeted figure. The sheet was slick with blood, and rolled towels had been placed around it, like sandbags along a levee, to stanch additional flow.

Marshall swallowed. He had dissected bodies in graduate-level physiology courses. But those bodies had been sanitized: drained, cleaned, anonymous, seemingly more synthetic than human. Josh Peters was none of those things.

He glanced at the others who had silently arranged themselves around the table. Wolff, his expression studiously neutral. Gonzalez, staring at the bloody sheet, jaw working. Sully, looking more uncomfortable than ever. And Conti, eyes darting toward the body, then away, and then back again, with the strangest mix of agitation, hunger, and impatience on his face.

"I'll need a couple of buckets and a sponge," Marshall said.

Gonzalez disappeared into a storage closet, returned with two white plastic tubs. Marshall placed one on the floor beside the table, half filled the other with water from the sink. A dusty lab coat hung from a peg on the door and Marshall put it on. Opening one of the portable medical kits, he pulled out a pair of latex gloves, snapped them over his hands. Then he turned toward Sully.

"Gerry?" he said.

Sully didn't answer. He was looking at the rolled towel pressed against Peters's sheeted head. It was so sodden that blood was dripping from it onto the floor.

"Gerry," Marshall said a little more loudly.

Sully started, looked at him.

"Would you mind taking notes?"

"Huh? Oh. Sure." And Sully searched his pockets for a pen and a bit of paper.

Marshall took a deep breath. Then he reached for the rolled towels on the near side of the corpse and dropped them into the tub. They made a wet slapping noise as they hit the plastic. Another, deeper breath. Then, grasping the edge of the sheet, he slowly peeled it away from the body.

A collective, involuntary groan issued from the observers. Marshall heard it rise in his own throat. The only person who remained silent was Gonzalez, whose jaw nevertheless worked more quickly.

It was even worse than he'd feared. Peters looked like he'd been through a thresher. His clothes were in tatters and there were cuts over almost all the exposed surfaces of his body, thin straight red lines razored through the pale flesh. There was a huge, vertical slashing wound across his chest, tearing it open, the lower ribs sprung and gaping, ends clean and bare as if a butcher had frenched them. The slash widened as it reached the abdominal region, exposing red-and-gray ropes of viscera. More horrifying was the trauma to the head, an attack that left it barely recognizable: a ruined, broken skull sagging flaccidly from the brain stem, gray matter leaking into the crushed remains of the sinus cavities.

Marshall turned away, blinked several times. Then he took half a dozen of the clean towels from the bench, rolled them tightly, and snugged them up against the body to stop the blood that still trickled from a hundred cuts. Reaching into the medical kit, he removed a metal probe. Then he turned his attention back to Peters.

"The body seems to be completely exsanguinated," he said. "There appear to be excoriations over almost its entire surface, along with numerous, perhaps hundreds, of narrow wounds with non-ragged margins. I am at a loss to explain how these smaller wounds were created. At least two of the other, larger wounds present could individually have proven fatal. The first of these fractured and exposed the—let's see—the eighth to the twelfth ribs on the left side, penetrating the pleura and causing massive hemorrhaging, then continued down to the abdominal area where it also penetrated the peritoneal cavity. In the wound channel there are indications of damage to the cardiac ventricles. The second large wound needs little description. Massive damage to the entire region of the neck and head, from the right internal jugular vein to the cerebrum to the parietal lobe to the frontal lobe, along both sides of the longitudinal fissure. Elsewhere, the patella and other bones of the left knee are crushed, the femoral artery pierced." A pause. "Damage to the clothing corresponds to the injuries noted. Further analysis will have to await toxicological and professional forensic analysis." He stepped away.

For a moment, nobody spoke. Then Gonzalez cleared his throat. "It's like I said. A polar bear attack. Now, can we get him wrapped up and stowed in a meat locker?"

"It could be human," Wolff replied. His voice was quiet but steady.

"Are you *crazy*?" Gonzalez said. "Look at the wounds!"

"People high on certain illegal drugs have been known to fall into ferocious, murderous rages. With the right kind of implement—weapon—this kind of damage could be inflicted." He turned to Marshall. "Isn't that right?"

Marshall glanced back at the body. "The chest wound is about ten centimeters wide, with a total depth of almost eight centimeters. The amount of pressure to inflict such a wound would be massive, requiring tremendous strength."

"Such as a polar bear," said Gonzalez.

"Frankly, I'm surprised even a polar bear could create wounds like that," Marshall replied.

"A killer could do it," said Wolff. "If given time to land enough blows."

"What about this, then?" With the probe, Marshall lifted the left leg at the knee. The foot swung loosely—too loosely—and hung at an odd angle. "It's bitten almost completely through, hanging by a few tendons."

"Simulated bite marks," Wolff replied. "Created to cause fear and unease."

"For what purpose?" asked Sully.

"To keep the curious away from the site where the cat's body has been cached."

Marshall sighed. "So you're telling us that whoever stole the cat is willing to kill—kill in the most outrageous and savage fashion imaginable—to protect his prize?"

"He or she was willing to come up here, pretend to be one of us," Wolff countered. "Willing to spend the time and the money, take a terrible risk. Why not?"

Marshall looked speculatively at him. "I don't see why you refuse to accept the far simpler, far more rational explanation: this man blundered into the path of a polar bear and got killed as a result. Polar bears are ferocious, known man-killers. Why can't you believe that?"

Wolff's eyes glinted in the harsh artificial light. "Dr. Marshall, you speak of simple, rational explanations. I can't accept that a polar bear did this for one very simple, very rational reason: if there is no thief—if a polar bear did this—then where did the cat go . . . and why is it missing?"

25

Throughout the meeting in the infirmary, Conti had remained silent, preferring to keep his observations to himself. As the group broke up, he stayed behind for a moment, watching Gonzalez and the newly returned Private Phillips carefully wrap the body in preparation for storage. From the soldiers' chatter he'd learned that, in order to isolate the corpse from the rest of the personnel, a spare meat locker in the south wing would be used. Now he began making his way slowly and thoughtfully back to the central section of the base.

As he reached the entrance plaza, he saw Fortnum and Toussaint approaching.

"Emilio," Fortnum said. "We heard you wanted to see us?"

Conti glanced around quickly before answering. The plaza was empty, the guard station temporarily unattended. Conti lowered his voice anyway.

"I have some assignments for you," he told them. "Some special footage I need."

The two nodded.

"Consider these projects to be under the radar. Surprise segments I'm going to insert for added effect. Don't take any others along. And nobody is to know—not Kari, not Wolff."

The cinematographers looked at each other, then nodded again, a little more slowly this time.

"Have you heard the news?"

"What news?" Fortnum replied.

"Josh Peters is dead."

"*Josh?*" the two men said in unison.

"How?" asked Toussaint.

"The scientists think a polar bear got him—it happened outside. Wolff thinks it was whoever stole the cat."

"Christ," said Fortnum. He'd gone dead white.

"Yes. And we have to capitalize on this while we still can."

The men looked at him blankly.

"Kari is going around right now, spreading the word of Josh's death." He turned to Fortnum. "Allan, I need you to find her. Get reaction shots from the crew. The more extreme, the better. But be subtle about it, try not to clue Kari in on what you're going for. If you don't get the reactions you want, wait until Kari has left and then embellish on her descriptions while the camera's running. I want to see naked fear. Hysterical tears would be even better."

A puzzled look had spread over Fortnum's pallid features. "This is our own crew you're talking about filming—right?"

"Of course. They're the only ones around who don't know about Peters yet." Conti waved an impatient hand. "You need to hurry up, Kari's out there already, playing Johnny Appleseed with news of the killing."

Fortnum opened his mouth as if to raise another objection. Then he closed it instead and—with one last curious look at Conti—walked off in the direction of the crews' quarters.

Conti watched him go. When the DP was out of sight, he turned toward Toussaint. "I have an even more important job for you. The body is currently being held in the infirmary. It's in the south wing, I'll sketch out a map for you. They're going to place it in cold storage, but I heard them saying that some repairs are needed to the unit; it won't be ready and chilled until tomorrow. That's our opportunity."

"Opportunity," Toussaint repeated a little uncertainly.

"Don't you *understand*? Once the body's in the freezer, it'll be locked up." Conti tried to master the almost frantic impatience and frustration that had been building within him since he'd first heard about the missing cat. "It's like this. Wolff doesn't want us filming Peters's corpse."

"Naturally." Toussaint's voice sounded detached, far away.

"But we *have* to. This is a fluid situation; it's changing all the time. The documentary has to change with it." Conti grasped the cameraman's sleeve. "Our livelihoods, our reputations, are on the line here. We were dealt a rotten hand. That cat was the heart and soul of our show—and now it's gone. But something new is beginning to happen. What started this morning as just a mystery has become a murder mystery. Do you see? Done right, this could be even bigger than *Raising the Tiger*. With the publicity that's already run we've got a built-in audience. And we can give them something nobody's given them before: a 'closed-box' documentary that suddenly morphs into something completely different. A crime drama that plays out *in real time*, among the actual crew."

Toussaint blinked in reply.

"But you can't have a murder mystery without a shot of the corpse. That's where you come in. I want you to wait until dinner. Things will have settled down a little by then. I'll make sure the soldiers are occupied—nobody will be around. It'll be quick. Consider it a recon: get in, get the shot, get out. Don't worry about the lighting or the framing or anything like that. It's the footage that's important. Do it in one long take; I can fix it on the DataCine back in New York. Okay?"

Toussaint nodded slowly.

"Good man. And listen—remember not to tell anybody. Not even Fortnum. It'll be our secret—until the final cut, and the applause of the network execs. Understood?"

"Understood," said Toussaint in a very quiet voice.

Conti gave a quick, birdlike nod. "Now, prepare your equipment. I'll make you that map."

26

The set of rooms was small and stripped as bare as a monk's cell. Only the skeletal frames of bunk beds and a few sad-looking metal cabinets remained. And yet as he looked around, Logan felt certain this had been the scientists' quarters.

Locating it had proven a challenge: C Level was cluttered with so much spare junk, it was hard to discern habitat from mere surplus bedding. But there were precisely eight beds here, arranged in attitudes that suggested an actual living arrangement rather than mere storage. There were four bunks in the central room, two above two. A single bunk in a good-sized room to one side—no doubt the chief scientist's quarters. Two more beds in a room on the other side. And one last bunk in a cramped space off the bathroom barely larger than a closet.

Logan switched on every available light. Then, hands behind his back, he strolled slowly through the suite of rooms, looking around, peering into the empty cabinets, silently cajoling the long-departed ghosts to whisper their secrets to him. He'd hoped to find something: tools, perhaps, or equipment, printouts, photos. But it was clear the quarters had been carefully searched long ago, every item of interest removed and—if standard operating procedure in such classified matters was followed—immediately incinerated. Two hangers hung forlornly in a closet; a button lay on the floor, trailing thread behind it like a kite string. A tube of toothpaste sat on the metal shelf above the bathroom sink, curled and desiccated. It seemed the space had little left to tell.

Logan returned to the central room. He had lived in a similar space himself once, years ago, on an archaeological dig near Masada. The Israeli army had loaned the team of scientists and his-torians a remote set of barracks to bunk in. Logan shook his head, recalling the aridity and the isolation. It had felt, he remembered, a million miles from anywhere. Just as this place did.

He settled slowly onto the wire springs of the nearest bunk. Empty rooms or not, scientists left trails. Their minds were always busy. They kept journals. They had ideas and observations to col-lect, and never more so than when away from civilization, far from phones or research assistants. There would be notes to jot down, things to come back to later in the comfort of private labs: ideas for experiments, theories for research papers. His wife had teased him about this very thing more than once, calling him a conceptual pack rat. "Other people hoard dish towels, greeting cards, spare toast-ers," she'd said. "You hoard theories." The scientists here would have been no different.

Except for one thing. They—and their theories—never got out.

He rose from the bed, looked around at the four bunks again. The chummiest guys, the socializers, would have slept in this room, played poker or bridge. He walked slowly through the other rooms, stopping at last in the cramped compartment. This dark and cave-like space would probably have been the least desirable berth. And yet it was the one he would have chosen: private, quiet, the ideal place to concentrate on one's thoughts.

Or to write a journal.

As he stood there—in the acute and watchful silence—an unexpected but strangely delicious shudder passed through him. All of a sudden he felt intensely alive. *Even if I don't succeed here,* he thought, *even if this whole wild-goose chase proves a failure, right now is what makes it all worthwhile.* There was something indefinably glorious about the hunt itself: here, in this room, three floors beneath the ice, trying to piece together the struggles of those men, fifty years ago; putting himself in their shoes; and maybe—just maybe—finding gold dust.

The room was utterly empty save for the bare bed frame. Kneeling quickly, he looked at it from below. Nothing. He pulled the lone, empty cabinet away from the wall, looked behind it, looked beneath it, pushed it back into place. In the rear of the room was a closet, barely big enough to stand in. He lifted the single metal rod that spanned it, peered into its hollow core, returned it. There was a narrow lip that ran along the closet walls, just below the ceiling; he reached up and drew a finger along it, finding nothing but dust. He stepped back into the room, looking around again: at the bare walls and ceiling, at the lone lightbulb.

If I'd been living here, he thought, *if I'd been keeping unauthorized notes of my findings—and I would have—where would I have stashed them?*

He pulled the bed frame away from the wall. The metal surface behind it was as bare as all the rest, save for an electrical outlet near the floor. With a quiet sigh, he pushed the bed back into position.

Then he paused. Pulling the bed away once again, he knelt beside the wall, retrieved a combination tool and a flashlight from his pocket, unscrewed the outlet plate, and shone the beam of his flashlight inside. What he saw surprised him. The outlet receptacles were disconnected and came away with the cover plate. Behind it was just a dark rectangular hole. Then, looking more closely, he noticed a strand of thick rubber wrapped around the ancient switch box. One end of the length of rubber disappeared down into the blackness behind the wall space. Gently threading it out, Logan found it was tied to a hole punched into the spine of a small note-book: yellowed, tattered, covered with mildew.

As carefully as if he was handling a Fabergé egg, Logan untied the little knot of rubber, wiped the dust from the notebook, and opened the cover. Faded, spidery handwriting covered the first page.

He smiled slightly to himself. "Karen, darling," he murmured. "I wish you could see this." But there was no response from beyond the grave—as Logan knew there wouldn't be.

27

The corridors of the south wing were dimly lit, and shadows striped the drab metal walls. It was 6:00 PM and Fear Base lay cloaked in utter silence. Ken Toussaint walked down the central passage of A Level, portable digital camera in one hand and Conti's hastily sketched map in the other. He hadn't seen any of the small detachment of soldiers—Conti had promised to keep them occupied through the dinner hour—but nevertheless he found himself walking almost on tiptoe. Something about the close silence unnerved him.

This was the strangest and most unpleasant photo shoot he'd ever been on. He'd been sent to some out-of-the-way places in his time; he'd been eaten alive by mosquitoes in Cambodia, dusted sand out of every imaginable orifice in Chad, flicked scorpions from his equipment in Paraguay. But this took the cake. Marooned on the roof of the world, hundreds of miles from anything resembling civilization, threatened by ice storms and polar bears, confined to an ancient, smelly military base. Not only that, but it seemed all the discomfort had been for naught.

Reaching an intersection, he stopped, consulted the map, turned right. And that wasn't the worst of it. What had been merely annoying had now turned abruptly lethal.

What was he doing here, anyway, sneaking around like this? When Conti had given him the assignment he was dazed by the news of Peters's death, still trying to process it. The implications of what Conti wanted hadn't really sunk in. But now, walking down this silent corridor, they had. Big-time. Now, when it was too late to object.

He'd only been in this wing of the base once before, yesterday, searching halfheartedly for the missing carcass. It seemed to house lots of engineering and technical apparatus, at least judging by the worn lettering stenciled on the doors he passed. On impulse, he stopped by a door labeled TRANSDUCER ARRAY—BACKUP I. He reached for the knob, jiggled it. Locked. He continued on.

It seemed almost cannibalistic, what Conti wanted: a gratuitous, sensationalist filming of a member of their own crew, now that he was dead and couldn't object. It was a gross invasion of privacy. What would Josh's family have to say?

On the other hand, he told himself as he started forward again, the network wasn't stupid, they'd make sure it was tasteful, nothing gory. And Conti knew what he was doing—he had to remember that. Conti might be a brilliant filmmaker, but he was a realist as well. If there was a way to turn this disaster around, to make something truly memorable, he'd find it. Toussaint reminded himself that he, too, had a reputation to worry about.

The fluorescent bulbs were less frequent now, and the intersection ahead was wreathed in intertwining shadows. And there was something else to think about: this was, at last, a truly unique assignment. Nobody but he and Conti knew about it. It could become a feather in his cap, something to add to his portfolio. For the entire production phase he'd been doing second-unit work, shooting inserts, getting the B shots. He'd always been distinctly in Fortnum's shadow. This was a chance to change that. He'd make sure to add audio commentary to the shot: if the network liked it, that could only help raise his profile further.

Reaching the intersection, he plucked the lens cap from the camera, switched it on, set the frame rate, fired up the supplemental illumination, adjusted the focus, checked the white balance and exposure, fitted the cord of the shotgun mic to his belt pack. He'd do this in one long take: sweep into the infirmary, move to the examination room, do a 360 of the body, zoom in for a few close-ups, maybe briefly pull back the sheeting he'd been told Peters was wrapped in. That would be it. He could be in and out in ninety seconds, the footage safe and secure on the camera's hard disk. Like Conti had said: get in, get the shot, get out.

He rounded the corner. There it was: second door on the left. Thrusting the map into his pocket, he fitted the viewfinder to his eye, lined up the shot. The beam of his camera light bobbed along the corridor with the movement of his shoulder, and he aimed the spotlight on the infirmary door. The door was closed.

An unpleasant thought suddenly struck him. What if it was locked? Conti wasn't in the mood to take no for an answer.

He hastily approached the door, looking through the lens as he walked. A quick try of the door reassured his jangled nerves: it was unlocked. He reached in, felt for the light switch, flicked it on, withdrew his hand.

Taking his eye from the viewfinder, he glanced up and down the corridor again, with the sudden, guilty movements of someone up to no good. But there was nobody; there was nothing. Nothing except the fine hairs on the back of his neck standing nervously on end; a faint high keening in his ears that signified, perhaps, he'd waited too long to take his blood pressure medication.

Time to do this. He cleared his throat quietly, fitted his eye to the viewfinder again, pressed the Record button, and pushed the door wide. "I'm going in now," he said into the microphone.

He moved quickly inside, careful to keep the camera level as he panned around the cramped space. His heart was beating faster than he liked, his motions jerky and abrupt. He cursed himself for not bringing the Steadicam, then reconsidered: an amateurish approach might be just the thing for this sortie. They could add some digital filters back in the lab, give the film the grainy look of a cheap camera rig, imitating shots taken on the sly . . .

The doorway to the next room came into focus in the viewfinder. The body, Conti said, would be in there.

"The body's in the next room," he murmured into the mic. "Beyond the office."

He felt his breathing accelerate, matching his heart. Ninety seconds. That's all. In and out.

He moved forward, sweeping the camera left and right as he went, careful not to trip over any obstacles. The doorway was a pool of blackness, perforated by the small yellow cone of the camera's light. Again his hand felt along the nearest wall; again he snapped on the old-fashioned bulky switch.

The lights came up and immediately the view through the lens went solid white. Stupid mistake—he should have turned the light on before he entered, given the camera time to compensate. As the saturated white faded somewhat and the room shapes resolved themselves, he saw the examining table in the center. The body lay on it, wrapped tightly in plastic sheeting. Thin smears of blood ran along the underside of the sheeting like stripes on a candy cane.

Breathing still faster now, he got a good establishing shot of the room, then maneuvered slowly around the table, panning the camera along the length of the sheeted corpse. This was good. Conti's instincts had been right. They'd edit the content down, add a few jump cuts, let the viewers' imaginations fill in the gaps. He laughed through his panting breaths, forgetting in his excitement to continue the audio commentary. *Wait until Fortnum sees this* . . .

That was when he heard it. Although "heard" wasn't quite right—it was more like a sudden change in air pressure, a painful sensation of fullness, felt through the pulmonary cavity of his chest and—especially—the deepest channels of his ears and nasal sinuses. Something nearby, something he instinctually understood to be per- ilous, made Toussaint take instant notice. His head jerked away from the viewfinder and—with the atavistic certainty of a million years of prey—locked his gaze onto the dark doorway in the far wall of the exam room.

Something lurked there. Something *hungry*.

His breath was coming even faster now, rough gulps of air that somehow weren't enough to fill his lungs. The camera was still rolling, but he no longer noticed. His mind worked frantically, try- ing to tell him this was crazy, just an attack of nerves, completely understandable under the circumstances . . .

What the hell was he so worried about all of a sudden? He hadn't seen anything, heard anything—not really. And yet something about the perfect blackness of that far doorway set his instincts ringing five-alarm.

He stepped back, swinging the still-whirring camera wildly, the beam of light lashing across the walls and ceiling. His retreating back bumped heavily against the corpse and it pushed back with the sickening stiffness of rigor.

Just turn around, he told himself. *You've got the shot. Turn around and get the hell out.*

He wheeled, preparing to flee.

And yet he could not flee. Deep inside he knew that if he didn't look now, he'd never dare to look, ever again. And he sensed some- thing else—something even deeper—telling him that, if his instincts were right, running wouldn't make the least difference anyway.

Lifting the camera, fitting the viewfinder to his eye, panting au- dibly now, Toussaint turned back and—very slowly—aimed the beam of light into the darkness beyond the far doorway.

And into the face of nightmare.

28

"I got your message," Marshall said as he stepped into Faraday's lab and closed the door behind him. "You've found something?"

Faraday glanced up at Marshall, then at Chen, then back at Marshall. The biologist's eyes looked wide and anxious behind the round tortoiseshell frames. But this in itself didn't disturb Marshall—Faraday wore a nervous look on even the best of days.

"It's more an interesting succession of facts than a hard theory," Faraday said. He was standing behind—almost hiding behind, it seemed—a bewildering array of test tubes and lab equipment.

"Not a problem."

"I can't corroborate any of it. Not from here, anyway."

Marshall crossed one arm over the other. "I won't tell the NMU board of regents if you won't."

"And I warn you that Sully's going to—"

Marshall sighed in exasperation. "Just let me hear it."

One last hesitation. "Okay." Faraday cleared his throat, straightened the soup-stained tie he insisted on wearing under the lab coat. "I think I understand. About the melting in the vault, I mean."

Marshall waited.

"I told you we went back up to get more ice samples from the cave. Well, we've been examining them with X-ray diffraction. And they're very unusual."

"Unusual how?"

"The crystalline structure is all wrong. For normally occurring precipitant ice, I mean."

Marshall leaned against a lab table. "Go on."

"You know how there are many different kinds of ice, right? I mean, other varieties beyond the kind we put in our lemonade or chop off our car windows." He began ticking them off on his fingers. "There's ice-two, ice-three, five, six, seven, and so forth, up to ice-fourteen—each with its own crystalline structure, its own physical properties."

"I remember something about that in my graduate-level physics course. It takes great pressure or extreme temperatures for the solid-state transformation to take place."

"That's right. But the really unusual thing about some of these types of ice is that—once they've formed—they can remain solid *well above the freezing mark*." He handed Marshall a sheet of paper through the forest of test tubes. "Look. Here's the structure diagram for ice-seven. Look at its unit cell. Under sufficient pressure, this form of ice can remain in solid form up to two hundred degrees centigrade."

Marshall whistled. "That hot? We could have used that kind of ice in the vault yesterday."

"But here's the thing," Faraday went on. "I read an article in *Nature* last month describing another type of ice that could theoretically exist: ice-fifteen. Ice that has just the opposite qualities."

"You mean . . ." Marshall paused. "You mean, ice that would melt *below* thirty-two degrees Fahrenheit?"

Faraday nodded.

"The key word is 'theoretically,' " Chen added.

"And the unusual crystalline structure of this melted cave ice—does it match ice-fifteen?"

"There's no way to be sure," Faraday said. "But it may well."

Marshall pushed away from the lab table, paced back and forth. "So possibly—just possibly—that ice melted on its own."

"They were slowly raising the temperature overnight," Faraday said. "And in all the commotion of finding their prize missing, nobody bothered to check the temperature in the vault. To verify it was actually *above freezing* inside."

"That's right." Marshall stopped. "Nobody would have thought it necessary. They just left the door wide open and went off searching."

"Allowing the temperature inside the vault to quickly return to the ambient level," said Chen.

"So there might have been no saboteur at all," Marshall said. "The thawing process was proceeding properly. It's the ice *itself* that was the culprit."

Faraday nodded.

"How would this unusual ice have formed?" Marshall asked.

"Therein lies the rub," said Chen.

A brief silence settled over the lab.

"That's a very interesting speculation," said Marshall. "But even if you're right, and there was no thief, no saboteur, the question remains: What happened to the cat?"

No sooner had he asked the question than he saw Faraday's nervous expression deepen. "No, don't tell me," he went on. "Let me guess. It let itself out."

"You saw my photographs of the vault flooring. Those marks were of something getting out, not in. And they weren't saw marks, either."

"True. They didn't look like saw marks. But they didn't look like cat claws, either. They were much too powerful for—" Marshall stopped abruptly. "Wait a minute. It's a very clever theory, ice melting below freezing and all. But there's an enormous problem. In order for the cat to break free of the remaining ice, to tear its way out of the vault, it would have to be alive. But it's been dead for thousands of years."

"That's the problem we were discussing the last time you came in here," Faraday said. "I've got an answer for that, too—again, a theoretical one."

Marshall glanced at him. "Ice crystals would have formed in the cells as the animal froze. It would be fatal."

"Maybe. Or maybe not. At an evolutionary biology conference in Berkeley last year, I listened to a lecture on the Beresovka mammoth."

"Haven't heard of it."

"It was a woolly mammoth, found in Siberia in the early part of the twentieth century. Frozen solid, with fragments of a buttercup between its teeth."

"And?"

"Well, the question is—how could the mammoth freeze so quickly in a spot warm enough for buttercups to bloom?"

Suddenly, Marshall understood. "A downdraft of cold air. Caused by an inversion layer."

Faraday nodded. "Super-cold arctic air."

"I see where you're going. Because when your mammoth froze, it must have been summer, based on the buttercup. But here—in the dead of winter—" Marshall stopped.

For a moment there was silence. Then Chen continued. "Flash-freezing."

"Terminal freeze," added Faraday.

"And the faster it froze—if, say, high winds were involved—the smaller the ice crystals that would form in its cells. If it happened quickly enough, the creature could conceivably be frozen alive." Marshall looked at them. "Do you suppose this terminal freeze could be reversed?"

Faraday blinked. "Reversed how?"

"If there could be a sudden downdraft of super-cold air in summer—couldn't there just as easily be a downdraft of super-*warm* air in winter?"

Faraday nodded slowly. "In theory."

"So what if the phenomenon *was* reversed? Sent down remarkably warm air? Don't you remember how tropical it felt that night before the documentary was to go live?"

Faraday nodded again.

"It must have been close to freezing." Marshall began to pace again. "The vault freezer would have kicked in—but if your ice-fifteen was involved, it wouldn't have mattered. It would still have been close enough to freezing to cause a massive thaw." He hesitated. "When you went back to get those ice samples in the cave, did the ice around the excavation site show any signs of melting?"

"No."

"But it's colder up there, by the glacier . . ." Then Marshall hesitated, shook his head. "I don't know, Wright. It's brilliant—but it seems pretty far-fetched."

Faraday held up the phase diagram. "The crystalline structure doesn't lie. We performed the X-ray test on the ice ourselves."

A brief silence settled over the lab. Marshall looked at the diagram, then quietly placed it on the table.

"If you're right about the reversal," Faraday said slowly, "about the heated air, then it could explain something else."

"What?" Marshall said.

"What we saw in the sky that night."

"You mean, the bizarre aurora borealis? You think it was a side effect?"

"A side effect," Faraday replied. "Or a causative agent. Or, perhaps, a harbinger."

Another silence. Faraday thought back to the old shaman's warning: *Their wrath paints the sky with blood. The heavens cry out with the pain.*

"What about the blood?" he asked. "That you found caked on the vault splinters?"

"We've been too busy analyzing the ice to check it yet."

Another silence fell over the lab.

"Well, you've been busy," Marshall said after a moment. "But this still begs two questions. If these unusual forms of ice require great pressure, or extreme temperature, how did they form *here* in the first place?"

Faraday took off his glasses, polished them on his tie, replaced them. "I don't know," he replied.

The three of them looked at one another a moment. "You said you had two questions," said Chen.

"Yes. If your speculations are right, and the creature is still alive—and on the loose—where is it now?"

The question hung in the air. And this time the lab remained silent.

29

As news of Peters's death spread through Fear Base, people—almost unconsciously—began leaving their quarters, gathering in the larger spaces of B Level, seeking consolation in the company of others. They sat around the tables of the officers' mess, speaking in low tones, sharing affectionate anecdotes: outrageous things he'd done or said, dumb technical mistakes he'd made. Others hung out in the Operations Center, drinking tepid coffee, speculating on when the blizzard would lift, promising darkly to assemble a hunting team and seek out the polar bear that mauled the production assistant. The sorrowful atmosphere only exacerbated the sensation of being marooned in an icy wasteland, cut off from all the reassuring comforts of civilization. As the evening lengthened and conversations began to falter, the groups nevertheless remained where they were, reluctant to return to their bunks and the private, unsettling silence of their own thoughts.

Ashleigh Davis did not share these sentiments. She sat disconsolately at a table in the officers' mess, elegantly coiffed head lolling on her hands, staring at the wall clock in its metal grill. This, she decided, was a living hell. Worse than a living hell. The place *stank*. The food was *beyond* vile. It was a million miles from the nearest spa. You couldn't get a decent cup of bergamot-infused espresso to save your life. And worst of all, it was a prison. Until the storm lifted, she was stuck here, twiddling her thumbs, her glorious career on hold. There was no way out except to walk. And if she had to stay here much longer, she thought morosely, she'd probably be driven to do just that: walk out into the snow and the dark, like that guy on Scott's antarctic expedition . . . she'd narrated a documentary on the subject but couldn't summon the energy to remember the poor chump's name.

And the time crawled by so slowly! The afternoon had lasted an eternity. She'd bullied the makeup staff into giving her a makeshift facial, doing her fingernails and toenails; she'd had her hair done; she'd run the costume girl half dead, bringing first one, then another, then still another outfit for her to try on while deciding what to wear to dinner. *Dinner.* That was too kind a word for it. "Slop" was more accurate, or maybe "pig swill." And the company at dinner, never entertaining to begin with, had tonight been absolutely *cadaverous.* Just because this idiot Peters was stupid enough to bump into a bear, everybody was acting like it was the end of the world. They'd forgotten they had a star in their midst. It was pathetic, truly pathetic; she was utterly wasted on this bunch.

She sighed with irritation, pulled a cigarette from her Hermès handbag, lit it with a snap of her platinum lighter.

"There's no smoking on the base, Ashleigh," came Conti's voice. "Military rules."

Davis gave an exasperated snort, plucked the cigarette from her mouth, stared at it, replaced it between her lips, took a deep drag, then stubbed it out in a dish of congealing tapioca. Blowing smoke through her nose, she looked across the table at the producer. She'd spent the better part of the last hour trying to beg, blackmail, or bluster an emergency airlift out of this horrible place and back to New York—all to no avail. It was impossible, he'd said; all flights, public or private, were suspended indefinitely. Nothing she said had budged him. In fact, he'd barely taken notice of her; he seemed to be preoccupied about something. She slumped in her chair, pouting. Even Emilio was taking her for granted. *Un*believable.

She pushed her chair back, stood up. "I'm headed for my trailer," she announced. "Thanks for a delightful evening."

Conti—who had looked down again at the notes he'd been scribbling—glanced up once more. "If you run into Ken Toussaint," he said, "please send him to me. I'll either be here or in my quarters."

Davis placed her coat over her shoulders, not deigning to reply. Brianna, her personal assistant, picked up her own coat and rose from the table. She'd been silent throughout dinner, knowing better than to speak when Davis was in a black mood.

"Are you sure you want to return to your trailer?" Conti asked. "I could get accommodations fixed up for you here."

"Accommodations? As in, share a bathroom, *bivouac* on some army cot? Emilio, darling, I can only hope you're joking." And she turned away with a contemptuous sweep of ermine.

"But—" he began to protest.

"I'll see you in the morning. And I expect a helicopter ready and waiting by then."

As she walked briskly toward the doorway, she became aware of someone approaching. It was the man who had trucked her trailer to the site. She glanced at him briefly. He wasn't bad-looking, with the tanned, lean body of a surfer. But his outrageously pastel Hawaiian shirt was in the worst possible taste. He was chewing, cudlike, on an enormous wad of gum.

"Ma'am." He smiled at her, nodded at Brianna. "We've never been formally introduced."

I've never been formally introduced to my chauffeur, either, she thought with a frown.

"The name's Carradine, in case you hadn't heard. I'm heading back to my cab, too, so I'll walk with you ladies—if you don't object."

Davis looked toward her assistant, as if to ask: *Am I to be spared nothing?*

"You know," the trucker said as they made their way toward the main stairwell, "I've been hoping to talk with you, Ms. Davis. When I heard it was your trailer I'd be ferrying up here, when I realized I might just get the opportunity to speak to someone in your position . . . well, it was like the kind of a happy accident you read about sometimes. Like Orson Welles meeting William Randolph Hearst."

Davis looked at him. "William Randolph Hearst?"

"Didn't I get that right? Anyway, I hope you don't mind if I take just a minute of your time."

You already have, Davis thought.

"See, I'm not just a trucker. The season's pretty short, you know—four months, I'm not usually up here this early, the lake ice isn't thick enough yet—so I have plenty of time to do other things. Oh, not like I'm busy all the time—life moves kind of slowly down in Cape Coral. But I've certainly kept busy with *something.*"

He seemed to want her to ask what it was. Davis climbed the stairwell in resolute silence.

"I'm a screenwriter," he said.

Davis glanced back at him, unable to conceal her surprise.

"That is to say, I've written *a* screenplay. See, I listen to books on tape while I'm driving—helps keep your mind off the ice—and I sort of got into the plays of William Shakespeare. The tragedies, anyway, with all that blood and fighting. My favorite's *Macbeth.* And that's the screenplay: my version of *Macbeth.* Only it's not the story of a king, it's the story of an ice-road trucker."

Davis walked quickly across the entrance plaza, trying to distance herself from Carradine. The man hurried to keep up. "The king of ice-road truckers, see. Except there's this other trucker that's jealous of him and his fame among the rest. Wants his girl, too. So he sabotages the king's route, fractures it, fractures the ice, know what I mean?"

They passed through the staging area and out the main entrance. Instantly, the wind and ice slapped them back with a giant, invisible hand. The exterior lights barely penetrated the swirls of snow, and it was hard to see beyond a few feet. Davis hesitated, remembering it was a polar bear that had killed Peters just outside the perimeter fence.

Seeing her hesitate, Carradine smiled. "Don't you worry," he said, lifting his shirt and displaying a huge revolver tucked into his waistband. "I never go out on a run without it."

Davis winced, wrapped her coat more closely around her shoulders, and allowed Brianna to go first and act as a windbreak.

They moved slowly across the apron, the sheds and Quonset huts around them mere specters in the roiling snow. Davis kept her head down, picking her way unhappily over the rivers of electrical and data cables that lay treacherously beneath the coating of white. Carradine walked alongside, oblivious to the cold. He hadn't even bothered to grab a parka from one of the lockers in the weather chamber. "As I was saying, the king's rig falls through the ice. And the other trucker, he becomes the new king."

"Right, right," Davis muttered. *God, only a dozen more steps to the trailer.*

"Anyway, it's a great story, real violent. The ice-road trucker angle is killer. I've got a copy of the screenplay in the cab. And I was wondering, with your connections and all, if you'd be willing to have a look and maybe recommend—"

He stopped speaking so abruptly that Davis glanced toward him. Then she heard it, too: a muffled thump, like a heavy, deliberate knock, coming out of the darkness ahead of them.

"What's that?" Davis breathed. She looked at Brianna, who returned the look nervously.

"Don't know," said Carradine. "Some loose piece of equipment, maybe."

Knock.

"It's just like the porter scene in *Macbeth*!" Carradine exclaimed. "The knocking at the gate, after they've wasted Duncan! I have that in my screenplay, too, when the new king of truckers is back down in Yellowknife, and he hears the son of the old trucker king at his door—"

Knock.

Carradine laughed. *"Wake Duncan with thy knocking!"* he quoted. *"I would thou couldst."*

Knock.

Davis took another step forward, then hesitated. "I don't like this."

"It's nothing. Let's take a look."

They moved forward, more slowly now, through the thick pall of snow. The wind whistled mournfully between the outbuildings, biting Davis's bare legs and plucking at the hem of her coat. She tripped over a cable, staggered, righted herself again.

Knock.

"It's coming from the back of your trailer," said Carradine.

"Well, tie it down, whatever it is. I'll never sleep through that racket."

Now the bulk of the trailer loomed ahead of them, a gray monolith in the snowy murk, its generator purring. Carradine led the way around the back end, shirt flapping and fluttering behind him. It was darker back here, in the shadows between the trailer and the perimeter fence. Davis shivered, licked her lips.

Knock.

And then there it was, directly before them: a body, hanging upside down from a support for one of the window awnings. It was coatless, its clothes torn in several places. The arms stretched limply toward the ground. The head, which was level with their own— too snow-covered to be recognizable—bumped slowly against the metal wall of the trailer at the caprice of the wind.

Knock.

Brianna screamed, took a step back.

"It's dead!" Davis shrieked.

The trucker stepped forward quickly, brushed the snow from the face that hung before them.

"Oh, *God!*" cried Davis. "Toussaint!"

Carradine reached up to unhook the body from the support arm. As he did so, Toussaint's eyes abruptly popped open. He looked at each of them, uncomprehending. Then, quite suddenly, he opened his mouth and screamed.

Brianna crumpled to the ground in a dead faint, her head hitting the trailer with an ugly thump.

As he hung there, Toussaint screamed again—a ragged, ululating scream. "It plays with you!" he shouted. *"It plays with you!* And when it's finished playing—it kills. *It's going to kill us all."*

30

The crowd in the Operations Center had grown even larger. The last time it had been this crowded, Marshall thought grimly, was when Wolff ordered the emergency meeting after the vault was found empty. At that meeting, there had been shock, dismay, disbelief. This time, the prevailing mood was fear. It was so strong that Marshall could almost taste its metallic bite in the air.

He stepped into the room and was at once approached by both Wolff and Kari Ekberg.

"How's Toussaint?" Wolff asked.

"He's half frozen, he's suffered a broken ankle, and he's sustained numerous nasty lacerations to the legs and arms. But he'll survive. He's raving—we had to sedate him heavily with some meds from the military's stockpile. Gonzalez has rigged up temporary restraints—even with the tranquilizers, he's been quite a handful."

"Raving?" Wolff echoed. "What about?"

"It's pretty incoherent. He said he was attacked in the infirmary, knocked about a lot, then dragged outside."

"Who would have done such a thing?" breathed Ekberg.

"According to Toussaint, it's not a who," replied Marshall. "It's a what."

Wolff frowned. "That's crazy."

"*Something* hung him up like a side of beef. That hook was a good ten feet off the ground."

"A polar bear wouldn't do something like that," said Wolff. "And it couldn't move in and out of the base with impunity. The man is clearly delusional. What was he doing in the infirmary, anyway?"

"It seems he was trying to sneak a shot of Peters's corpse."

Wolff started. Then his face darkened. "Did he get it?"

"Hard to say. There was a camera in the infirmary—Gonzalez had his men check just now. But it was badly damaged, the video feed was blank. All you could hear was the audio, Toussaint murmuring 'no, no, no' over and over again."

"Did he describe what attacked him?" Ekberg asked.

"Not in any detail." Marshall paused, trying to recollect the frantic torrent of babbling he'd heard while stabilizing Toussaint. "Said it was huge—big as a station wagon."

Wolff looked skeptical.

"He said it had more teeth than you could count. Not big, but sharp as razors. He said they wriggled."

Wolff's look of skepticism increased. "Not likely, is it?"

"I don't know. Razors would account for all those marks on Peters's body." Marshall paused again. "And the eyes. He kept talking about the eyes."

Ekberg shuddered.

"He said it sang to him," Marshall added.

"I think I've heard enough." And Wolff turned away.

"There's something else," Marshall called after him.

The network rep stopped without glancing back.

"Peters's body is missing."

Marshall and Ekberg watched Wolff exit the room. They stood for a moment in silence. People were huddled in small knots, heads together. Their tones were muted, barely whispers. In marked contrast to the rest was Davis, whose shrill complaints and expostulations had been instrumental in spreading the news in the first place. She was standing in a far corner, loudly demanding personal military protection.

Ekberg nodded toward Carradine, who was sitting in a corner by himself drinking cocoa from a Styrofoam cup. "He's offered to take everybody back," she said.

"You mean, back down to Yellowknife?"

"Wherever. Away from the base. He said he'd be able to fit almost everyone in Ashleigh's trailer."

"Might not be a bad idea—if he sticks to a safe route and doesn't do any hotdogging."

"Wolff overruled him. Said it was too dangerous."

"Well, being around here is getting more dangerous by the minute." Marshall glanced at her. "Would you leave? If Carradine got the green light, I mean."

"Depends on what Emilio does."

"You don't owe him anything. Besides, now I know what you really think of him."

"What *I* really think of him?"

"You didn't exactly make a secret of it this morning."

Ekberg smiled ruefully. "I can't deny he's something of an ass. But most directors I've worked with are. You need an inflated ego if you're going to put your personal stamp on something as big and complex as a prime-time documentary. Besides, I didn't just sign on with Conti—I signed on with the show. That's how it works in this business. I'm the field producer. I stay through the final cut."

Marshall smiled back. "You're a brave woman."

"Not really. Just a very ambitious one."

Marshall became aware that somebody was standing at his elbow. Looking over, he saw Jeremy Logan watching them. *He may be an academic,* Marshall reflected as he nodded at him, *but he's like no professor I've ever known.*

"I'm sorry to interrupt," Logan said. "I was hoping to have a few words with Dr. Marshall."

"Of course. I've got to do what I can to reassure the troops anyway. I'll speak with you later, Evan." And Ekberg moved away.

Marshall turned to Logan. "What's up?"

"A great deal, it would seem. Let's find some place a little more private. We can talk there." And Logan motioned toward the exit.

31

Marshall's lab was just half a dozen doors from the Operations Center, but nevertheless the walk seemed to last an eternity. Marshall kept thinking about the torn, sprawled figure of Peters, the wild-eyed rantings of Toussaint. It was all he could do to resist glancing over his shoulder.

Reaching the lab, Marshall removed his MIDI keyboard from the spare chair, waved Logan to sit down, closed the door carefully behind them. Then he took a seat on the lab table.

"Private enough for you?" he asked.

Logan glanced around. "It'll do." He paused. "I heard what happened. How are people taking it?"

"Hit-and-miss. There's an awful lot of fear. I've seen several who are pretty close to the breaking point. One of the makeup crew got hysterical and had to be sedated. If this storm doesn't pass soon . . ." He shook his head. "People don't know what to believe, don't know what's going on—and that's probably the hardest thing of all."

"I want to know what *you* believe. You scientists, I mean. I have a hunch you're on to something—and I need to know what it is."

Marshall glanced at him thoughtfully a moment. "I'll tell you what I don't believe. I don't believe a human could have torn Peters apart like that. And I don't believe a polar bear could have hung Toussaint up by his ankles."

Logan crossed one leg over the other. "That doesn't leave very much, does it?"

Marshall hesitated. Logan, he recalled, had already taken him into his confidence, told him why he was here, explained about the ill-fated scientific team. "Faraday has a theory," he began after a moment.

Briefly, he sketched out what Faraday had explained to him: about the unique low-temperature melting qualities of ice-fifteen; about the possibility the creature had been flash-frozen in the ice; how there was a chance—a remote chance, but a chance nevertheless—that it had not been killed but instead placed in a form of cryogenic sleep.

Logan listened intently, and Marshall noted the historian didn't once look skeptical. When it was over, he nodded slowly. "That's very interesting," he said. "But it still doesn't answer the biggest question of all."

"Which one is that?"

Logan leaned back in his chair. "What is it?"

"We've talked about that, as well. Have you heard of something called the Callisto Effect?"

Logan shook his head.

"It's a biological theory of evolutionary turbulence. According to the theory, when species become too comfortable in their niche—when they stop evolving, or start to overburden the ecosphere—a new creature is introduced, a killing machine, to cull the population, jump-start the evolutionary process. Ecologically speaking, a perfect weapon."

"Another fascinating theory. Except it's hard to imagine a population explosion needing to be culled up here."

"Don't forget, we're talking about the local ecology as it existed thousands of years ago—when the creature was originally frozen. And even then, given the climate, it probably wouldn't have taken a large population to overtax such a barren habitat. But in any case the theory goes on to say that the Callisto Effect is, by and large, an evolutionary aberration. Because such a killing machine seems to be *too* effective. Ultimately, it becomes its own worst enemy. It kills *everything*—leaving itself without sustenance."

Logan nodded again, even more slowly, as if fitting a piece into some mental puzzle he was constructing. " 'A perfect weapon,' you called it. Interesting you should use those words, because I just came across them myself. You see, this morning I found a notebook one of the old scientists left behind. He'd hidden it away in his quarters." And he patted his shirt pocket with a little smile.

"This morning? And you're only telling me now?"

"I didn't realize I *had* to tell you anything."

Marshall waved his hand, conceding the point.

"The truth of the matter is, I delayed telling you because the thing is about as hard to read as the Linear A texts of Agia Triada. It's written in code."

Marshall frowned. "Why would the scientist do that?"

"No doubt he felt it wasn't enough just to hide the notes, he had to encrypt them as well. This was the fifties, remember—the cold war was white-hot. People were serious about security; the fellow probably didn't want to spend twenty years in Leavenworth. In any case, I've been working on decrypting it all day."

"You're a cryptanalyst, too?"

Logan smiled again. "It comes in very handy in my line of work."

"And just where did you pick that up?"

"I was once employed by—how should I put it?—by the 'intelligence services.' In any case, I've had only limited success so far—words, the odd phrase here and there. It's polyalphabetic, a variant of the Vigenère cipher, but with a nasty twist. I think he combined it with a book cipher, but of course they took all the books away when they cleared out his quarters." He reached into his pocket, pulled out a tiny notebook—battered and dusty and furred with mildew—and placed it on the lab table beside Marshall. He opened it and extracted a folded sheet of paper.

"Here's what I've managed to decipher so far." Logan unfolded the sheet and glanced over it. "A couple of the entries are quotidian, talk of poor meals and spartan accommodations and working conditions that were less than ideal—I'll skip those. For example: 'We've had to work very quickly. Unpacked sonar equipment underfoot everywhere.' And here: 'The secrecy makes it all so difficult. Only Rose has been briefed.'"

"Rose?" Marshall repeated.

"He was the officer in charge of Fear Base at the time, remember?" Logan scanned down the sheet. "Here we go: 'It is horrifying. Wonderful, but horrifying. It truly is the perfect weapon—assuming we can harness its power. That will be'—two words I haven't yet deciphered—'challenge.' Toward the end, the writing gets more rapid, agitated: 'It killed Blayne. God, it was awful; so much blood . . .' And then there's one other that I haven't gotten quite right: 'The Tunits have the answer.' 'Tunit' is clearly a garble of some kind, I have to work some more on that."

"It's not garbled. The Tunits are the local Native Americans."

Logan looked up quickly from the sheet. "Are you sure?"

"Absolutely. They came here to see us, just after we made the discovery in the ice cave. Warned us to leave in no uncertain terms."

Logan's eyes narrowed. "I've never heard of the Tunits. And I know a lot of Alaskan tribes. Inuit, Aleut, Ahtena, Ingalik—"

"They basically went extinct a thousand years ago, when their lands were overtaken and they were turned out into the wilderness. Over the years, those few that remained either died off or were absorbed into the mainstream population. I'm told this is the last remaining camp."

Logan chuckled. "I knew coming to you wasn't a mistake. Do you see what this means?" And he slapped the sheet of paper. "This might be the answer we've been looking for."

"You think there's a connection between the dead scientists and what's been attacking this base? There can't be. That creature we discovered has been frozen—*under a glacier*—for more than a thousand years. The evidence of that is absolutely incontrovertible."

"I realize that. But I don't believe in coincidence." Logan paused. "There's only one way to find out."

For a long moment, Marshall did not reply. Then he slowly nodded. "I'll take the Sno-Cat," he said. "It's the only way to get through this blizzard."

"You can drive one?"

"Sure."

"Do you know where the Tunit settlement is?"

"I know the rough location. It's not far, maybe thirty miles to the north."

Logan folded the sheet, slipped it back into the small journal, and returned them to his pocket. "I'll come along."

Marshall shook his head. "It's better if I go alone. The Indians strongly disapprove of our presence here. They're suspicious. The fewer who go, the better."

"It isn't safe. If you get injured, there will be no one to help."

"There's got to be a radio in the Cat. I'll be careful. At least the Tunits have met me before. They don't know you. Your time would be better spent here, bringing my colleagues up to speed."

"The powers that be may take a dim view of your appropriating the Sno-Cat."

"That's why we won't tell them. I'll be as quick as I can. I doubt they'll even notice, under the circumstances."

Logan frowned. "You realize, of course, it's possible the Indians are responsible for what's been going on. You said it yourself: they don't want us here. You could be walking right into a trap."

"That's true. But if they can shed any light on what's happening—any at all—it's worth the risk."

Logan shrugged. "I guess I've run out of objections."

Marshall stood up. "Then come and see me off." And he nodded toward the door.

32

It seemed that Conti spoke up almost before Fortnum knocked on the door. "Come in."

The cinematographer stepped inside and closed the door softly behind him. Conti was on the far side of the room, in the makeshift screening area, absorbed by a video playing on his huge LCD screen. The image was choppy and scratchy, but nevertheless instantly recognizable: the *Hindenburg,* afire and crumpling to the ground at Lakehurst Naval Air Station.

"Ah, Allan," the director said. "Have a seat."

Fortnum walked over and settled into one of the comfortable armchairs before the screen. "How's Ken?"

Conti tented his fingers together. He was still staring at the screen. "I'm sure he'll be just fine."

"That's not what I heard. He's out of his mind."

"Temporary. He's had a bad shock. And that's what I wanted to speak with you about." Conti pulled himself away from the newsreel footage long enough to look at Fortnum. "How are you coming?"

Fortnum had assumed Conti summoned him to discuss Toussaint's condition. Instead, it seemed the director wanted to talk business. He told himself he shouldn't be surprised: with high-powered directors like Conti, business always came first. "I've got half a dozen decent reaction shots to Peters's killing. I'm rendering them now."

"Good, good. That's an excellent start."

Start? Fortnum was under the impression these were wrap shots: the rather distasteful final footage for a documentary *about* a documentary—a study of a project that had gone tragically wrong.

The image on the screen faded to black. Conti picked up a remote, pressed a button, and the newsreel began again: the *Hindenburg* gliding serenely in toward its berth, a huge silver cigar floating over the grassy fields of New Jersey. Suddenly, flames shot from its underside. Dark palls of smoke began roiling skyward. The zeppelin slowed; hung in the air for a horrible moment; then began sinking to the ground, fire devouring its skin, exposing wide black ribs one after another.

Conti gestured toward the screen. "Look at that. The framing's horrible, the camera movement's choppy. It's completely lacking in mise-en-scène. And yet it's probably the most imperishable image ever captured on celluloid. Does that seem fair?"

"I don't think I follow you," Fortnum replied.

Conti waved a hand. "Here we are, year in and year out, refining our technique, creating ever more subtle and beautiful shots, worrying endlessly about three-point lighting and non-diegetic inserts and eyeline matches. And to what end? Somebody with a box camera just happens to be in the right place at the right time—and in five minutes shoots something more famous than all of our carefully orchestrated hours of film put together."

Fortnum shrugged. "That's just the way it goes."

"Not necessarily." Conti fiddled with the remote.

"I still don't see what you're getting at."

"It's just that—this one time—maybe fate has put someone with the skills and the tools *in* the right place."

Fortnum frowned. "You're talking about whatever mauled Josh Peters. The thing Ken was raving about."

Conti nodded slowly.

"Are you buying into that? You don't believe it was sabotage anymore?"

"Let's say I'm keeping my options open. And if there's an opportunity here, I plan to seize it. We'd be fools not to."

Fortnum paused. *He couldn't be talking about . . . No, of course not. Not even Conti is cold-blooded enough for that.*

The film ended and Conti started it yet again with a flick of the remote. "Allan, let me ask you a question. Why do you think the *Hindenburg* footage is so famous?"

Fortnum thought. "It was a huge tragedy. You don't often get to see that."

"Precisely. And you phrase it exactly right: one doesn't often *get* to see it. Did anyone capture the St. Valentine's Day Massacre on film? No. The Triangle Shirtwaist Factory fire? No. If somebody had, would those be just as iconic today as the *Hindenburg* film? Probably." Conti turned to look at him, and Fortnum—with a growing sense of dismay—saw the director's eyes were alive with excitement. "And the real tragedy is that the few films we have of such disasters are crude and unsophisticated. We've been given a chance to change that. Now do you understand what I mean by *opportunity*?"

Fortnum could barely believe what he was hearing. His worst fears about Conti's motivations and intentions were proving true. "You expect me to catch this thing—whatever it is—in the act of *killing* somebody? Try to get it on film? Is that it?"

Instead of answering directly, Conti looked back at the screen.

"You know what the most popular videos on YouTube are? Animal maulings. And the documentary with the best Nielsen numbers last year? *When Sharks Attack*. People have this primitive urge to see others die. I can't explain it. Maybe it's some reflexive form of schadenfreude. Maybe it's a primitive fight-or-flight instinct, something programmed into our amygdala. But we've been given a chance here, a chance filmmakers rarely get: we're present at a moment of real crisis. Is this what we came here for? No. Did we plan it this way? Of course not. But we owe it to ourselves, to the network—to *posterity*—to document it."

Fortnum stood up. "So you want me not only to expose myself to extreme risk but to actually film the creature in the act of mauling our crew. Film it, instead of doing all I can to save lives."

"Who knows? There may be no more attacks. There may not even be an animal. The storm may clear prematurely, and we'll be out of here tomorrow. But we need to be prepared, Allan—*just in case.*"

Fortnum felt his shock and disbelief giving way to anger. "Why was Ken Toussaint's camera found in the infirmary, not ten yards from where Peters's body was stowed? That was the assignment you gave him back in the entrance plaza, wasn't it: to film Josh's torn-apart corpse."

"A shame the video feed was destroyed." Conti's eyes turned back to the screen, where once again the great dirigible was sinking to the ground in a slow, strangely formal gesture, engulfed in flames and smoke. "Primitive," he murmured. "Amateurish. But not this time. I plan to take this documentary—this *autobiography*—and immortalize the unfolding tragedy on film. A crisis as memorable, in its way, as the *Hindenburg* . . . yet, this time, it will be art."

"Mining Peters's death for reaction shots was bad enough. But this . . ." Fortnum stiffened. "I won't have any part of it. And I think you're a monster for even suggesting such a vile thing."

It took Conti a moment to tear his eyes from the screen and look at Fortnum. "You're working for me," he said. "If you don't have what it takes to do this, you're not fit to be a documentary cinematographer. I'll see to it that you're finished in the business."

"Somehow," Fortnum replied, "I think one or the other of us already is." And he turned on his heel and strode out of the room without another word.

33

Private First Class Donovan Fluke walked glumly along the B Level transverse corridor of the south wing, weighted down by no fewer than three heavy duffels. At first he hadn't believed his luck, catching the assignment of escorting Ashleigh Davis to her new temporary quarters. She might be a bitch, but she was most definitely hot—by far the prettiest woman he'd seen in four months. In fact, not counting the rest of the documentary crew, she was just about the *only* woman he'd seen in four months. Before joining the engineering corps he'd been something of a womanizer—in fact, he'd enlisted primarily to escape trouble with an angry husband—and he knew how to chat up the skirts. And Davis's personal assistant was in her own temporary quarters, recovering from a bad concussion. He'd definitely caught another break there because now he had Davis all to himself. She had asked to be housed near the soldiers' quarters for extra protection. And so he figured he'd use the escort to turn on the charm, smile his patented aw-shucks-ma'am smile. And if that didn't do the trick, he'd scare her a bit, talk up the rumors going around about the vicious polar bear running amok. Either way—romance or a case of nerves—he'd see if he could get himself invited into her room, spend a little time. Maybe more than a little time.

It hadn't worked out that way at all. Davis had proved impervious to his every amorous strategy. She'd remained silent, deflected his sallies, refused to respond to his hints or leading questions. Exiting the base, they'd gone initially to her trailer, where he'd had to wait—outside in the cold—nearly fifteen minutes while she packed up a few things for the overnight stay. Standing there on the trailer steps, sidearm in hand, thinking about the bloody and savagely mauled body of Josh Peters he'd first observed not a hundred yards from this spot, had gone a long way toward dampening his ardor. Then to top it all off, he'd had to carry the "few things"—three duffels full—by himself as they returned to the base and made their way into the south wing.

They reached an intersection and Fluke let the duffels slip to the floor.

"What's the problem?" Davis asked immediately.

"Need to rest a moment, ma'am," he replied.

Davis sniffed disdainfully. "How much farther?"

"Another couple of minutes." The only suitable room they could have ready on short notice, the duty officer's bunk, was at the far end of the enlisted men's quarters. Fluke had initially looked forward to the long walk—more time to chat. Now it seemed an intolerable slog.

His radio chirped, and he plucked it from his nylon duty belt. "Fluke."

"Fluke, this is Gonzalez. What's your status?"

Fluke glanced around at the shadow-haunted doorways. "We're outside the Intercept Array Center."

"Report in once Ms. Davis is secured."

"Roger." He snapped off the radio, returned it to his belt, heaved up the duffels. "We go left here," he said.

He led the way through the section of the base that had housed the support services for the military population: gym and library, medical and dental. The actual platoons were long gone, and the spaces were now disused and cheerless. They passed the open door leading to the library, the empty, bookless shelves unrelieved lines of black in the gloom. Fluke believed himself to be used to all the silence. But tonight it seemed more oppressive than usual, almost a tangible thing. He tried whistling, but it struck a false, strident note and he stopped immediately.

Walking half a step behind him, Davis shivered. "It's so dark."

So it was getting to her, too. Fluke decided he'd give it one more shot. "That's the infirmary just ahead," he said. "Weird, isn't it, how the body of that guy, Peters, has gone missing? Makes a person wonder who took it—and *why*?"

Davis's response was to wrap her fur coat more tightly around her narrow shoulders. Fluke opened his mouth to offer another chilling salvo, then decided against it—if she got too creeped out, instead of inviting him in she'd probably insist on going back to the others . . . and the last thing he wanted to do was lug the duffels all the way back to the Operations Center.

As they walked past the infirmary door, Fluke's thoughts remained on Peters, the dead production assistant. The shredded head, brain exposed and eyestalk dangling ridiculously; the explosion of blood over the permafrost . . . despite his horny advances toward Davis, those images never strayed far from his mind.

He shot a glance at the door. *And just where the hell was Peters's body now?*

Past the infirmary—the only spot in this section that had seen use recently—the hallway grew still darker. It felt oddly cold here, given the usual hothouse temperatures inside the base. Fluke stopped to fasten the top button of his uniform. "Not much farther now," he said in what he hoped was a helpful tone. "Right up ahead and down a set of stairs. I'll get your blankets and linen, then see what I can do about getting some of these lights working."

Davis replied with a muttered monosyllable.

The stairway lay at the end of the corridor in a pallid pool of light. As they approached, Fluke tried to forget his aching arms by mentally checking off what he needed to do next: make sure the room was aired and reasonably presentable, get the linens and lightbulbs from the quartermaster's stores, go over the floor plan so—

Suddenly he stopped dead.

Davis looked at him, startled by the abrupt halt. "What is it?"

"There's something wrong." Fluke gestured ahead and to his left, where a heavy metal door was hanging ajar. "That door—it's supposed to remain locked at all times."

"Well, close it and let's get going," she said uneasily.

Fluke put down the duffels, plucked the radio from his belt. "Fluke to Gonzalez."

There was a crackle of static, then the sergeant's voice came on. "Gonzalez here."

"Sir, the door to the powerhouse staging room is open."

"Then secure it. Report anything suspicious."

"Yes, sir." Fluke glanced at Davis. "Any of your people been wandering around this quadrant?"

"How would I know? They searched a lot of places. Come on, do what he said and let's get out of here."

Fluke approached the door. Something about the way it hung in its frame looked odd to him. He pulled a flashlight from his pocket, switched it on, and ran its beam along the doorframe. Then he quickly unshipped the radio again.

"Sergeant?" he spoke into it. "Sergeant Gonzalez?"

"Go ahead, Fluke."

"The door—it looks like somebody's kicked it open. The lock's broken."

"Are you sure, Private?"

"Yes, sir. Not only that—it appears to have been kicked open from the inside."

"We're on our way."

"Roger, out."

Fluke stepped closer now, moving slowly, the beam of his light licking over the linoleum flooring, up the damaged door, into the thin black wedge of the room beyond.

"Can we go now?" Davis asked. "Please?"

"Just a minute." The chill he'd noticed—it came from here. He could feel it seeping out the crack, as if the room itself was exhaling.

He kicked the door gently open. It moved awkwardly, groaning on sprung hinges. He felt along the inside wall, found the light switch, snapped it on.

The overhead fluorescent flickered into life, lending a feeble illumination to the space beyond. It was a large, spartan-looking metal cube, containing ganged power conduits bolted to metal housings leading in from the powerhouse outside, with step-down transformers to attenuate the voltage entering the base. The room thrummed with current; Fluke could feel it almost tingle his skin. He looked around, frowning. There it was: the source of the chill air.

"What the *hell*?" he muttered.

On the far wall was an access panel. It was about four feet square and set just above the floor; it was used to reach the repair and maintenance crawl space for the length of conduit between the room itself and the base's external shell. Normally, this was kept securely closed. But now it yawned open, the panel sagging loosely on twisted pins. Arctic air from outside was pouring in.

"My ears," Davis said. "They hurt."

Fluke walked quickly across the room and knelt before the damaged panel. Grasping its edge, he tried to push it closed, but it was folded back on itself and refused to budge. He tried again, heaving with all his strength. No luck. He stopped to warm his fingers and catch his breath. As he did so, his gaze fell on the crawl space that lay beyond the frame of the access panel.

It was a dark hole perhaps ten feet deep. At the far end, the exterior panel had also been torn away and Fluke could see outside: the outline of an equipment shed, ribbons of snow swirling like dust devils in the banshee wind. Staring, he realized that his ears hurt, too. But it wasn't a pain he'd felt before—it was a strange, deep ringing, almost felt more than heard, accompanied by an unpleasant sensation of pressure, as if his inner ears were swelling within his skull . . .

And then—as he crouched, staring—the swirls of snow at the far end of the maintenance crawl space were abruptly blotted out.

He peered down the tunnel in confusion, wondering if the exterior panel had just been shut from the outside. But then the darkness *shifted*—and he realized what had suddenly blocked his view was a large shape, moving stealthily toward him down the crawl space.

He fell backward onto the floor with a neigh of terror. He pulled his sidearm from his holster but his fingers were suddenly fat and stupid and it clattered to the floor. He tried to marshal his wits, to rise to his feet and run, but he was paralyzed with shock and disbelief. The thing was closer now, filling the wide crawl space with its bulk, and as he stared Fluke felt the pain in his head swell until it was almost unbearable. There was a sudden flood of warmth around his thighs as his bladder let go.

And then it was in the room. Davis screamed—a sharp, piercing sound—and the thing turned toward her. Fluke just stared. There was absolutely nothing in his understanding or experience, no nightmare, no fever dream, no creation either of the Almighty or the Prince of Darkness that could account for what was now with them in the room.

Davis screamed again, wildly, a dreadful, larynx-shredding scream, and then instantly the thing was on her. The scream escalated in pitch and volume, then changed to a desperate, bubbling gargle. Fluke felt himself lashed with a warm, viscous spray. Quite abruptly, he realized he could move. He staggered to his feet and wheeled desperately toward the door, weapon forgotten. Distantly, as if from very far away, he thought he heard shouts; a cry of warning. But then it was on him and suddenly there was nothing at all left in his universe except pain.

34

The front windows of the Sno-Cat 1643RE were vast—they took up the entire face of the cab—and from his vantage point in the driver's seat Marshall had a panoramic view of the storm. Although the heavy glass and metal shielded him from the worst of the fury, he was all too conscious of how the big vehicle swayed under the fierce gusts and of the ice pellets that hammered incessantly against the roof and sides. The wind cried and moaned constantly, as if frustrated in its desire to peel back the steel and get at him.

Marshall took his eyes off the swirling whitescape long enough to glance at his watch. He had been driving now for almost forty minutes. Once he'd cleared the immediate area of the camp and its labyrinth of lava fissures, he had made good time. The permafrost was quite level, and he'd managed a steady thirty miles an hour: he didn't know the maximum safe operating speed and was playing it safe. He'd lied to Logan about his expertise—he'd never driven a Sno-Cat in his life—but the vehicle had proven mercifully easy to handle, its controls similar to a truck or tractor, with extra switches for the plow, winch, rotating beacon, and transmission-pan heater. The hardest thing to adjust to had been the four independently sprung steel tracks, hydraulically steered by the front and rear axles, which—combined with the cab's alarming amount of glass— gave him a lurching, almost vertiginous sense of being perched far too high off the ground.

The Cat's half-dozen halogen headlights lanced ahead, barely penetrating the murk. Marshall peered along their beams into the raging storm, then glanced over at the GPS mounted onto the control panel. He knew the Tunit camp was situated near a frozen lake; Gonzalez had mentioned as much. There was only one such lake in the GPS unit's database within a thirty-mile radius to the north, but it was sizable. That made fuel his biggest concern. The Cat had half a tank. That meant twenty-five gallons to reach the lake, find the village, and get back to the base. And Marshall had no idea how much fuel the enormous machine used.

He drove on, wipers flailing at the whirlwind of snow and the needles of ice peppering the window. He shook his head blearily, trying to clear it, wishing he'd brought a thermos of coffee. Was it really only thirty-six hours since he'd discovered the creature was missing?

Again, Marshall found himself wondering why exactly was he making a trip that could well prove a wild-goose chase at best—and ruinous at worst. If he broke down out here in the Zone, lost power, he'd never be found in time.

The Tunits have the answer. Some scientist had written those words, fifty years ago. The man had felt them important enough to commit to paper, to encrypt, to conceal within his quarters. And now, today, someone had been savagely killed. And another assaulted in the most bizarre way. Almost forty people were in grave danger. If there was even the merest chance the Tunits knew something—an old myth, some oral tradition, anecdotal evidence, *anything* that could shed a little light on what was afflicting the base—it was worth the risk.

And there was another, more personal reason. No matter where he'd gone or what he'd done over the past seven days, it seemed to Marshall he'd never quite been alone. There was a presence, always there, always watching: two yellow eyes, big as fists, with pupils like bottomless black pools. Since he'd first seen them looking back at him through the ice, those eyes had haunted him. The paleoecologist in him wanted—*needed*—to understand this creature better. Even if Faraday was right, even if it was somehow still alive and behind the recent atrocities, Marshall felt a yearning to decipher its mysteries. And he would travel a lot farther than thirty miles in a blinding snowstorm to accomplish that.

The cab shook violently once, then twice—the terrain was growing uneven. Marshall cut his speed. The GPS showed the lake directly ahead now: a vast wall of blue that took up the entirety of the tiny screen. And then there it was, beyond the windows: a dim line in the howling murk, covered with drifting snow, recognizable as a body of water only by its uninterrupted and featureless horizontal line.

Marshall slowed the Cat. Turning the wheel, he began to cruise along the edge of the lake, scanning carefully for any sign of habitation. He'd used ten gallons of gas already; that meant he could spare only two or three more in his search. The frozen ground sloped down steeply toward the lakeshore, and he had to keep a tight hand on the wheel and a steady pressure on the foot throttle to maintain forward traction.

Suddenly the Cat sheered violently to one side. Realizing a crevasse yawned ahead, Marshall turned the wheel sharply in the opposite direction and stepped on the gas. The cab shook as the metal tracks crabbed along the slick ice sheet. Marshall feathered the engine, trying to find the balance between traction and forward motion, struggling to keep the tracks from slipping sideways into the widening crevasse. The big vehicle whipsawed back and forth, at last struggling over the lip of the ice sheet and falling heavily forward onto level ground once again.

Marshall let the Sno-Cat roll to a stop. He sat there, idling, as his heart gradually slowed. Then, applying pressure to the throttle again, he eased forward, moving gently away from the steep shoreline.

Then, through the swirling snow, he saw something—or thought he saw something: gray shapes in the strange late-summer twilight. He stopped the Cat, staring hard through the glass. They were off to the side, away from the lake. Twisting the wheel, he inched the Cat forward. As he approached, the dim shapes resolved themselves into rudely built igloos: two of them, snow-scoured and pathetically small, surrounded by vortexes of swirling ice.

Marshall stopped the vehicle, killed the engine, zipped his parka tight. Then he exited the cab and clambered down the trapezoidal tread. Turning his head away from the teeth of the wind, he approached the first igloo. It was dark and cold, its entrance tube a black void. He staggered over to the second igloo, knelt before its doorway. It, too, was tenantless, the fur blankets and skins within cold and stiff.

Beyond, Marshall could now make out three additional igloos and a larger snowhouse. There were no other structures around, and he realized with surprise just how small the last Tunit community really was.

These three igloos were just as deserted as the first two had been. The ice walls of the snowhouse, however, danced with a faint, flickering orange glow. A fire was burning inside.

For a moment, the winds slackened, as if to rest from all their blowing. As the clouds of snow subsided, Marshall could once again make out the strange, blood-red northern lights lowering in the sky. They cast an eerie crimson glow over the tiny village of ice.

Taking a deep breath, he made his way to the snowhouse, drew back the caribou skin that served as a door flap, and stepped cautiously inside. The interior was dark, low-ceilinged, and full of smoke. A profusion of skins and blankets covered the floor. Marshall brushed the ice and snow out of his face and looked around. As his eyes adjusted, he realized there was only one occupant: a figure in a heavy caribou-skin parka, kneeling before a small fire.

Marshall took another deep breath. Then he cleared his throat. "Excuse me," he said.

For a long moment, the figure remained motionless. Then, slowly, it turned toward him. The face was a dark hollow within the fur-lined hood. The figure raised a hand to the hood, pulled it back with an unhurried, deliberate motion. A wizened face marked with intricate tattoos stared up at Marshall. It was the old shaman who had come to the base, warned the scientists to leave. He held a reindeer antler in one hand, decorated with fantastical lines and curlicues, and an intricately carved bone in the other. There were several small items scattered across the reindeer skin before him: polished stones, tiny fur fetishes, animal teeth.

"Usuguk," Marshall said.

The man gave a faint nod of his head. He didn't seem surprised to see him.

"Where are the others?"

"Gone," the man replied. Now Marshall remembered the voice: quiet, uninflected.

"Gone?" he repeated.

"Fled."

"Why?"

"Because of you. And what you have awakened."

"What have we awakened?" Marshall asked.

"I have spoken to you of it already. *Akayarga okdaniyartok.* The anger of the ancient ones. And *kurrshuq.*"

There was a pause in which the two men regarded each other in the flickering light of the fire. The last time they met, the old man had seemed anxious, frightened. Now he looked merely resigned.

"Why did you remain?" Marshall asked at last.

The shaman continued to look at him, his black eyes shining in the reflected firelight. "Because I knew you would come."

35

The weeping wasn't particularly loud, but it refused to abate: a continuous drone of background noise, mingling with the tap of the heating pipes and the distant hum of generators. When Wolff closed the door of the officers' mess, it faded from audibility. Yet it remained a presence in Kari Ekberg's mind; a presence as real as the fear that gnawed and refused to go away.

She glanced around at the people in the mess: Wolff; Gonzalez and the corporal named Marcelin; Conti; the academician, Logan; Sully, the climatologist; a handful of film crew. On the surface, everyone seemed calm. And yet there was something—in the furtive expressions, in the way people started at unexpected sounds—that spoke of controlled panic.

Gonzalez glanced at Wolff. "You've got them all locked down?"

Wolff nodded. "Everyone's in their bunks, ordered to remain there until we tell them otherwise. Your private, Phillips, is standing guard."

Ekberg found her voice. "You're sure they're dead?" she asked. "Both dead?"

Gonzalez turned toward her. "Ms. Ekberg, bodies just don't get any deader than those two."

She shuddered.

"Did you get a look at it?" Conti asked, his voice a low monotone.

"I only heard Ms. Davis's screams," Gonzalez replied. "But Marcelin did."

Wordlessly, everyone turned toward the corporal, who was sitting alone at a table, an M16 slung over one shoulder, aimlessly stirring a cup of coffee he'd forgotten was there.

"Well?" Conti urged.

Marcelin's youthful face looked pink and shocked, as if someone had just ripped the guts from his belly. He opened his mouth but no sound came.

"Go on, son," Gonzalez said.

"I didn't see much," the corporal said. "It was rounding the corridor when I—"

He stopped dead again. The room was silent, waiting.

"It was big," Marcelin began again. "And it had a head with . . ."

"Go on," Wolff urged.

"It had a head with . . . with . . . *don't make me say it!*" Abruptly the pitch of his voice spiked wildly.

"Steady there, Corporal," Gonzalez said gruffly.

Marcelin gasped for breath, the hand that held the plastic stirrer stiffening. After a minute he mastered himself. But he shook his head, refusing to say more.

For a long moment, the room remained silent. Then Wolff spoke up. "So what do we do now?"

Gonzalez frowned. "I don't see that we have a lot of choices. Wait for the weather to clear. Until then, we can't evacuate—and we can't get reinforcements."

"You're suggesting we wait around to get picked off, one by one?" said Hulce, one of the film techs.

"Nobody's going to get picked off," snapped Wolff. He turned to Gonzalez. "What's the weapons status?"

"Plenty of small arms," replied the sergeant. "A dozen M16s, half a dozen larger-caliber carbines, twenty-odd sidearms, five thousand rounds of ammunition."

"The scientific team brought along three high-powered rifles," said a voice. Ekberg glanced toward it. It was Gerard Sully, the climatologist. He was leaning against the rear wall by the steam trays, one hand nervously drumming on the steel railing. He was very pale.

Wolff glanced around the room. "We'll need to make sure anyone on the move travels as part of an armed group."

Gonzalez grunted. "Even that may not be enough."

"Well, what else can we do?" Wolff countered. "We can't just cower behind locked doors."

"You can use my truck," came another voice.

Everyone glanced toward it. It was Carradine, sitting in a plastic chair tipped back on its rear legs. Ekberg hadn't noticed him before; she wasn't sure if he'd been there the entire time, listening, or if he'd come in during the conversation.

"It's like I offered before," he continued. "My rig's the only thing that can get people out in a storm like this."

Wolff sighed in irritation. "We've been over this. It's not safe."

"Oh?" Carradine replied. "And staying here is?"

"You couldn't fit everybody inside."

"I could fit them in Ms. Davis's trailer." The trucker lowered his voice. "It's not like she needs it anymore."

"He's right," Gonzalez said. "You've got—what, thirty-three, thirty-four crew? With the scientific team that's still less than forty. Everybody will fit inside that trailer."

"What if they get lost?" Wolff asked.

"I never get lost," replied Carradine. "GPS, baby."

"Or break down? Or have a flat?"

"Ice-road truckers always carry spares and redundant equipment. And even if I can't fix it—well, that's what God invented CB radio for."

"It's simply too dangerous," said Wolff. "I said no earlier, and I'm saying no now."

"The situation has changed," Gonzalez growled.

Wolff turned to him. "How so?"

"Because this time I'm overruling you."

Wolff's look darkened. "You—"

"What we're dealing with goes beyond any and all conditions mandated for your stay. Your documentary has gone down the tubes. Three people are dead. There's no reason to compound the tragedy." He turned to Carradine. "How long will it take you to ready the rig?"

The trucker stood up. "Half an hour, tops."

Gonzalez glanced toward Marcelin. "I want you to escort Mr. Carradine here to his truck. Don't take any chances, fall back here at the first hint of any trouble."

Marcelin nodded.

"Then I want you and Phillips to start evacuating the film crew. We'll use this mess as the staging area. Bring them in half a dozen at a time. Carefully, do it by the book."

"Yes, sir." Marcelin unshouldered the M16, nodded to Carradine. The trucker stood up, pulling a large handgun out of his waistband as he did so. Stepping to the door, Marcelin opened it, did a quick scan of the corridor beyond, then slipped out. Carradine followed and the door closed tightly behind him.

Gonzalez reached into one of the deep pockets of his fatigues and pulled out two radios. He tossed one to Wolff, the other to Sully. "You can contact me with these. I've preset the emergency frequency." He stood up, grabbed his own M16. "Lock up behind me. I'll be back in five minutes."

"Where are you going?" Wolff asked.

"To the armory. I'll be needing more firepower."

"Why?"

"Because I'm going hunting."

After the door shut behind Gonzalez, Wolff walked over and locked it. He stood a moment in silence, facing the closed door. Then, quite abruptly, he turned and walked to the center of the room. "Well?" he said to nobody in particular.

"I can't leave." It was Sully, the climatologist, who spoke. His voice shook slightly. "I'm the expedition leader. I can't just leave all our experiments here. Besides—Evan's missing."

Ekberg started at this. "Missing? But I was just talking to him, not two hours ago."

Sully nodded grimly. "He hasn't been seen since. He's not in his lab. And he's not in his quarters."

"He'll be back," said Logan.

Everyone turned toward the academician.

"Excuse me?" Sully asked.

"He borrowed the Sno-Cat."

"In a blizzard?" Ekberg asked. "Where did he go?"

"The Tunit village, to the north."

"Why?" Sully demanded.

Logan glanced around at his inquisitors. "To get answers. Look, let's find Faraday and talk about it. In your lab."

Sully sighed, shook his head. "All right. Once Gonzalez gets back here with the firepower."

"And when he does get back here, he may have something to say about your little plans." Wolff glanced around. "The rest of you?"

"Are you kidding?" It was Hulce. "I'm out of here." There was a murmured chorus of assent from around the room.

Wolff looked at Conti. "Emilio?"

Conti didn't reply. Since asking about the creature, he had remained silent, his gaze far away.

"Emilio?" Wolff asked again.

As Ekberg watched, Conti became slowly aware he was being addressed. "Excuse me?"

"Can you be ready to leave in half an hour?"

Conti blinked, frowned. "I'm not going anywhere."

"Didn't you hear Gonzalez? He's ordering everyone to head south in Carradine's truck."

The producer gave his head a little birdlike shake. "I have a documentary to finish."

Wolff's eyes narrowed in disbelief. "Excuse me? There is no more documentary."

"That's where you're wrong." And Conti smiled faintly, as if at some private joke.

"Emilio, Ashleigh is dead. And in about half an hour, your entire staff will be heading in the direction of Fairbanks."

"Yes," Conti murmured. "It's all up to me now."

Wolff raised one arm in an exasperated gesture. "Didn't you hear? You've *got no crew*!"

"I'll do it myself. The old way, the classic way. Like Georges Méliès, Edwin Porter, Alice Guy Blaché. Fortnum will be leaving with the rest of them; I know he will." And he glanced toward Ekberg.

Ekberg understood the significance of that glance; understood what he was asking of her. Despite what she had told Marshall in the Operations Center, despite her uncompromising commitment to both Conti and her career, she felt a cold thrust of fear at the mere thought. Nevertheless, she returned his look and—holding his gaze—nodded slowly.

36

The old shaman gestured to a pile of caribou skins on the far side of the fire. "Sit," he said.

Marshall, painfully aware that time was of the essence, also understood this encounter—whatever it might produce—could not be hurried. He sat down.

"How did you know I was coming?" he asked.

"In the same manner I knew you were angering the ancient ones. My spirit guide told me."

The shaman picked up the scatter of items before him, placed them in a small leather pouch, drew the drawstring tight.

"The others—where did they go?"

Usuguk stretched his palm northward. "To our brothers along the sea."

"Another Tunit camp?" Marshall asked.

Usuguk shook his head. "Inuit. We are the last of our kind."

"There are no other Tunits?"

"None."

Marshall looked over the fire at the old shaman. *So it's true, then.* "When will they return?"

"Perhaps never. Life is much easier beside the sea. It has been difficult to keep them here since their mothers and fathers died."

Marshall sat for a moment, collecting his thoughts. It was hard to believe that this sad little encampment was the last vestige of an entire Native American tribe. It was galling to think that his own arrival at the glacier might be partly responsible for scattering it, even temporarily.

"Those markings you made, outside the base," he said at last. "What were they for?"

"A warding of protection. To compel the *kurrshuq* to spare you." The shaman returned Marshall's gaze. "Your presence here means the warding was unsuccessful."

Marshall hesitated again. He had come all this way, yet he did not know exactly how to begin—or even what to ask. He took a deep breath. "Listen, Usuguk. I know we have already caused you anxiety and difficulty, and I am very sorry for that. It was never our intent."

The Tunit said nothing.

"Now we are in trouble. Serious, serious trouble. And I have come here in hopes that you can help."

Still, Usuguk did not reply. His expression was stolid, almost taciturn.

"The mountain," Marshall continued. "The one you told us was evil. We found something there, as we were doing our experiments. A creature bigger than a polar bear, encased in ice. We . . . we cut it from the ice. Now it's missing."

As Marshall said this, the shaman's expression changed. A look of something close to shock blossomed over the weathered features.

"We don't know exactly what it is. I can only tell you that it has caused injury. It has caused death."

The look of shock subsided, replaced by the same mix of fear and sorrow Marshall recalled from their first meeting. "Why do you come to me?" the Tunit asked.

"There was a scientific expedition at the base, fifty years ago. It met with tragedy. Most of the scientists died. But we recovered one of their journals. It contained the following words: 'The Tunits have the answer.' "

Usuguk sat motionless, staring into the fire. Marshall waited, uncertain whether to speak or keep silent. After about a minute, the shaman reached over, rummaged slowly through an assortment of ritual objects, and grasped the bone handle of what appeared to be some kind of drum: a narrow hoop about a foot in diameter, leather stretched tightly across it. Slowly he began tapping it against the palm of his other hand, flipping the instrument with each beat, back and forth, back and forth. He accompanied the rhythm with a chant, quiet at first, then louder, the sound filling the snowhouse like the smoke of the fire. At last, after several minutes, the chant subsided. The shaman's face was once more at peace. Putting the drum aside, he unstrung the leather pouch, dipped in his hand, and took out two greasy pellets of a soft material, one blue, the other red. He carefully dropped them into the fire, one after the other. Bi-colored smoke roiled upward, blending to violet at its edges.

"*Tashayat kompok,*" he murmured, examining the smoke. "As you will it." Marshall did not think the shaman was speaking to him.

Marshall repressed the urge to glance at his watch. "Do you know what the scientist meant?" he asked. "About the Tunits having the answer?"

Usuguk said nothing. His eyes remained on the fire.

"I know you've seen something of the world," Marshall went on. "Your command of English says as much. If you can help, if you know anything about this, *please* tell me."

"It is not my place. You have brought this darkness upon yourself. I've already done what I could. I made a long journey—a sun, a moon, and a sun—to warn you. You paid no heed."

"If that is true, I apologize. But I think violent death is too high a price to pay for our ignorance."

Usuguk closed his eyes. "The circle you have begun is yours to complete. Even the Circle of Death can be beautiful."

"There was no beauty in Josh Peters's death. If you know something, no matter how insignificant or unrelated it may seem—you owe it to us as fellow human beings to aid us."

"You are of the world," Usuguk replied slowly. "I am of the spirit. I left that life behind long ago. I cannot go back."

Marshall sat, wondering what else there was left for him to say. At last he cleared his throat. "Let me tell you something. I once left a life behind, too. My best friend's life."

Slowly, Usuguk opened his eyes.

"It was twelve years ago. I was an Army Ranger, stationed in Somalia. My unit had been under fire for three days from rebel skirmishers. It was house to house, room by room. My friend was establishing a forward post. The orders were garbled; he got ahead of the detail. I saw him moving across a square. It was dark. I thought it was an enemy sniper. I shot him." Marshall shrugged. "After that, I swore I'd never pick up a gun again."

Usuguk nodded slowly. Another silence settled over the snowhouse, broken only by the crackling of the fire, the mournful cry of the blizzard outside.

"It was not a frag," the shaman said, opening his eyes.

Marshall looked at him in surprise. "Were you in the service?"

Usuguk ignored the question. "It was a mistake."

"My unit had never lost a soldier to friendly fire. I was ordered to lie, to cover it up. When I refused, my commanding officer arranged for me to get a dishonorable discharge. I—I had to break the news of my friend's death to his wife."

Usuguk grunted quietly. Reaching into his medicine pouch, he pulled out several small artifacts. Smoothing the skins before him, he tossed the items onto them and scrutinized the way they fell. "You said you swore not to pick up a gun again. Such an oath is not to be taken lightly. And now? What will you do now?"

Marshall took a deep breath. "If there's something out there—something bent on killing all of us—I'll do my very best to kill it first."

Usuguk looked into the fire. Then he turned his seamed and inscrutable face toward Marshall. "I will go with you," he said. "But the only lives I take now are those necessary to sustain my own. My hunting days are over."

Marshall nodded. "Then I'll hunt for both of us."

37

Penny Barbour had wanted to take all the data critical to the expedition: a network image; the accessions and samples database; the online lab journals of her fellow scientists. In the end, she'd taken nothing. The two soldiers, Marcelin and Phillips—looking nervous despite their M16s—did not allow any time. Barbour, Chen, and the four others assigned to their group were instructed to change quickly into their warmest clothes and to grab some form of ID. They were assembled in the officers' mess, their names checked off against a master list of everyone at the base, then they were escorted to the staging area. Phillips took point, Marcelin brought up the rear. They moved quickly and in complete silence through the corridors, halting at each intersection while Phillips reconnoitered. Reaching the central stairwell, they crept upward and crossed the entrance plaza—spectral in the nighttime half-light—to the weather chamber. The chamber was as crowded as the rest of the base had been empty: as they opened its door, a sea of tense faces turned quickly toward them.

Gonzalez stood at the head of the group. He had a handcart full of weapons and ammunition—enough for a small army—and he was methodically checking each in turn. He nodded to the soldiers, then racked the slide of the handgun he'd been inspecting, holstered it.

"This is the last of them?" he asked.

"Yes, sir," Marcelin replied. He passed the list of names to the sergeant, who inspected it, grunted his approval, and put it aside.

Gonzalez glanced at his watch. "Carradine will be ready to load in five minutes." He turned toward the group. "All right, everybody—listen up. I want you to don your weather gear now. We're issuing extra gloves, scarves, and balaclavas—you'll find them in this box. When I give the signal, we'll head outside. You are all to follow me and make directly for the trailer. Maintain silence at all times. Any questions?"

Nobody spoke.

"Then get busy."

There was a squeal of metal against metal as three dozen lockers were opened almost simultaneously. Opening hers, Barbour shrugged into her parka, draped a scarf around her neck, then grabbed a balaclava from a large carton in the middle of the room and fitted it over her ears. She pushed an extra scarf into one pocket and a pair of gloves into the other.

"I have a question," a gruff voice said. It was the foreman of the roustabouts, Creel. He alone had not put on a parka, and was against the wall, burly arms crossed.

Gonzalez eyed the man, nodded.

"Just what is it you're planning to do after the truck leaves?"

"We're *planning* to put a stop to all this killing."

"You mean, you're going to hunt it."

"Whatever this thing is, I think it's done its fair share of hunting. Now it's our turn."

"Just the three of you," Creel said.

Gonzalez eyed the cache of weapons, then smiled mirthlessly. "Why? You think our force is insufficient?"

"Given the state of your intel, I think the larger the force, the better."

Now Gonzalez examined the man more carefully. "Were you in the service, mister?"

Creel threw out his chest. "Third Armored Cavalry, Desert Storm."

Gonzalez stroked his chin. "You're not part of this little group, right? You're the local foreman."

The man nodded. "George Creel. Out of Fairbanks."

"Ever do any hunting?"

The foreman grinned crookedly. "Only uniformed humans."

"That's sufficient. Want to join the party, Mr. Creel?"

Creel's grin widened. "And let me do this for free? Are you kidding?"

"Very well."

Barbour heard her own voice almost before she realized she was speaking. "I think that's a mistake."

Gonzalez turned toward her. "What, exactly, is a mistake?"

"You're hunting it with so little information. Sully and Faraday are in the lab, analyzing its blood, learning what they can. The more you know, the better equipped you'll be to do it harm."

Gonzalez's eyes narrowed. "What can they possibly learn that will help us?"

"They can find a weakness. Learn its vulnerabilities. Make observations."

"They're welcome to make all the observations they want—of its carcass." Gonzalez glanced around the weather chamber. "All right, people. Follow me."

They passed into the staging area, where Gonzalez paused to line them up three abreast. Then the outer doors were opened and they marched into the storm. The ragged procession huddled close together, tramping through drifts that curled around their ankles.

Gonzalez led the way, M16 at the ready, while Corporal Marcelin brought up the rear, lugging an improvised sled stowed with cases of water and emergency supplies.

Barbour heard the eighteen-wheeler before she saw it: the snarl of an idling diesel, filtering back through the gloom. She kept staggering forward through the storm, head bowed, until she bumped heavily into the person in front of her. Looking up, she realized the procession had stopped. There was the truck, covered with tiny yellow lights like some immense holiday offering, its headlights lancing the coruscating snow. Carradine had attached Davis's trailer and was framed in its wide doorway. He was busily throwing objects out of the trailer and into the snow: hatboxes, racks of expensive designer dresses, a vanity table. As Barbour watched, a small leather suitcase went cartwheeling out the trailer door. Hitting the ground, it sprang open, sending forth an explosion of cosmetics. The wind caught a flimsy negligee and scooped it up into the air, flapping and rippling like a silken kite. It got caught briefly on the trailer's antenna before floating away and disappearing in the dark sky.

Carradine brushed one hand against the other in satisfaction. "That's better," he said over the rumble of the diesel. "Okay. Bring 'em on."

Gonzalez did one last head count. "Get inside," he told the first row of people. "Find a comfortable spot to stow yourselves."

"Don't all bunch up together," Carradine added. "Distribute the weight as evenly as possible." He jumped down into the snow. "I've placed a spare battery-powered CB radio inside to communicate with the cab. Somebody will need to take charge of it."

A tentative hand went up. "I will." It was Fortnum.

Barbour watched as the two casualties were helped into the trailer: Toussaint, slumping, clearly under heavy sedation, babbling quietly to himself, and Brianna, her head bandaged, silent and looking terrified. As the line slowly shuffled closer, Barbour could feel the heat radiating out the open door. No doubt Carradine had it cranked all the way up, warming the trailer while he still could.

"I'll need somebody up front," he said. "To feed me directional up-dates if things get hairy."

"I'll do it," Barbour said.

Carradine looked at her. "Can you program a GPS unit?"

"I'm a computer scientist."

"Good enough for me. Let me check the belly tarp and the alco-hol evaporator, and we'll be on our way."

She stepped out of the line and into the relative shelter beneath the cab. As the last of the group climbed into the trailer, Marcelin handed up the cases of water and the emergency supplies. Carra-dine made a final inspection of the rig. Then he climbed onto the trailer and, after briefly surveying the interior and showing Fort-num the CB, he closed the door. Walking around to the rear, he dis-connected the power conduit. Instantly, the trailer went dark save for the running lights at the rear.

"Ready?" Gonzalez asked.

The trucker gave him a thumbs-up.

"Then good luck and Godspeed."

Carradine helped Barbour up into the cab, then trotted around the front and clambered into the driver's seat. He did a quick equip-ment and instrument check against a clipboard list that hung on the wall behind him, buckled his seat belt, then plucked the CB hand-set from the dash. "You with me back there?" he spoke into it.

"We're here," came the reply.

"Ten four." He replaced the radio, glanced over at Barbour. "Ready?"

She nodded.

"Then let's go." He released the air brake, shifted into gear, eased off the clutch. The truck shuddered, then began rolling slowly for-ward.

Barbour looked out the window, into the scudding snow. As they headed into the wastes and the dark, her last view of Fear Base was of the three soldiers—Gonzalez, Marcelin, and Phillips—standing by the empty sled, weapons ready, watching them depart.

38

For the last hour, the officers' mess had been a scene of frantic activity. One by one, groups had been assembled, their readiness checked, and the soldiers had escorted them to the staging area. At one point Gonzalez had radioed, making a final appeal for Conti to see reason, to leave with the rest. Conti, watching rough takes on the digital video camera Fortnum left behind, barely listened. At last, Gonzalez muttered something about Conti not being worth the time it would take to force him into the truck and warned him to stay put. "You want to film something? Film the mess once we've killed it." Marcelin and Phillips returned to escort the final group of six to the staging area.

That left the three of them alone.

Kari Ekberg glanced at the other two occupants of the mess. Conti, having finished watching the rough takes, was now feverishly scrawling notes on the clipboard he never seemed to be without. Wolff had secured two heavy-caliber sidearms from the military store and was toying with them. The way he jammed rounds into the extra clips with his thumb, as if filling an oversize Pez dispenser, made it seem as though he could be relied on to handle them properly.

This hardly made Ekberg feel better. She had been growing less and less confident of her decision to remain. Loyalty to a project was one thing; ambition was one thing; but being marooned here with some killing machine seemed increasingly like a questionable career move.

She tried to shake her reservations away. After all, hadn't two of the scientists elected to remain behind with their data and their samples? Logan had chosen to stay with them. And Marshall—Marshall was out in the storm somewhere. He'd be returning, too. Besides, there was the military contingent to think about—combat-trained and sporting a very impressive arsenal of weaponry, ready to hunt the creature down once the truck had departed. She told herself that her chances were better here, warm and dry, than in an eighteen-wheeler out on the ice.

Conti put down his pen, scanned the notes he'd just taken, then glanced up at the clock. "The truck will have left by now," he said. "It's time."

Wolff put down the guns. "Time for what?"

"To film the hunt, of course. It'll start any moment. I can't take the risk of losing them."

Wolff frowned. "Emilio, you can't be serious."

Conti picked up the video camera, examined its settings. "I would have liked to shoot the truck leaving, but I couldn't take the chance—Gonzalez might have forced me to board it. But we can always stage that later." He put down the camera. "The hunt, however, can't be staged. It's the moment we've been waiting for, what everything has been leading up to."

"But that's crazy." The words were out almost before Ekberg had spoken them.

The director turned toward her. "What do you mean? I'll stay well back from the soldiers. I'll shadow them, follow them by ear—they'll never know I'm there until the action starts and it's too late to do anything about it."

"But you won't be safe—" Ekberg began.

"Do you think I'm safer here? Personally, I'd rather be close to the machine guns."

"But Kari's right," said Wolff. "The soldiers are intentionally walking into danger. That means you'll be exposed, as well."

"Then come along." Conti nodded toward the guns. "Bring those. We're better off sticking together."

Wolff didn't reply.

"Listen to me," Conti said. "We came up here to film that beast. Don't you see the opportunity we've been given? This is a new story, and a far greater one than we ever expected. Do you really believe I'll stay in this room, sitting on my hands, while the shot of a lifetime—maybe the shot of *all* time—is taking place a stone's throw away?"

When nobody replied, he stood up and began to pace the room. "Of *course* there's a degree of danger. That's just what will make this the most exciting documentary ever. We're living the actual events as they unfold; the raw materials are all around us. We three—the director, the field producer, the channel rep—we *are* the documentary. It's experiential in the way no film has ever been before. Don't you understand? We're witnessing the dawn of *an entirely new genre of film.*"

As he spoke, Conti's face flushed and his eyes glittered. His voice trembled with an almost messianic conviction. Despite her fear, Ekberg began to feel stirrings of excitement. Wolff listened in silence, his eyes following the director as he paced back and forth.

"And there's something else," Conti said. "Ashleigh is dead. She gave her life for this project. We should do it for her. *I* will be the narrator now."

There was a moment of silence. Then Wolff spoke. "Do you really think you could pull it off?"

"I trained as a cinematographer, didn't I? I'll get shots that will make Fortnum retire his camera in shame." Conti turned to Ekberg. "I'll do the filming, but it will be a smoother sequence if you handle the sound equipment."

She took a deep breath. "I'll get the field mixer wired up."

Conti nodded. "I'll prep the rest. Kari, you hold the radio. We'll leave in five minutes."

39

Marshall maneuvered the Sno-Cat as quickly as he dared through the spume of snow and ice. The snow had slackened somewhat but the wind was worse than ever, screaming around the doors and windows of the big vehicle. The half dawn could not be far away, but time seemed strangely irrelevant in this no-man's-land of mono-chromatic gray. At times it felt like being underwater, as if earth and air had been merged by the violence of the storm into some strange new element, some chemical suspension through which the Cat was forcing its way.

He glanced into the rearview mirror. Usuguk sat cross-legged in the back of the cab, medicine bundle on his lap. He had left his bat-tered carbine behind and was unarmed. Hood pushed back and weathered face exposed, the man seemed dwarfed by the parka that surrounded him. Although Marshall had tried to draw him into conversation several times, the Tunit had said little during the trip south, instead swaying gently—with a motion that had nothing to do with the bouncing of the Sno-Cat—and now and then chanting softly to himself.

He tried once more. "Back at your village, you told me your hunting days were over. You used to be a hunter?"

Usuguk roused himself. "I was. I was a great hunter. But that was years ago, when I was still a little man."

Little man? "There's something I don't understand. Why do you live so far inland, away from the sea? You can't grow anything in this climate. There's no food to harvest except the occasional polar bear. You said it yourself: life would be so much easier if you lived near the coast."

Again, it took Usuguk a moment to answer. "I have no interest in an easier life."

"Do you mean to say that, if the others don't return, you'll just live out here in the wilderness by yourself?"

A long silence. "It is my *roktalyik*."

Marshall glanced again in the rearview mirror. The man knew something—that seemed clear—but would it be of use? Would it turn out to be a tapestry of myth and ritual, interesting but completely useless? He could only hope not.

They continued southward in silence, Marshall keeping one eye on the GPS and the other on the swirling snow. Mount Fear was close now, and he reduced speed, straining to spot any lava tubes or magma fractures that might yawn treacherously before them under a concealing mantle of snow. Within ten minutes a tiny pinpoint of light winked out of the darkness to the left; then two; then half a dozen. Marshall corrected course and moments later the perimeter fence appeared, skeletal in the headlights. Instead of parking at the motor pool, he maneuvered his way past the gate and between the outbuildings, nosing the Cat toward the central entrance. To his vast surprise he noticed that both Carradine's rig and Davis's trailer were gone. A large vacant spot just inside the fence marked where they had sat, footprints and tread marks scoured clean by the wind.

He parked as near the double doors as he could, then killed the engine and nodded to Usuguk. The Tunit came forward and together they exited the vehicle, ducking through the icy squall. Marshall opened the doors and stepped inside. After a pause, Usuguk followed.

The weather chamber looked like a war zone: a dozen lockers hanging open, cold-weather gear and ration boxes strewn across the floor. A large cache of weapons and ammunition stood in one corner. Marshall walked over and—feeling a huge reluctance—picked up an M16 and a couple of thirty-round magazines. He stuffed the magazines into his parka pockets and slung the semiautomatic over his shoulder.

The entrance plaza beyond was dark and empty. Marshall paused a moment, listening. The base seemed almost preternaturally silent; there was no hollow echo of footsteps, no distant chatter of conversation. He led the way to the central staircase, heading toward the living quarters on B Level. Usuguk followed him at some distance, looking neither left nor right. The Tunit seemed disinterested in his surroundings. In fact, he seemed to be trying to notice as little as possible. There was a remote, almost pained look on his face, as if he was in the midst of some internal struggle.

B Level seemed just as deserted. As they passed by rooms that in previous days had been abuzz with activity—the Operations Center, offices, and the living quarters—Marshall grew increasingly puzzled. What had happened? Where was everybody? Had they all retreated to someplace deep within the base, a safe haven—or last redoubt?

There was one spot he felt certain would be occupied: the life-sciences lab. And as he approached it he found he was correct: faint voices could be heard inside. When he opened the door he found not only Faraday but Sully and Logan as well. All three jumped as he entered. Logan stood up quickly, looking curiously at Usuguk. Sully, who was sitting at an adjoining table, just nodded, his fingers drumming a nervous tattoo. One of the high-powered rifles used to guard against polar bear attacks was leaning beside him. Faraday looked from Marshall to Usuguk and back again.

"You did it," Logan said. "Good man."

"Where is everybody?" Marshall asked.

"They left," Logan replied. "In the trailer."

"The thing got Ashleigh Davis and one of the soldiers," Sully said. "Slaughtered them both."

A chill went through Marshall. "My God. That's three it's killed now."

"Gonzalez and his boys are out hunting it," Sully added.

Logan waved a hand toward Sully and Faraday. "I told them about the journal. Why you made the trip to the village."

"What about the journal?" Marshall asked.

"I've deciphered a few more fragments. Nothing of use."

Marshall turned toward the shaman. "We know about the science team here fifty years ago. There were eight of them. Seven died under sudden and it seems violent circumstances. I told you what one wrote: 'The Tunits have the answer.' To what, we don't yet know. So, can you help us?"

As he spoke, a change seemed to come over Usuguk. The pained expression slowly left his face, to be replaced by something Marshall thought might be resignation. For several moments, he remained silent. And then, slowly, he nodded.

"You can?" Logan asked eagerly. "Then you know about what happened?"

"Yes." Usuguk nodded again. "I was the one who got away."

40

When he first pulled duty at Fear Base, as a green buck private back in 1978, Gonzalez had participated in the occasional infiltration exercise. They—there had been six of them back then—were told to assume a Russian sabotage unit had penetrated the base, and they were tasked with interdiction. Of course, since even at that time the base had been closed almost twenty years, it was nothing more than a war game. Yet it was considered good training, especially for those who transferred out of the engineer corps and into the regular army. And it stayed with you: Gonzalez still vividly recalled the whispered orders, the readied weapons, the doors knocked open with sudden kicks.

This felt pretty much the same.

After the semi and trailer had departed, the team had readied their weapons and—after a short briefing and a few words of caution from Gonzalez—deployed into the south wing. They moved down the corridors in near-total silence, Gonzalez indicating his wishes with a gesture or single word. They had passed the infirmary and were approaching the spot where Fluke and Davis were attacked. It was the second time in an hour he'd taken this particular walk. The last time, he missed the action by seconds. Fluke was dead, torn literally into pieces, but Davis lingered a little while. It hadn't been a pretty sight. Now both bodies were occupying the infirmary's examining room, rolled in plastic sheets, replacing the missing Peters.

"Okay," he muttered. "We'll take up position outside the staging room. Phillips, you do a quick recon."

Phillips, who was on point, gave a thumbs-up. Gonzalez glanced back at Marcelin, who nodded his understanding.

Privately, Gonzalez was relieved at how Marcelin was holding up. He was the only one to catch a glimpse of the creature, and it had almost unmanned him. But either he'd rallied or he was putting up a good front. A rotation like this, stuck in the ass end of nowhere, didn't generally pull the cream of the crop, but he was pleased with his present team. True, they were "camp slugs," engineer corpsmen without combat experience under their belts. But they weren't whiners and they weren't prima donnas. They understood that every day at Fear Base would be just like every other day.

That is, until now.

Gonzalez looked over Marcelin's shoulder at Creel. The burly foreman was grinning like an idiot, two handguns jammed in his waistband, brandishing his M4 grenade launcher–equipped carbine like he was goddamned Rambo. Creel was a wild card: Gonzalez was a little skeptical about the Third Cav claims but at least the man knew how to handle a weapon. And though three machine guns seemed like plenty, Sergeant Gonzalez was a conservative man. An extra trigger finger felt like a good precaution.

He'd considered calling this one in and waiting for orders. But waiting for a reply to filter through the chain of command would have taken hours, maybe longer, and Gonzalez was in no mood to wait. Besides, he didn't particularly relish trying to explain what it was, precisely, they were after. There had been three deaths already on his watch, and he'd been given broad discretion at this far remove from authority. Better to let the bullet-riddled corpse provide its own explanations.

The powerhouse staging room lay directly ahead now. In the dim light of the corridor, Gonzalez saw the door yawning open, hanging at a crazy angle on twisted hinges. "Remember," he told Phillips. "Low and slow."

"Yes, sir." The private unshipped his M16. Weapon at the ready, he drew himself up to the doorframe, slipped around it. Ten seconds later he gave the all clear.

Gonzalez motioned the others to step inside, then he followed. The room was as they'd left it: a hurricane of bloodstains, looping in fantastic arcs and jets across the floor and the footings of the step-down transformers. They had managed to close the access panel to the maintenance crawl space, but the room was still uncomfortably cold.

He glanced at Marcelin. The corporal was studiously averting his eyes from the bloodstains. He looked a little green about the gills.

"Corporal?" Gonzalez spoke over the hum of the transformers.

Marcelin's eyes darted toward him. "Sir?"

"You okay?"

"Yes, sir."

Gonzalez nodded and turned his gaze once more toward the rivers and tributaries of blood. Dozens of bloody footprints traced desperate lines, testament to the frantic activity that had taken place here shortly before. Some of them led into the corridor and back in the direction they'd come from, toward the infirmary. But there was another set of prints—if you could call them prints—that led off in the other direction, deeper into the base. Pulling his flashlight from his service belt, he snapped it on and examined them. They were huge, distorted rosettes. Recurved hooks, long and cruel-looking, sprouted from the front of each rosette.

He stared a long time.

Gonzalez considered himself a simple man, a man with few needs and fewer pretensions. He had never had much use for the company of others, and the only kind of pride he knew was the pride of doing a good job. That was why he'd never sought out promotion; why he'd never felt any strong desire to advance beyond the rank of sergeant. Sergeant, he felt, was his ideal niche: high enough to impose his own small vision of order on things, but not so high as to court unwanted responsibility. It was also why he was the only soldier to have remained longer than eighteen months at Fear Base. The fact was, he'd been here now almost thirty years. He would never forget the look on the face of the major at Fort McNair when, returning from a furlough after his first tour at Fear Base, Gonzalez asked to be posted there again. He could have retired years ago, but he couldn't imagine doing anything else other than making sure this installation, mothballed and forgotten, was well cared for. He had no family and few possessions beyond a Bible and the tall stack of mystery novels he read over and over again in the evenings, alphabetically by title. He'd spent so much time in the company of his own thoughts that it had become the company he most preferred. It was a simple existence but well-ordered, rational, predictable—just the way he liked it.

Which was why the bloody print now illuminated in the flashlight beam gave him such a disagreeable feeling of unease.

His thoughts were interrupted by Creel snugging a grenade into the under-barrel launcher of his M4. "You know, my uncle won an African safari once," he said. "No kidding. First prize in an Elks raffle. Bagged a cape buffalo on it. Boy, he boasted about that damn hunt for years."

This is one hunt you won't ever be allowed to brag about, Gonzalez thought. He glanced at his men. Phillips was shining his light over the floor and walls, spatters of blood appearing and disappearing as the beam traveled. Marcelin was standing in the doorway, looking out into the corridor, head cocked as if listening.

"We ready?" Gonzalez asked quietly.

"Hell, yes, we're ready," Creel said. "Let's take this thing down."

They regrouped just inside the doorway, then moved into the hall. Phillips once again took point, supplementing the faint corridor illumination with slow sweeps of his flashlight, following the bloody, disquietingly large prints. There seemed to be occasional droplets of blood on the floor here, too—drops that had nothing to do with the tracks. Had the creature been wounded somehow?

"Jesus," he heard Phillips say. "What the hell kind of prints are those?"

The hall dead-ended at an intersection. To the left lay a series of unused and empty offices; to the right, the corridor led to the radar-support spaces. They paused while Phillips carefully shone his light around. The prints were growing less distinct, the droplets of blood less frequent, but they clearly led to the right.

Gonzalez felt his heart sink. The radar-support spaces were a warren of small, equipment-heavy galleries and storage nooks. If the thing was in there, it would be a bitch to flush it out.

"Let's go," he said. "Weapons at the ready. Don't speak unless it's absolutely necessary."

He looked at them in turn, lingering briefly on Marcelin. The greenish cast had left the corporal's face, to be replaced by pallid anxiety.

As they moved forward again, Gonzalez took a quick mental inventory of his own emotions. He realized that he, too, was afraid. Not of being killed or injured—their overwhelming firepower would protect them from that—but of the unknowns this thing they were tracking represented. He remembered the photographer, Toussaint: the way he had raved, shrill and loud and with hardly a break for breath, until sedated. He recalled the panicky edge to Marcelin's voice, back in the mess. *Don't make me say it . . . !* Gonzalez was simply too old, too set in his ways, to have his understanding of the natural world roughly unseated.

The corridor was a receding rectangle of black, punctuated by pools of yellow light. Phillips kept his flashlight on the tracks while the others licked theirs left and right in loose, unchoreographed patterns. They passed the stairwell leading to C Level and the enlisted men's quarters, then the set of rooms used for data acquisition and identification. All four doors were closed and showed no signs of tampering, their small metal-grilled windows undamaged.

"Where should we aim?" he heard Creel pipe up, almost eagerly, from behind. "The head? The heart? The guts?"

"Just keep shooting until it falls down," Gonzalez replied.

Ahead was the narrow opening that led to the radar-support spaces. It was pitch-black. Phillips entered first, sweeping left past the doorway. Gonzalez followed, reaching over and flipping on the lights with the palm of his hand.

Radar support was a series of three large rooms, one after another, all filled with monolithic metal racks arranged in a parallel line—a library of technological obsolescence. The first rack lay directly before them like a wall, its high shelves covered with ancient equipment for radar scanning, acquisition, and interpretation: dark CRT screens, logic boards festooned with vacuum tubes, multicolored tumbleweeds of tangled wire.

"Where does this lead?" Creel whispered.

"Nowhere," Gonzalez replied. "It's a cul-de-sac."

"Sweet. So if the thing's in here, we've got it cornered."

Nobody answered.

Gonzalez peered along the tall metal casing, looking first left, then right. Then he turned to Phillips and Marcelin. "You two take the right-hand edge," he said. "And watch your six."

They nodded, then turned and crept down the narrow space between the wall and the first rack, weapons at the ready.

Gonzalez motioned to Creel. "We'll go down the left. Meet us at the rear door. If you see anything—anything at all—sing out."

"Got it."

Gonzalez walked alongside the storage rack until he reached the left-hand wall of the room. Then he turned the corner quickly, raking the area with his eyes. The end caps of the other storage racks retreated toward the back of the room, the narrow corridors between them dark. To the left, along the wall, were deep niches for additional storage. Gonzalez took a slow breath, then started forward again, glancing down each row of storage racks as he passed it. At the far end of each he could make out the forms of Phillips and Marcelin doing the same, advancing up the right side.

It was the work of a minute to reach the rear of the room. He turned and walked along the back wall until he met up with the others at the doorway leading to the second storage area. "Anything?" he asked.

Phillips shook his head.

Gonzalez nodded. The room had not only looked empty; it had felt empty. Searching radar support began to seem like a waste of time. The creature had probably retreated down the staircase to C Level. Why would it be here, in this dead end?

"Let's take the next," he said, reaching through the doorway and snapping on the lights in the room ahead. "Same procedure."

The second room seemed identical to the first: tall shelves full of long-forgotten equipment. It was as dead as the first room except for a faint humming noise, pitched very low, almost more felt than heard—excess air in the heating system, no doubt. Again, Gonzalez and Creel took the left-hand side, walking slowly and quietly along the storage racks, while the other two took the right. They reached the rear—which thanks to a burned-out bulb was only dimly illuminated—and once again rejoined Phillips and Marcelin at the doorway to the third room.

Gonzalez peered into the blackness ahead. "We'll check, just to be thorough. Then we'll go back to stairwell 12 and try C Level. Let's go, same procedure."

"Smell that?" Creel asked.

"Smell what?" said Phillips.

"I don't know. Hamburger or something."

Gonzalez reached in, snapped on the lights once again. A few fluorescent bulbs flickered into life. Then, seconds later, the nearest one dimmed with a quiet sizzle.

He frowned. *Shit. What a time for the ballast to go.* Now the distant part of the room lay in half-light, while the area directly ahead of them was shrouded in gloom.

Phillips snorted. "You picked a strange time to be hungry," he told Creel.

Gonzalez stepped through the doorway, the others following.

"No, man. I didn't mean *cooked* hamburger."

Gonzalez turned to the left, preparing to walk yet again along the storage rack, Creel right behind him. Then he stopped.

Ahead, where the walls met, he could make out the first of several equipment niches. Except this niche didn't contain the metal-sided radar units he'd observed before. Instead, something lay in the bottom; something that shone dully in the faint light.

"My head hurts," said Marcelin.

Gonzalez reached for his flashlight, stabbed its beam toward the niche. The light illuminated a twisting of clear plastic, something caked with dried blood inside.

Peters.

At that precise moment, Marcelin began to whimper.

Gonzalez wheeled around. *Something* was peeping out at them from around the opposite corner of the storage rack. In the brief moment that he saw it, Gonzalez registered a heavy, shaggy pelt of dark hair; a large ear, heart-shaped like a bat's and set at an angle lateral to the head; and a single yellow eye.

And there was something else. The head was too *high,* too high off the ground . . .

There was a roar in his ear as Creel's grenade launcher exploded. The shell rocketed along the storage case and exploded against a shelf half a dozen feet short of where the head had been. The room shook. Red-and-yellow smoke roiled back toward them and pieces of metal and vacuum-tube glass rained everywhere.

"Back!" Gonzalez yelled.

They scrambled back into the second room.

"Take up positions in the corners!" Gonzalez ordered. "Phillips, Marcelin, cover the door! Careful of crossfire!"

He retreated to the rear left corner of the second room and hunkered down, using the end cap of the last storage rack for cover, aiming his M16 at the darkened doorway. His heart was beating faster than it ever had in his life.

Creel was jabbering beside him. "Oh, God. Oh, God."

"Get behind me," Gonzalez said. "If it comes for us, aim at the door. The door, you hear me? If you shoot my men by accident, I'll shoot you."

But Creel didn't seem to hear. "Oh, *God* . . ."

"Ready yourselves!" Gonzalez shouted to the soldiers. There was no response from the far side of the room save a faint whimper that was probably Marcelin.

He sighted down the barrel of his M16, struggling to control the sudden, unfamiliar panic that had at first almost overwhelmed him. A dreadful minute passed, then two. Gonzalez tried to blink away the sweat coursing down his forehead. The low sound he'd noticed before was louder now, filling his ears and even his head with a dull ache that . . .

A headache. Marcelin had mentioned that, too—

Gonzalez went rigid. In the darkness of the doorway, something moved.

He blinked again, passed a hand quickly over his eyes. It was some trick of the dim light. But no: there *was* movement in the shadows, gray against gray. For a moment, it stopped. Then it started again and—slowly, slowly—the head slid out. A low noise, like the gargle of a drowning man, began to sound in Creel's throat. Gonzalez stared, paralyzed like the rest. Christ, it just seemed to keep on coming, dark and bullet-shaped, with a massive crest of bone at the rear leading to a set of incredibly powerful, high-set shoulders. It was like nothing Gonzalez had ever seen. It was magnificent. It was terrifying.

The head was fully through the doorway now, staring in the direction of Marcelin and Phillips. As Gonzalez watched, the head moved again and—with an agonizing, insolent slowness—turned to look at him. The yellow eyes seemed to hold his own eyes in thrall.

Then the jaw opened and Gonzalez's gaze dropped to it and—*sweet Jesus, what the hell were those* . . .

Abruptly he felt the hinges of his sanity begin to loosen. His finger twitched spasmodically against the trigger guard.

The gargle in Creel's throat changed to a low keening, then rose abruptly to a ragged scream.

And then the thing leapt toward them.

Everything happened at once. Creel yelled incoherently, falling backward instinctively while simultaneously raising his weapon. Phillips and Marcelin opened fire from the far corner, their bullets ripping along the wall and ricocheting over Gonzalez's head with sharp whines. Gonzalez felt himself brutally knocked to one side as the thing fell upon Creel: there was a low crunching, like the sound of a chicken joint giving way, and the foreman gave another terrible scream—this time of pain. Gonzalez leapt to his feet, room spinning, grabbed his gun, and whirled around, taking aim. He saw right away it was too late for Creel. The creature was taking him apart like a rag doll, coronas of blood and gore rising in a red mist. The others had stopped firing. As Gonzalez stared, the thing looked up at him, its face a mask of red. In the faint light, Gonzalez thought he saw the edges of its mouth raise in what could only have been a smile. And then he was running, running, past the storage racks and out the door in the wake of Phillips and Marcelin, through the first room and into the corridor and on, running, running . . .

41

The air in the life-sciences lab seemed to freeze. For a long moment, everybody in the room simply stared at Usuguk. For his part, the Tunit stood close to the doorway, motionless, his sealskin boots and his parka of caribou skin and blanket cloth in stark contrast to the drab metal walls and prosaic instruments.

"You," said Marshall, surprise thickening his voice. "You're the eighth scientist."

"That is what they called me," replied Usuguk.

Across the room, Logan frowned. "What do you mean?"

For a long time, Usuguk said nothing. His dark eyes looked at each of them in turn. Then they focused on a spot beyond all of them, a spot that to Marshall seemed far, far away. "I am an old man," he said. "May I sit?"

"Of course." Marshall hurried to get him a chair. The shaman lowered himself onto it, placed his medicine bundle on his knees.

"I was a specialist," he said in his uninflected accent. "Army specialist. I grew up a hundred miles from here. In the old days, my people lived in a settlement near Kaktovik. I lived with my cousin's family. My mother died giving birth to me, and my father starved to death when I was six, out on the ice, looking for caribou. I grew up foolish, full of *quiniq*. Back then, sitting for hours at a breathing hole, waiting to spear a seal—it was not enough for me. I did not respect the old ways. I did not understand the circle of beauty, the glamour of the snow. An army recruiter came through Kaktovik once a year, full of talk of far places. I had learned your language; my arm was strong. So I enlisted." He shook his head slowly. "But I spoke Inuit; I spoke Tunit. So after six months at Fort Bliss they sent me back here, to this base."

"Was the base operational?" Marshall asked.

"*Ahylah.*" The Tunit nodded. "All except the north wing. That was still being completed. It had to be built below the level of the snow."

"Why?" Logan asked.

"I do not know. It was a secret. For tests. Some experiments with sonar." Usuguk paused. "The army put several of us Tunits to work, digging out the ice for the north wing and placing supports. All Tunits knew the mountain to be a bad place where the evil gods dwell. But we were few, and poor, and the money of the *kidlatet*—white man—was hard to resist. My uncle was one of the workers. It was he who found it."

"Found what?" asked Marshall.

"*Kurrshuq,*" Usuguk said. "Fang of the Gods. The Devourer of Souls."

The others exchanged glances.

"What exactly is *kurrshuq*?" Logan asked.

"It is that which you have awakened."

"What?" Sully spoke up. "The same creature? That can't be."

The Tunit shook his head. "Not the same. Another."

Marshall felt surprise burn its way through him. *Was this possible?* Silence settled briefly over the group. "Go on," Sully said at last.

"It was encased in ice in a small crevasse at the base of the wing," Usuguk continued.

"Probably frozen by the same phenomenon," Faraday murmured.

"My uncle was very agitated. He came to me. And I went to Colonel Rose."

"The base commander," said Logan.

Usuguk nodded. "No one else was to know. My uncle had me tell the colonel that the army must leave the spot at once. It was forbidden ground. And the *kurrshuq* was its guardian." He paused. "But they did not leave. Instead the colonel sealed off the crevasse and summoned them."

"Them?" Marshall repeated.

"The special scientists. The secret scientists. They arrived before the new moon. Two cargo planes, their bellies full of strange instruments. These were all placed in the north wing, under darkness."

"So the north wing was re-tasked," Logan said. "Its original purpose set aside while the new discovery was examined."

"Yes."

"What of your uncle?" Logan continued. "The other Tunits?"

"They left immediately."

"But you stayed."

Usuguk bowed his head. "Yes. To my everlasting shame. I told you I had little use for the ways of my tribe. And the scientists needed a helper, someone who understood the operations of the base. Someone who could also act as—as protection. Since I already knew of the *kurrshuq,* I was selected. They were kind to me, included me in their work. They called me 'the little scientist.' One of them, the *kidlatet* called Williamson, was interested in . . ." He paused, apparently hunting for the word. "In sociology. I shared with him some of the legends of my people, our history and beliefs."

"And what of the . . . the creature?" Marshall asked.

"It was cut very carefully from the ice, taken from the crevasse, put in a freezer in the north wing. The scientists were to study it, measure it, then thaw it. But it soon thawed itself."

"Thawed *itself*?" Sully repeated.

"Of course." Usuguk shrugged as if perplexed by Sully's incredulous tone.

Marshall and Faraday exchanged glances. "It was alive?" Marshall asked.

"Yes."

"And it was hostile?"

"Not—not at first. *Kurrshuq* is a crafty demon. It plays with you, like the fox cub plays with a vole. The scientists were intrigued. Once they had recovered from their fear, they were intrigued."

"Their fear?" Marshall asked.

"The *kurrshuq* is terrifying to behold."

Logan pulled out a leather notebook. "Will you describe it?"

"No."

Another brief silence.

"Tell us what happened," Marshall said. "To the scientists."

"As I told you, it pretended to humor us. Pretended to be friendly. The scientists continued their observations and tests. They tested its strength and speed. They grew more and more excited— especially by its ability to defend itself. They talked of testing its intelligence, of finding ways to—what was the word they used?—of weaponizing it. But on the third day it chose to do the will of the evil gods. It wearied of toying with us. One of the scientists, the *kidlatet* named Blayne, was testing its . . . its instinct for the hunt. What they wanted it to hunt they would not tell me. He had a tape recorder, with the sounds of animals in distress—marmots, snowshoe rabbits. When he played the tape, it grew angry. It tore him to pieces. We heard his screams and came running. When we arrived his body was all over the audio lab. And the *kurrshuq* was asleep on the floor, Blayne's head between his forepaws. It had eaten his soul."

Marshall glanced at Logan. The historian had a small leather notebook open and was writing furiously.

"The scientists left without touching the body and returned to their quarters to talk. Some said that the creature should be killed immediately. Others said, no, it was too valuable a find. Maybe, they said, the death of Blayne was an accident. The creature was confused, acting in self-defense. They agreed to continue their study."

"Williamson, the one interested in sociology," Logan said, looking up from his notebook. "Did he discuss this with you?"

Usuguk nodded. "He asked me many questions. What my people knew of *kurrshuq*, why it was here, what it wanted."

"And what did you tell him?"

"I told him the truth. That it was the guardian of the forbidden mountain. That the Devourer of Souls could not be killed."

"What was his reaction?"

"He spent a lot of time writing in his little book."

Logan rummaged in his pocket, pulled out the faded journal, passed it to Usuguk. The Tunit opened it carefully, turned the yellowed pages, passed it back with a nod.

" 'The Tunits have the answer?' " Logan quoted. "Perhaps it was a question—not a statement."

"What happened next?" Sully asked.

"The next day, when we went back in, I was armed. It acted . . . differently. It was unresponsive, hostile. When the scientists pushed it, it attacked."

"It killed them all?" Sully went on.

"No. Not . . . not at once."

"How, then?"

As he talked, the Tunit's gaze had slowly lowered. Now he suddenly looked up, fixing them one after another with eyes haunted by memory. "Do not ask me," he said, voice trembling. "I do not wish to remember."

The room fell silent. Slowly, Usuguk let his gaze return to the distant point. His face relaxed, grew resigned once again.

"Did you shoot it?" Marshall asked as gently as he could.

Usuguk nodded without looking at him.

"What happened?"

"The bullets annoyed it."

Now Logan spoke. "How did you get away?"

"It was . . . stalking us. Those who remained alive tried to escape the north wing. It cut us off, once, twice. At last there was only me and Williamson. We were hiding in the electrical room, not far from the north wing exit hatch." His speech slowed, became halting. "It came out of the shadows . . . Williamson screamed . . . it leapt on him . . . he tumbled backward onto an electrical coupling . . . there was great light and smoke . . . I ran as quickly as I could out of the north wing."

There was a long pause in which nobody spoke.

"Colonel Rose sent for a special team," Usuguk continued at last. "When we returned to the north wing, we found the *kurrshuq*, still lying on Williamson's body. It no longer moved."

"Dead," Sully breathed.

Usuguk shook his head. "It chose to move on. To leave its corporal being."

"What did they do with its body?" Marshall asked.

"The body vanished."

"What?" Sully asked.

"They returned later with a body bag. By then it was gone." The Tunit looked at them in turn. "It is as I told you. It chose to return to its spirit form."

Sully shook his head. "Probably crawled off to die. They were in a hurry to close the place, cover up the whole incident—I'll bet they didn't look too hard for it."

Marshall looked at the shaman. "And you? What did you do?"

"I left the military. I took a few from my village who would listen and started a new community, out on the ice. We strove to live the old, true way of my people, the way they had lived for thousands of years, before the *kidlatet* came. I left the things of the physical world behind."

Sully wasn't listening. "Don't you see?" he said. "It's susceptible to electricity. That's its Achilles' heel. We need to get word to Gonzalez."

The Tunit looked up quickly. "Have you heard nothing I told you? This is not an animal. It is of the spirit world. You cannot kill it. That is the reason I came back—to tell you this. You did not listen to me the first time. You must listen now. Because I speak the truth. I am the *only one* who lived."

Sully did not respond. He walked across the room, picked up the radio Gonzalez had given him.

"There is a second reason I came back," Usuguk said, turning to Marshall. "The creature you found. You said it was larger than a polar bear, did you not?"

Marshall nodded. "That's right."

"The creature the scientists cut from the ice fifty years ago was the size of an arctic fox."

There was a shocked silence. For a moment, nobody stirred. Then Sully raised the radio, pressed the Transmit button. "Dr. Sully to Sergeant Gonzalez. Do you read me?"

The radio buzzed static.

Sully tried again. "Sully to Gonzalez. Do you read? Over."

More static.

As Sully tried again, Usuguk rose from the chair and came over to where Marshall and Faraday were standing. "After you came here—when the sky rained blood—I feared you had wakened another," he said. "That is why I warned you all to leave. I am a shaman. I have one foot in the physical world, and the other in the spirit world. You must believe that I understand these things."

"Another," Marshall repeated. He was still having trouble taking it in.

"Perhaps we shouldn't be surprised," said Faraday. "Game theory predicts that the least optimal result is the one most likely to occur."

"The size of a fox," Marshall said. "And it killed seven men."

Usuguk nodded. "Now do you believe me? This *kurrshuq* is an even more important spirit. It will not leave as the last one did. You cannot kill it. You cannot conquer it. You can only leave. There is still a chance it might allow that."

"But we can't leave," Marshall said. "There are too many of us for the Sno-Cat. We're trapped here, by the storm."

The Tunit looked at him with glittering eyes. "Then I am very sorry for you."

42

"It's supposed to be this rough?" Barbour asked through gritted teeth. "The ride, I mean?"

"Nope. Normally they cover the winter road portages in a layer of ice. But we're making our own road. Just grab the 'oh, shit!' handle."

"The what?"

"That stabilizer bar over your door."

Barbour reached up and took hold of the horizontal metal bar, then glanced at Carradine. The cab of the big truck was so large that the man was actually out of reach. It seemed his hands were constantly moving—over the steering wheel, to the gearshift, to one of the innumerable buttons on the dash. She had never ridden in an articulated lorry before and was astonished at how high off the ground they were—and just how rough it was.

"Have to keep our speed down to thirty," the trucker said, omnipresent wad of gum bulging one cheek. "Don't want to damage the trailer coupling. We'll have to slow down even more when we reach the lake, but at least the ride will be smoother then." He chuckled.

Barbour didn't like the sound of that chuckle. "What lake?"

"We'll have to cross one lake on the way to Arctic Village. Lost Hope Lake. It's too wide, can't be avoided. But it's been nice and cold, we shouldn't have any problems."

"You're joking, right?"

"Why do you think they call it ice-road trucking? On the regular winter road, eighty percent of the route is over ice. The portages only count for twenty percent of the trip."

Barbour didn't reply. *Lost Hope Lake,* she thought. *Let's hope it doesn't live up to its name.*

"We're lucky we've got this wind," Carradine went on. "It keeps the snow cover down, helps me find the most level route across the permafrost. We have to be very careful—can't risk getting a blowout, all those people back there without heat."

Barbour glanced into the rearview mirror. In the reflected running lights she could just make out the silver bulk of the trailer. *Thirty-five people inside.* She imagined them sitting in there, probably speaking very little, with only a flashlight or two for illumination. The heat would be waning by now.

Carradine had shown her how to use the CB radio to communicate with Fortnum. She plucked the handset from its cradle, made sure the proper frequency was selected, pressed the Talk switch. "Fortnum, you there?"

There was a brief crackle. "Here."

"How is it going back there?"

"Okay so far."

"Is it getting cold?"

"Not yet."

"I'll give you updates as we get farther south. Let me know if you need anything."

"Will do."

Barbour didn't know the proper etiquette for ending the conversation so she simply replaced the handset onto the transmitter. The last part of the exchange had been only for morale—there was of course nothing she could do to help them. She glanced over at Carradine. "How much farther?"

"To Arctic Village? It's two hundred and ten miles from the base to the northern outpost. That's where we're headed."

Two hundred and ten miles. They'd already been on the road nearly an hour. Barbour did a little mental calculation. They still had almost six hours to go.

Outside the broad windshield, the storm was a confusion of white flakes against a screen of black. The wind whipped huge skeins of snow up from the ground, exposing the featureless gray moonscape of permafrost beneath. Carradine had turned on every fog light and headlamp on the truck, and despite his light tone and joking manner she noticed just how carefully he watched the landscape ahead, gently turning the truck well before encountering a potential obstacle.

The cab bounced and shook until it seemed her teeth would loosen. She wondered how Sully and Faraday were getting on back at the base, whether or not Marshall had returned. Maybe she shouldn't have let Sully talk her into leaving. It was just as much her expedition as anybody else's; she wasn't only the computer specialist, she had important research that shouldn't be abandoned just because . . .

Something had changed. She glanced over at Carradine. "Are we slowing?"

"Yup."

"Why?"

"We're approaching Lost Hope Lake. Fifteen miles per hour, *maximum,* on the ice."

"But there's no heat back in the trailer. We can't delay."

"Lady, let me explain. Driving over a frozen lake creates a wave beneath the ice. That wave follows us as we cross. Drive too fast, the wave gets too large and breaks through the ice. If that happens, we sink to the bottom. The ice refreezes overhead in minutes and, presto, you've got a premade grave that—"

"Right. I get the picture."

Now, out of the darkness ahead, something glinted dully in the headlights. Barbour sat up, peering intently—and nervously. Ice, stretching into the distance until it became lost in the storm.

Carradine slowed the truck still further, working his way down through the gears, then let it roll to a stop with a chuff of air brakes. He reached back into the sleeper cabin, pulled out a long tool shaped like a svelte jackhammer. "Be right back," he said, opening his door.

"But—" she began to protest.

The trucker stepped out and shut the door behind him, dropping down out of sight, and she fell silent. A moment later she saw him again, trotting out ahead of the truck, an incongruous sight in his tropical shirt, tool balanced on one shoulder. The wind had eased, and skeins of snow curled around him almost caressingly. As she watched, he stepped onto the ice, walking perhaps fifty yards out. He unshouldered the tool, fired it up, and applied it to the ice. It was, she realized, a power auger. Within thirty seconds he had broken through and was trotting back toward the cab. He climbed up, opened the door, and swung in. He was smiling widely. A thin coating of ice covered his hair and shoulders.

"You're just bloody daft, you know that?" she said. "Going out into a storm, dressed like that."

"Cold is a state of mind." Carradine threw the auger into the back, then rubbed his hands together—out of chill or anticipation, Barbour couldn't guess. "The ice is twenty-two inches thick."

"Is that bad?"

"That's good. Eighteen inches is the minimum. We're ahead of the season. This here is good for twenty-five, maybe thirty tons." He jerked a finger toward the auger, chuckling. "I know this trip's kind of low-tech. No continuous profiling, no ice radar, like they have on the real winter road. But hey, we don't have any load restrictions or pain-in-the-ass dispatchers, either."

He looked at her a minute. "Okay. I'll tell you something now, just so you'll be prepared. Driving on ice isn't like driving on a normal road. It bends with the truck. And it makes a lot of noise."

"What?"

"It's better if you hear it for yourself." He released the brake, put the truck in gear. "Now I'm going to ease us onto the lake. You don't want to hit it too fast and stretch the ice."

"Stretch it? No, no, you certainly don't want to do that." Barbour looked out at the seeming limitless span of ice that lay ahead. Were they really going to drive an eighteen-wheel truck onto *that*?

"All right." Carradine let the truck creep forward toward the shore, then glanced at her again and winked. "Here's where you cross your fingers, ma'am."

They crept forward onto the ice at little more than ten miles per hour. Barbour tensed as she felt the shaking and pounding of the permafrost give way to the far more unsettling sensation of ice flexing beneath them. Carradine frowned with concentration, one hand on the wheel, the other grasping the gearshift. The engine whined as they moved forward. "Gotta keep the RPMs high," he muttered. "Helps prevent spinning out."

As they ventured farther onto the ice, Barbour could hear a new sound—a faint crackling that seemed to come from all around her, like the sound of cellophane being torn from a Christmas toy. She swallowed painfully. She knew what that sound was: the ice, protesting under the massive weight of the big-rig truck.

"How far across?" she asked a little hoarsely.

"Four miles," Carradine replied, not taking his eyes from the ice.

They kept on at what seemed a snail's pace, the crackling growing louder. Snow skittered along the ice, forming eddies and cyclones and odd phantasmal shapes in the headlights. Now and then Barbour heard sharp pops and booms from beneath. She bit her lip, mentally counting the minutes. Suddenly, the truck yawed sideways, sliding to the right. She looked quickly at the trucker.

"Gust of wind," he said, turning the wheel very gently to compensate. "No traction out here."

The CB radio chirped. Barbour reached for the handset. "Fortnum?"

"Yes. What's all that noise outside? People back here are getting a little worried."

She thought a moment before replying. "We're going over an icy patch. Should just be a couple of minutes more."

"Understood. I'll pass the word."

She replaced the handset, exchanged glances with Carradine.

Five minutes crawled by, then ten. Barbour realized her right hand had gone numb from gripping the stabilizer bar. The faint give of the ice, the constant crackling and snapping sounds, made her so tense she feared she'd go mad. The wind moaned and cried. Now and then a stronger gust would shove the truck sideways, forcing Carradine to compensate with the greatest of care.

She peered ahead through the murk. Was that the far shore in the distance? But no—it was just a dark wall of icy pellets that hung in the air, shifting and throbbing in the wind like a rippling curtain.

"Ice fog," Carradine explained. "The air can't hold any more moisture."

The strange mist began to envelope the truck like a cloud of black cotton. The visibility, poor to begin with, abruptly dropped to near zero.

"Can't see a bloody thing," Barbour said. "Slow down."

"Can't," the trucker replied. "Can't lose momentum."

This new blindness, combined with the awful flexing and crackling of the ice beneath them, was simply too much for Barbour. She felt herself hyperventilating, drowning in anxiety. *Hold on, luv,* she told herself. *Just hold on. Only a minute or two more.*

And then they were through the cloud of ice—and now she could see the rocks of the far shore, at the very limit of the headlight beams. Relief flooded through her. *Thank God.*

Carradine took his eyes from the ice long enough to glance at her. "That wasn't so bad, was it?"

Suddenly the truck gave a sharp lurch downward. At the same time there was a loud crack, like the report of a gun, just behind them. "Soft spot," said Carradine, stepping heavily on the accelerator. "Weak ice."

They pushed forward faster now, the big diesel whining. Another crack, louder, this one from directly below. Barbour saw that a split had formed in the ice and was now shooting out ahead of them with increasing speed, the two sections pulling apart. Carradine immediately compensated, maneuvering the truck so the crack stayed between the front wheels. But ahead the crack forked, once, twice, spreading across the ice at crazy angles like summer lightning. Carradine turned the wheel sharply, moving laterally over the webbing of cracks. The popping and snapping spiked abruptly in volume. Just then a brutal gust of wind caught the side of the truck. Barbour cried out as she felt the rear of the truck twist, then tilt alarmingly, threatening to jackknife and overturn on the collapsing ice.

"Spinout!" Carradine shouted. "Hold on!"

Barbour clung desperately to the stabilizer bar as the trucker fought to keep the big vehicle from rolling. Slowly, forward momentum brought them level to the ice. The far shore was just ahead now, less than fifty yards away. But the truck was still in a barely controlled spin. It collided with one of the shoreline rocks in a shuddering crash, lurched away, then stabilized. Carradine goosed the throttle again and the truck roared off the ice and back onto the washboard surface of the permafrost.

Barbour exhaled a long, shivering breath. Then she reached for the CB handset. "Fortnum, it's Penny Barbour. Everyone all right back there?"

After a moment, Fortnum's crackly voice replied. "A little shaken up but otherwise okay. What happened?"

"A gust of air caught us. But we're off the ice now, and it should be clear sailing the rest of the way."

As she replaced the handset, she happened to glance at Carradine. He was peering into his rearview mirror. Seeing the expression on his face, her anxiety returned.

"What is it?" she asked.

"That rock we hit," he replied. "Looks like it holed our left tank."

"Petrol tank? But don't you have two?"

"The left tank was full. The right one isn't. It's only a third full."

The feeling of anxiety spiked sharply. "But we've got enough to get to Arctic Village—don't we?"

Carradine didn't look at her. "No, ma'am. I don't believe we do."

43

They had worked quickly, in as little light as possible. Precisely how much the beast relied on sight, Gonzalez didn't know—but there was no point making it any easier for the goddamned thing.

He tapped Phillips on the shoulder, then gestured toward the dimly lit intersection ahead. "Cover that corner," he whispered. "I'll make the final connections."

"Yes, sir."

"Signal the minute you hear anything."

"Sir."

He watched Phillips move down the hallway—a shadow among shadows—and take position near the intersection. Then he glanced at the hastily constructed setup immediately before him: half a dozen thick copper wires, hanging from the ceiling and suspended a foot over a shallow pool of water. Crude, but lethal enough once he'd finished. Then he slipped back through the doorway marked MOTIVIC POWER STATION.

He stopped just inside, looking around at the complex arrays of cogs, couplings, shafts, rotors, and hydraulics. The substation housed the giant machinery once used to turn the radar dishes. He had chosen this particular room for three reasons: it was nearby, it had sufficient power, and it lay along the lone hallway that led out of this section of B Level. Sooner or later, the creature would have to come this way.

His eyes drifted to a far corner of the room, where Corporal Marcelin stood, weapon at his feet, trembling, eyes downcast. Then, picking up the loose ends of the copper wires—he and Phillips had run them over the pipes of the hallway ceiling and through the transom above the door—he headed toward the main electrical panel. Though the radar dishes hadn't been spun up in almost half a century, the electrical connections that fed them were still operational. He'd just tested them himself: the fuses were a little powdery, the connections rusted, but they were still capable of plenty of current. Besides, he didn't need to use the radar dishes—he just needed to run power to them.

How and why Sully and the others in the life-sciences lab thought electricity was the beast's particular weakness, Gonzalez didn't know and didn't care. He was simply relieved—relieved as hell—to know it had one. Coming up with a plan, putting it into action, had taken fifteen minutes. And during that fifteen minutes he'd been too mercifully busy to think.

The main panel was set into the closest wall, fixed to the metal by four ceramic insulators. He opened its cover plate and shone his light inside. Four rows of heavy-duty fuses glinted back at him. He checked to make sure the mains were off, then used his pocketknife to strip the heavy insulation from the ends of the eight-gauge wires. As quickly as he could, he affixed the wires directly to one of the bus bars. He swept his gaze over the panel, ensuring that all the safeties were disconnected. Finally, he reached over, grasped the fail-safe lever beside the panel, and thrust it into the On position. There was a faint hum as the circuit went live.

Now the wires were crawling with six thousand volts and twenty amps of juice. That kind of voltage—three times the amount of an electric chair—would seize the heart of any beast, no matter how big. And Gonzalez wasn't taking any chances: the twenty amps would cook it nicely, to boot.

He shifted the fail-safe lever back into the Off position and turned to Marcelin. "Come here, Corporal."

For a minute, Marcelin didn't seem to hear. Then he picked up his M16 and came forward on wooden legs.

"Wait here. When I give the word, throw this lever. Do it *quickly*. Got that?"

The corporal nodded.

"Take up position by the doorway. Wait until the thing has stepped into the water, made contact with the wires. Then open fire—and keep firing."

Marcelin moved next to the electrical panel. Gonzalez took one last look at the jury-rigged connection, then stepped out into the hallway and took up his own position, careful to keep well away from the wires. He checked his weapon, ejected the magazine, knocked it gently against the ground, slapped it back into place. Now there was nothing to do but wait.

He gave his plan a quick run-through. It had been more than thirty years since he'd studied elementary engineering, but he remembered the basics well enough. Electricity passes easily through water. Organisms are mostly water, making them good conductors of electricity. So: hang enough live wires from the ceiling that the creature would have to come in contact with at least one, and hang them low enough so that it couldn't crawl beneath. Pour enough water on the floor to create a shallow pool, and make sure it reached from wall to wall. Position the wires over the water and apply positive current. When the beast walked through the wires, it would complete the circuit—and good night, ladies.

It seemed foolproof enough. Now all they needed was for the thing to show up.

He crouched lower, minimizing his profile. He could see the dim form of Phillips up ahead at the intersection. Phillips was the lure. The private had a good vantage down both corridors; he'd see the beast when it was still far away. Once he was sure he'd been spotted, he would retreat down the hall, past the wires and over the water, to the spot where Gonzalez waited. As the beast approached, they'd signal Marcelin to throw the lever—and the frigging thing would fry.

Gonzalez snugged the stock of his M16 against his cheek, sighted along the barrel. While he'd been checking the electrical box, running the wires, he had been all too aware that the creature might surprise them at any moment. Now that everything was in place, he had time to think. And he did not want to think. Because he knew where his thoughts would stray: to the sight of the thing tearing Creel into dog food; to those horrible moments of mad, mindless flight away from radar support, never knowing if the next moment, he'd feel teeth sink into his back, feel those claws rip his limbs from his body . . .

He shifted position. No point in maintaining silence anymore now that the trap was set. "Phillips," he called out. "Anything?"

From the pool of light at the intersection, Phillips shook his head, formed an X with his forearms.

Gonzalez shifted again in the darkness. Creel's rocket had been sadly off target; it wasn't surprising that it didn't stop the creature. But the hail of bullets that had followed: Was it possible they all missed? Because if they hadn't missed, then that meant . . .

Gonzalez didn't want to think about what that meant.

Maybe it was dead. Maybe that was it. It had been mortally wounded, and its carcass was lying back there somewhere in the dark passages. Or maybe it had gone down to C Level. Maybe they'd be sitting here for hours, in the dark, waiting . . .

Gonzalez shook his head savagely to clear these thoughts. He glanced into the substation, toward the motionless figure of

Marcelin. The corporal was in bad shape. He was confident—reasonably confident—the man could be relied on to pull the fail-safe switch. It was a chance he had to take. He couldn't be in two places at one time, and Phillips needed him to . . .

Movement at the corner of his eye made him glance back down the corridor. Phillips was gesturing frantically, a stricken look on his face.

"Is it coming?" Gonzalez called. "You see it?"

Phillips fumbled one-handed with his gun, dropped it, frantically picked it up again. And all the time he was holding his other hand over his head, waving it, looking for all the world like a New Year's Eve reveler twirling a noisemaker.

"Get the hell back here!" Gonzalez cried out. "Marcelin, get ready with that switch!"

But Phillips didn't move. He just stood there, mouth working, as if terror had snatched his voice from him.

Gonzalez squinted into the darkness, frowning, trying to get a better look at Phillips. Focusing on the upraised hand, he could see now that it wasn't just waving. It was pointing. Pointing at a spot *behind* Gonzalez.

Fear gripped the sergeant's vitals. He looked quickly over his shoulder, back down the corridor behind him.

It was there: black against black, perhaps fifty feet away, moving with a stealthiness Gonzalez would never have guessed possible for such a huge creature. He stared in horror. For a moment, his heart faltered in his chest. Then it exploded into life again, hammering against his ribs. He tumbled backward, splashing through the water, electrical wires dancing crazily as he half ran, half fell down the corridor toward Phillips. *It's not possible,* a voice was saying in some distant part of his brain. *This corridor is the only way out. There's no way for it to have gotten past us.* And yet somehow it had. As Gonzalez took up a position beside Phillips, gasping, he saw the thing pause briefly, its unblinking yellow eyes staring coldly at them, before creeping forward again.

"Marcelin!" Gonzalez cried. "Marcelin, *now!*"

There was no response from the substation.

"Marcelin, *throw the goddamn switch*!"

Was that the low hum of the transformer applying the load? It was hard to tell over his gulps for breath, over the painful pressure that once again seemed to suddenly fill his head. The creature was still creeping toward them. Another few seconds and it would pass the door to the substation . . . and reach the wires. Gonzalez fell forward on the ground, the butt of the outstretched M16 snugged against his cheek. He tried to aim at the thing but the barrel of his weapon kept rising and falling with the beat of his heart. The beast was moving more quickly now, as if abandoning any pretense of stealth.

"Oh, my God," Phillips was saying, in a voice that was half prayer, half whimper. "My God. My God . . ."

Another step. Then another. As it approached, the creature never took its gaze from them, never blinked, never hesitated. There was something so awful about that look that Gonzalez felt himself go slack with dread. It was all he could do to keep the rifle from slipping through his fingers and clattering to the floor.

And then the creature reached the water. As Gonzalez watched, it hesitated a moment. Then it thrust itself between two of the dangling wires.

For a moment, nothing happened. And then the corridor filled with a tremendous, ear-splitting crack. Livid lightning danced from wire to wire, arcing over the creature's massive haunches, spitting a hundred forking tongues toward the ceiling. The air filled with the smell of ozone. Gonzalez felt the small hairs on the back of his neck stand on end. Gray smoke billowed up in angry waves, filling the corridor, blotting the creature from view. There was a rising whine as the transformer tried to draw more current. The lights flickered—once, twice—followed by a hollow *boom* as the transformer overloaded. The corridor fell into utter blackness.

"My God," Phillips was still repeating, tonelessly, like a mantra. "My God."

The lights snapped on again as a secondary transformer picked up the load. The wires jerked and danced, raining fitful showers of sparks. Gonzalez peered through the roiling pall of smoke, searching desperately for a glimpse of the thing. It had to be dead. It *had* to. Nothing could live through that . . .

The creature's head poked through the leading edge of the smoke. Gonzalez gasped, tightened his grip on his weapon. As the smoke began to slowly dissipate, more of the creature became visible. Black scorch marks were seared across its withers. For a moment it remained as still as death.

And then it opened its mouth.

Inside the substation, Marcelin began to scream.

The creature swiveled toward the noise. It reared back on powerful haunches. Then it turned and—slowly, deliberately—disappeared inside the doorway. And as he watched, unable to move, unable to act, Gonzalez's heart seemed to accelerate with the pitch of Marcelin's screams.

44

"What was that?" Conti turned suddenly, camera tilting dangerously on his shoulder.

Once again, all three paused to listen.

Wolff cocked his head to one side. "I don't hear anything," he said. "This is the third time you've done that."

"I tell you, I heard something. A shout, I think. Or maybe it was a cry." Conti pointed down the corridor. "It came from that direction."

Kari Ekberg followed the director's outstretched finger with her eyes. The corridor led into blackness. It was so dark she couldn't make out its end. It was as if it led on forever, into the icy wastes beneath the arctic night. She shivered despite the humid warmth.

They had been looking for Gonzalez's team, unsuccessfully, for half an hour now. They had first tried the staging area, only to find it deserted save for a large cache of weapons. After that they had moved around the central wing in widening circles. As the minutes passed, Conti had gotten increasingly restless: complaining bitterly about the time he had squandered in convincing them to assist him, fretting over and over that he was missing his "window of opportunity." As their search shifted to the southern wing of the base, Ekberg felt herself growing more and more uneasy. It seemed to her just as likely they'd find the creature as Gonzalez's party.

"Let's keep moving," Conti said. "The infirmary's just ahead."

"I know," Wolff said. "I was there, too—remember? What makes you think the sergeant came this way?"

"I heard them saying that Ashleigh and that soldier were killed not far from it," the director replied.

"Seems to me a good reason to stay away," Ekberg said.

Conti didn't bother to answer. Instead, he snapped on the camera's supplemental illumination. Yellow light filled the corridor, throwing the old equipment scattered against the walls into sharp relief.

"If you're so eager to find them," Wolff said, "why not just use the radio?"

"Can't do that," Conti replied. "That sergeant doesn't believe in my work. None of them do. They'd probably give us false directions, just to throw us off. Or confiscate the camera. We can't take the chance."

He led the way down the hallway. Most of the doors they passed were closed; the ones that were open gave onto shadow-haunted spaces full of unidentifiable gear. They descended a staircase, turned a corner.

"That's it, right?" Conti said. "That door on the left?"

Wolff nodded.

Ekberg followed the two into a small waiting room. She had never been in this section of the base and, despite her unease, looked around curiously at the dusty medical supplies and ancient, fading labels of the bottles stored behind glass fronts. Conti had already walked into the next room, and when she heard his sharp intake of breath she knew he had found something. Peering in after him, she saw two sheeted bodies lying on an examination table. One was abnormally short, as if made up of parts rather than an intact corpse. The plastic coverings were so thickly smeared with blood and fluids that the remains were utterly obscured. Ekberg quickly looked away.

"Kari," Conti said.

She was so overcome with horror that she did not reply.

"Kari," he repeated. "Turn on the sound pack."

It was all she could do to switch on the mixer, plug in the microphone cable. Conti hovered over the bodies, the glare from his camera raking them pitilessly. "They're here," he said into his lavalier mic, his voice fraught with the gravity of the moment. "The newest victims. One was a simple soldier, doing his part in the service of our country, who gave his life trying to protect others. The other was one of our own, Ashleigh Davis, who was also doing a service—a service in its way no less vital. She came to this godforsaken place in order to solve a great mystery. She was an intrepid journalist who never shirked danger, never hesitated to put her life on the line for others, whether for enlightenment or entertainment. The thing that killed them is still out there—as is the party of soldiers bent on its destruction."

He fell silent, but his camera lingered over the sheeted bodies, passing back and forth, zooming in, panning out.

"They'll never let you show that on the air," Wolff said.

"I'm thinking of the DVD to follow," Conti said. "The director's cut." He lowered the camera. "This was a lucky break."

"A lucky break?" Ekberg asked. "What are you talking about?"

"Finding them here. I was afraid they'd be in cold storage already."

Wasn't so lucky for them, Ekberg thought. She began to object but held her tongue. It wouldn't do any good.

They returned to the corridor and continued, their footsteps echoing hollowly on the floor. Now and then Conti called a halt and stood motionless, listening intently. There was an expression on his face she'd never seen before: a strangely furtive eagerness. His eyes shone with it. She glanced uneasily at Wolff. In the reflected light of the camera, his face was set in a dubious frown.

Another intersection, another endless hall. Conti stopped once again. "Look," he said, pointing the camera down the hall like an oversized flashlight. "Isn't that blood on the floor?"

Ekberg followed the beam of light. He was right: maybe twenty yards ahead, sprays of what could only be blood covered the floor of the hallway. They seemed to have come from an open doorway marked P-H STAGING ROOM. A confusing welter of bloody footprints led in and out of the room and down the far end of the corridor. Ekberg felt a spike of anxiety.

Conti trotted ahead, fitting the camera's viewfinder to his eye. Ekberg watched as he pointed the lens at the blood, panning left to right in a long, lingering take. Then he stepped up to the door—bloodying his own shoes in the process—and began shooting the interior of the room. He motioned for Ekberg to run the sound again.

"This is where the outrage occurred," he intoned. "This is where the unspeakable finality of death overtook them. Death at the hands of what can only be described as a monster—a monster whose secrets we are now committed to uncovering . . . and putting to an end."

He gestured for Ekberg to kill the sound. Lowering the camera, he pointed excitedly at the ground before him. "Look. Those tracks—there are three sets at least! That's got to be Gonzalez and his men." He paused, scrutinizing the floor more carefully. "My God. Is this the monster's spoor?" He raised the camera again, panned ahead of them along the corridor.

As Ekberg came forward, she avoided looking into the room where Ashleigh and the soldier named Fluke had died, focusing instead on the bloody splotch Conti was staring at. It couldn't be the tread of a creature—it couldn't. It was too big; its shape was too unnatural. Something about it disturbed her violently and she looked away.

"Beautiful," Conti murmured as he filmed. "Just beautiful. The only thing better would be if—" Remembering himself, he fell silent. He lowered the camera and shot a hooded gaze in the direction of Wolff and Ekberg.

The faint lighting in the hallway dimmed, brightened, dimmed again. Then it went out completely. And Ekberg found herself in utter darkness. She heard a surprised hiss from Wolff. A few seconds later, the light came back on, somewhat fainter than before.

Conti heaved the camera back onto his shoulder. "Ready?"

"I'm not sure this is a good idea," Wolff said.

"What are you talking about? We know where they went now. This is precisely what we came for—we have to hurry." And he trotted forward. After a moment, Wolff followed. Ekberg swung in behind, hugely reluctant.

The corridor ended at an intersection, where the bloody tracks clearly went right. They passed several doors and a stairwell leading down to C Level before the tracks petered out. They stopped at the point where the last faint fleck of blood was visible on the floor.

"Well?" Wolff asked.

Conti pointed ahead. "The hallway dead ends in that room, there." And again he fitted his eye to the camera and moved forward.

Ekberg remained motionless, watching the director as he proceeded toward a double door stenciled RADAR SUPPORT. The doors were open and—surprisingly—a few lights were on within. As she watched, Conti stepped through. He looked first right, then left. And then he froze. For a long moment he remained motionless. At last he turned on the camera, filmed for perhaps fifteen seconds. Then he glanced out into the corridor.

"Kari?" he said in a strange, thick voice. "Could you come here a moment?"

She walked down the corridor, stepped through the doorway. Directly before her was a huge metal rack full of ancient, dusty equipment. When she looked at Conti inquiringly, he simply nodded over her shoulder. She turned, looking in the indicated direction. At first she saw nothing. But then she looked down, in the corner, where the floor met the adjoining walls. A head lay there, upturned, staring at her with an expression that almost seemed accusatory. She staggered backward, reeling under a double blow of shock and horror. A part of her registered that this had been Creel, the foreman of the roustabout team they'd hired from Anchorage. The head had been torn rudely from its shoulders, and arterial blood sprayed in a wide corona around it. A few feet away, two booted feet peeped out almost impishly from behind the edge of the metal rack.

She groaned, stepping backward quickly. As she did, she bumped roughly into something. Turning, she looked directly into the wide lens of Conti's camera. He had been filming her. She could see the reflection of her face in the glass—a small face, pale, vulnerable, frightened.

"Stop it!" she heard herself cry. "Goddamn you, stop it, stop it, *stop it*!"

45

"I've finished my analysis of the blood from the vault shards," Faraday said quietly.

Marshall glanced over at him. The biologist was staring up from his position at the fixed-angle centrifuge. He had spent the last several minutes moving from the stereozoom microscope to the centrifuge and back again, and the eyepieces of the microscope had left marks that made him look like a raccoon.

"And?" Marshall prompted.

"It's unlike anything I've ever encountered."

Sully sighed impatiently. Gonzalez hadn't reported in, and he was taking the wait badly. "Specifics would help, Wright."

Faraday replaced his glasses and blinked at Sully. "It concerns the white blood cells. Mostly."

Sully waved his hand, as if to say, *we're waiting*.

"You know white blood cells are all about infections, inflammation, and the rest. The neutrophils, lymphocytes, basophils, etcetera—they're tasked with defense, with wound healing. Well, this organism has a hyper-developed white blood cell line. It's like a healing machine on steroids. There's an incredibly high concentration of monocytes. And they're not at all typical—they're *huge*. They're clearly capable of transforming into macrophages and dumping a ton of cytokines and other chemicals into the bloodstream, promoting almost instant healing."

When nobody replied, Faraday continued. "There's something else. The tests indicate a chemical compound in the blood and cell tissue very similar to arylcyclohexylamine."

"Come again?" said Marshall.

"It's the causative agent in PCP. And it's present in the creature's blood in a remarkably high concentration—more than one hundred nanograms per milliliter. I believe it's an NMDA receptor antagonist, acting as both a stimulator and an anesthetic. What I can't understand is how the creature could produce such a chemical—I've never seen anything like it before in nature, certainly not in these concentrations. Assuming it's not exogenous, perhaps the anterior pituitary gland is releasing it into the bloodstream as a response to stress. Anyway, such a flood of exotic chemicals in the bloodstream would account for its apparent imperviousness to bullets and other injury. It simply doesn't feel the wounds, and—"

"This is all very interesting," Sully interrupted. "But it doesn't get us any closer to the real goal: finding the damn thing's Achilles' heel."

"He's right," Logan said. "The most important thing is learning how to stop it."

"Maybe it's been stopped already," Marshall said. He glanced around the life-sciences lab with eyes made bleary by the long trek through the snowstorm. "Maybe it's dead. Electricity worked last time."

"Last time, the beast they were dealing with was much smaller," Sully replied. "We don't even know if it was the same species."

"It was the same," Usuguk said. "*Kurrshuq* is *kurrshuq*. The difference is size, power, capacity for evil."

Marshall glanced over at the Tunit, sitting cross-legged on the floor of the lab. He had taken several fetishlike items from his medicine bundle and arrayed them on the ground before him. Picking up each in turn, he spoke to it in a low, singsong tone, full of pleading and urgency. Then he carefully replaced it on the ground, gave it a loving half turn, and picked up the next.

"What are you doing?" Marshall asked.

"Performing a ceremony," was the response.

"I gathered that. What kind?"

"This has become a place of unrest. Of evil. I am asking my guardian spirits for help."

"Why don't you ask them to send down a couple of bazookas while you're at it?" said Sully. "M20s, preferably."

There was a noise in the corridor outside. The speed with which everyone save Usuguk turned toward it drove home to Marshall just how much tension was in the air. The knob turned and the door pushed open. Sergeant Gonzalez and a private—the one named Phillips—stood outside. They came in slowly and closed the door behind them.

"Well?" demanded Sully.

Gonzalez walked stiff-legged into the center of the room. He unshouldered his M16 and let it drop to the floor. Phillips simply stood where he was, ashen-faced.

"Is it dead?" asked Marshall.

Gonzalez shook his head wearily.

"And the trap?" asked Logan. "The electricity?"

"The electricity made it mad," replied Gonzalez.

"Why don't you tell us what happened?" Marshall asked quietly.

The sergeant's gaze drifted toward the floor. For nearly a minute he said nothing. Then at last he fetched a deep breath.

"We set it up just like you said. Standing water on the floor, atop a metal plate. A curtain of bare wires hanging down from the ceiling, attached to a high-voltage source. In a corridor the beast would have to traverse if it wanted to reach the rest of the base."

"And?" Marshall prompted.

"It flanked us somehow. Came up from the rear. I don't know how it got around our position, but it did. We managed to fall back. It approached, hit the wires. Took the full electrical load." He shook his head at the memory.

"What kind of current?" asked Logan.

"Six thousand volts."

"That's impossible," said Faraday. "You must have mis-wired it somehow. Nothing could take that kind of charge and survive."

"I didn't mis-wire it. It went off like a goddamned explosion."

"And the creature?" asked Marshall.

"Charred its pelt here and there. That's about it."

A brief silence ensued.

"How did you get back?" Sully asked.

"Marcelin was inside the substation, controlling the current. He began to scream. The creature went for him. We managed to run past while . . ." Gonzalez didn't bother finishing the sentence.

Another, longer silence settled over the room. Marshall glanced around again at the deflated faces. Not until now—when faced with failure—did he realize just how much he'd been relying on Gonzalez and his team to succeed. He had put so much faith in the Tunit's story, on electricity being the way to combat the creature, that this setback seemed almost unbearable. And yet there was something in what Gonzalez had just said that sounded a familiar ring. He searched his memory for a connection.

And then, quite suddenly, he realized what it was.

"Just a moment," he said aloud.

The others turned toward him.

"Maybe it wasn't the electricity that made it mad."

"What are you suggesting?" asked Logan.

"This creature is a complete mystery to us, right? It's a freak of nature, a genetic aberration. Its blood is completely abnormal. Conventional weaponry doesn't seem to have much effect on it. So why should we presume to understand its motivations—or its emotions—or anything else about it?"

"What's your point?" asked Sully.

"My point is this. All along we've been assuming this creature is only interested in murdering us all. What if it didn't start out that way? Remember what Toussaint said? That it plays with you. Maybe that's actually what it was doing: playing."

"Usuguk said the same thing," added Logan. "About the other one. It played like a fox cub plays with a vole."

"Playing?" repeated Sully. "Was the thing playing when it first killed that production assistant, Peters?"

"Maybe it didn't know what it was doing. Or didn't care. That can be part of playing, too—a cat doesn't have any feelings for the pain of a mouse. The point is, maybe the creature wasn't *deliberately* trying to kill. Not at first. When Peters's body was placed in the infirmary, it came and took it back—like it would a plaything. And look at Toussaint—he was hung up like a toy. And there's something else. It has killed, it has torn to pieces—but it hasn't eaten any of its victims. Not a one."

"Something we did angered it," said Logan.

Marshall nodded. "And I think I know what it was. What did everyone who's been killed so far have in common? They *all screamed*."

"Kind of a normal reaction when you're faced with a blood-thirsty monster," said Sully.

"Marcelin screamed," Marshall went on. "Didn't Sergeant Gonzalez here imply that's why the creature went after it instead of him?"

"And Ashleigh Davis," Logan added. "The soldiers heard her scream, as well."

"Creel screamed, too," Gonzalez said. "It went right over me to get at him."

Marshall turned toward Usuguk. "And you said that the first beast, the smaller one, didn't become angry until it was played tapes of animals in distress. Rabbits screaming. But Toussaint *didn't* scream. We heard him on the camera's audio track. He just murmured under his breath: no, no, no."

"This is nothing but arrant speculation," said Sully.

"It's not speculation when every action conforms to a pattern," replied Logan.

"For all we know, the screams simply caught its attention," Sully went on.

"Clearly all its senses are exquisitely acute," said Marshall. "It wouldn't need sound to catch its attention."

The room went silent. All eyes, Marshall saw, were on him. Even Usuguk had put down his totem and was regarding him intently.

"I think sound is painful to this creature, perhaps exquisitely so," Marshall said. "Specifically, sounds of a certain frequency and amplitude—such as a scream. Look at its ears, how closely they resemble a bat's. Sound might have a completely different effect on it than it has on us. I think the creature perceives a scream as a threat, an act of aggression . . . and acts accordingly."

"And after it's been screamed at enough," Logan added, "it assumes we are hostile—and grows angry."

Marshall nodded. "Instead of killing us as a side effect of play, it begins to kill in earnest. For self-protection."

"This is too much," said Sully. "What do you suggest—that we kill it with sound?"

"I suggest that we look into the possibility, yes," Marshall said. "At least, hurt it enough to drive it away."

"Even if we could, just how would we do that?" Sully went on. "This is a radar installation. Radar uses electromagnetic waves, not sound waves."

For a moment, nobody answered. Then Logan spoke again. "There's the science wing."

"What about it?" Sully asked.

"I know from that old journal its original use was something to do with sonar technology. I don't know what, and Usuguk here couldn't provide anything beyond a confirmation. Maybe it was some new submarine equipment, and they needed a remote place to research it undisturbed. Maybe it was meant to somehow supplement the phased radar arrays of the base. But remember: this research was abandoned when the creature was found, and the north wing re-tasked."

"But for all we know the original equipment was already in place before the creature was discovered." Marshall turned to Usuguk. "Do you remember seeing instruments, tools, in the north wing?"

The Tunit nodded. "Much was covered with sheets or tarps. Others were still in crates. And there was a room, large, round, with padding on the walls like caribou fur."

"Perhaps an echo chamber of some sort," said Faraday.

"But even if there are instruments stored there," asked Logan, "who has the acoustic experience to put them to use?"

"That's not the problem," said Sully. "All of us took the requisite electrical engineering courses in graduate school."

"You've seen my keyboard," said Marshall. "I built an analog synthesizer in college."

"I was a ham radio operator," added Faraday. "Still have my license."

Logan turned toward Gonzalez. "So how about it? Now will you let us in?"

"Nobody has been inside the north wing in fifty years," the sergeant replied.

"That's not an answer," said Logan.

For a moment, Gonzalez said nothing. Then he gave a curt nod.

"What about Kari Ekberg and the others?" Marshall asked.

Gonzalez pulled out his radio. "Gonzalez to Conti. Repeat, Gonzalez to Conti. Come in."

No response but static.

"Hold on a minute," said Sully. "We don't know for certain whether there's truth to any of this. It's just a theory."

"Would you rather wait here for that thing to kill us all?" Marshall said. "We're fresh out of options." He stood up. "Let's go. Time's running out."

46

They stood in the dim hallway outside radar support. Ekberg kept her head averted, hands clenched and fingers interlaced, shivering despite the warm air. Wolff glanced at her, then looked away again. Conti stood apart, reviewing the footage he'd recently shot on the camera's small viewscreen.

"Why didn't you let me respond to Gonzalez's call?" she asked.

"He probably just wants to smoke out our location," the director murmured. "He clearly retreated following the attack, and now he wants to pull us back as well."

"He probably fell back to the life-sciences lab," replied Wolff. "Rejoined the others. If he was smart, that's what he did."

"I doubt it. Gonzalez is a soldier; he wouldn't have let a setback like this stop him."

"Is that what you call it?" Wolff retorted. "A *setback*? That creature just killed another of his men."

Conti flicked a switch on the camera and the viewscreen went dark. "Gonzalez wouldn't take it lying down. He probably got jumped. Now he's learned from his mistake—trying to take the fight to the beast was a bad move. Better to choose your place of engagement. Let the enemy come to you."

Wolff looked at him in disbelief. "Emilio, what do you think this is? Some film you can script to your satisfaction?"

But Conti didn't seem to hear. "Let's check out that stairwell we passed. He might have taken his team down there, set up a killing field." Hoisting the camera back onto his shoulder, he began to walk down the corridor. Wolff stepped in behind him, still protesting.

Ekberg watched them walk away. The corridor was wreathed in interlacing shadows that seemed to grow more oppressive by the minute. She could not get the image of Creel out of her mind: the torn and staring head, the spreading blood, the dismembered corpse. Woodenly, she moved to follow them.

"Either we radio Gonzalez or we head back to the science lab," Wolff was saying. "Wandering out here, with that killing machine on the loose, is madness."

"You won't say that when we're accepting a Best Documentary Oscar. Besides, you've got a weapon."

"Creel had a weapon, too. A nice, big weapon. And look what happened."

"We don't know what happened. It could have been anything. Perhaps he got separated from the others. Perhaps he lost his nerve and ran off—straight into the jaws of the beast."

They were approaching the stairwell. The metal-walled shaft was a maw of blackness, only a small glimmer of light from below illuminating the treads and risers. Ahead, the corridor ran back to the intersection leading to the infirmary. Conti stopped at the top of the stairs to adjust the camera lens and switch on its supplementary light.

"I won't let you go down there," Wolff said.

Conti continued to fiddle with the camera. "Didn't anything I said earlier sink in? This is simply too important. If they're down there, I have to film it."

"We should never have left the officers' mess." Wolff looked back at Ekberg as if to demand her agreement.

She said nothing. She was too full of grief and horror. The memory of being back in the mess, agreeing to run sound for Conti, already seemed a lifetime away. The notion that the good of the documentary outweighed all other considerations now filled her with revulsion.

"It won't take me long to check," said Conti. He lifted the camera back onto his shoulder. "Wait here if you want. Kari, I'll need your help."

Ekberg shook her head. "Sorry, Emilio. I'm not going."

Wolff put his hand on the camera. "You're coming back with us. Now."

"You can't order me around," Conti said, wheeling away, his voice abruptly spiking. "This is my shoot."

"I'm the Blackpool representative—"

Suddenly, Wolff fell silent. He gave a low grunt of pain and covered his hands with his ears. A moment later, Ekberg felt it too: a painful pressure that seemed to radiate from the center of her skull.

"I don't like this," she said.

"We need to get out of here," Wolff replied. "Get out of here fast, before—"

Once again he stopped speaking. His jaw went slack and his frame seemed to sag. He was staring past Conti, down the corridor. Ekberg turned to follow his gaze with huge reluctance, fear buckling her knees, afraid to look but even more afraid not to.

Ahead, at the corridor intersection, the webbed darkness had begun to shift.

47

They made their way down through the levels in almost complete silence. Gonzalez led the way, M16 slung over his back and powerful flashlight illuminating a path through the clutter. A heavy monkey wrench hung from a cloth ring stitched to his fatigues. Logan and the scientists came next: Sully with a weapon in each hand, Marshall and Faraday carrying khaki duffels of hastily gathered tools and equipment that might or might not come in handy. Next came Usuguk, his tattooed face expressionless. Phillips brought up the rear, darting frequent looks over his shoulder.

They moved past the storage spaces of D Level, racks of ancient instruments and redundant sensor arrays like watchful sentinels in the faint light. As Gonzalez's torch swung in an arc, catching new objects in its beam, sudden shadows darted at them from open doorways and storage niches.

The gloom and silence began to wear on Marshall's nerves. He hadn't really wanted to leave Ekberg, Conti, and Wolff behind, but the possibility of fashioning a weapon that might harm the creature made it a chance worth taking. He slowed his pace, falling back slightly until he was beside the Tunit. "Usuguk," he said, eager to turn his mind elsewhere. "Why do you call this mountain a place of evil?"

It took the Tunit a moment to answer. "The story is very old. It has been handed down from father to son, generation to generation, for longer than living memory can tell."

"I'd like to hear it."

Usuguk paused again before continuing. "My people believe in two sets of gods, the gods of light and the gods of darkness. Just as everything has an opposite—for happiness there is sorrow, for day there is night—it took both sets of gods to fashion our world. The gods of light are supreme. They are the ancient ones: the gods of goodness and wisdom. They bless the hunt, fill the sea with fish. They watch over the natural order. The gods of darkness are different. They control sickness and death, the human passions. They dwell in dreams and nightmare. Over time, their own veil of darkness began to poison them. They grew envious of the gods of light. The evil that was their instrument, their source of power, seduced them. And they themselves became evil."

They turned a corner, continued past a series of repair bays.

"The gods of darkness tried to undermine the gods of light, twist their deeds into evil, pollute the land, turn the healing sun dark. When this failed they tried to use their evil to corrupt the gods of light, turn them against themselves. Although the gods of light were benevolent, this worried and angered them. And that was when Anataq spoke up."

"Anataq?"

"The trickster-god. He is neither light nor darkness, but acts as a balance between them. He had seen the acts of the dark gods and knew them to be disruptive, dangerous to the order of nature. So he offered to help. He went to the gods of darkness and told them of a secret Tunit cave; a place, he said, where the fifty most beautiful and unspoiled women of the tribe were kept. Their beauty, he said, was of such rare quality that they were not to be had by men, but to be admired and revered. Their cave was deep within a mountain. This story aroused the lustful interest of the dark gods, and their blood burned hot."

Following Gonzalez, they descended a stairway to E Level, lowest in the central wing, their feet ringing softly against the metal steps. "The gods of darkness asked Anataq where this mountain was. But the trickster-god would not tell them. He said only that he visited the mountain once a year, each midsummer eve, when the guardians of the women were away at the purification ceremony. That year, on midsummer eve, he went to the hollow mountain. The gods of darkness followed him, as he knew they would. And once they were within its deepest chamber, Anataq poured liquid fire down upon them, sealing them inside."

"Lava," murmured Marshall.

"The anger of the dark gods was terrible. They bellowed and shrieked, and again and again the mountain spit fire. Their violence was such that the sky was rent from horizon to horizon and the heavens bled. For thousands of years they raged. But Anataq had sealed them in too well, and at long last they grew weary. The mountain no longer belched red fire. The heavens no longer bled."

Until now, Marshall thought. With such a legend as part of his belief system, it was no wonder Usuguk had grown agitated at the return of the strange, crimson-colored northern lights. It was remarkable to think that the man had been able to work at this base at all—in particular, to work with such a terrifying and dangerous creature. But then, he reflected, Usuguk had been young and full of doubts about his people's traditions. Too bad it had taken such a shocking episode to transform him.

"And the *kurrshuq*?" he asked. "You called it the guardian of the forbidden mountain."

"Once the gods of darkness were imprisoned in the mountain, Anataq called on the *kurrshuq* to guard it, to make sure there was no escape. The *kurrshuq* are creatures of the spirit world, not gods but powerful beings who do not deign to involve themselves in the ways and lives of the People. For many years, a group of them guarded the mountain. But slowly, very slowly, the darkness of the imprisoned gods corrupted them as well. And they became evil things."

"Eaters of souls," Marshall said.

The Tunit's eyes darted toward him momentarily, then looked away again.

E Level was even more crowded with cast-off detritus than the higher floors had been, and completely dark, and their progress slowed considerably. Gonzalez led them past mechanical spaces and an auxiliary control room, then stopped at an electrical chamber just beyond. Motioning the others to wait, he stepped inside. Marshall watched as he opened an electrical panel, twisted a series of heavy fuses into place, then closed it and threw a fail-safe switch. He grunted his satisfaction, stepped back out into the corridor.

"The north wing should have juice now," he said.

They passed a series of smaller rooms, then turned right at an intersection. Ahead the passageway ended, barred by a heavy hatch, dogged and padlocked. Marshall glanced a little uneasily at the unlit red bulb above it, at the warning sign that barred all save those with the proper clearance.

Gonzalez glanced back at Phillips. "You guard our six while I try to get this open."

As Marshall watched, the sergeant opened the heavy dogs with the monkey wrench, one at a time, the cleats squealing in protest after half a century of disuse. After freeing the last cleat, Gonzalez pulled a huge key ring from one pocket. It took half a dozen attempts to find the correct key. Lock open, Gonzalez grasped the circular hasp and pulled the hatch toward him. It opened with a low pop. Powdered rubber rained down from the nearly mummified gasket, and stale air eddied outward, freighted with a desiccated mustiness.

Beyond lay utter blackness. "It's like looking into King Tut's tomb," Logan muttered. Marshall knew what he meant: nobody had so much as looked through this hatch in fifty years.

Gonzalez felt around the inside wall and snapped on a switch. There was another series of pops as some of the overhead bulbs failed. But enough lights still worked to illuminate a narrow metal hallway, receding back into dim space. They all stepped through and Gonzalez shut and dogged the hatch behind them.

"Looks like a pretty secure redoubt to me," Sully said, nodding at the heavy hatch with approval.

Gonzalez shook his head. "That thing got past us once before— I still don't know how. And this wing has ventilation ducts and service ports, just like the others."

They moved slowly down the corridor toward the first set of open doors. To Marshall, the air tasted of dust, overlaid with a coppery, metallic tang.

Gonzalez stopped at the nearest doorway, flashed his light inside. The beam revealed two wooden desks with old-fashioned manual typewriters: a forward office of some kind. A half-written memo was still visible in one of the typewriters, the yellowed paper curled around the platen. Gonzalez withdrew the light and they moved along to the next doorway. He glanced inside and Marshall heard him catch his breath sharply.

Marshall stepped up for a look. A vast storm of some dried dark liquid covered the floor and arced over banks of what appeared to be electrical equipment in wild trajectories. In one corner stood a coupling apparatus, burned and half fused.

"The electrical room," said Usuguk in a monotone.

"They didn't even bother to clean up the bloodstains," said Sully.

The sergeant snapped off his light. "Can you blame them?"

They continued down the narrow corridor, turning on lights as they went. There were labs full of oscilloscopes and black, boxlike devices, some on tables and in racks, others still in their wooden crates.

"This must be the sound equipment," murmured Faraday.

They stopped at a control room of some sort, with a mixing console and a variety of amplifiers. Gonzalez's flashlight revealed that the far wall was of glass, overlooking a small soundproofed studio.

Beyond, corridors led off to the left and right, and past this intersection the central hallway ended in another heavy hatch. Gonzalez opened it, shone his flashlight within, and snorted in surprise. He snapped on the light. Marshall followed the others in—then immediately stopped.

They were standing on a narrow walkway—a catwalk, really—that spanned the center of a large, circular room. At the far end of the span was a landing, perhaps ten feet by ten, enclosed by glass walls. The entire inner surface of the sphere was covered in a dark-colored knobby padding. Here and there, small spikes projected in from the walls.

"My goodness," breathed Faraday. "It *is* an echo chamber. No doubt to be used for testing the sonar device."

"If they'd gotten that far," replied Sully.

"True. I suppose the experiments were conducted elsewhere once this place was sealed up."

Logan leaned in toward Marshall. "Only one exit."

Marshall glanced around. "That's right."

"Echo chamber. Is that what it looks like to you?"

"Yes." Marshall turned to look at the historian. "Why. You don't think so?"

Logan paused. "Actually, no. It looks more like Custer's Last Stand to me."

48

Very slowly, the thing resolved out of the blackness. Striped shadows flexed to the motion of muscled flanks. Ekberg stared in horror as—creeping inch by inch into the half-light, like a swimmer emerging from a dark pool—outrageous and terrible details gained form. The huge, shovel-shaped head, covered with short black hair, coarse and glistening. The overhung upper jaw, fronted by an array of huge fangs and flanked by two tusks, behind which—horribly—hung hundreds of narrow, razor-sharp tendrils, like the vibrissae of a walrus. The wide mandible, small and set back by comparison yet anchored to the skull by a massive hinge of bone. And—most shocking because she had seen them before, at least a lifetime before, encased in ice—the unblinking eyes that stared back at them with a mixture of lust and malice.

"Christ," Conti murmured beside her. "Christ. It's magnificent."

Slowly—very slowly—he aimed the camera, armed the Record button, and began to film.

Wolff was standing right behind him. He began to raise his gun, but he was shaking so badly Ekberg could hear his teeth rattling. "Emilio," he said in a strangled voice. "For the love of God—"

"Quick, Kari," Conti interrupted in a whisper. *Sound.*

But Ekberg could not move. She could only stare.

Moving so slowly she could not be sure it was even moving at all, the thing began its approach down the dappled hallway. Its massive forelegs were bowed slightly, like a bulldog's, tapering to bulbous, hooflike paws barbed with cruel talons. It was fully visible now, the length of a young horse. The line of its back tapered from high broad shoulders down to squat, powerful haunches matted with coarse hair. She stared, mouth agape. Then, almost unwillingly, her gaze returned to the mouth: the curved fangs; the countless, unutterably hideous mass of tendrils that hung down behind them. She noticed that the tendrils did not just shake gently in time to the monster's steps, but seemed to slither among themselves *with independent movement* . . .

The pain in her head was spiking cruelly, her heart laboring in her chest. And yet she could not retreat, could not even move. She was transfixed by fear. Now the creature stopped again, crouching, maybe twenty feet from them. But not once did it blink or look away. It seemed to Ekberg that its eyes were hard and deep as topaz, burning with fierce inner fire.

It remained motionless for perhaps sixty seconds. The only sound was the low whirring of Conti's camera, her own strained breathing. And then, once again, it began creeping toward them.

This was too much for Wolff. With a low groan he wheeled around and went tearing back down the corridor, gun clattering unheeded to the ground.

The thing paused again, more briefly this time. A narrow tongue, forked and pink, peeped out from below the vibrissae. It extended—farther, farther—licking first one tusk, then the other.

It was at this point Conti seemed to go a little mad. He began to laugh, softly at first, and then louder. At least, in her paroxysm of horror and disbelief, Ekberg thought it must be a laugh: a strange, high sound.

Eeeeeee, Conti keened, still louder now, the camera tilting visibly as his shoulders shook: *Heeee-eeeeeeeeeee . . .*

"Emilio," she whispered.

"I've got it!" Conti cried, almost hysterically. "It's a wrap. *It's a wrap! Eeeeee-heeeeeee—*"

In two bounds the thing was on him, knocking him violently into the air. The camera sailed down the hallway, hitting a wall and then falling to the floor, shivering into pieces. As he fell, the creature caught Conti between its enormous front paws and began to spin him, like a craftsman using a lathe, clutching him close and running the wriggling razor tendrils hanging from its upper jaw back and forth along his form, from head to foot and back again, working him like a cob of corn. Gobbets of blood began raining out in all directions, spattering the walls and ceiling and causing nearby light-bulbs to pop and sizzle. Conti's banshee laughter morphed into a sharp scream, rising violently in pitch. Abruptly, the creature jammed the director's head into its mouth and bit down. There was a low crunching sound and the scream stopped. The beast opened its mouth again and Conti dropped heavily to the ground. And then at last Ekberg found her feet and began to run, past Conti and the nightmare beast that was hunched over him, heedless of the dark, heedless of any obstacles in her path. And as she hurtled headlong down the shadow-haunted corridor and away from the insanity, Conti began to make noise again: not laughter or screams, not this time, but the sharp snapping of bone: crack, crack, *crack . . .*

49

When Marshall stepped into the control room, black metal box in hand, he could see Sully and Logan in the studio beyond the glass partition, bending over a wheeled cart of stainless steel. As he looked at the cart, his heart sank. The contraption sitting on it looked more like a child's erector set than a weapon for killing a two-ton monster. On its upper tray sat a small forest of analog and primitive digital equipment: potentiometers, voltage-controlled filters, low-frequency oscillators, long-throw fader and control pots, all connected by a cloud of multicolored wires. On the lower tray was an old vacuum-tube amplifier, connected by thin red leads to a woofer and a high-frequency driver.

The group had spent the last thirty minutes ripping open crates and breaking apart racks of unused instrumentation, frantically trying to cobble together a machine capable of generating a wide variety of high-frequency sound waves at as great an amplitude as possible. They had ultimately taken the tweeter from a much larger piece of sonic equipment than the woofer, on the assumption that high frequencies would most likely prove harmful to the creature. Although Marshall had been a proponent of the scheme—mostly because it was the only plan that seemed to have a chance—he was well aware what a gamble it was: whether the device would work at all, or whether in fact it would deter the beast. They were assembling it on a movable cart so that it could be placed anywhere— ideally, far outside the science wing—allowing them a fallback position in case it failed.

He handed Sully the metal box. "Here's the ring modulator. Faraday managed to liberate it from an active sonar emitter."

Sully placed it on the upper tray, connected two wires to it, grunted in satisfaction. As the sonic weapon had come together, the climatologist had grown less dubious and increasingly excited about its potential. "We should try emitting white noise first. A signal of equal power within a set bandwidth—that would give us the most efficient burst of sonic pressure." He glanced over at Marshall. "Where is Faraday now?"

"Back in the equipment room, gathering spares."

"Well, this just leaves the dry-cell batteries. You didn't happen to see any, by chance?"

"No. But I wasn't looking. I was too busy tearing apart that transducer array."

"I'll go find some, then." And the climatologist straightened up, walked through the control room and into the corridor. He glanced briefly over his right shoulder before disappearing to the left.

Marshall knew why Sully had glanced to the right. He had glanced that way himself before stepping into the control room. That way led to the main hatch of the science wing: where Gonzalez and Phillips were standing guard, machine guns at the ready, watching for any sign of the creature.

He became aware that Logan was looking at him. "Any idea what kind of secret research was meant to go on here?" the historian asked.

Marshall shrugged. "So little of the equipment was actually assembled or unpacked, it's difficult to tell. But from the variety of passive sonar devices—I haven't seen much active sonar equipment here—I'd guess they were hoping to supplement the early warning radar with a stealth sonar emitter."

"As in, much closer to Russia."

Marshall nodded. "Possibly even within. Active sonar would give you an object's exact position. But an installation like Fear Base wouldn't need to know that—at least, not right away. They'd be more interested in whether an object was simply headed for them—and passive sonar could do that, silently, using TMA to plot a missile's trajectory."

"TMA?"

"Target motion analysis. Its solution would give range, speed, even course—long before the radar here could get a positional lock."

"And all in a package small and quiet enough to escape notice. Interesting." Logan paused. "The real question, I guess, is whether it's going to save our asses."

Marshall glanced down at the mad-scientist device on the tray between them. "I think we have a fighting chance. Of the five senses, hearing is the only one that's a completely mechanical process. A sound wave actually changes air pressure, causes vibration. Extreme low-frequency sound can cause shortness of breath, depression, even anxiety in humans. High-frequency noise has been thought by some to interfere with normal heart rhythms or even cause cancer. There are all sorts of rumors of infrasonic or ultrasonic weapons that can injure, paralyze, even kill." He shrugged. "Who knows? Perhaps that kind of research was the real intent of this installation."

"That would be ironic." Logan patted the side of the cart. "And now this is complete?"

"Except for the batteries, yes. Sully's out gathering those."

"So we've got our weapon. Now we just need the target."

"There's no guarantee it's heading this way—we may need to find a lure of some kind."

"Or perhaps the proper term would be 'bait.' " Logan paused again. "There's something else I've been thinking about. These two creatures—the one you found, and the one they found fifty years ago: Do you suppose they're related?"

"Good question. I've only glimpsed a bit of it, through a block of occluded ice. But Gonzalez's descriptions seem to match Usuguk's, and—"

"I didn't mean it that way. I meant, are the creatures *related*?"

Marshall looked at him. "You mean—like father and child?"

Logan nodded. "Or perhaps mother and child. Separated, then flash-frozen in the same freak climatological event."

"Jesus." Marshall swallowed. "If that's the case, let's hope the parent doesn't find out what happened to junior."

Logan rubbed a hand over his chin. "Speaking of junior—have you wondered what did kill it the first time?"

"You mean, if it wasn't electricity?"

"Right."

"Yes. And I don't have any answers. Do you?"

"No. But I find it very interesting that neither creature has eaten any of the people it killed."

"I told you. It did not die. It chose to leave the physical world."

It was Usuguk who spoke. He had been sitting, cross-legged, in a corner of the studio, the backs of his hands balanced on his knees, so silent and motionless that Marshall hadn't even been aware of his presence. Seeing the Tunit's tranquil, reserved expression, sensing his quiet yet granitelike conviction, Marshall felt himself almost ready to believe this, as well.

"That tale you told me," he said to the shaman. "About Anataq and the gods of darkness. It was unsettling, even to me, an outsider. I have to ask: If you truly believe we are dealing with a *kurrshuq*—a devourer of souls—why did you agree to come back with me?"

Usuguk glanced up at him. "My people believe that nothing happens without a reason. The gods had a destiny for me, foreordained from the day I was born. When I was a young man, they led my step away from my people—led me to this place—knowing that in the end it would bring me back, stronger and closer than before. By turning my back on the spirit world, I embraced it."

Marshall returned the look thoughtfully. And then he understood. All these years, by living—even by the most traditional Tunit values—an ascetic, monastic, spiritual life, Usuguk had been atoning for temporarily betraying his faith. And returning here—the very place of that betrayal—was his final act of atonement.

"I'm sorry it's come to this," Marshall said. "I didn't mean to expose you to such extreme danger."

The Tunit shook his head. "Let me tell you something. When I was a very young child, back when the hunts still took place, my grandfather would always return with the largest walrus. People wanted to know his secret, but he would never tell. Then, finally, when he was an old, old man, he confided in me. He would take his kayak out past the straits, he explained, into the deep ocean currents, farther than anyone else ever dared go. I asked why he would do such a thing—as you say, expose himself to extreme danger—just for the largest catch. He told me that the hunt itself was danger. If you are going to walk on thin ice, he said, you might as well dance."

There was a noise from beyond the glass partition and then Faraday entered, loaded down with electrical and mechanical equipment. "Here are the spare oscillators and potentiometers," he said. He glanced over the apparatus on the cart. "Where are the batteries?"

"Sully went to find some," Marshall replied.

"Good. Once we have those, we can start the test runs, and—"

At that moment there was a sharp crackling noise from the control room. Marshall looked over. It was the radio Gonzalez had issued them, balanced on the top edge of the mixing board.

The radio crackled again. "Hello?" It was Ekberg's voice. *"Hello?"*

Marshall stepped out of the studio and into the control room. He grabbed the radio, pressed the Transmit switch. "Kari? It's Marshall. Go ahead."

"Oh, God. Help me!" Her voice was ragged, pitched at the edge of hysteria. "Help me, *please*! That thing—it got Emilio. It picked him up, it picked him up, and it—"

"Kari. Calm down." Marshall tried to modulate his voice, keep it reasonable. "Now I want you to tell me: Where are you?"

He heard a series of panicky breaths. "I'm . . . oh, *God* . . . I'm at the entrance plaza. By, by the sentry station."

As Marshall pressed the Transmit button again, Logan and Faraday came in from the studio and took up positions around the radio. "Okay. Do you have a flashlight?"

"No."

"Then head down to the stairs to the officers' mess. Quickly and quietly as you can. You'll find spare flashlights there. Weapons, too. Do you know how to use a gun?"

"No."

"That's okay. Now go there right away. Once you're there, radio me again."

"It's going to come for me, I know it is. When it's done with Emilio. It's going to come, and it's going to . . . *it's going to*—"

"Kari. I'm coming to get you. I'll lead you to my position. Just keep your head. And don't lose that radio."

There was another crackle, then the radio fell silent.

Marshall turned to Faraday. "Find Sully. Help him with the batteries. Then move the sonic weapon out of here, into the corridors of E Level. We'll need this science wing as a fallback if it doesn't work."

Faraday nodded, then quickly left the control room. Marshall looked over at Logan. "Remember what you said about bait? Looks like it's going to be me." And without another word he snugged the radio into his pocket and raced out of the room, heading for the hatch to the central wing.

50

Kari Ekberg stumbled down the corridor of C Level, the flashlight slick in her sweaty hands. Her shins ached from where she had barked them on protruding ducts and storage crates; her knees were skinned from half a dozen falls onto unforgiving steel and linoleum floors. Thank God the light and radio still worked. Yet again she forced the dreadful images from her mind: Conti screaming as blood flew in all directions like spray from a rotary sprinkler. Yet again she told herself, over and over, like a mantra: *Don't look back. Don't look back.*

It had taken fifteen minutes to descend the two decks from the officers' mess: fifteen minutes of unadulterated terror. Now she passed the laundry, ancient washers and dryers standing in silent rows below curling posters exhorting cleanliness. Next was the tailoring shop: a nook barely large enough for a desk, a sewing machine, and a tailor's dummy. Beyond, the hallway divided. She stopped and fumbled with the radio. Her hands were shaking so badly it took three tries to depress the Transmit button.

"I'm at the hallway junction by tailoring," she said, hearing the quaver in her voice.

Marshall's voice crackled back. "I just reached D Level. Hold on, I'll radio Gonzalez for directions."

She stood, gasping for breath, in the close darkness. This was the worst time: standing, waiting for instructions—and waiting for that strange full feeling in the ears, the stealthy tread that signaled the approach of nightmare . . .

"Make a left," Marshall's electrified voice said. "At the end of the hall, make another left. You'll see a staircase: go down it. I should be waiting there. If not, radio me."

Ekberg pushed the radio back into the pocket of her jeans. Turning left, she shone the light around briefly, searching for obstacles, then took off at a jog. She passed the food-preparation areas: empty kitchens, huge porcelain sinks gleaming and spectral. A dozen doorways flashed past, yawning onto rooms black and mysterious. Her knees and shins throbbed fiercely, but she pushed the pain to the back of her mind. Ahead, illuminated by a single bulb, she could see the hallway divide again. *Go left, he said. Go left, and you'll see a . . .*

Suddenly, her foot caught against something and she fell headlong to the floor, her radio clattering away down the corridor, the flashlight rolling against the wall and winking out. *God, no, no . . .*

Crawling on hands and outraged knees she felt around frantically for the flashlight. One hand closed over it and, heart in her mouth, she pressed the switch. It flickered, went out, then brightened. *Thank you. Thank you.* Pulling herself to her feet, she shone the light ahead, searching for the radio. There it was: on the ground maybe ten feet ahead. She raced to it, knelt, scooped it up.

"Hello!" she said, fumbling with the Transmit button. "Hello, Evan, are you there?"

Nothing. Not even static in reply.

"Evan, hello!" Her voice spiked sharply with anxiety and dismay. *"Hello—!"*

Suddenly she stopped. Something had just set off her instinct for self-preservation, five-alarm. Was that the padding of feet from the darkness behind, heavy and yet horribly stealthy? Was that blood rushing through her ears, or some faint, strange—almost unearthly—singing? Terror coursed through her afresh, and with a sob of despair she jammed the broken radio back into her pocket and forced herself to start running once again. The light at the end of the corridor drew closer. And then she was at the intersection, veering left, shining the light wildly ahead, searching for the stairwell.

There it was: a well of blackness. She dashed up to it and raced down the steps, flashlight clattering against the metal handrail, no longer making any attempt to conceal her panicky flight.

She paused at the bottom step, looking about. Another dim corridor stretched on ahead, desks and tools piled up on either side. It was empty.

She blinked hard, wiped the back of a hand across her eyes, looked again. Nobody.

"Evan?" Ekberg said into the emptiness.

She felt her breathing grow shallower. *No, no, no . . .*

And there it was again: that low singing noise, almost like a whisper in her ears. Whimpering, she took a step forward, off the bottom step and into the corridor. She felt an overpowering need to look over her shoulder, up the stairwell. The light twitched in her hand . . .

"Kari!"

She glanced down the corridor again. A figure had come into view at the far end, a dark silhouette in the low light. With a cry she ran toward it. As it approached she recognized Marshall, worried expression on his face, an automatic rifle slung over one shoulder.

"Kari," he said, coming up to her. "Thank God. Are you all right?"

"No. It's after me, the monster, I heard it just now—"

"Hurry." And with an urgent tug of his hand he led the way back down the hall.

Despite her growing exhaustion, Ekberg followed closely as Marshall traced a circuitous path past storage spaces and repair bays. Once they stopped at an intersection as he tried to recall the correct route. Another time they radioed back to Gonzalez for directions through the labyrinth.

"Where are we going?" she panted.

"The science wing. It's one deck below. It's protected by a thick hatch. It's much safer than the upper decks. And we've assembled a weapon, a sonic weapon, that we hope to test on the beast. But first things first—let's get you safely behind the hatch."

They reached another stairwell and Marshall practically dove down it, three steps at a time. Ekberg followed as quickly as she could. E Level was a tomb, its low ceilings covered by thick rivers of conduit and cabling. They jogged past several rooms, Marshall's light illuminating the way. They turned right at a T junction. And then Marshall stopped so abruptly that Ekberg almost plowed into him.

Ahead the corridor ended at a massive hatchway, thrown wide open, brilliantly lit from the spaces beyond. Just inside was a strange contraption on a wheeled cart, all wires and antennas and electrical components like a confection from a 1950s science-fiction film. Two of the scientists—Faraday and Sully—were toiling over it. Beside them stood Sergeant Gonzalez, machine gun at the ready, pointed in their direction.

"What's wrong?" Marshall said. "Why isn't the weapon out here, away from the hatch?"

"No batteries," said Faraday. "We had to connect it to the power supply inside. This is as far as the wires will reach."

"Well, for God's sake," said Marshall, "find a connection out here!"

"No time," replied Sully.

"You're damn right there's no time! That thing's behind us, and we can't compromise the safety of the science wing with an open—"

Marshall stopped in mid-sentence. Then Ekberg became aware of it, too: a creeping presentiment, more sixth sense than sensation, that raised the hairs on the back of her neck and sent fresh fear coursing through her. Once again, every instinct cried out for her to turn and look back. And this time she yielded, glancing over her shoulder.

Around the corner, just within eyesight, a black shape was crawling stealthily down the staircase toward them.

51

"Move, *move!*" And Marshall physically propelled Ekberg down the corridor and through the reinforced hatchway. The M16 that thumped against his back as he ran was an unfamiliar—and yet too familiar—weight. Just inside the hatchway, Sully—white-faced but determined—was manning the controls of the sonic weapon. Long power cables led away from it back into the electrical room, pulled taut, at the limit of their range. The big drivers sitting on the bottom tray crackled and hummed with latent power, the woofer trembling slightly. Directly behind were Faraday and Logan, looking on anxiously. They were flanked by Gonzalez and Phillips, both kneeling, automatic weapons pointing out through the hatchway and down the corridor. Usuguk stood behind them. He was holding his medicine bundle in both hands and chanting a low monody.

Marshall looked around quickly. This was exactly the situation he had hoped to avoid: hatchway wide open; weapon inside the science wing, untested and unproven; all of them now utterly exposed and vulnerable to attack. "We should close the hatch," he said. "Just close it, now."

"We'll have time," Sully replied. "If it doesn't work, if it doesn't stop the creature, we'll have time."

Marshall opened his mouth to protest again but at that moment there was movement at the corridor junction. All eyes turned to the dim hallway beyond the hatch. Slowly, a huge form came into view. Marshall stared in disbelief at the features: the wide, spade-shaped head; the teeth that gleamed wickedly; the dozens of razorlike tentacles that hung beneath. It was the creature of his nightmare, only worse: he'd seen the top of the head through the ice, but the dark occlusions had mercifully hidden the hideous lower half from view. Although perhaps it *wasn't* merciful, after all, because surely if they could have seen those dreadful teeth through the ice, those vibrissae that slithered like a nest of snakes, they would never, *never* have allowed such a horrible beast ever to be unfrozen . . . For a moment he simply stared in horror and surprise. Then he unslung the weapon and pulled Ekberg over to Faraday.

"Take her deep into the science wing," he said. "Find the safest, most secure spot you can. And lock yourselves in."

"But—" Faraday began.

"Do it, Wright. Please."

The biologist hesitated a moment. Then, nodding, he reached for Ekberg's elbow and together they retreated back down the passageway, past the soldiers and the softly chanting Usuguk, rounded the corner, and disappeared from view.

Marshall turned back to the nightmare that was now crouched, fully exposed, at the corridor junction. From over his shoulder he could hear somebody breathing stertorously. "No," said Phillips in a high desperate voice. "No, God, please. Not again."

"Steady, soldier," growled Gonzalez.

Sully—also breathing loudly—wiped his hands on his shirt, replaced them on the potentiometers and oscillator pots. Marshall crept forward half a dozen paces to the inner fairing of the hatch-way, ducking behind the metal lip. He smacked the bottom of the ammo clip to make sure it was properly seated, pulled back the slide rod at the top of the weapon to chamber the first round, felt around the handle for the safety and toggled it off.

The creature took a step forward, looking at each of them in turn with unblinking eyes.

"Any time you're ready, Doctor," said Gonzalez.

The creature took another stealthy, deliberate step. There were bare streaks here and there in the matted hair that lay across its powerful shoulders—bullet tracings—and through those streaks Marshall could see the dull gleam of what looked like a snake's scales.

Sully's hands were shaking badly. "I'll, I'll try the wash of white noise first."

For a moment, all Marshall heard was Phillips's labored breathing and the rattle of another weapon being cocked. Then a squeal of static came from the drivers.

The creature took another step.

Sully's voice was high and tight. "I'll raise the sound pressure to 60 decibels, apply a low-pass filter."

The volume abruptly increased, filling the narrow corridor. Still the creature came on.

"No effect," said Sully over the wash of noise. "I'll try a simple waveform instead. Sawtooth, fundamental frequency of 100 hertz."

The sound of static faded, replaced by a low hum, rising quickly in pitch.

In the hallway, the creature stopped.

"Square wave next," Sully said. "Raising frequency to 390 hertz at 100 decibels."

The sound broadened, grew more complex. And as it did, Marshall began to hear—or thought he heard—a strange, faint singing, like the low tone of some sinister organ, borne on a distant wind: a complex, exotic, mysterious sound that had nothing to do with the waveforms created by Sully. His head felt strangely full, as if with some internal pressure.

The creature hesitated, one massive forepaw raised in mid-step.

"Adding the sine oscillator now," came Sully's voice. "I'll raise the frequency, 880 hertz."

"Goose the decibels," Marshall called over his shoulder.

The sound grew louder still, until the metal walls of the corridor seemed to vibrate with noise. "Passing the threshold of pain!" shouted Sully. "At 120 decibels!"

The maelstrom of sound, overlaid with the fullness in Marshall's head, threatened to grow maddening. The creature took a step backward. Its haunches jerked slightly, as with involuntary tremors. It shook its shaggy head: once, twice, violent shakes of obvious pain.

"Just the sine wave now!" Sully cried. *"It's working!"*

And then—suddenly—the creature gathered itself into a crouch, preparing to spring.

A dozen things happened simultaneously. Phillips and Sully cried out in dismay and fear. The volume of the device spiked still further, broadening and swelling. Gonzalez gave an almost inaudible command to fire. And then bullets were singing past Marshall's head, ripping down the corridor in strafes of gray smoke as they whined off walls and tottering piles of surplus equipment. Marshall raised his own gun and depressed the trigger. He could see his bullets running true; see them impact the creature, then ricochet off; watched fresh streaks of chitinous obsidian appear on the beast's withers and flanks as the slugs exposed more exoskeleton. At this moment of crisis, of absolute extremity, time seemed to slow and reality fade: it was as if Marshall could almost see each individual bullet fly down the corridor on its violent, futile journey.

And then the beast charged. Instantly, Marshall flung himself toward the hatch in a desperate attempt to shut it, heedless of the fire being laid down by Gonzalez and Phillips. But the creature moved with remarkable speed. In a heartbeat it was past the hatch and through, knocking Marshall aside, throwing him against the wall with a sickening impact, leaping over the sonic weapon and overturning it in the process as—with single-minded ferocity—it seized Sully in its forepaws and, with two savage twists of its head, tore his arms from their sockets.

52

Marshall raised himself onto one elbow, momentarily stunned by the force of the blow. The central corridor of the science wing had been transformed into a bedlam of sound and violence: the beast, ripping into the shrieking Sully; blood, spraying from the climatologist's ruined limbs, spraying the walls and floor in a maelstrom of crimson; Gonzalez and Phillips, scrambling backward, trying to get in a clear shot at the creature; the tray that held the sonic weapon lying on its side, wheels still turning; Usuguk, stepping forward past the soldiers, shaman's charm held out before him as his chanting rose in pitch and urgency.

As Marshall watched, ears ringing with the impact, he saw the beast bat Sully—still screaming—into the air with one powerful swipe of a forelimb. A second swipe knocked the scientist through a doorway and into the forward office. The creature bounded in after him, disappearing from view. An enormous din—the crash of furniture, the impact of a body slamming against walls—erupted from inside. Sully's screams grew ragged.

Marshall tried to rise to his feet, staggered, pulled himself up. It was too late—Sully was going to die. They were *all* going to die. For a second he wondered if there was time to get them out of the science wing, to close the hatch on the monster, but he quickly dismissed the thought. There was no time. It was over, the thing would kill Sully and then it would turn on them, one at a time, and—

His eyes fell on the sonic weapon, its pieces in disarray on the hallway floor. And yet *it had worked.* That last waveform Sully had tried, the sine—it had clearly affected the creature. He tried to drown out the ferocious din, the shouts of the soldiers, the painful pressure in his head. Tried to think, to concentrate, in the few seconds he had left. Why would a sine wave work when a sawtooth wave or a square wave didn't?

He stopped. Maybe it wasn't the waveshape at all. Maybe it was something else entirely . . .

He dashed toward the cart, righted it, and frantically began picking up the electronics that had shaken free and reassembling them.

"What are you doing?" Logan cried. Sully's screams had now stopped but the terrible crashing and banging in the forward office continued.

"Trying again." Marshall checked the connections from the amplifier to the drivers, snapped a loose potentiometer back into place. "It's the harmonics; it has to be. That's the only answer. But we need proper acoustics if we're going to maximize—" He looked around wildly a minute. "Come on, give me a hand. That thing will be back out any second. We have to get this into the echo chamber."

"You don't have time for that shit!" Gonzalez said. "What's the point of moving it?"

"It's like adding poison to an arrowhead. We're maximizing the payload."

With Logan's help, Marshall wheeled the cart down the corridor, slipping repeatedly on a floor made slick with Sully's blood. Usuguk followed in their path, still chanting, shaman's rattle in one hand and a bone fetish in the other. With difficulty the two men trundled the cart past the control room, past the corridor intersection, and through the rear hatch into the echo chamber itself.

"Gonzalez!" Marshall cried. "I'm counting on you to slow it down!"

Motioning to Phillips, Gonzalez fell back to a spot just outside the echo chamber and took up a defensive position.

The crashing and banging from within the forward office stopped.

"We'll need to set it up in the center to get the greatest effect," Marshall told Logan.

Together, they pushed the cart to the middle of the catwalk. The electrical cables stretched taut, and for a dreadful moment Marshall thought they would not reach. But there was just enough play in them to position the weapon precisely in the center of the chamber, a spot marked on the floor of the catwalk with a label reading "0 dB."

Marshall glanced at Usuguk. "You might be safer in that monitoring booth," he said, gesturing to the glass-enclosed landing at the rear of the catwalk.

The Tunit stopped his low chant, shook his head. "Do you forget already what I taught you? If you are going to walk on thin ice, you might as well dance."

"Your call." Marshall turned the cart so the drivers were facing down the corridor, checked the connections, snapped the machine back on. No response. Frantically, he reseated vacuum tubes, tightened leads, and tried again. This time a low hum sounded from the massive woofer. He scanned the device, recalling the basics of sound generation on a synthesizer, reacquainting himself with the controls for amplitude, frequency, oscillator waveshape, filter envelope. He grabbed the amplitude knob, turned it sharply right. The cart began to tremble.

He noticed Logan was looking at him. "I calculate I've got about three minutes left to live," the historian said. "If I'm lucky, it'll happen quickly. In that case, I've probably only got two minutes. I'd like to die knowing what it is you tried to do."

"That last waveform Sully tried," Marshall replied, eyes back on the controls. "The one that caused the creature to react. It was a sine wave. That's the purest sound wave possible. No harmonics, no overtones. So I'm going to pick up where he left off—I'll use Fourier addition to complicate the pattern. Maybe it'll hurt the creature enough to drive it away. If we can keep it away long enough, maybe we can create more portable—"

He fell silent. The creature had emerged from the forward office. Now it slowly turned to face them. Its forelegs and paws were sopping with blood, and its fangs and vibrissae were flecked with gore.

Marshall took a deep breath, tried to steady his shaking hands.

The creature took a step toward them. Quickly, Marshall set the waveform of the first oscillator to sawtooth, the frequency to 30 hertz, verified the amplitude of the master output was at 100 decibels. He pressed the tone button. The room rumbled with a low tone just above the threshold of hearing.

The creature sprang forward.

Marshall did a frantic mental calculation. *A second note, overtone free, several octaves higher . . .*

Even as he did so, the creature picked up speed, coming toward them at great leaps down the corridor. He set the second oscillator to sawtooth, dialed its frequency to 800 hertz.

"Christ!" Logan shouted.

Gonzalez and Phillips were firing now. Over the whine of the speaker, Marshall could just make out Phillips's ragged cry, his weapon firing wildly, up and down and side to side as he lost the last remnants of his shattered nerves. The creature reached the soldiers, paused once again to shake its head violently, vibrissae dancing madly left and right. Phillips dropped his gun, rose to his feet, and ran down the corridor, wailing. The creature ducked its head, raised it again, and with a dreadful swipe of its foreleg knocked Gonzalez—still firing, point-blank—back into the echo chamber, a dreadful blow that sent him cartwheeling over the heads of Marshall and Logan. The sergeant hit the rear wall of the echo chamber with a crash, then slid down the curve of the wall to the floor twenty feet below, where he lay in a confusion of insulation and sound foam, stunned.

Marshall's hands were shaking badly now and he fumbled to set the third and final oscillator: sine wave again, this time at a very high frequency—60,000 hertz. A quick glance ensured that the amplitude envelope was fully front-loaded. Then, grasping the master fader, he pulled it all the way down. The eerie *screeeeeee* of the sine wave grew fainter, then stopped altogether.

"What are you *doing*?" Logan asked through gritted teeth. "You turned it off—and now we're trapped!"

"I want to draw it inside the chamber," Marshall replied. "We're only going to get one chance at this. It has to count."

With a precise, almost finicky movement that seemed wildly out of place for such a massive beast, the creature lifted one foreleg over the lip of the hatchway. The other foreleg followed. It glanced first left, then right, yellow eyes taking in the chamber. The strange low wash of singing in Logan's ears increased, and the pain in his head grew almost unbearable. Now the creature was fully inside the chamber, stepping out onto the catwalk. It groaned beneath its weight. One step, two . . . the creature crouched back on its haunches, tensing for another—and final—spring.

You might as well dance. With a quick movement, Marshall grasped the amplitude dial, set it to 120 decibels, and threw up the fader.

Instantly, the echo chamber came alive with sound. It was as if the sphere filled with a million wasps, all droning together, their hum amplified and re-amplified. The creature began to leap even as its entire frame convulsed. Marshall twirled the dial, raising the volume to 140 decibels. The creature convulsed again in midair, more violently this time, curling in on itself as it hurtled toward them; this arrested its jump and it fell heavily to the ground, shaking the catwalk alarmingly. Marshall's entire universe now seemed to be the frantic, terrible hum that echoed through the chamber, feeding on itself and building with an independent crescendo of power and intensity that seemed to penetrate his very pores. The creature scrabbled on the catwalk, clawing forward, first one paw, then the next, the bloody talons digging into the metal plating. Grasping the dial, his breath coming thick and fast, Marshall steeled himself, then twisted the dial all the way: 165 decibels, the amplitude level of a jet engine. Beside him, Logan covered his ears with his hands; the historian opened his mouth but any cry he made was completely masked by the barrage of noise—a *screeeeeeeee* that now seemed to be part of Marshall's very essence. His hands, too, went instinctively to his ears, but they were scant defense against the excruciating violation of sound. Spots danced before his eyes, and he felt himself grow faint.

The creature went rigid. Another violent trembling shook it from forepaw to hindquarter. It raised its head, opening its terrible jaws wide, the fangs still dripping with Sully's blood, the vibrissae undulating fiercely. It turned sideways, banged its jaws against the catwalk with a horrifying impact: once, twice. It gathered its limbs, reared back. And then, as Marshall watched, its head came apart in an eruption of gore and matter, spattering them with a rain of blood, collapsing virtually at their feet. Drenched, the sonic weapon arced and squealed, then fell silent in an explosion of sparks.

For a long moment, Marshall simply stood there, trembling. Then he glanced over at Logan. The historian was looking back, blood trickling from his ears. He was speaking but Marshall could not hear him—could not, in fact, hear anything. Marshall turned away, stepped over the motionless creature—black blood still flooding from its ruined skull—and began walking toward the hatch leading out of the science wing, his limbs leaden. All of a sudden he felt a need to get out of this dark place of horrors, to breathe clean air. He sensed, more than heard, Logan and Usuguk swing into place behind him.

Slowly, painstakingly, they made their way up to the surface: to D Level; to the more familiar spaces of B Level; and finally to the entrance plaza, shadowy and lifeless. Still deaf, sodden with the creature's blood, Marshall walked into the weather chamber, not bothering to don a parka. Stepping through the staging area, he pushed open the double doors leading to the concrete apron beyond.

It was dark, but a faint blush at the horizon line hinted dawn was not far away. The storm had subsided and the stars were coming out, lending a spectral brightness to the snowpack. Vaguely, as if from far away, Marshall recalled an Inuit proverb: They are not stars, but openings where our loved ones smile down to reassure us they are happy. He wondered if Usuguk believed this as well.

As if in response, he felt the Tunit touch his sleeve. When he looked over, Usuguk wordlessly pointed one finger toward the sky.

Marshall glanced up. The deep, unearthly crimson of the northern lights—the lights that had haunted them since the nightmare began—was quickly ebbing. Even as he watched, it faded away to nothing, leaving only the black dome of stars. There was no indication, even the faintest, that it had ever been there at all.

53

"Mr. Fortnum? It's Penny. How are you back there?"

This time, the response was slow to come. "We're cold now. Very cold."

"Hold on," she said into the handset. "We're only—" she glanced over at Carradine.

"Twenty miles," the trucker muttered. "If we make it."

"Twenty miles," she said, then replaced the handset onto the CB unit. "We *have* to make it. How's the petrol?"

"Left tank drained awful fast." Carradine tapped the instrument panel. "Says we've got enough for another ten."

"Even if it runs out, we can walk the other ten miles."

"In *that*?" He pointed out over the steering wheel into the wasteland of the Zone. "Beg pardon, ma'am, but cold as they are already, those in the back wouldn't last two hundred yards."

Barbour glanced out through the windshield. A red smudge of dawn smeared the horizon line. The storm was quickly abating: the wind had died to almost nothing, and the surrounding landscape was now coated in a fresh mantle of powdery snow. But as the storm receded, the temperature had plummeted. The instrument panel read minus twenty-two degrees.

The truck shook roughly and she grabbed the stabilizer bar. Twenty miles. At current speed, that meant over half an hour.

She glanced at the GPS device mounted on the dashboard. She was used to seeing the unit in her own car, always bristling with streets, highways, and landmarks as she drove around Lexington, Woburn, and the greater Boston area. But the GPS in Carradine's truck was utterly blank: a screen as white and featureless as the snow outside, with only a compass heading and latitude-longitude reading to indicate they were moving at all.

"You look tired," Carradine said. "Why don't you rest?"

"You must be joking," she replied. And yet this tense and seemingly endless vigil—on the heels of so many sleepless hours at Fear Base—had exhausted her. She closed her eyes to rest them, just for a moment. And when she opened them again, everything was different. The sky was a little brighter, the snow around them sparkling with sunlight. The sound of the truck had changed, too: the RPMs were lower, the speed dropping noticeably.

"How long was I asleep?" she asked.

"Fifteen minutes."

"How's the fuel?"

Carradine glanced at the instrumentation. "We're on fumes."

The truck was still slowing. And now, glancing again at the GPS, Barbour noticed it was, in fact, displaying something: a band of unrelieved blue, filling the top half of the screen.

"That's not another—" she began, then stopped.

"Yup. Gunner Lake."

Fear—which had ebbed to a dull sense of anxiety—surged afresh. "I thought you said we were only going to cross one lake!"

"I did. But we don't have the gas to detour around this one anymore."

Barbour didn't reply. She swallowed, licked her lips. Her mouth felt very dry.

"Don't worry. Gunner Lake is broad, but it ain't wide."

She looked at him. "Why had you planned to go around it, then?"

Carradine hesitated briefly. "The lake's only about forty feet deep. It's littered with big rocks, glacial erratics, and the like. In these conditions, with the snow cover, sometimes they can be hard to see. If we hit one by mistake . . ."

He didn't finish. He didn't need to.

She glanced out through the windshield. The lake was clearly visible just ahead. Carradine worked his way down the gears as they approached the shore.

"Aren't you going to stop?" she said. "Test the ice depth with your power auger?"

"No time," the trucker replied. "No gas."

They crept out onto the ice. Once again, Barbour squeezed the stabilizer bar with all her might at the sensation of ice flexing under their weight; again, she felt the tension rise as the dreadful crackling began once more, spreading out from beneath the wheels in all directions. A few rocks were clearly visible, poking above the snow cover like fangs, their black tops shining in the morning sun. Others were hidden beneath drifts. The retreating wind had tucked and piled the snow into fantastic shapes: ridges and peaks and miniature buttes. Carradine made his way across the surface, threading the truck carefully between the rocks and snow formations. Barbour kept glancing from the GPS to the frozen lake and back again, willing the display to update, to show white once again.

Three minutes passed, then five. The crackling grew louder, fractures forking away before them in spastic lines. The engine hiccupped; Carradine feathered it and the RPMs returned to normal.

Barbour could guess what would happen if they ran out of gas while on the ice.

"Nearly there," the trucker said, as if reading her thoughts.

A low ridge of snow appeared directly ahead, perhaps forty yards wide, scooped and scalloped by the wind until it resembled a cresting wave. "That's got to be pure snow," Carradine said. "Can't risk veering around it, might spin out again. We'll plow straight through, clear the path for the trailer. Hang on."

Barbour was already hanging on with a grip that could not possibly be tightened. She held her breath as Carradine aimed the truck directly at the snow ridge. As it shuddered under the impact, Carradine goosed the throttle, maintaining speed.

Suddenly, the front of the truck kicked violently into the air. Barbour was thrown forward, her head almost impacting the dashboard despite the seat belt. "Christ!" Carradine said, turning the wheel to the left. "Must have been a boulder hidden under that ridge!"

There was a second impact as the rear right wheels of the cab went over the boulder. The truck rose, then fell heavily onto the ice. There was a sound like the retort of a cannon and the big vehicle suddenly slowed. Barbour felt herself pressed back against the seat.

"We're going down in the rear!" the trucker yelled. "Get on the horn—tell everyone in the trailer to move forward, *now*!"

Barbour fumbled for the CB handset, dropped it, picked it up again. "Fortnum, we've broken through the ice. Get everybody to the front of the trailer. Hurry."

She replaced the handset as Carradine frantically gunned the diesel. The truck strained forward, listing to the rear, splitting the frozen surface, the back end of the trailer literally forcing its way through the spreading ice. Barbour felt them tilt back still farther, the angle increasing. "No!" she heard herself crying out. "God, *no*!"

Carradine shifted gears and jammed the accelerator to the floor. There was another crack, almost as loud as the first, and with a shriek of effort the truck shook itself free of the hole in the ice and shot forward. Quickly, Carradine throttled back, careful not to lose control on the slick surface. Barbour slumped in her seat, almost overcome by relief.

"They don't get any closer than that," Carradine said. He glanced at the gasoline indicator. "Tank's bone dry now. I can't imagine what we're running on."

Barbour looked at the GPS indicator. And now at last she saw a white line of dry land a quarter mile directly ahead.

Clearing the last set of rocks, the truck roared up onto the shore and accelerated. Carradine fetched a huge, shuddering breath, plucking his floral shirt away from his skinny frame and fanning himself with it. Then he sat up, pointed ahead. "Look!"

Barbour peered through the windshield. In the distance, where the sky met the horizon, she made out a low cluster of black shapes, a blinking red light.

"Is that—" she began.

The trucker nodded, grinning hugely. "Arctic Village."

Quickly, she picked up the CB handset. "Barbour to Fortnum. We made it. Arctic Village is just ahead."

And as she replaced the handset she thought she could hear—floating forward, over the grinding of the diesel—the sound of cheers.

EPILOGUE

The day was as clear and bright as crystal, as if the elements—ashamed of their ferocity—were eager to atone for the storm. The air was absolutely still, without a breath of wind, and if Marshall looked away from the base—toward the broad icepack and the perfect dome of sky above it—he could almost imagine that, in this remote and wild place, nature had a palette of only two colors: white and blue.

The morning had seen a steady procession of comings and goings: medevac and morgue choppers, a confusion of military helicopters, and one small plane full of men in dark suits that, for some reason, had made Marshall very uneasy. Now he stood with Faraday, Logan, and Ekberg on the apron before the base entrance. They had gathered to say their farewells to Usuguk, who was about to make the journey back to his empty village.

"You sure you don't want a ride?" Marshall asked.

The Tunit shook his head. "My people have a saying: the journey is its own destination."

"A Japanese poet wrote something very similar," said Logan.

"Thank you again," Marshall said. "For agreeing to come despite everything. For sharing your knowledge and your insight." He put out his hand to shake, but instead of taking it Usuguk reached out and clasped Marshall's arms.

"May you find the peace which you seek," he said. Then he nodded to the others, picked up the small duffel of water and supplies they had prepared for him, drew the fur-fringed hood around his face, and turned away.

They watched, not speaking, as the old man made his way north across the snow. Marshall wondered if the women would return to the village, or if Usuguk would live out the rest of his life alone, in monkish solitude. Somehow, he knew the man would accept either outcome with stoic philosophy.

"Are you searching for peace?" Ekberg asked him.

Marshall thought a moment. "Yes. I guess I am."

"I suppose we all are," she replied. She hesitated. "Well, I'd better get back. The Blackpool representative and insurance people will be here after lunch. I've got a lot to do before then."

"I'll look in on you later," Marshall said.

She smiled. "You do that." Then she turned and slipped through the doors into the staging area.

Logan glanced after her. "Is that a relationship you plan to pursue?"

"If I can find an excuse," Marshall replied happily.

"There's always an excuse." Logan glanced at his watch. "Well, I guess I'm next to leave. My helicopter is due any minute."

"We're leaving tomorrow," Marshall said. "You could have waited a day, saved yourself some money."

"I got a call from my office. Something's come up."

"Another spook hunt?"

"Something like that. Besides, the black-ops types who did all the interrogating this morning know where I live. I doubt I've heard the last of them." He paused. "What did you tell them?"

"Exactly what happened, as best I could remember," Marshall replied. "But it seemed every answer I gave just spawned more questions, so in the end I basically shut up."

"Did they believe you?"

"I think so. With all of us as eyewitnesses I don't see why they wouldn't." He looked at Logan. "Don't you think?"

"I think it would have helped if there was a carcass."

"Yes, that is strange. Certainly left plenty of blood behind. I'd have sworn up and down it was stone dead, its skull the way it was."

"It must have crawled off to die," said Faraday. "Just like the first one."

"You know what Usuguk would say about that," Marshall replied. He looked toward the horizon, where the Tunit was already dwindling to a brown speck between the broad smears of white and blue.

"I'm damned glad it died," Logan said, "but I still don't understand the mechanics. How the sound waves killed it, I mean."

"Without a corpse we can't be sure," Marshall answered. "But I knew that high frequencies irritated it. A pure sine wave, without harmonics, seemed even more painful."

"But don't most sounds produce harmonics?"

"That's right," said Faraday. "So-called 'imperfect' instruments, like a violin or oboe—or a human voice—all do. It's ironic, because those harmonics are what make sounds rich and complex."

"But certain sine waves *don't*," Marshall said. "I had the machine produce a series of waves that would reinforce the fundamental tone. I hoped that if we found a sound sufficiently painful, we could drive it from the base."

"It had a much greater effect than that," said Logan.

Marshall nodded. "It's interesting. Fish and whales have internal air bladders, which can be disrupted by sonar. Some scientists believe dinosaurs had organs in their brains for making incredibly loud, trumpeting noises that could be heard miles away. I wouldn't be surprised if this creature had some similar organ or cavity in its skull—for mating, or communication, or something else. I believe these high frequencies triggered a sympathetic resonance within that organ, and ultimately caused it to burst."

"I'm a historian, not a physicist," said Logan. "I've never heard of sympathetic resonance."

"Think of glass shattering when a soprano sings a high note. There's a natural frequency at which that glass vibrates. If the soprano keeps singing the same note, it keeps adding energy to the glass. At some point the glass can't dissipate the energy quickly enough and it breaks." Marshall glanced back toward the base. "In this case, I guess we'll never know."

"A pity." Logan turned to Faraday. "And what did *you* tell our uniformed interrogators?"

Faraday looked back with his perpetually startled expression. "I tried to explain it from a purely biological perspective. How the two creatures were frozen separately during a single event: an atmospheric inversion causing a downdraft of super-cooled ice, flash-freezing the animals before ice could form in their bloodstreams, keeping them alive in suspended animation. I explained how the ice melted: its unique composition, ice-fifteen, that melts a few degrees below zero centigrade. I explained the second causal agent: the opposite phenomenon to a terminal freeze, a downdraft of unusually warm air that helped revive the creature—and how both events could have triggered the bizarre crimson northern lights that upset Usuguk. I gave them the example of the Beresovka mammoth as a precedent."

"What did you say about the creature itself?" Logan asked.

"I told them about the Callisto Effect. How the creature could well have been a genetic mutation, or perhaps something as simple as an unknown species. And I told them about the creature's hyper-developed white blood cell line, how it would promote healing that was almost instant. How beneath the fur it had a chitinous exo-skeleton, but scaled almost like a snake, allowing for rapid and flexible movement—and the deflection of bullets. And its unique neurological makeup: even high doses of electricity didn't disrupt its nervous system or stop its heart. Yet, ironically, sound—of a certain amplitude and frequency—was lethal: aided, perhaps, by weakness brought on due to starvation."

"So that explains everything," said Logan.

"Everything—and nothing," Faraday added.

Logan frowned. "What do you mean?"

"Because everything I just told you—except for the blood work—is mere theory and speculation. The fact is, strange types of ice, like ice-fifteen, require a great deal of pressure to form. The fact is, the creature survived being frozen in ice—whatever kind of ice—for thousands of years. It was transcendentally strong. It was impervious to even high doses of electricity . . ." Faraday shrugged.

Marshall looked at him thoughtfully. The biologist had just constructed a plausible explanation to everything—and then, quickly, pulled the rug out from under it. "Maybe Usuguk was right, after all," he said.

The two men looked at him.

"Are you serious?" asked Faraday.

"Of course—partly, anyway. I'm a scientist, but I'd be the first to admit science can't explain everything. We're a long way from civilization. This is the top of the world. A different set of rules is in place here, rules we don't have the least idea about. This isn't man's environment—but the men who *are* here have seen a lot more than we have, and we should listen to them. If any land could be called the land of the spirits, wouldn't it be here—this strange, sacred, distant spot? Do you really think the way the northern lights winked out just when the creature died was utter coincidence?"

The question hung in the cold air, unanswered. In the silence that followed, Marshall heard the distant *whap-whap* of helicopter blades.

"That would be my ride," Logan murmured. He hoisted the duffel at his feet.

"What about you?" Marshall asked.

"What about me?" Logan slung his laptop over his shoulder. "If either of you are ever in New Haven, look me up."

"That's not an answer. Which theory do you subscribe to—the scientific or the spiritual?"

Logan looked at him for a moment, eyes narrowing slightly. Instead of answering, he asked a question of his own. "Where did you grow up, Dr. Marshall?"

This was the last thing Marshall expected to hear. "Rapid City, South Dakota."

"Have any pets?"

"Sure. Three dachshunds."

"Ever go on long driving trips as a kid?"

Marshall nodded, mystified. "Practically every summer."

"Ever lose any of those dachshunds at a roadside rest stop?"

"No."

"I did," said Logan. "Barkley, my Irish setter. I loved that dog more than just about anything. He ran off at a picnic ground in the middle of Oklahoma nowhere. My family looked for three hours. Never found him. Finally, we had to leave. I was inconsolable."

The helicopter was landing now outside the security perimeter, beating up diaphanous skeins of powdery snow. Marshall looked at Logan, frowning. "I don't understand what losing a pet has to do with—"

All of a sudden Logan's implication hit home. Marshall blinked in surprise as the light dawned. "Except that the travelers you're talking about were from much farther away than Rapid City, South Dakota."

Logan nodded. "Much, much farther."

Marshall shook his head. "Is *that* what you believe?"

"I'm an enigmalogist. It's my job to exercise my imagination. As your friend Faraday here said—mere theory and speculation." He grinned, shook their hands in turn, then walked toward the waiting helicopter. As the pilot opened the passenger door, he turned back.

"It's a hell of a speculation, though—isn't it?" he called over the whine of the engine. Then he clambered in and closed the door. The helicopter rose; wheeled over the Fear glacier—blue against the blue of the sky—and then turned sharply south, toward civilization, away from the land of the spirits.

An excerpt from Lincoln Child's

THE THIRD GATE

Forthcoming from Doubleday in Summer 2012

The doctor helped himself to a cup of coffee in the break room, reached for the cylinder of powdered creamer on a nearby counter, thought better of it, then poured in some soy milk from the battered lab refrigerator instead. Stirring the coffee with a plastic swizzle, he walked thoughtfully across the pale linoleum floor to a cluster of identical heavy-sided chairs. The usual sounds filtered through the door: the rattling of wheelchairs and gurneys, bleats and beeps of instrumentation, the drone of the hospital intercom.

A third-year resident named Deguello had sprawled his lanky limbs across two of the threadbare chairs. Typical, thought the doctor—a resident's ability to fall asleep instantly, vertical or horizontal, in no matter how uncomfortable a position. As the doctor settled into a chair beside him, the resident stopped his faint snoring and opened one eye.

"Hey, doc," he murmured. "What time is it?"

The doctor glanced up at the industrial clock, set over the line of lockers along the far wall. "Ten forty-five."

"God," Deguello groaned. "That means I've only been asleep ten minutes."

"At least you've managed some," the doctor said, sipping his coffee. "It's a quiet night."

Deguello closed the eye again. "Two myocardial infarctions. An open-skull fracture. An emergency C-section. Two gunshot victims, one critical. A third-degree burn case. A knife wound with renal penetration. One simple and one compound fracture. An old gent who stroked out on the gurney. Oxycodone OD. Meth OD. Amphetamine OD. And those were all in"—he paused—"the last ninety minutes."

The doctor took another sip of coffee. "Like I said—quiet night. But look on the bright side. You could still be doing grand rounds at Mass General."

The resident was quiet for a moment. "I still don't understand, doc," he mumbled. "Why do you do this? Sacrifice yourself on the ER altar every other Friday. I mean, I've got no choice. But you're a big-time anesthesiologist."

The doctor drained his cup, tossed it in the trash. "A little less curiosity in the presence of your betters, please." He pushed himself to his feet. "Back into the trenches."

Out in the hallway, the doctor glanced around at the relative calm. He started toward the operations desk on the far side of the ER when he suddenly noticed an increased bustle of activity. The head nurse came jogging up. "Car accident," she told him. "One victim, arriving momentarily. I've set aside Trauma Two."

The doctor immediately turned toward the indicated bay. As he did so, the trauma doors buzzed open and a paramedic team wheeled in a stretcher, followed by two police officers. Instantly, the doctor could see this was serious: the urgency of their actions, their expressions, the blood on their coats and faces, all telegraphed desperation.

"Female, thirtysomething!" one of the paramedics bawled out. "Unresponsive!"

Immediately, the doctor waved them in and turned to a waiting intern. "Get a suture cart." The intern nodded and jogged away.

"And call Deguello and Corbin!" he called after him.

The paramedics were already wheeling the stretcher into Trauma Two and positioning it beside the table. "On me," said a nurse as they circled the body. "Careful with that neck collar. One, two, *three*!" The patient was lifted onto the table, the stretcher pushed away. The doctor got a glimpse of pale white skin; cinnamon hair; a blouse, once white, now soaked with blood. More blood made a drip trail on the floor, leading back toward the trauma area.

Something alarming, like a cold electric current, began to tingle in the back of his brain.

"She was T-boned by a drunk driver," one of the paramedics said in his ear. "Coded once on the way in."

Interns piled in, followed by Deguello. "You got a type?" the doctor asked.

The paramedic nodded. "O negative."

People were busy now, attaching monitors, hanging new IV lines, trundling in crash carts. The doctor turned toward an intern. "Get the blood bank, call for three units." He thought of the spatter trail across the linoleum. "No, make it four."

"O_2's full," called out one nurse as Corbin, the other ER doc, hurried in.

Deguello came around to the head of the table, peered down at the motionless victim. "Looks cyanotic."

"Get a blood gas in here," the doctor rapped. His attention was fixed on the woman's abdomen, now bared but slick with blood. Quickly, he peeled back the temporary dressing. A dreadful open wound, hastily sutured by the paramedics, was bleeding copiously. He turned toward a nurse and pointed to the area. She swabbed it and he looked again.

"Massive abdominal trauma," he said. "Possible supine subpulmonary pneumothorax. We're going to need a pericardial tap." He turned toward the paramedic. "What the hell caused this? What about the air bag?"

"Slid beneath it," the man said. "Dashboard snapped in two like a twig and she got hung up on it. They had to come in from the top with the Jaws. Awful scene, man, her Porsche was totally flattened by that drunk bastard's SUV."

Porsche. The cold little current in his head tingled more sharply. He straightened up, trying to get a view of the head, but Deguello was in his way. "Significant blunt trauma," Deguello said. "We're gonna need a head CT."

"BP's down to eighty over thirty-five," said a nurse. "Pulse ox is seventy-nine."

"Maintain compression!" Deguello ordered.

The exsanguination was too great, the shock too severe: they had a minute, maybe two at most, to save her. Another nurse came in, hanging blood packs on the IV rack. "That's not going to do it," the doctor said. "We're gonna need a large-bore IV—she's bleeding out too fast."

"One milligram epi," Corbin told an intern.

The nurse turned to the suture cart, grabbed a larger needle, pulled the woman's limp hand forward to insert it. As she did so, the doctor's gaze fell upon the hand: slim, very pale. The hand bore a single ring: a platinum wedding band inlaid with a beautiful star sapphire, whiskey colored against a field of black. Sri Lankan, very expensive. He knew, because he'd purchased it.

Suddenly, a sharp tone sounded throughout the trauma room. "Full arrest!" cried a nurse.

For a moment, the doctor just stood there, paralyzed by horror and frozen disbelief. Deguello turned toward one of the interns, and now the doctor could see the woman's face: hair matted and askew, eyes open and staring, mouth and nose obscured by the breathing equipment.

His dry mouth worked. "Jennifer," he croaked.

"Losing vitals!" cried the nurse.

"We need lido!" Corbin called. "Lido! *Stat!*"

And then, as quickly as it had come, the paralysis fell away. The doctor wheeled toward a hovering ER nurse. "Defib!" he cried.

She raced to a far corner of the room, wheeled the cart back. "Charging."

An intern approached, injected the lidocaine, stepped back. The doctor grabbed the paddles, barely able to control his trembling hands. This couldn't be happening. It had to be a dream, just a bad dream. He'd wake up and he'd be in the break room, slumped over, Deguello snoring in the next chair.

"Charged!" the nurse called out.

"Clear!" The doctor heard the desperate edge in his own voice. As the workers fell back he placed the paddles on her bare, bloody chest, applied the current. Jennifer's body stiffened, then fell back onto the table.

"Flatline!" cried the nurse monitoring the vitals.

"Charge it again!" he called. A fresh beeping, low and insistent, added its voice to the cacophony.

"Hypovolemic shock," Deguello muttered. "We never had a chance."

They don't know, the doctor thought, as if from a million miles away. *They don't understand.* He felt a single tear gather in his eye and begin to trickle down his cheek.

"Recharged!" the defib nurse said.

He reapplied the paddles. Jennifer's body jumped once again.

"No response," said the intern at his side.

"That's it," Corbin said with a sigh. "Guess you need to call it, Ethan."

Instead, the doctor threw the paddles aside and began heart massage. He felt her body, unresponsive and cool, moving sluggishly under the sharp motions of his hands.

"Pupils fixed and dilated," the monitoring nurse said.

But the doctor paid no attention, his heart massage growing increasingly violent and desperate.

The sound in the trauma room, which had been growing increasingly frantic, now began to die away. "Zero cardiac activity," said the nurse.

"You'd better pronounce her," said Corbin.

"*No!*" the doctor snapped.

The entire room turned at the anguish in his voice.

"Ethan?" Corbin asked wonderingly.

But instead of responding, the doctor began to cry.

Everyone around him went still, some staring in incomprehension, others looking away in embarrassment. Everyone except one of the interns, who opened the door and walked silently down the corridor. The doctor, still crying, knew where the man was going. He was going to get a shroud.

Three Years Later

Growing up in Westport, currently teaching at Yale, Jeremy Logan thought himself familiar with his home state of Connecticut. But the stretch through which he now drove was a revelation. Heading east from Groton—following the e-mailed directions—he'd turned onto US 1 and then, just past Stonington, onto US 1 Alternate. Hugging the gray Atlantic coastline, he'd passed Wequetequock, rolled over a bridge that looked as old as New England itself, then turned sharply right onto a well-paved but unmarked road. Quite abruptly, the minimalls and tourist motels fell away behind. He passed a sleepy cove in which lobster boats bobbed at anchor, and then entered an equally sleepy hamlet. And yet it was a real village, a working village, with a general store and a tackle shop and an Episcopal church with a steeple three sizes too large, and gray-shingled houses with trim picket fences painted white. There were no hulking SUVs, no out-of-state plates; and the scattering of people sitting on benches or leaning out of front windows waved to him as he passed. The April sunlight was strong, and the sea air had a clean, fresh bite to it. A signboard hanging from the doorframe of the post office informed him he was in Pevensey Point, population 182. Something about the place reminded him irresistibly of Herman Melville.

"Karen," he said, "if you'd seen this place, you'd never have made us buy that summer cottage in Hyannis."

Although his wife had died of cancer years ago, Logan still allowed himself to converse with her now and then. Of course it was usually—though not always—more monologue than conversation. At first, he'd been sure to do it only when he was certain not to be overheard. But then—as what had started as a kind of intellectual hobby for him turned increasingly into a profession—he no longer bothered to be so discreet. These days, judging by what he did for a living, people expected him to be a little strange.

Two miles beyond the town, precisely as the directions indicated, a narrow lane led off to the right. Taking it, Logan found himself in a sandy forest of thin scrub pine that soon gave way to tawny dunes. The dunes ended at a metal bridge leading to a low, broad island jutting out into Fishers Island Sound. Even from this distance, Logan could see there were at least a dozen structures on the island, all built of the same reddish-brown stone. At the center were three large five-story buildings that resembled dormitories, arranged in parallel, like dominos. At the far end of the island, partly concealed by the various structures, was an empty airstrip. And beyond everything lay the ocean and the dark green line of Rhode Island.

Logan drove the final mile, stopping at a gatehouse before the bridge. He showed the printed e-mail to the guard inside, who smiled and waved him through. A single sign beside the gatehouse, expensive looking but unobtrusive, read simply *CTS*.

He crossed the bridge, passed an outlying structure, and pulled into a parking lot. It was surprisingly large: there were at least fifty cars and space for as many more. Nosing into one of the spots, he killed the engine. But instead of exiting, he paused to read the e-mail once again.

Jeremy,

I'm pleased—and relieved—to hear of your acceptance. I also appreciate your being flexible, since as I mentioned earlier there's no way yet to know how long your investigation will take. In any case you'll receive a minimum of two weeks' compensation, at the rate you specified. I'm sorry I can't give you more details at this point, but you're probably used to that. And I have to tell you I can't wait to see you again after all this time.

Directions to the Center are below. I'll be waiting for you on the morning of the 18th. Any time between ten and noon will be fine. One other thing: once you're on board with the project, you might find it hard to get calls out with any degree of certainty, so please be sure you've cleared your decks before you arrive. Looking forward to the 18th!

Best,

E. R.

Logan glanced at his watch: eleven thirty. He turned the note over once in his hands. *You might find it hard to get calls out with any degree of certainty.* Why was that? Perhaps cell phone towers had never made it beyond picturesque Pevensey Point? Nevertheless, what the e-mail said was true: he was "used to that." He pulled a duffel bag from the passenger seat, slipped the note into it, and got out of the car.

Located in one of the central dormitory-like buildings, Reception was an understated space that reminded Logan of a hospital or clinic: a half-dozen empty chairs, tables with magazines and journals, a sprinkling of anonymous-looking oil paintings on beige walls, and a single desk occupied by a woman in her midthirties.

The letters *CTS* were set into the wall behind her, once again with no indication of what they might stand for.

Logan gave his name to the woman, who in response looked at him with a mixture of curiosity and uneasiness. He took a seat in one of the vacant chairs, expecting a protracted wait. But no sooner had he picked up a recent issue of *Harvard Medical Review* than a door across from the receptionist opened and Ethan Rush emerged.

"Jeremy," Rush said, smiling broadly and extending his hand. "Thank you so much for coming."

"Ethan," Logan replied, shaking the proffered hand. "Nice to see you again."

He hadn't seen Rush since their days at Johns Hopkins more than fifteen years before, when he'd been doing graduate studies and Rush had been attending the medical school. But the man who stood before him retained a remarkable youthfulness. Only a fine tracery of lines at the corners of his eyes bore testament to the passage of years. And yet in the simple act of shaking the man's hand, Logan had received two very clear impressions from Rush: a shattering, life-changing event and an unswerving, almost obsessive, devotion to a cause.

Dr. Rush glanced around the reception area. "You brought your luggage?"

"It's in my trunk."

"Give me the keys, I'll see that somebody retrieves it for you."

"It's a Lotus Elan S four."

Rush whistled. "The roadster? What year?"

"1968."

"Very nice. I'll make sure they treat it with kid gloves."

Logan dug into his pocket and handed the keys to Rush, who in turn gave them to the receptionist with some whispered instructions. Then he turned and motioned Logan to follow him through the open doorway.

Taking an elevator to the top floor, Rush led the way down a long hallway that smelled faintly of cleaning fluid and chemicals. The resemblance to a hospital grew stronger—and yet it seemed to be a hospital without patients; the few people they passed were dressed in street clothes, ambulatory, and obviously healthy. Logan peered curiously into the open doorways they walked by. He saw conference rooms, a large, empty lecture hall with seats for at least a hundred, laboratories bristling with equipment, what appeared to be a reference library full of paperbound journals and dedicated terminals. More strangely, he noticed several apparently identical rooms, each containing a single, narrow bed with literally dozens—if not hundreds—of wires leading to nearby monitoring instruments. Other doors were closed, their small windows covered by privacy curtains. A group of men and women in white lab coats passed them in the hallway. They glanced at Logan, nodded to Rush.

Stopping before a door marked director, Rush opened it and beckoned Logan through an anteroom housing two secretaries and a profusion of bookcases into a private office beyond. It was tastefully decorated, as minimalist as the outer office was crowded. Three of the walls held spare postmodernist paintings in cool blues and grays; the fourth wall appeared to be entirely of glass, covered at the moment by blinds.

In the center of the room was a teakwood table, polished to a brilliant gleam and flanked by two leather chairs. Rush took one and ushered Logan toward the other.

"Can I offer you anything?" the director asked. "Coffee, tea, soda?"

Logan shook his head.

Rush crossed one leg over the other. "Jeremy, I have to be frank. I wasn't sure you'd be willing to take on this assignment, given how busy you are . . . and how closemouthed I was concerning the particulars."

"You weren't sure—even given the fee I charged?"

Rush smiled. "It's true—your fee is certainly healthy. But then your, ah, work has become somewhat high-profile recently." He hesitated. "What is it you call your profession again?"

"I'm an enigmalogist."

"Right. An enigmalogist." Rush glanced curiously at Logan. "And it's true you were able to document the existence of the Loch Ness monster?"

"You'd have to take that up with my client for that particular assignment, the University of Edinburgh."

"Serves me right for asking." Rush paused. "Speaking of universities, you *are* a professor, aren't you?"

"Medieval history. At Yale."

"And what do they think of your other profession at Yale?"

"High visibility is never a problem. It helps guarantee a large admissions pool." Logan glanced around the office. He'd often found that new clients preferred to talk about his past accomplishments. It postponed discussion of their own problems.

"I remember those . . . *investigations* you did at the Peabody Institute and the Applied Physics Lab back in school," Rush said. "Who would have thought they'd lead you to this?"

"Not me, certainly." Logan shifted in his seat. "So. Care to tell me just what CTS stands for? Nothing around here seems to give any clue."

"We do keep our cards pretty close to our vest. Center for Transmortality Studies."

"Transmortality Studies," Logan repeated.

Rush nodded. "I founded CTS two years ago."

Logan glanced at him in surprise. "You founded the Center?"

Rush took a deep breath. A grim look came over his face. "You see, Jeremy, it's like this. Just over three years ago, I was working an ER shift when my wife, Jennifer, was brought in by paramedics. She'd been in a terrible accident and was completely unresponsive. We tried everything—heart massage, paddles—but it was hopeless. It was the worst moment of my life. There I was, not only unable to save my own wife . . . but I was expected to pronounce her dead, as well."

Logan shook his head in sympathy.

"Except that I didn't. I couldn't bring myself to do it. Against the advice of the assisting doctors I continued heroic measures." He leaned forward. "And, Jeremy—she *pulled through*. I finally revived her, fourteen minutes after all brain function had ceased."

"How?"

Rush spread his hands. "It was a miracle. Or so it seemed at the time. It was the most amazing experience you can imagine. It was revelatory, life-altering. To have pulled her back from the brink . . ." He fell briefly silent. "At that moment, the scales fell from my eyes. My life's work was suddenly revealed. I left Rhode Island Hospital and my practice as an anesthesiologist, and I've been studying near-death experiences ever since."

The life-changing event, Logan thought. Aloud, he said, "Transmortality studies."

"Exactly. Documenting the various manifestations, trying to analyze and codify the phenomenon. You'd be surprised, Jeremy, how many people have undergone near-death experiences and—in particular—how many similarities they share. Once you've come back from the brink, you're never quite the same. As you might guess, it's something that stays with you—and with your loved ones." He swept his hand around the office. "It was almost no effort to raise the money for the Center, all this. Plenty of people who have had near-death experiences are passionately interested in sharing those experiences and learning more about what they might mean."

"So what goes on at the Center, exactly?" Logan asked.

"At heart, we're a small community of doctors and researchers—most with relatives or friends who have 'gone over.' Survivors of NDEs are invited here to stay for a few weeks or months, to document precisely what happened to them and undergo various batteries of tests."

"Tests?" Logan asked.

Rush nodded. "Although we've been operational only eighteen months now, a great deal of research has been conducted already—and a number of findings made."

"But, as you say, you've kept it all pretty hush-hush."

Rush smiled. "You can imagine what the good residents of

Pevensey Point would say if they knew exactly who had taken over the old Coast Guard training base down the road, or why."

"Yes, I can." *They'd say you were tampering with fate*, he thought. *Messing with people brought back from the dead.* Now he began to have some idea why his own expertise had been called for. "So exactly what's been going on here that I can help you with?"

A look of surprise briefly crossed Rush's face. "Oh, you misunderstand. Nothing's happening *here*."

Logan hesitated. "You're right—I do misunderstand. If the problem you're experiencing isn't here, then why was I summoned?"

"Sorry to be evasive, Jeremy. I can tell you more once you're on board."

"But I *am* on board. That's why I'm here."

In reply, Rush stood and walked to the far wall. "No." And with a single tug he opened the blinds, exposing a wall of windows. Beyond lay the airstrip Logan had noticed on his arrival. But from this vantage, he could see the runway wasn't empty after all: it was occupied by a Learjet 85, sleek and gleaming in the noonday sun. Rush extended a finger toward it.

"Once you're on board *that*," he said.